Castles in the Sand

Sally John

HARVEST HOUSE PUBLISHERS

EUGENE, OREGON

Scripture quotations are taken from The Holy Bible, 21st Century King James Version (KJ21®). Copyright © 1994, Deuel Enterprises, Inc., Gary, SD 57237, and used by permission, and from The New Jerusalem Bible, copyright © 1985 by Darton, Longman & Todd, Ltd. and Doubleday, a division of Random House, Inc. Reprinted by Permission.

Some quotations are also taken from *The Book of Common Prayer.*

Cover by Garborg Design Works, Savage, Minnesota

Published in association with the literary agency of Alive Communications, Inc., 7680 Goddard Street, Ste #200, Colorado Springs, CO 80920.

Cover photos © Ross Anania / Photodisc Red / Getty Images; Krzysztof Nieciecki / istockphoto; Ron Hohenhaus / istockphoto

This is a work of fiction. Names, characters, places, and incidents are products of the author's imagination or are used fictitiously. Any resemblance to actual persons, living or dead, or to events or locales, is entirely coincidental.

CASTLES IN THE SAND
Copyright © 2006 by Sally John
Published by Harvest House Publishers
Eugene, Oregon 97402
www.harvesthousepublishers.com

Library of Congress Cataloging-in-Publication Data
John, Sally, 1951-
   Castles in the sand / Sally John.
     p. cm. — (The beach house series ; bk. 2)
   ISBN-13: 978-0-7369-1317-1 (pbk.)
   ISBN-10: 0-7369-1317-3 (pbk.)
   Product # 6913173
   1. Pregnancy, Unwanted—Fiction. 2. Clergy—Family relationships—Fiction. 3. Fathers and daughters—Fiction. 4. Mothers and daughters—Fiction. 5. Seaside resorts—Fiction. 6. Domestic fiction. 7. Psychological fiction. I. Title. II. Series.
PS3560.O323C37 2006
813'.54—dc22
                                              2006004026

Printed in the United States of America

06 07 08 09 10 11 12 13 14 / BC-MS / 10 9 8 7 6 5 4 3 2 1

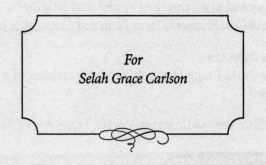

For
Selah Grace Carlson

Acknowledgments

I am so very grateful to my "walking encyclopedias" who responded to a myriad of requests for information throughout the writing of this story and to my encouragers who read early drafts—
Cindi Cox; Elizabeth, Tracy, Patti, and Christopher John.

Special thanks to~
Dave and Peggy Hadacek, for the provision of a writing table.

William Payton, for an uncommon expression of the faith.

Much appreciation to~
All the wonderful people at Harvest House Publishers, who tenderly care for my work.

Heartfelt thanks to my gracious collaborator~
Editor Kim Moore.

And, as always, thanks to my Tim.

The Beach House Ladies

Susan Starr ~
   Wife of Drake; mother of Kenzie, 19; wedding coordinator; singer

Natalie Starr ~
   Susan's sister-in-law; wife of Rex; mother of two boys; soccer coach

Kenzie Starr ~
   Susan's daughter; girlfriend of Aidan Carlucci; barista; musician

Pepper Carlucci ~
   Wife of Mick; mother of six, including Aidan, 25; bookstore clerk

The "Martha Mavens" ~
   Mildred and Leona: 77-year-old twins; widowed
   Tess: wife; mother; director of church women's ministries
   Gwyn: divorced; paralegal
   Emmylou: wife; pregnant with first child; hairdresser

Yahweh your God is there with you,
the warrior-Saviour.
He will rejoice over you with happy song,
He will renew you by His love,
He will dance with shouts of joy for you,
as on a day of festival.

–Zephaniah 3:17-18 NJB

Prologue

New Year's Day
San Diego, California

A few minutes after seven o'clock in the evening on January first, the year her daughter was nineteen years old, Susan Starr nearly fainted for the first time in her life.

"Mom?"

Susan's head felt cotton stuffed, but she heard concern in Kenzie's voice. The sight of her only child dimmed as if a gauzy curtain had dropped between them. Black shadows pawed at the edges of the curtain. She leaned forward until her head hung between her knees.

"Dad! Do something!"

"Young lady, after what you just told us, there isn't a thing I can do. What did you expect? You're out of the country for four months, and then you come home with…with…with *this!*"

Even in her half-coherent state, Susan realized her husband was about to launch into a tirade. It meant civil, three-sided conversation was over.

She sat up and blinked, pretending she could see straight. "Drake, I'm fine."

"You are not fine." He rose from his armchair and drew all six slender feet and three inches of himself upright, stiff and straight as the fireplace poker on the hearth behind him. "Our unwed, unemployed daughter has just announced that she's—" He clamped his mouth shut.

7

Pregnant. Susan filled in the blank and gazed at Kenzie, seated all alone in the center of the couch. She resembled an imp, especially now with her short dark brown hair spiked every which way. Some people judged her insolent before she uttered a word. They would say the silliest things about her attitude, even when she was a baby.

A baby.

Tears stung Susan's eyes, and she put a hand to her mouth. Her baby was having a baby!

Drake propped his hands on his hips. "Mackenzie, how could you?" Though his height and glower intimidated, he never raised his voice during a rebuke. When extremely agitated he lowered the volume to just above a whisper. Like now, it commanded more attention than an out-and-out, top-of-the-lungs roar.

He went on. "Shock and dismay do not begin to describe our reaction! How do you think your mother will ever be able to show her face again? And how do you think I can ever preach again? What am I supposed to say to my congregation? 'By the way, forget everything I've ever taught in the past ten years about parenting. My single, jobless, sometimes-college student of a daughter is—'" Again he locked his jaw, cutting off the key word.

"I'm sorry I've hurt you." It was Kenzie's third reiteration of an apology. She had opened and closed her confession with it: *I'm sorry. I have to tell you something, and you're going to be upset. But—I'm pregnant. I'm sorry.*

"Honey." Susan paused, not sure how to delicately phrase the question. "Who...who's the father?"

"Aidan."

Drake plunked back onto his chair as if rammed there by something.

Susan said, "Oh."

Aidan Carlucci. The guy from the band. Sort of...grungy-looking. Older. By what? Five or six years? Long hair. Susan met his parents once. The father wore his hair in a ponytail. The mother had a peculiar name.

"Mom, I love him." Unlike her flat tone of voice, her eyes pleaded.

They were pale blue like Susan's and outlined in Drake's deep gray color. Slanted in a curious, almost foreign way, they aided and abetted the elfin image. "He loves me."

Drake huffed. "Love. What could you possibly know about love at your age? It has nothing to do with one-night stands. You have to be friends first. For goodness' sake, we don't even know his family. There are more than a thousand people in the church, and you take up with some stranger."

"It wasn't a one-night stand."

He went speechless again. His face reddened.

"And we are friends." She turned to Susan. "Give him half a chance. You'll like him."

"Does he know?"

"Why wouldn't he? We're in this together. He's totally committed to the relationship."

"Oh." Susan twisted a piece of hair dangling loose from the French twist Kenzie had arranged just hours ago, before dinner. They had giggled...

The fire crackled. Rain beat against the windows with a steady staccato sound. Lights twinkled on the Christmas tree in the corner.

Susan could not get her mind around Kenzie's news. The ramifications were endless. But...the situation was not all that uncommon, even among their congregation. Off the top of her head she counted three couples—good, solid people—who housed out-of-wedlock grandchildren and—

She gasped. "I'm going to be a grandmother!"

Kenzie flashed a smile. "Yeah. Grandma Susan."

A brand-new knowledge burst inside of her. She loved this unborn soul! Loved him with all her being. Flesh of her flesh...of her flesh. Another generation had begun.

She felt her heart leap across the room, flying toward the grandchild. She longed to literally dance after the feeling and embrace Kenzie and—by extension—the little one. But she hesitated...and then the moment was gone and Drake was speaking.

"Kenzie, I cannot marry you in the church. You know that, right? I do not perform the ceremony for anyone who has had relations."

"Drake!" Susan sputtered his name. "This is our daughter!"

"I'd look like a hypocrite."

"But—"

"No, we will not discuss it further. The people know my stance. I have to live out what I preach."

"You married the Malcolms in the chapel. We could—"

"Perhaps, but I—"

"Mom! Dad!" Kenzie held up a hand. "It doesn't matter. We're not getting married."

"What?" Drake's low-keyed voice took on an edge.

"Oh, honey," Susan whispered. The worst of her fears had just become reality. Not only was her child unwed and pregnant, she planned to remain unwed. How had such upside-down social norms taken hold of her?

"Mackenzie." Drake put his elbows on his knees, laced his fingers together, and hunched forward. The reasonable tone prevailed again. "I don't like what I'm about to do, but you leave us no choice."

Susan anticipated his words. She had heard them often enough in his sermons. Time ground into slow motion as she stared at the two people she loved most in the world, sensing that they were about to break her heart.

Drake, always the epitome of a respected public figure, scrambled for control. His shoulders, elegantly nestled in powder blue cashmere, sagged. His long tan face, more handsome at forty-eight than twenty-five, creased with tension. Even his short silver-streaked dark brown hair, moussed in a stylish stand-up fashion, seemed to droop. His mouth worked as if his tongue pressed chewing gum against the back of his teeth, readying it for bubble blowing. It was an old nervous habit, long ago trained away.

Only Kenzie could push the right buttons to make it surface again.

Of course, he pushed her buttons as well. There she sat, her mouth in its perpetual half-open position, giving the impression she was eager to laugh or suggest mischief…or smart off to her dad. She seldom did the latter, choosing instead to express herself with moderation. Like him, she could withstand incredible pressure.

But tonight the button pushing soared to new heights.

Years before, Susan had created a way to diffuse her own discomfort when they went at it like this, fussing at each other. She envisioned teensy, pearly buttons lodged in the identically upturned tips of their noses. In her imagination Drake and Kenzie tapped forefingers against each other's buttons. The image distanced Susan from the tense situation. Sometimes it even made her smile.

At the moment it wasn't working.

Drake cleared his throat. "You leave us no choice. If you insist on having a child out of wedlock, you are not welcome in this house."

Susan lost all feeling in her limbs. Anticipated or not, the words drained life from her, melding her body into the upholstery. Incapable of processing what was happening, her mind shut down as well.

Kenzie uncurled her slender self from the couch and stood. "Well, that was no surprise. I'll get my things."

"I don't mean tonight. We'll sort through details in the morning."

"No, Dad. There's nothing to sort through. I didn't expect any support from you."

Drake narrowed his eyes. The button had been pushed too far. "The car stays here."

"That's not fair. I paid for half of it!"

"So take half of it."

"Fine!" With a glance at Susan, she stomped from the family room.

Drake covered his face with his hands. "We had to do that. We had to. How can she learn if she doesn't suffer the consequences of her choices?"

Burning logs in the fireplace snapped and crackled. A gust of wind slammed a sheet of rain against the windows.

Her baby was having a baby.

Like a robot, Susan stood.

"Don't go after her."

"It's dark and cold and raining."

"She'll get a ride to a friend's. And tomorrow or the next day she'll come to her senses. We just have to gut this out."

Susan hesitated. Kenzie was, if nothing else, resourceful. She'd been on her own, more or less, for years. Even as a youngster she spent nearly as much time with friends' families as with her own. Since working as a babysitter at the age of twelve, she had seldom asked for money. She graduated from high school at seventeen and soon after moved out—

From the entryway came the sound of the front door opening and closing. Her daughter traveled lightly.

Drake lifted a mournful face to her and held out a hand. Tears pooled in his eyes.

She went to him.

One

Late March, Lenten Season

On a sunny afternoon in late March, Susan trailed behind her sister-in-law through a narrow passageway between two beach houses. Not far beyond the sidewalk's end, ocean waves rushed toward shore.

"I don't feel right about this." Susan's thoughts were not on the surroundings.

Natalie Starr, wife of Drake's younger brother and confident to an almost annoying degree, halted her brisk steps and turned. "Which part don't you feel right about? Five days at the beach in hopes of preventing a nervous breakdown? The feeling that you've abandoned Drake? The fact that you sent your daughter packing? Or that you lie to people at church concerning her whereabouts?"

"I don't exactly lie. I just tell them she returned from the band's European tour excited as a puppy—which she was—and is living with friends again. Which she is, I assume, since she hasn't come home."

Natalie cocked her head and pursed her lips. Sunbeams shone in her dark curly hair, highlighting reddish tones.

Susan diverted her attention to her little pug dog gaily crisscrossing the walkway, sniffing flower beds on both sides, oblivious to any tension. Pugsy, fawn colored and chubby, had originally been Kenzie's dog that short season she attended college and lived in a pets-allowed apartment. Somehow, somewhere along the way, responsibility for the dog fell to Susan. She didn't mind.

"Come on, Susan. Spit it out."

There was no escaping Natalie's prodding. "Well, in truth, I guess all of the above. A few days here without Drake, sending Kenzie off, and keeping her situation a secret from the congregation, from friends. I don't feel right about any of it."

"That's what I thought. You know, wallowing in guilt is overrated. Confess the sending and the lying as wrong and forget the rest. You need some R and R. It was Drake's choice not to come. Smell this salt air, listen to the beat of those waves. Give your mind a break." She sighed. "And call the boy's parents tomorrow."

"The gospel according to Natalie."

"Yep. I'm going to give my brother-in-law heart failure yet." She turned and resumed pulling the suitcase alongside the beach house. It clickety-clacked over the uneven concrete.

Susan called to the dog and followed, carrying a large shoulder bag. Although Natalie's opinions drove Drake up a wall, for Susan they often shed light into tunnels of confusion.

They rounded the corner of the house and stepped onto the cobble-stone patio, which served as the beachside front yard. A low picket fence separated the patio from a broad public walkway. Beyond that was the sand and then, a mere stone's throw away, the Pacific.

Natalie paused again, this time gazing at the house. She snorted. "This place always cracks me up. I mean, look at it. A squished red chili pepper of a cottage still holding its own against progress. It probably looked exactly the same in 1940."

Susan couldn't help but smile. The place was an anomaly in a neigh-borhood of large million-dollar-plus homes. A three-story white stucco towered over one side of it. At the other, three stories of phenomenal engineering rose with curved glass instead of corners.

The humble abode appealed to both women. Natalie and her husband, Rex, had been renting it for themselves every August for some years now. They treated Drake and Susan to a week at it every spring after Easter.

A feeling of peace washed over Susan, the first since Kenzie left two months, three weeks, and five days ago. Except for one brief, explosive phone conversation on the fourth of January—Day Three of that first heartsick week—Susan had not talked with her daughter. Kenzie called for the sole purpose to let Susan know she was okay and with friends. She offered no address, no phone number. Her stinging blast against her father and against her mother for siding with him still echoed in Susan's ears.

Guilt avalanched her now like a load of rock crashing all around her from an upended dump truck. She sat down on the suitcase.

"Hey, Suze," Natalie said. "You okay?"

"No."

"You will be. Come on. Let's get you settled."

~

While Natalie put away groceries in the kitchen, Susan took the suitcase into a bedroom and thought again at how odd the situation was, her being there without her husband.

Drake's prediction had not come true. Kenzie did not "come to her senses" and return home.

On Day Two after hearing the news, Susan thought she would drown in her despair. Natalie called. Aunt Nattie, as Kenzie referred to her, wanted to speak with her favorite niece and hear all about Europe. The story poured from Susan.

Drake was not a happy camper. His sister-in-law always told his brother everything, and Rex withheld little from their sons, Eric and Adam, who in turn had friends in the youth group at church. Word would get out.

On Day Six, a Sunday, Susan's capacity for "gutting it out" peaked. That morning Drake calmly declared he would remain mum on the subject; he had no idea how to spin the news to his congregants. Unable to mask her pain, Susan skipped church and spent the entire day in bed. Drake comforted her as best he could.

On Monday though, Day Seven, he reached the end of his own rope. He announced a moratorium on the topic—even with his wife.

A curtain dropped between them.

Adept at hiding real emotions, Susan got by…for a while…up until last week.

She was in a large outlet store on some errand and inadvertently walked through the baby department. Whatever the thin thread was that held her together unraveled right then and there. Slowly at first, then faster and faster, spinning her in a circle.

She found her way to a pay phone and called Natalie, who immediately picked her up.

That night her sister-in-law and brother-in-law convinced Drake that Susan needed a break, at least a week's worth. Drake said a retreat for five days was acceptable, perhaps even a good idea. An entire week was out of the question. Had she forgotten? There was the Hathaway wedding rehearsal Friday night and then the wedding Saturday afternoon. Not to mention Sunday church. He needed her on Sundays. She was his anchor on Sundays.

Susan acquiesced. She liked the Hathaways immensely. Her work as coordinator of their daughter's wedding had been a joy and not nearly the stress of many she did. It had probably been what held her together the past couple months.

The vacation rental was located less than an hour's drive from home, but Drake said he simply could not get away. It was the Easter season. His flock needed him and counted on his availability until his official vacation date after the holiday, three weeks from now. He promised to make excuses for her at meetings she normally attended. He would forward wedding-related calls to his capable director of women's ministries.

So many lives disrupted. All because of her.

The guilt alone might very well suffocate her before she'd even unzipped her bags.

Two

She didn't suffocate. Instead, Natalie handed her a cup of tea and she settled into an overstuffed chair. The front end of the house combined kitchen and living room. Two large windows faced the ocean; the dining table sat in front of one, and two comfy chairs and an ottoman were by the other.

While Natalie finished putting away groceries, Susan studied the familiar surroundings and sipped chamomile from a delicate bone china cup.

"Nothing about this place ever changes, does it? We've used these pretty cups and teapot for seven years. And, as usual, the white canister is full of all kinds of tea." She toed off her loafers and tucked her legs beneath herself. Pugsy jumped up and snuggled beside her.

Natalie plopped down in the other chair, water bottle in hand, and stretched her legs across the ottoman. "Yep. It probably looks exactly the same as it did the day Faith Fontaine moved into it. Except for the furniture. That couch can't possibly be forty years old. Though it does remind me of my grandmother's when I was a kid. All puffy and flowery."

"Don't you wish Rex would tell us who inherited the house from her?" Her brother-in-law had been the attorney for the deceased owner and handled her will.

"He said he'd have to shoot me if he told me."

"It's almost as if a thoughtful woman is still around in charge of all the little touches. Like the fresh lavender potpourri and candles. The herbs and spices in the cupboard. Rental property managers don't stock kitchens, do they? And the bone china cups. I think there was one with wisteria on it. I don't see it now. This yellow rose pattern is new, though, and it's from England just like the others."

"How on earth do you notice such things? Or why?"

Susan shrugged. She noticed details. And chattering like a chimp about them postponed the inevitable.

Natalie shifted in her chair. "I think this was a good idea for you to come, even if only for five days. A little time away will make a huge difference."

Susan glanced around the room. The place was full of cozy paraphernalia. Knickknacks and books, afghans and pillows, paintings and wall hangings. It was a grandmother's home. If welcome could be a physical sensation, the air was thick with it.

Maybe it was thick enough to choke the life right out of her guilt?

Natalie went on. "You can sit back and hopefully come to terms with Kenzie's news. Get used to the idea that my favorite niece is going to make me a great-aunt." She winked. "Grandma Susan."

"Easy for you to say."

"Suze, what can you do to change the situation? Not one thing. Kenzie is pregnant with or without a ring on her finger. At least she's not fifteen. At least she's not an alcoholic or a drug addict."

"As far as we know, anyway. She's looked the part for years with all that black clothing, all those earrings up and down her ears. The tattoo."

"A tiny rose out of sight on her hip. Come on. Those things are just Kenzie expressing herself."

Susan couldn't connect self-mutilation with positive self-expression, but she said nothing. That wasn't the point now. Her hands shook and the teacup clattered against the saucer as she set it on the end table. "I sent her away on a cold rainy night without so much as a hug."

"Drake's responsible for that, not you."

"I could have done something. I could have at least given her a ride. That wouldn't have exactly been interfering with the process. I mean, we think this is the best way to love her. To let her suffer the consequences

of her choices. It's just that the memory of that night unnerves—
Sorry. You've heard all this."

"Once or twice." Natalie smiled briefly. "Have you heard it though,
Suze? You keep saying 'we think.' *We?* What do *you* think?"

"That we have to present a united front."

"Okay, scratch that question. Tell me what you feel. What is your
heart saying?"

There it was. The inevitable. The place she didn't want to go. "I
don't know."

Natalie cricked her neck, moving her head in a half shake, and raised
her brows. It was a gesture of disbelief or disgust. Susan never was sure
which. Natalie easily spoke her mind, but Susan still thought she held
back a lot.

"Susan, I love you. Drake is a brilliant teacher and full of good practical advice. You are the epitome of a helpmate. But I swear, I am not
tracking with you here on this Kenzie business. Do you want my opinion?"

"All right." Her sister-in-law would give it anyway.

"Call Aidan's folks. If he's committed to the relationship like Kenzie
said he is, then she's probably still with him and they might know where
that is."

"Drake doesn't think we should."

"But you looked up their phone number."

"I can't go behind his back and undermine the process of letting her
suffer the consequences."

"But you looked up their phone number."

A tightness in her chest nearly cut off her voice. "I feel like I'm dying.
I have to know if she's all right."

Natalie gave a tiny smile. "Ah. There's your heart, Suze. Go with it."

～

Behind the house, Susan waved goodbye as Natalie drove down the
one-way street no wider than an alley. Half a block away, she turned a
corner and three-story town houses whisked her from view.

Now what?

Now do what you came to do, she admonished herself. Which was...
what?

Drake recommended a mini-retreat. To him that meant prayer and
Bible study and reaching Spirit-led conclusions within five days. She
agreed. She should gather her notebook and Bibles—three translations,
one paraphrase—and concordance and commentary and pen and get
to work. Expect God to show up.

A bird-of-paradise plant caught her attention. It was at least four feet
wide and just as tall. Five flowers bloomed among the mass of long slender green leaves. Orange petals sprouted upward like plumage, braced
underneath by indigo petals that jutted sideways like beaks. No question
why they were nicknamed "birds." How did so much life thrive from a
mere crack in the concrete?

"Susan?"

She turned and saw the neighbor in his patch of backyard on the
other side of a low wall. Probably in his mid-fifties, Julian lived in the
towering three-story.

"Hi." She smiled and stepped over to meet him at the wall.

"I heard you were coming." He kept tabs on the house for the property manager and knew when to expect guests. "A little early this year,
aren't you?"

"Yes." She shook his outstretched hand.

"Welcome."

"Thank you."

A feeling of peace washed through her as if it flowed from Julian's
fingertips to hers and on up her arm until it filled her. And then she
remembered. It was his usual effect.

Julian was unlike anyone she knew. He spoke with a Scottish accent
in a deep mellow timbre. His rectangular wire glasses often deflected
light, masking brown eyes she had found a little too intense on occa-
sion. As far as she knew, his entire wardrobe consisted of shorts, jeans,
T-shirts, and sandals. Though casual in appearance, his tight brown
curls were always neatly trimmed.

"Is Drake around?" he asked.

"No. Not yet. Not until..." She fluttered her hand, wondering how to explain. "Um, later. Our usual time. Monday after Easter. Three weeks."

"Ah. Pugsy with you?" Only Julian would remember the dog's name.

"Yes. He's keeping me company. Of course, he's already tired out and sleeping away the afternoon. We're just here for a few days, until Friday, a little private sabbatical before a big wedding at the church and Easter functions. So what's new at the beach?"

They chatted about the neighborhood and a recent storm that left sand displaced and strewn with seaweed all the way up to the retaining wall.

"Well," he said, "be sure to let me know if there's anything you need." His crow's-feet crinkled, and he turned to go.

"Julian!"

He faced her again.

"There is, um, one thing. I might...I might need to use a phone." It was an amenity the beach house did not offer.

"You're welcome to use mine anytime."

"I don't have a cellular. There just never seemed to be a reason for me to get one. I mean, I'm usually at home or at the church. People can reach me fairly easily. Drake, on the other hand, can't possibly survive without his, so he couldn't loan it to me. I could use the pay phone at the 7-Eleven." She paused to take a breath and recognized her chimp routine again.

"No problem."

Her lower lip trembled. She bit it.

"Susan, I don't mean to pry, but are you all right?"

"I'm fine." She cringed. She truly did hate that perky tone, the gushy soft rah-rah twist she employed in almost every conversation.

In truth she wanted to pour out the story to Julian's sympathetic ear. But how could she? Drake thought it best they not share the news with anyone. It was a private matter, not yet settled. It wasn't ready for public viewing. He said he would tell people in his own way in his own time. The situation had to be presented with dignity. A repentant Kenzie, wedding invitations in hand, wouldn't hurt matters.

As far as they knew, word had not gotten out. Absolutely no one knew about Kenzie besides Natalie and Rex.

It couldn't be helped.

But then neither could it be helped that she was not fine. Two months and three weeks and five days were too long to pretend her world was hunky-dory. To pretend it had not, in fact, swiveled right off its axis and spun out of orbit, leaving her with a sense that she was free-falling.

Julian slid his thumbs into his jeans pockets. "One time Faith Fontaine and I stood back here, almost in this very same spot. She could tell I was agitated, though she didn't pry. And I didn't want to talk. After all, it wasn't any of her business. She didn't know I was fiddling with a bullet in my pocket, thinking about going inside and playing Russian roulette until I lost."

Susan gawked at him. "My goodness. What happened?"

"I didn't play." He smiled. "I don't know exactly what happened. I'm sure she was praying. Suddenly I realized I had two choices: Russian roulette or tell her my life was a mess. Obviously I chose the second option. She didn't have any startling revelations of how to fix it. It was just in the telling that my weight lessened. Considerably."

"Well." She fingered a piece of paper in her skirt pocket and attempted a smile. "I don't have a bullet. Only a phone number."

Julian leaned forward.

Without the perky tone, her voice was so soft it was nearly inaudible.

"My life is a mess. No, it's not that bad. Comparatively speaking, it's really all right. Probably average. I mean, we hear so many heart-rending stories at the church and—"

"Susan, I forgot to mention the one conversational rule."

She waited.

"You can only talk about your own mess. Other people's heartrending stories don't count."

She felt awash in safety. "Kenzie, our daughter, is…pregnant." Intense heat obliterated the safe feeling, but she continued. "She's not married, though she says the young man is committed. And…and…"

He nodded. "That tends to create a mess."

"Yes. I'm having a hard time with it. I just need to get used to the idea. And to…well, Drake and I believe Kenzie should suffer the consequences. She does not want to get married. Drake says that is unacceptable."

"If she married, things would be different? Acceptable?"

"Y-yes."

Why? He didn't ask it, but she heard it.

Poof. A flash of white lit up a dark corner of her mind and the answer came. *Because if she married, then the matter of her having a baby within a few months wouldn't matter as much. People would not see us as parental failures.*

Susan's entire body felt smothered with heat. She and Drake had not voiced the explanation, but there it was.

"Kenzie has only called once since she told us on New Year's Day. She didn't leave a number. I don't know who her local friends are anymore… So I want to call the boy's parents to find out what they know."

"Of course you do." Pure compassion. Understanding. Nonjudgmental. "How about right now?"

She stared at him.

He nodded. "And if you talk to an answering machine, leave my number." He gestured toward his house. "The back door's open."

Three

In her rush to answer the ringing telephone, Pepper Carlucci smashed a toe against a pint-sized pickup truck and wondered, not for the first time, why it was at the age of forty-five she had yet another toddler in the house?

"Ow." She punched the phone's "on" button. "Ow, ow. Excuse me. Hello?"

"Uh, hello. This…this is…"

Before the woman finished the sentence, Pepper intuited who she was. *Susan Starr.* Kenzie's mother. The other grandma. For more than two months Pepper had both dreaded and hoped that she would call.

"Susan Starr."

"Yes, hello." She tilted the phone away from her mouth and inhaled deeply. Sinking onto the couch, she blew out the breath, pulled her foot up on the cushion, and repositioned the phone. "This is Pepper Carlucci. Aidan's mom." She rubbed her big toe.

"Hi."

The silence stretched, but Pepper vowed not to break it. She wasn't the one who had called. She wasn't the one who had banished her child from home.

Now that was a crummy attitude. Evidently she was still a tad bit angry about things.

"Um." Susan Starr's voice was barely a decibel above a breath. "I don't know where to be—" A sob cut her off.

24

Pepper sighed. "Kenzie is fine."

"Oh, thank God."

Well, thank Him and her husband, Mick, and Aidan and herself. Why not throw in the other five kids too? They all helped. They all loved Kenzie as though she were family.

"Is she there?"

"No." Pepper ran her fingers through her short hair. "But she's fine."

"Do you know where she's staying?"

Duh. The woman was a fruitcake right out of the fifties. Where would the girl be staying except with the guy?

Oh, Lord! Forgive that. "She's living with Aidan."

There was a rustling noise, like paper being rubbed between a nose and the phone's mouthpiece. "Um. May I have the phone number?"

"Susan, look, I'm really sorry, but she asked me not to give it to you. She said she will call you when she's ready. She's just hurting right now." *For good reason.*

The silence lasted a long moment. "How is she? With the pregnancy?"

"The morning sickness has subsided." Pepper deliberately closed her mouth to prevent herself from revealing more. This was Kenzie's battle.

Except for an immature little stubborn streak, her semi-daughter-in-law was a beautiful girl, inside and out. Courageous. A go-getter. One week back in the country she had taken a job as waitress in a coffee shop—make that *barista*—and seen a doctor. And her voice! An angel's. Pepper could not have chosen a better partner for her eldest son. God indeed had heard and answered her prayers. Well, not the pregnancy before marriage part, but then life never did fit into her version of perfect.

Susan said, "Will you give her a message, please? Tell her I'm at the beach house this week. Alone. Till Friday. But there's no phone here."

"Sure." The Starrs had a beach house? La-di-da. How much did superchurch pastors make, anyway?

"Mrs. Carlucci, may I ask you something?"

The woman's hesitant manner was getting on Pepper's nerves. "Shoot."

"Are you okay with this?"

"With what?" She knew with what, of course, but she was ornery enough to force Susan Starr to put it into words.

"With…with…" Susan sighed. "With them not being married. With them living together."

She waited a beat, measuring her words. "I find it best to be okay with things I can't possibly change. I sleep better at night."

There was another long silence. At last Susan spoke. "Can we meet? For tea? Or something? Just to talk a few minutes?"

Pepper wrinkled her nose. She really didn't want to get into it. If and when the Starrs made amends with their daughter, then she might consider a cordial relationship—for the baby's sake.

Susan was still speaking, rushing her words together. "The truth is, I'm not okay with this. I'm not sleeping. I'm not eating. I can't think straight. I don't know how to process the situation. Please. Tell me how you do it?"

Pepper suppressed a sudden urge to giggle. *Nah. No way, Lord. This one is totally Yours. I'd bite her head off and have fun doing it.*

Susan said, "I'm sorry. That was awfully presumptuous to ask. Will you just tell Kenzie that…that…I miss her and I'm here."

"Of course." Why wasn't the woman pounding on the Carluccis' front door to find Kenzie instead of stammering over the telephone? Their address was in the book!

"All right. Thank you. Goodbye."

If you forgive others their failings, your heavenly Father will forgive you yours; but if you do not forgive—

Nuts. She really had to quit studying Matthew's Gospel.

"Susan, wait. Where are you? What beach?"

Again a reply did not come immediately.

Pepper gazed at her ceiling and noted cobwebs.

"Mission Beach."

"Okay." That was further than she wanted to drive, and she wasn't ready to have her cobwebs scrutinized by the wife of the illustrious

Reverend Drake Starr. She calculated a midway point, not too private. "We could meet at the Fashion Valley mall. At the Starbucks on the second level."

"When?"

"Tomorrow? Say nine thirty?"

"Yes. Thank you. Uh, we met once, but it was a long time ago. I don't look like Kenzie. I have dark blond hair."

And, I bet, the expression of a woman watching a rattlesnake coiled at her feet. "I'll recognize you."

∽

Later that evening after dinner, Pepper enlisted Aidan's help in the kitchen. As he washed dishes, she playfully bumped a shoulder against his. "So, you want to come with me tomorrow? Meet your semi-mother-in-law for coffee?"

"Mom." Aidan, hands deep in sudsy water, shook his head. "Where do you come up with these phrases?"

"It's a gift. You know you didn't get your ability to write song lyrics from your dad." She picked up a plate and towel-dried it. "I guess I could say 'the mother of your live-in girlfriend who's not exactly just a girlfriend because she is the mother of your child, now about twenty weeks old in womb age.' "

"Yeah, right. How about 'the witch who wouldn't leave her dog outside on a rainy night but shoved her daughter through the door'?"

Pepper grasped his bristly chin and turned him to face her. "Hush," she whispered. "We all make mistakes, and she didn't shove Kenzie."

He closed his eyes briefly.

Nose to nose with him, she could have been looking at a photo of herself. He had the same narrow face as she, the same long nose, the same sapphire blue eyes set deep and close together under bushy brows. No laugh lines creased his twenty-five-year-old skin, though. No extra weight rounded out his neck. His dark hair was longer, thicker, and curlier than hers, and he stood shoulders and head taller. She let go of his chin.

"Yeah, Mom, we all make mistakes."

"You remember my first reaction to your news."

He smiled. "You were ecstatic about being a grandma."

She picked up a handful of flatware with the dish towel. "All right. Go to the second and third reactions. I wanted to ground you for life."

"Thank you for not doing that."

"Like I could." He no longer lived under her roof.

The day of his announcement she had exhausted her anger outdoors so as not to alarm the younger children. Walking round and round the high school's track, she fussed and fumed. How could her son have been so stupid? He knew not to play with fire. He *knew*.

That night her husband held her tightly and they consoled each other. Their Aidan understood his choices made his future more difficult than it needed to be, but he was a good kid. Not perfect as in angelic. He was too much a chip off the old block to be anything but just plain human.

Make that a chip off two old blocks. Pepper and Mick weren't exactly sainthood material. Not even close.

She laid the last fork in the drawer and closed it. "So what about coffee tomorrow?"

"I think I'm busy."

"Chicken." She hung the damp towel on the oven door's handle. "I'm going to make sure the little ones aren't terrorizing Kenzie. It's way too quiet back there."

She walked through the modest house, sidestepped a laundry basket overflowing with clean towels, and wondered what Susan Starr's five-bedroom home looked like. Kenzie had mentioned the size once and said the extra rooms weren't used much for guests. Maybe Pepper could rent space and ship the younger girls over there. They'd love not having to share a bedroom.

She found Kenzie in the middle of a twin bed, six-year-old Davita curled up on one side of her, three-year-old Mickey Junior on the other, both fast asleep. Kenzie's lids were shut as well.

Pepper paused in the doorway. A corner of her mind still wished to condemn the young woman as a blasphemous tramp who had ruined her son's life. It was so much easier to blame someone else's kid instead of one's own flesh and blood.

But that someone else's kid now carried Pepper's own flesh and blood.

She walked to the bed, and Kenzie's eyes fluttered open.

The girl smiled and shut a storybook propped on her lap. "Hi."

"Hi, yourself. How did you do this? Pj's, no less."

"Your kids are so sweet." She yawned.

"Occasionally, but you bring it out in them." She sat on the edge of the bed. "You are a natural with children."

"Nope. I'm just a PK." Kenzie often referred to herself as a Preacher's Kid. "I did not attend Sunday school. I always taught it. I think I was about a year old when I stood up in the nursery crib and exposited to the other kids about this dude named Moses telling the Red Sea to split."

Pepper chuckled as much at Kenzie's humor as at her delightful face. Whenever she poked fun at herself, her chin rose slightly so the tip of her nose appeared conspicuous. Its upward tilt made Pepper think that God had lifted His paintbrush just a millisecond too soon. But of course He didn't make mistakes. The nose fit just so.

And the baby fit just so as well.

"Kenzie, you are going to be an excellent mother." She patted her leg. "Now I want to ask this one more time. Are you sure you want me to meet your mom tomorrow without you?"

She nodded. Her eyes sparkled with tears. "I'm not ready. Please, just tell her I miss her."

Pepper blinked at her own tears and felt again squeezed in the middle of someone else's life. Her son owed her for this one. He owed her big time.

Four

Natalie Starr blew out an exasperated sigh. "Rex," she addressed her husband across the dining room table. "Why do you have to be such a *man* about this whole thing?"

His brows rose a notch as he sipped his after-dinner coffee. "You're emoting enough angst over Susan for the two of us."

"She's all alone down there!"

"She'll be fine. She's stronger than she looks. Or sounds."

"Oh! I have to tell someone else besides you!"

Rex set down his cup. "Nat."

She made a growling noise. "Don't talk lawyer to me."

"What'd I say?"

"You don't have to say a thing. It's your tone. All business and practical and full of reasonable argument designed to win over a jury. You're going to tell me to butt out. I don't want to hear it."

He smiled.

And she almost gave in. She loved his analytical mind. It usually complemented her own thinking. Their greatest joy was creating solutions to problems, whether big, small, irrelevant, personal, or business. World affairs were settled over morning coffee and their sons' adolescent woes over dinner decaf.

But now they were talking about Drake and Susan. Natalie's feminine side was riled up, a side she usually relegated to the back burner. Except when it came to Drake and Susan.

In spite of Rex's less than empathetic attitude, she felt nothing if not gratitude for his solid character. He did not resemble his older brother in the least. Instead of being tall with dark hair and light eyes, he was stocky in build with caramel brown eyes and blondish hair worn in a crew cut. The siblings' appearances provoked snide comments about a milkman's genes. Personality-wise, they were even more dissimilar, a fact that always triggered a jet stream of thankfulness in her.

"Rex, what happened to him?"

"It's what didn't happen to him."

The exchange was an old rerun. Natalie agreed that as young men in their early thirties, both brothers were smart, goal-oriented, hard chargers with a magnetism that drew people to them. They were both headed toward what she considered greatness: Rex in law, Drake in the church. Their goals centered around helping people. The irony was that the more they succeeded in helping others, the less time they devoted to their roles as husbands and fathers.

Seven years ago, life-threatening injuries from a ski accident changed Rex forever. As soon as his casts were removed, he went down on his knees. Seven years later he still did so on a daily basis. And it showed loud and clear in his compassionate ways.

Meanwhile, Drake spent the years feeding his public persona and distancing himself further and further from his family.

"I want to strangle him, Rex."

"I know, but it wouldn't help. And going against his wishes and telling people about Kenzie will not budge him. Only prayer will."

"But we've been praying that for months and Susan is hurting so badly."

"She has to make her own choices. And keep in mind, she is not like you. You never would have taken his nonsense sitting down. All we can do is pray her quiet demeanor wins him over."

"And that Kenzie is not lost in the process."

"Yes."

"We need more people praying."

"This is not for the gossip chain. Not without Drake's knowledge."

"I'm calling the Prayer Warrior."

Rex opened his mouth as if to protest more.

"I won't tell her details."

His lips relaxed back into another smile. "Mildred Murray. All right, totally different story from the gossip…I mean, prayer chain. Where would we be without those special older women who really know how to pray?"

His question was rhetorical. He referred not only to seventy-seven-year-old Mildred Murray, but to Faith Fontaine, the deceased owner of the beach house. When Faith learned that he lay near death in the hospital, she went to him and prayed. The doctors called it a miracle. So did Natalie.

She said, "Mildred is discreet. She will only tell the Father. Gwyn Fairchild knows discreet too."

"Natalie." His tone was back to *let's just hold on here a minute.* "Gwyn too?"

"I won't tell her details, either. Gwyn is the only woman who doesn't intimidate Susan to the point of speechlessness."

"Not like you."

She harrumphed. "No, not like me. That's why I have to tell Gwyn. She knows how to love Susan in a gentle way. I only harangue my poor sister-in-law. I don't know why she even talks to me."

"Harangue isn't the word. You simply suggest solutions. Like she needs time away. Aw, Nat. You're crying." He backed his chair from the table and held out his arms. "Come here."

Fighting back tears, she walked around the table and slid onto his lap.

"I promise you Susan will be fine."

"It hurts so bad seeing them like this."

"I know." He wrapped his arms around her, and she leaned into him. "It's too easy to imagine us in the same situation. Me being so consumed with my image that I would shut you and the boys out. But for the grace of God, there go I."

She put her face against his crisp white shirt. It worked pretty well as a handkerchief.

Five

On Tuesday, her first morning at the beach house, Susan awoke at four. Despite the early hour, she followed her usual routine: She showered, ate two soft-boiled eggs and lightly buttered toast, drank a cup of tea, engaged in a quiet time—at least a feeble attempt at it; the open Bible laid in her lap for a few minutes—and walked the dog.

Going through the motions was easier than worrying about what the day held in store for her. The routine was probably a close cousin to her chimp chatter.

Now she sipped another cup of tea in the big armchair by the front window and cuddled with Pugsy. The long beach walk in the brisk predawn hour had worn him out. Wouldn't Drake have a conniption if he knew she was outdoors at that time of day?

But he wasn't there to explain her lapse in good judgment.

She watched the tide make its way inland. Big waves had already enticed surfers into the deep. Though they were only specks on the horizon, she could see them because the house sat high enough to afford a view over the seawall straight to the ocean.

Julian surfed. Perhaps he was one of them. The previous day he showed her where he hid a door key on his patio. She was welcome to use it and his telephone anytime day or night, whether or not he was home. Julian was a nice man. Very compassionate.

Should she call Drake and tell him of her uneventful evening and the morning beach walk?

Best to spare him.

Should she tell him of her phone conversation with Pepper Carlucci? Of their meeting scheduled to take place in three hours?

Better to wait. Why borrow worry for him over something that had not yet happened?

Lord.

The prayer stopped.

She remembered how her mind had shut down the night Kenzie left. Nearly three months later, it hadn't fully restarted. It was like a dirty CD that got stuck on a smudge and played one word over and over and over.

She couldn't get past His name. *Lord.*

She couldn't pray.

The most she could do was go through the motions of everyday tasks and count the minutes until she met Aidan Carlucci's mother.

The closest link to Kenzie.

Closest? She was the only link.

~

Standing in a warm sunny space outside the coffee shop, Susan twisted the strap of her handbag around her fingers. She was fifteen minutes early.

Except for classical music pouring from loudspeakers hidden in flowerbeds, the second level of the open-air mall was quiet under a brilliant blue sky. A group of seniors clothed in cozy jogging suits sat at one of the food court tables. Occasional shoppers walked by. None resembled what she remembered of Aidan's mother.

They had met two years ago when Kenzie joined Aidan's band, Glory Traxxx. Drake deplored their rock style and thought it not true worship music, but he admitted it seemed to connect with teenagers. So he allowed them to perform at the church for a special youth group rally. Mr. and Mrs. Carlucci had attended along with parents of the ten or so other band members.

All in all Susan thought the evening a spectacular success. She didn't stop grinning and tapping a foot from the moment of their energetic opening downbeat until the next morning when Drake announced things had been just a bit too wild, a bit too vague when it came to the gospel, not quite suitable for his tender flock.

Soon after that, their youth pastor resigned. A mega-church in Texas hired him. Kenzie had seen him last year when Glory Traxxx performed there. He was happy.

Some days, when Drake was at the office, Susan listened to the cassette recording Kenzie had given her. She would grin, tap her foot, and feel astonishment at her daughter's voice coming through the sound system.

A woman approached. Her appearance fit the memory of Pepper Carlucci: shorter than average, not fat but roundish in a pleasant way, black hair cut almost as short as a man's and not styled, really. A small toddler accompanied this woman, though. Surely at her age—

"Susan?" Still several feet away, the woman called loudly and waved. "Is that you?"

Susan lifted a hand in greeting.

The towheaded child skipped alongside her. A boy? His hair curled to his shoulders, and he wore overalls with a long-sleeved red plaid flannel shirt. Mrs. Carlucci wore denim as well, jeans and a white tunic top.

Susan felt self-conscious in her floral skirt and blazer. She probably looked stiff and formal.

They neared. The woman shifted an oversized canvas bag to the other shoulder and held out a hand. "Hello." A smile lit up her entire face, and her blue eyes seemed to dance. "I'm Pepper."

She returned the smile and shook her hand. "Hello. And who is this?" She crouched down until face-to-face with the child.

He held out his hand before she could offer hers and smiled into her eyes. "I'm Mickerson Matthew Carlucci Junior. Pleased to meet you."

"Pleased to meet you, Mickerson Matthew Carlucci Junior. I'm Susan." She took his little hand into hers and couldn't help but giggle.

He glanced up at his mother, a look of concern on his face.

"I told him we're meeting Mrs. Starr."

"Well, Mickerson, I am Mrs. Starr, but you may call me Susan if you like."

"You can call me Mickey."

"All right. How old are you, Mickey?"

"Four, Susan."

"My, you are the most polite four-year-old I have ever met."

"Thank you." He smiled. "Mickey Senior says I'm a prodigy."

Pepper groaned. "Prodigy. Nemesis. The jury is still out."

He turned. "Mom, is it time for my Starbucks muffin treat?"

Susan laughed with Pepper and an odd thought struck her. Would her grandchild be as cute as Mickerson Matthew Carlucci Junior?

~

They sat outdoors in the sunshine.

Susan thought Mickey was a perfect buffer. His precocious conversation eased them through the first awkward moments of meeting. By the time they sat at a patio table and Pepper unloaded a bagful of books, markers, and miniature trucks, Susan felt able to sip her herbal tea without choking.

"Pepper, how many children do you have?"

"Six. Do you believe it?" She chuckled. "Aidan is the oldest, and—thank goodness—Mickey is the youngest."

The boy, engrossed in drawing and eating his muffin, didn't respond.

Pepper said, "We have the twins, Lisel and Sari. They're working on their masters' at UCLA. When they were in middle school, we started our second family." Her smiled was self-deprecating. "Carys is ten, Davita is six."

"I'm sorry. I mean, I'm not sorry that you have six—I think that's wonderful—we never could have more— Anyway, I'm sorry I don't know anything about you. Kenzie never mentioned being…well, I just didn't know she was particularly interested in your son. She spoke of him, of course, as a band member. As the leader, the songwriter. My, he is talented. Are all six of yours prodigies?" The perky tone reared its ugly inflection complete with chimp chatter.

But Pepper chuckled again. "Not exactly. Aidan is gifted in music, like Kenzie. Her voice belongs to an angel. And her fingers fly across a keyboard like it's an extension of herself."

"She's played by ear since she was four."

"Well, you have a prodigy for sure. Her lead vocals are my favorite of all their songs." She smiled. "You were saying you didn't know Kenzie and Aidan were an item?"

"She never spoke of him in…in that way."

"Their friendship just seemed to develop naturally. You know, from working together. Aidan moved out of the house ages ago, but sometimes the band still practices in our garage. Sometimes they just hang out, like family. Our home is what you'd call laid-back. Really laid-back. I guess with six kids it has to be. People come and go at all hours, all days of the week. After a while, I noticed Kenzie would come and go even if the band wasn't around."

Susan bit her lip and waited a moment for her vocal chords to untangle. "So you've known her for some time."

"Yes."

And I don't know Aidan because they didn't hang out at our house. They didn't do that because…because why?

Kenzie and that independent nature of hers was why! She rarely came herself and only called sporadically.

She said, "When did they start dating?"

Pepper shrugged. "A year ago, maybe."

A year. A whole year and she didn't know? What else didn't she know? "Did they…did they live together?"

Pepper turned to her son. "Mickey, you can go run around. Just stay between those tables and that wall there. Okay?"

"Okay," he mumbled, brushing crumbs from his mouth. "Thanks for the treat. 'Scuse me." He grabbed a handful of trucks and hopped down from the chair.

Pepper turned to Susan. "As far as I know they did not live together."

"He thanked you!"

"What?"

"Mickey just thanked you and excused himself!"

"He's a polite little thing."

"He's amazing."

"He has five siblings who think they're surrogate parents. We seem to share the role. Someday, though, we will have to let him go and he will make his own decisions."

The shift in Pepper's tone drew Susan back to the subject at hand.

"Aidan has been making most of his own for years now." She paused. "I saw no evidence in his apartment that Kenzie was living with him. I think he would have told me. I do know they fell in love somewhere along the way. They're crazy about each other. One thing led to another and now here we are."

"But Kenzie is a Christian!" The words tumbled out, at last naming a confusion that had plagued her since January first. "Your son writes worship music!" Maybe it wasn't worship music. Maybe Drake was right. He had studied Aidan's lyrics. Maybe the opaque references to love and peace and joy had nothing whatsoever to do with God.

Pepper tilted her head in a questioning gesture. "Yeah?"

"Well, I think something is terribly wrong with this picture!"

"You think Christians don't stumble?"

Susan blinked. "How...how can you condone what they've done? What they're doing?"

"Oh, goodness." Pepper laughed in disbelief. "I don't condone it. They've made some incredibly stupid decisions and created humongous bumps in their road. They've done things their own way, kind of like a hundred percent of the world's population does. But I accept these two children of ours." Her tone grew urgent, almost argumentative. "They are wounded human beings who are bringing another one into the world who will need that same acceptance and not condemnation for being born."

Susan's heart pounded. "What about consequences? How can they learn from their mistakes if we simply welcome them with open arms? That communicates they can do whatever they please."

Pepper opened her mouth and then quickly shut it. Her lips disappeared as if she were pulling them inward and sealing them together. She closed her eyes for a brief moment. "Susan, I'm sometimes accused of being too blunt. Tact just isn't one of my gifts. I blame my parents. I mean, for goodness' sake they named me 'Pepper.' My personality was doomed from day one to be irritating. Please forgive me if I come across hurtful. I don't mean to."

What on earth...? "All...all right."

"I think the question is, does Jesus welcome us with open arms? With our faults? Did He die on the cross for us because we did everything right?"

"No, of course not, but...but what does that have to do with Kenzie's situation?" Susan felt as though she was racing through a maze, turning one blind corner after another and getting nowhere.

"You kicked Kenzie out of the house. On a cold rainy night. Without a car."

An overwhelming sense of horror slammed into her like a physical blow to the chest. Hearing the truth from a stranger multiplied the awfulness of what she had done.

Pepper said, "I'm sorry. In all fairness, she said you didn't kick her out that night. She's the one who decided to leave right then. She knew Aidan was waiting outside in his car for her."

Aidan was waiting? Thank goodness.

"And Kenzie said it was her dad who sent her, not you."

"But," she whispered, "I sat there and let it happen."

Compassion etched furrows in Pepper's brow, around her mouth.

A sense of loss overwhelmed Susan. "I miss her. I think I've missed her for years. She never was around much and then she moved out right after high school..."

"She is a strong, determined young woman. I didn't even have to suggest she see a doctor. She found a clinic for low-income women."

A flush crept up her neck. Drake made a decent salary! Their daughter shouldn't have to go to a clinic! How absurd! Should she give Pepper money? But he would never approve. Not welcome in their home meant not one penny would go to Kenzie or toward the baby's care.

"Susan." Pepper's voice grew soft. "Kenzie said to tell you that she misses you."

The words thwacked her like another harsh blow. In about two seconds she was going to fall apart.

Quickly, Susan twisted around and unhooked her handbag from the back of the chair. In one swift motion she shoved the seat from the table and stood. "I must go."

Without one polite phrase or even a glance in Pepper's direction, she hurried away.

Six

"Oh, man!" Pepper groaned and slid down the chair until her nose was level with the table. She spoke aloud, oblivious to people sitting nearby in the food court. "I did not mean to do that! I told You, Lord! I told You. You shouldn't have trusted me with this one. I wanted to stick it to her, and I did. I surely did."

"Mom?" Mickey tugged at her arm.

"Hi, honey." She widened her eyes at him and met his gaze. "Do you see a log in one of my eyes?"

Somberly he inspected each and then he shook his head. "Nope. No log."

She smiled. "Thanks." At the prodigious rate he was growing, he'd gain spiritual eyes soon enough and be only too eager to point out all sorts of logs.

"Where's Susan?"

"She had to go home. How about we pack up your toys and shop?"

He scrunched his nose in distaste.

"To buy a maternity shirt for Kenzie."

"For Kenzie? Yay!" As fast as his short legs would carry him, he tore off and collected the trucks he'd parked around the area.

He so obviously loved Kenzie. What was wrong with her parents?

"Oh, Lord. As I was saying, I am sorry."

Pepper raised a hand and then held it aloft, knuckles bent inches from the door. Dropping in unannounced at Aidan's apartment had taken on a whole new complicated dimension. Visions danced in her head. They were of herself and Mick as newlyweds behind closed doors and not expecting the in-laws.

Nope. The situation was not quite the same. She wasn't an in-law. The kids were not newlyweds. They had no business acting as such.

Eww. If that didn't smack of a Reverend Drake Starr judgmental attitude, she didn't know what did.

Beneath her raised arm, little Mickey whomped his body against the door and banged his fist on it. "Kenzie! Open up!"

He must have drained his courtesy tank on Susan. "Mickerson, that is not polite."

"Oops. Sorry."

Kenzie opened the door, a wide grin across her face, and knelt. "Mickey J!"

The boy jumped right into her arms, not slowed in the least by the shopping bag in his hand.

Thank You, Pepper breathed a prayer of relief. Kenzie's hair was in place, each spiky spring goop-laden to perfection. She was completely dressed in black jeans and a gray midriff sweater that hit just above the slightly rounded tummy. She wore shoes even. Those chunky heels. Murder on a back supporting a baby. Give her a couple months—

"Hi, Pepper. Come on in."

"Hi." She smiled. "Don't mean to interrupt."

"You're not. I'm just getting ready for work." She shut the door behind them. "I am so not a morning person. Thank goodness the coffee shop keeps me on the afternoon/evening shift. Sit down."

Pepper crossed the dinky living room and noticed that the door to the bedroom was shut. She pictured Aidan behind it, headset on, playing the electronic keyboard—its sound off—and composing music. Worship music. Nontraditional, but still a proclamation that God offered hope to everyone.

Mickey jumped up and down. "Kenzie! Kenzie! Open this." He pushed the shopping bag at her. "It's a tourney shirt!"

Pepper laughed and sat on a worn secondhand upholstered chair. "There goes that surprise."

Kenzie sat cross-legged on the threadbare carpet and dug into the bag. "Tourney shirt?" She pulled out a red plaid flannel. "Mickey! It's just like yours!"

He shook his head vehemently. "No. It's a tourney shirt. Boys don't wear tourney shirts."

Kenzie raised her brows at Pepper.

"Maternity." She eyed Kenzie's bare midriff again.

"Maternity? Really? Oh, wow! My very first!" She slid her arms into it. "Thank you!"

"You're welcome."

Kenzie sprang to her feet and whirled around. "It's great. I'll wear it today." She leaned over and hugged Pepper. "Thank you. And thank you." She knelt to squeeze Mickey.

He squeezed her back, and she held him tight, her eyes shut.

In that pose, Kenzie resembled her mother. It was not so much a physical thing but rather a vague impression. Both women sent out a subtle message of vulnerability. Fragility.

Pepper thought too of how they responded to Mickey in the same way, crouching down to his level, conversing with him like the real person he was. They both expressed obvious enjoyment of his personality. Not everyone did that. Then there was the hair. Granted Susan's was in an uptight-style bun that fit her personality and Kenzie's in its wild springs and a different color, but each was styled in such a way that held every hair perfectly in place.

Interesting. Like mother, like daughter.

Uh-oh.

The bedroom door opened and Aidan entered the living room. "Hey, Mom. Mickey, my man!"

Her youngest rushed at her oldest. They exchanged high and low fives before Aidan grabbed Mickey in a hug and lifted him toward the ceiling. The fact they had just seen each other the previous night didn't hamper their enthusiastic greeting.

Pepper waited. Finally Mickey settled into a corner with a stack of books. Aidan and Kenzie sat on the only other seat in the room—a fourth-hand loveseat of no identifiable color—and turned their attention to her. Expectant.

Well, yes, that was the word. In more ways than one.

"How'd it go, Mom?" Aidan took Kenzie's hand.

"Fairly…all right. We got to know each other a little better. Bottom line, she is upset about sending you away, Kenzie. The guilt is eating her up."

"She said that?"

"Not exactly." She thought of the moment Susan's mask slipped and her preacher-wife tone disintegrated. "She got very real when I said— almost in the same breath—that Jesus welcomes us to the cross when we're in our direst need and that she sent you away."

Aidan thrust a fist in the air. "Way to go, Mom!"

"No, not way to go, Mom. I got huffy. I hate being huffy. I especially don't want to be huffy with Kenzie's mother, with your semi-mother-in-law. Good grief, in the near future we'll have to share the same waiting room in the maternity ward. Not to mention birthday parties and holidays for the rest of our lives."

Kenzie's mouth formed an O shape. "I hadn't thought of that."

It's called consequences, my dear. "Anyway, I broke the ice. I filled her in on how you are. I found out she's hurting and regrets her actions. But the next step is up to you." She pressed her lips together before another huffy tone slipped out.

"Did she have my dog with her?"

"No."

"I bet Pugsy is there, though, at the beach house. Dad would never take care of him. Actually it's really weird Mom's at the beach without Dad. They always go right after Easter. My Aunt Nattie and Uncle Rex rent the house for them." She smiled. "It's a funky place. You'd never guess it was south of the Mission restaurant. It looks like a squished red chili behind a white picket fence. Right on the boardwalk between all this cool modern stuff."

So the house didn't belong to the Starrs. They didn't even pay for the rent. *Okay. I can live with that.*

Kenzie went on. "Mom loves it, but I can't believe she's there by herself. She never does anything without my dad. Why would he allow her to go alone?"

Allow her? Eww.

The girl shook her head. "I know I've hurt her. Hurt both of them. But I always seem to hurt them without even trying. I've never lived up to their standards. They hate my music. They—"

"Hon," Pepper said, "back up to 'I know I've hurt her.' Start and stop right there."

Kenzie gazed at her for a long moment. "You're saying I should apologize. But I already have!"

Pepper shrugged. "That first time hardly counts. Right, Aidan? I don't even think I heard the 'I'm sorry' until twenty-four hours later."

He raised his brows in reply.

Pepper knew the expression. It meant *Back off. Give me some space.* She glared, hoping he read her mind as well. *You little twerp.*

Since when had they become mind readers?

Since Kenzie.

In that split-second Pepper realized something had changed forever. She had refused to read the tea leaves, but it had been coming for months. The offbeat style of rapport she shared with her son vanished on the spot. Aidan had a wife—so to speak. All dialogue encompassed her. He didn't communicate "Give *me* some space." He meant "Give *her* some space." He spoke for Kenzie because his mother had stepped over a boundary she didn't know was there. Until now.

Pepper felt...displaced. She wasn't so sure she liked that.

Seven

Half a block from a busy intersection, Susan stood outside a bakery at a pay telephone. The scent of cinnamon rolls swirled with that of sea salt. Pugsy sat at her feet, content to soak up sunshine and watch people eat lunch at a sidewalk café across the street.

Susan arranged stacks of coins on the little shelf beneath the phone. She picked up the receiver and enough quarters for a toll call. She dropped them into the slot. They plunked. She listened to the dial tone, pressed the "1," and held her finger above the "8." It hovered there momentarily.

And then she replaced the receiver. The money clanked into the opening at the bottom of the phone. She scooped it out and carefully stacked it on the little shelf.

It was her fourth such repetition of the activity.

Or was it the fifth?

The definition of insanity is doing the same thing over and over and expecting a different outcome.

Was she going insane?

She wasn't sure.

Lord.

Her daughter was fine. Living in sin, yes, but physically safe and sound. Pepper seemed like a nice woman. She would be a mother's eyes and ears and make sure Kenzie had enough to eat and was warm enough. Food and shelter—the basics were covered.

Drake should be informed.

I don't want to tell him.

The thought sprang from nowhere and waggled around a bit.

Was it something a submissive wife would think?

She wasn't sure.

But there it was.

Susan gathered the coins and placed them in her blazer pocket. Kenzie was fine. That was enough for one day.

She only wished she had remembered to ask Pepper how it was she managed to sleep at night.

Pugsy's insistent yip woke Susan. It still felt odd to awaken in a chair in the middle of the day. Up until three months ago, she had been a stranger to sleepless nights and afternoon catnaps.

"What is it, Pugs?"

He quieted and tilted his head. At home he only barked when the doorbell rang. The noisy beach world confused him.

Movement at the window caught her attention. Susan leaned forward to see more clearly.

Good grief. There stood Gwyn Fairchild at the front door. Had she spotted Susan asleep? In a chair? In the middle of the day?

Thoroughly embarrassed, she straightened her skirt and smoothed back her hair into its bun. After a quick pinch to her cheeks, she forced a smile and opened the door.

"Gwyn! Hi!"

The other side of the screen door, her friend stared, unblinking, unsmiling, a bouquet of fresh flowers in her hand.

Susan's stomach twisted. Natalie was to blame. Her sister-in-law could not keep her big mouth shut. She had blabbed everything about Kenzie to Gwyn.

Without a word Gwyn entered, wrapped her arms around Susan, and squeezed.

Half a foot shorter than the drop-dead gorgeous 5' 10" paralegal, Susan returned the hug, her chin against Gwyn's shoulder. "How on earth did you find—"

The squeeze turned fierce. "Knock off the cheery bunk. You're exhausted and on a mini-retreat. That's all Natalie told me."

Maybe Natalie hadn't spilled the entire story.

Gwyn released her. "I would never interrupt whatever is going on except that when Natalie told me you were here, she was absolutely furious." The corners of her mouth went up gently. "You know how she can be." She handed her the flowers. "For you. Shall I make us some tea? Go sit down and smell the roses. Are there roses in that bouquet? Pugsy, shoo along with your mother. I'm sure you understand by now I don't like you in the least. I'll find a vase."

In her ever-elegant way, Gwyn pronounced the word *vahz*. Of course "cheery bunk" was said with equal aplomb in a cool tone that seldom varied in pitch. Continuing her small talk and not waiting for answers, she stepped into the kitchen area and began preparing tea. She moved like flowing liquid.

Susan returned to the chair by the window. If Natalie hadn't disclosed all, then the story would hold. She played yet another rerun. *Yes, I am so tired, that bout with the flu and all. Couldn't wait three more weeks for a break. Yes, Kenzie is still on her own, still singing with the band that plays alternative Christian rock music. Glory Traxxx. With three x's. I don't know why they spell it that way. She'd go back to Europe in a New York minute. Yes, she always planned on returning to school. Sometime.*

All of it true.

All of it so very exhausting.

Gwyn put the flowers in a crystal vase and set them on the kitchen table. When the tea was ready, she handed Susan a cup and sat in the other chair by the window. "Susan, I'm not very good at this." Her cool tone wobbled.

"At what?"

"At being there for you. Or here, I guess I should say. You know, like how you're always there for me. I'm not sure how to go about doing it."

The tangled knot in Susan's stomach had traveled upward into her chest. She could scarcely breathe.

Gwyn removed her heels and tucked her stockinged legs up under her knee-length skirt. Thick mascara and eyeliner defined her almost violet eyes. Every single lock of jet black hair hung perfectly together in a short bob. That was Gwyn, perfectly put together.

No. Susan knew better. She eyed the scar nearly invisible under makeup. It was a three-inch slash, parallel to her ear. The old wound reminded Susan that despite Gwyn's outward appearance, inside she resembled a war zone under reconstruction.

"Gwyn, there's nothing to do."

"Of course there is. For now we'll just sip our tea and wait for the others to come show me what to do."

"The others?"

"The Martha Mavens." She raised a brow. "I simply had to call for reinforcements. They'll be along shortly. Have some tea, Susan."

The last thing on earth Susan wanted to do was put on her game face, drink tea, and converse with Gwyn or others, even if they were the women who most closely resembled what she could call friends.

On second thought, that wasn't the last thing she wanted to do. The last thing had already happened.

She sipped her tea.

∽

Within the hour, the others Gwyn referred to descended upon the beach house like a storm-tossed wave that jumped over the seawall and flowed right on through the picket fence, across the patio, and under the door and windows. Susan's very pores felt drenched with the overwhelming presence of the Martha Mavens.

Gwyn had nicknamed the group in honor of the New Testament woman. Martha was overly occupied with kitchen matters while her sister, Mary, ignored dirty dishes in favor of sitting at Jesus' feet. The moniker was used tongue-in-cheek. Although it was Martha-type behavior that originally brought them together, what kept them truly linked over the years was a nearer resemblance to Mary. When all was said and done, spiritual concerns superseded the ability to bake a blue-ribbon lemon meringue pie.

A fact which always put Susan a bit on edge.

As the women entered the beach house, lifting the corners of her mouth required every ounce of strength.

I'm fine. Just fine.

Tess Harmon entered first. Typical leader. Short bouncy hair, streaked a light brown, matched her personality. She spoke in short, energetic phrases, a useful tool for the director of women's ministries at the church. Drake had nicknamed her "Boss," a title she adored.

The twins followed. Seventy-seven-year-old widows, Leona and Mildred were identically cute and roly-poly with white hair and doe eyes behind silver-rimmed glasses.

Young Emmylou Bainbridge entered last, a shy Mississippian who had followed her Marine boyfriend to San Diego when she was seventeen. Thirteen years later, they were now married and...

Susan wanted to crawl into a hole. Emmylou was more than eight months pregnant. Her abdomen literally protruded into the room while the rest of her remained outside on the patio.

"Sit," Tess commanded after Susan had greeted everyone with a hug.

Fighting the urge to flee to the bedroom, she once again did as she was told. Tess was more formidable than Gwyn.

Emmylou waddled over, her face beaming. "Susan, feel this." She took Susan's hand and placed it on her roundness. "It's his foot. Isn't that awesome?"

She nodded, tried to smile, and pulled back her hand. The impression of a hard little heel lingered in her palm.

Mildred's arthritic legs caused her to teeter along like Emmylou. She slowly lowered herself into the other chair by the front window and fixed her big eyes right on Susan. "Now, dearie, we are not here to intrude. But let's invite the Lord to visit." Not waiting for an answer, Mildred—nicknamed the Prayer Warrior—bowed her head and said, "Father."

That was all she said.

Susan clenched her fists until she felt the pain of fingernails digging into her flesh.

Eight

Sitting there in the beach house living room with her eyes closed, Mildred Murray prayed in silence for some time. At least Susan thought she prayed, although she really wasn't sure. Maybe the woman simply listened. Whatever went on in those quiet moments, things happened afterward. Susan had witnessed the phenomenon more than a few times. The elderly woman personified Martha's sister, Mary.

Meanwhile, the others quietly rearranged furniture, moving the love-seat nearer the two chairs by the front window. Leona and Emmylou sat on it with Pugsy between them. Gwyn and Tess sank nimbly to the floor like the yoga devotees they were. Then they all waited for Mildred to finish.

At last she straightened. The rosy glow on her face suggested she was a jogger just in from the brisk January air. A happy jogger at that. Her grin pushed cheeks back into many laugh folds.

She always appeared so after her prayer times. Susan described it once to Drake. He pooh-poohed that one's face would actually change in a physical manner during prayer.

Mildred said, "The Lord is here, and He wants to bless us."

She always announced that too. And then she waited for someone else to share whatever was on her mind.

Apparently Tess felt the nudge to speak first. "I've been thinking lately about how we Martha Mavens got our start. Gwyn, I hesitate to bring it up."

"It's all right," Gwyn said. "Ten years have passed."

Emmylou shuddered visibly. "It was the most horrific night of my life. Oh, Gwyn. I don't mean that. I mean, it was for me, but it was something much worse for you. I don't mean to make light of it."

"Of course you don't. But think of the good God brought from it." Gwyn spread her arms. "The Martha Mavens."

Tess said, "Right. I think that's why it's important to rehearse the past, like the Jewish people do with their history, so we don't forget."

A long silent moment passed.

Susan found her voice. "Drake and I were new at Holy Cross Fellowship that year."

Mildred said, "Such a floundering group we were before he became our pastor! A bunch of fish flopping around in a dried-up sea. We women were hardly acquainted before that night. Our paths seldom crossed. Tess, you'd recently been hired as director of women's ministries. And Emmylou." She smiled. "You were a darling teenager, all moony over your Marine and working as our janitress. Leona and I hadn't really gotten a chance to know you yet."

Tess said, "Natalie wasn't around much before then. But that night we were all there."

Leona nodded. "Six busy little Martha bees. Tess, you were working late in your new office. Mildred and I were packing up gifts for missionaries in Peru in the ladies' circle room. Susan, you were singing, practicing for a Sunday morning solo, and Natalie was trying to keep that old sound system going for you. Emmylou, you were vacuuming by the front door."

They went quiet again. Susan wondered if recounting history meant speaking aloud the horrific details.

Gwyn broke the silence. "And I was being raped and knifed behind the building." She touched the scar by her ear.

That answered Susan's question.

Emmylou said, "When I turned off the vacuum, I saw you through the glass doors, all huddled in a heap. You should not have been able to crawl that far."

"By God's grace alone." Gwyn paused. "And you came outside and screamed loud enough for everyone to hear."

"Can we say the rest is history?" Emmylou turned to Tess.

She shook her head.

Gwyn said, "Let me tell it. I was semiconscious, but I know you all stayed by my side. Waiting for the ambulance. Talking to the police. And Tess stayed even through the night in the hospital. You took turns for weeks after caring for me in my apartment. I named you the Martha Mavens and eventually came to church and heard about Jesus, who sounded exactly like each and every one of you. What wasn't to believe?" She smiled. "All right, now we can say the rest is history."

Mildred held up a hand. "Except to add that all seven of us bonded in a special way through this experience. Since then we've been there for each other. Through the good times, yes, but most especially through the grievous ones. There were the deaths of my husband and of Leona's."

Gwyn said, "My divorce."

"For me," Emmylou said, "all those years of infertility tests and surgery and miscarriages."

Tess said, "My son-in-law fighting overseas. And I might add for Natalie, her husband's near-fatal skiing accident."

Intimidation settled on Susan's shoulders like a coat of heavy mail. She felt eighteen again, at Bible college, sitting in a circle of young women. They all took turns to pray aloud with great fervency. All, that was, except quiet Susie Anderson. She didn't have a thing to say.

After a few such meetings, she realized that if she didn't contribute at least a few words, the others would think her spiritually impoverished. A far cry from Bible college material capable of snagging an up-and-coming pastor for a husband.

And so she adopted her chimp chatter routine. Mimicking the more vocal students proved an easy assignment. Now, at forty-three, she no longer needed to pretend herself worthy. She had indeed snagged the guy and she was indeed the pastor's wife.

A new set of expectations arrived with the marriage. The job description dictated she keep a corner of herself even more aloof than Susie Anderson ever had. Airing dirty laundry would never do. It encouraged congregants to lose respect for the pastor. Did it really matter that her husband never picked up after himself in the bathroom? Or excused himself from the table? Or offered a hand in the kitchen? No reason to share that sort of information. As Drake often said, she could make or break him in those little details.

But the job description also meant she owed something to the present conversation.

And so she said, "For me, there was Kenzie's smoking at the school in seventh grade and later all those holes pierced in her ears." Had she ever mentioned to any of them the tattoo she glimpsed beneath her daughter's hip-hugging waistband? Probably not. "And, um, there was the time Drake had to cancel his trip to Israel."

As Kenzie would say, *lame.* But the recap would have to suffice. No way was she about to match stories of death, divorce, rape, and infertility. Not that she couldn't. It just wouldn't be appropriate.

No one said a word.

Avoiding eye contact, she busied herself with lifting the teacup from the end table. Her hand shook so badly tea sloshed over. The cup slipped from her hand, clattered against the saucer, and landed on its side.

She sprang to her feet and righted the cup. "How clumsy. Oh, no! It's chipped. And cracked!"

Tess appeared at her side with a kitchen towel and proceeded to mop up the liquid.

"Susan," Mildred said.

She turned to the Prayer Warrior.

"You remind me of that china cup. I think a chip has been knocked off your heart and now it's cracked. Dearie, something needs to spill out before it can be glued back together. It can't hold things in any longer."

Again she thought of how she had seen things happen after Mildred's prayers. People unburdened themselves. They confessed all manner of trouble. Mildred then would point them to Jesus, the one and only source of forgiveness and healing.

But those things happened to other people. Never to the pastor's wife. There was, after all, her and Drake's reputation to protect.

Susan looked at the teacup in her hands, retreating from Mildred's searing gaze. She knew the right answers without the older woman's direction. She and Jesus would get together privately. Later. When she was ready. For the moment, in the presence of others, she could offer but one thought.

She cleared her throat, but her voice still came out scarcely above a whisper. "I have an…an unspoken prayer request."

Nine

"An unspoken prayer request?" Natalie couldn't help it. Annoyance shot through her tone loud and clear. "That's what you said to them, Susan? Give me a break!"

Susan turned around and wiped off the kitchen counter with a dishcloth.

"I'm sorry, Suze." She folded her arms and leaned sideways against the refrigerator. "I just don't get it. I mean, we're talking Mildred Murray."

"You know saying that much—an unspoken request—was a major concession for me, even to Mildred and the others. It was probably too much. This is such a personal matter. You're family, but Drake and I can't possibly open up to everyone else. They'd lose all respect—"

"That's absolute gibberish! He's the pastor, not God. He's human."

"He's the leader. He has to be strong."

"But he doesn't have to be perfect!" How many times had they had that conversation? Rex thought Natalie an optimistic nutcase, talking as if Drake would ever agree with her opinion. He was unbendable when it came to his view of pastor.

Susan's profile sagged. "I appreciate you trying to help, but sometimes we just need your support, a hundred percent of it, without sibling rivalry entering into the picture."

Natalie twisted her lips together so tightly her jaw popped. Rex was younger than Drake by five years. Susan chalked up their differences to typical issues of family rank. Drake saw himself as carrying an extra load of responsibility while their parents spoiled Rex rotten. How could Rex possibly understand Drake's role?

It was another tired topic, best to avoid it.

"Natalie, I really wish you hadn't told them where I was." Susan rinsed the dishcloth and wrung it out.

Natalie let the sibling rivalry comment go. It had nothing to do with the issue at hand. "Susan." She grasped her elbow and steered her around. "I love you. The Marthas love you. You're hurting. We want to express our love by being here for you in whatever way might help ease your pain."

"They were all here for me." She turned back to the sink, folded the cloth, and laid it over the faucet. "It doesn't matter that you had to coach soccer practice and couldn't come until they'd left." She faced her again. "You're here now and you listened to what I said about my meeting with Mrs. Carlucci without comment. You ate dinner with me. And just think. The food was all Martha-type gifts of love. We had Mildred's chicken soup, Emmylou's veggie pizza, Leona's brownies." She glanced at the coffeemaker steaming away. "There's Tess' hazelnut coffee for you to drink while I enjoy the new herbal tea Gwyn left—"

"Coffee." That was it. "Why don't you drink it anymore?"

"Why don't I—? What? You know why. It affects me adversely. I haven't indulged for years."

"It affects Drake adversely."

Susan went to the stove to flip off the burner under the teapot, but she didn't move to pick it up. "I'm really tired."

"I know." Natalie poured herself a mug of coffee. Why couldn't Susan accept their love? Why couldn't she be real with the others about Kenzie? It all kept coming back to Drake. Why? Determined to explore things further, she had to buy time. Rex swore her middle name was bulldog. *Speaking of dogs…*

"Suze, let's go walk Pugsy. Then I promise I'll leave. Just let me love on you a little longer?"

Her sister-in-law was clearly exhausted, but a corner of her mouth went up. "I don't know if I can handle any more being loved on."

Natalie chuckled. "I'll work on my delivery. Maybe a little more tenacity and less belligerence will help?"

"I'll get the leash."

⌣

With Pugsy in the lead, Natalie and Susan strolled through the dark. Yellowy lamplight lit the boardwalk at regular intervals. An overcast sky hid stars from view and kept the temperature mild.

They walked in a comfortable silence. Natalie thought how they'd been friends since the Thanksgiving Day fifteen years ago when Rex took her home to meet his family. She and Susan had connected instantly, an odd thing considering their disparate personalities. Susan was older, totally feminine, already a mother and married for eight years. To Natalie, she defined "pastor's wife" in her compassionate ways. On the other hand, Natalie was a high school phys ed teacher and a girls soccer coach and wore shorts all the time.

They always got along. But slowly and subtly, a wall went up between them. Susan laughed less and less and started wearing her beautiful naturally blond hair in a tight little bun.

Natalie believed the change coincided with Drake's ascension in popularity. Not that he didn't deserve all the kudos and attention. His was a fresh voice in the church. Even now, people still loved him. He still offered God's truth from the pulpit. Inside of him, though, something changed. Unable to explain why, Natalie and Rex felt their connection with him severed.

His connections with his wife and daughter had been affected as well, twisted and turned upside down. And now the collateral damage was coming to the surface.

Natalie said, "Want my opinion?"

Susan tugged smartly on Pugsy's leash and he barked. "You always ask that. Like I'd bother to say no."

"You can say no."

"Would you not give your opinion if I did?"

"Doubtful." She paused. "I think this dilemma is not so much about Kenzie. It's about you and Drake."

Susan shivered visibly.

"Today," Natalie said, "when you didn't run plans by Drake and just followed your heart, you met with Aidan's mother and you learned about Kenzie. The operative phrase is *you didn't run plans by Drake.*"

"I should have, though." Unmistakable guilt filled her voice.

"Not necessarily." She halted and faced her.

Susan stopped as well. "It's called submission. He is the head. We agreed not to interfere with Kenzie facing consequences. I went against that."

"Where you went was after your daughter, to learn about her welfare like you would any other homeless unwed mother-to-be who walked through the church doors. If that's anti-submission, sign me up."

"Drake says—"

"My question is, what would you do if Drake were not in the picture?"

"What do you mean?"

"What if he were dead?"

"Natalie! What a horrible thing to say!"

"Okay, imagine him out of the country for an extended period of time. He's a missionary in some godforsaken Latin American country and a tribe of heathens kidnap him and lock him away in the jungle for months and months. There's no contact. What would you do?"

"I can't fathom such a concept. He's not a missionary type and besides, we've been like one person for more than twenty-three years."

Natalie said, "My guess is you would make amends with Kenzie. You would not condone her actions, but neither would you pretend she and her baby do not exist."

Susan shook again as if chilled to the bone.

"Drake screens every jot and tittle of what you do."

"That's not true."

Despite her sister-in-law's unconcealed discomfort, Natalie refused to back down. "He doesn't even have to be in the same room. You listen to him in your head all the time. Oh, Suze. Imagine listening to your own voice instead! Or imagine God's voice. He's sitting there and He's laughing and saying things like 'You go, girl. You don't need anyone else's permission to do what you think is right. You've got Mine.'"

"The gospel according to Natalie."

"I think it's biblical. God alone is the audience we play to."

Susan's teeth chattered.

Natalie embraced her and squeezed tightly. She'd said enough. "I talk too much, but just imagine, Suze. Just imagine God right here and now speaking. You go, girl…"

Ten

Pepper Carlucci snuggled at her husband's side as they sat in bed. Mick draped one arm around her shoulders and held a John Grisham novel in his other hand. It was opened to page 85.

The scene typified their life since the birth of the twins. Reading, hugs, and catch-up on the day's events occurred only after ten and most often simultaneously.

"So in conclusion," Pepper spoke toward the book, "I'd say Kenzie's mother is one uptight lady. Not just personality-wise. It showed all the way from her hair wound in its neat little bun down to her business suit, panty hose, and heels."

Mick turned the page. "I didn't know women still wore panty hose."

"Real women don't." The long-standing joke between them was rooted in her opinion that the struggle to get into the things was not worth the silky result. They were high on her list of torture clothing designed by men.

He kissed the top of her head and resumed reading.

Pepper resumed her rendition of the morning's meeting with Susan Starr. "Mickey liked her."

"Hmm. That says something."

"I admit, she was good with him. Knew how to communicate. I bet she runs the Sunday school. I would even bet she has run the Sunday school ever since Drake was first hired by a church. I think she's probably a picture-perfect pastor's wife."

"Try saying that five times fast. 'Picture-perfect pastor's wife.' Better yet, 'picture-perfect pastor's partner.'"

She ignored his suggestion. "Kenzie said a strange thing. She said her father must have allowed her mother to go stay at this beach house. *Allowed.* Isn't that awful? It sounds like a nightmare version of submission."

"Mmm." He turned the page.

Pepper hadn't finished reading it, but multitasking was not within reach tonight. "It spells trouble, Mick. If Kenzie grew up observing a screwy version of marriage, that's exactly what she'll bring to her own marriage. Semi-marriage."

"You're going negative."

"No, I'm being realistic. She believes she's tossing out that version of marriage by simply not getting married. But mark my words, their relationship will look like her parents' before everything is said and done. Kenzie will kowtow to Aidan. I see signs of it already."

"Why would she do that?"

"Because that's what her mother does. Susan does it because that's how she gets her identity. Kenzie will try to get hers in the same way."

"Baloney. She has an identity. She's a lovely young woman, fun, great with Mickey, helpful around the house here, a musician who speaks the same language as our offbeat son. In all his twenty-five years, we haven't met one female who comes even close to what she's like."

"Do you think she got pregnant on purpose?"

"It took both of them." He slid a marker into the book and closed it. "You remember how it works." Mick used his deepest voice.

The one, Pepper was convinced, that directly accounted for her own six pregnancies.

He set the book aside and shifted his weight in order to make eye contact with her. "You're getting huffy. What's really going on here?"

A few years older than her own forty-five, Mick wore the extra pounds that usually came with age. But the biceps and pecs that caught her attention twenty-eight years before remained muscular, a consequence of his lifelong work in road construction. Gray had woven itself through the black hair he still preferred to wear nearly to his shoulders and in a ponytail. Only in California. Though he shaved less than an hour before, a five o'clock shadow colored his jaw. Warm topaz eyes softened his features.

"Hmm, Pepper Sprout? What's really going on?"

She melted into him. He smelled of fresh-scented soap. The man was her best friend.

As she turned her face sideways against his chest, he wrapped his other arm around her.

"Aidan and I had one of our exchanges."

"That's not new." Mick had witnessed their odd rapport often enough.

"But it was nonverbal. We couldn't say it out loud." Her lower lip whipped outward, all by itself. Mickey Junior's would do the same.

"Are you sulking?"

"Yes."

He gave her a quick squeeze. "Talk to me. Why did you two go nonverbal?"

"Because Kenzie was there."

"Ah. That intruder. How dare she!"

"Don't make fun."

"Never. What did our son say without words?"

"At first I thought he said to back off and give him some space. But then I realized he was telling me to back off and give *her* some space. Or *them*."

Mick chuckled.

"Don't."

He only laughed louder. "Oh, come on. Remember? I told my mother the same thing. Several times, as a matter of fact, and it wasn't nonverbal. It was a few decibels above a shout. She was not hard of hearing and she understood English perfectly well by then."

"She was upset because I don't have Italian ancestors."

"No, she was upset because you changed the dynamics between her and me. You stole her son."

Pepper's bottom lip moved outward again.

"We've talked about this since you were pregnant with Aidan, about the fact we would have to let him go someday."

"Yeah, and we have let him go."

"But not until now to another woman."

"Well, I don't like it."

"Nobody said you had to like it." Mick turned off the nightstand lamp. "It's just the way it is, Pepper."

She wriggled down and under the covers with him, still within the confines of his arms.

He kissed her. "Goodnight, you hussy, you."

"What?"

"Hussy. My mother's favorite name for you." His laughter ended abruptly in a snore.

Since the time he first relayed that tidbit years before, Pepper thought he teased. Now she wasn't so sure. She might easily replace the name "Kenzie" with the derogatory noun.

I'm sorry, Lord. This is more than I signed up for when I said Aidan was Yours. Letting him go is one thing. Welcoming this almost stranger into my family is another.

Exhausted as she felt, she wasn't sure sleep would come easily.

I find it best to be okay with things I can't possibly change. I sleep better at night.

Famous last words, full of bravado cleverly disguised as faith.

Yeah, right. She was as pathetically inauthentic as Susan Starr.

Was that mother able to sleep tonight?

Eleven

Early Wednesday morning, a storm whipped the tide far up onto the beach. Furious whitecaps nearly obliterated the sea's pewter color. Rain fell steadily, a persistent drumming against the windows.

The wet weather did not stop Susan from going through the motions of her everyday routine. Shower, two soft-boiled eggs, lightly buttered toast, tea, prayer—which hadn't progressed beyond "Lord" and one minute of sitting still in case more words followed—and walk the dog.

They went south. Pugsy loved the rain. Traipsing briskly along at the taut end of his leash down the concrete boardwalk, hood tied firmly beneath her chin, she wondered how on earth she'd had the presence of mind to pack rain gear. She doubted any presence of mind remained whatsoever within her grasp. Between Pepper Carlucci's comments the previous morning, the Martha Mavens' prayer time, and Natalie's late-night prodding, her head spun like a whirligig.

"Good morning!"

She squinted through raindrops and recognized Julian approaching. He wore a drab fisherman's hat pulled low over his ears and a windbreaker.

"Morning." She called above the wind and tugged the leash to halt Pugsy.

Julian reached her. "Perfect day for reading in front of a fire, eh?"

The whirligig cruised into slow motion. "Yes. Perfect."

"I noticed the tarp has blown off the woodpile behind your house.

The logs are probably too wet. I'll bring some dry stuff over if you like. Have you built a fire yet this week?"

"No, though it has been cool enough," she shrugged.

"Not to sound chauvinistic—I'm quite sure women can build fires—but perhaps you'd like help?"

What was it about Julian that made her feel safe enough to admit she needed help? "Actually," she said, "the gas starter thing terrifies me. Pretty silly, huh?"

"Not in the least. Why don't I get a cozy fire going for you? Then all you'll have to do is add wood."

"I don't really need a fire."

"Of course you do. It's in the rule book."

The man was full of imaginary rules. She said, "Is this the same book with conversational rules?" She turned and together they walked toward their houses.

"No, totally different. This is the Life at the Beach House Rule Book. Hundreds of rules are listed. I believe this one is number one-zero-seven. Quote, 'A fire must be built on rainy March days. Hours and hours must be spent relaxing in front of it with a book. Only fiction or outlandish biographies are allowed to be read.' Unquote."

"And what's the penalty for not doing so?"

"A very grumpy attitude."

She laughed out loud. "I think I've already got that."

"Well, now you know the fix for it."

A day of leisure was probably not the primary fix. Her first morning thought had been of the two people she loved most in the world. Overnight they took on jumping monkey qualities, one for each shoulder. Drake weighed down one, Kenzie the other. A children's rhyme sang in her head. *Five little monkeys jumping on the bed. One fell off and bumped his head. Mama called the doctor and the doctor said, "No more monkeys jumping on the bed." Four little monkeys...*

Maybe she should call a doctor to settle them down. Or at least call Drake.

"Julian, do you mind if I use your phone?"

"Of course not. I'll get a fire built for you while you make calls. Since you're here on sabbatical— By the way, have I mentioned I'm a sabbatical expert?"

"No."

"I am. It's what the beach is all about, you know. Especially Faith's house. As I was saying, since you are here on sabbatical, you might want to let the world know you are totally off limits for the day."

"Tucked away at the beach, miles from home without a phone— isn't that off limits enough?"

"I noticed you had company yesterday. A true sabbatical means totally, completely off limits to long conversations."

"I'm not sure what that looks like." No jumping monkeys, maybe? "Is it allowed?"

"Oh, definitely. As a matter of fact, it's required. Rule number seventy-three."

She smiled, and the whirligig puttered to halt.

~

Drake's secretary wanted to put Susan on hold while she went looking round the church for him, but Susan declined. The toll call was on Julian's nickel. He wouldn't hear of her paying for it or of her standing in the rain to use the public phone down the street. She didn't want to overstay her welcome.

Besides, she was eager to finish the business at hand. *Two little monkeys...*

The woman patched her to voice mail.

"Drake," she spoke in the perkiest of tones, the one he always accepted without question. Chimp chattering to Monkey Number One. "I just wanted you to know I'm fine, honey!"

Should she mention yesterday? Maybe not. It seemed somehow unkind to let him learn of Kenzie or Pepper or the Martha Mavens via a recording. She'd save all that for later.

"I will be home for the wedding rehearsal Friday."

The instant she said "Friday," her stomach roiled as if someone had punched it.

She didn't want to go home. Not yet.

But she must.

"On second thought, maybe I will just go straight to the church. I won't need to stop at the house. Rehearsal starts at five. It's raining here. Have a nice day."

She disconnected the call and then dialed Pepper Carlucci's number for the second time in her life. She already knew it by heart.

Another automatic voice message ended the ringing.

"Carluccis." It was a man's voice. "Pepper Sprout and Mick are unavailable. You know what to do."

In the background a female voice protested. "Mick! Don't say that!"

"Everybody knows what to do with an answering machine."

"I mean don't say 'Pepper Sprout'! That is not my name! Start it over!"

The teasing voices faded into muffled laughter and then the machine beeped.

"Uh, Pepper. This is Susan. Kenzie's mom. I mentioned I'm leaving the beach house on Friday? I, uh, I plan to head out around four o'clock." The chirpy tone trickled away. "I wanted to remind you just in case Kenzie was…thinking of coming down." She paused. So much to say.

But she didn't have the words.

"Thank you."

She hung up the phone and pressed a hand to her stomach. The pain was still there, but the Drake and Kenzie monkeys had hopped off her shoulders. *No more monkeys jumping on the bed.*

Not true. There was one more clutching at her damp coat tails.

She called Natalie's cell number and was surprised when her busy sister-in-law answered.

"Hello?"

"Natalie, it's me."

"You okay?" Immediate concern.

"Yes, I'm fine."

"I didn't recognize the number."

"I'm at Julian's."

"Suze, I know the fire hydrant struck again last night."

Susan smiled. Natalie's reference was to an old joke about how listening to her talk could be like taking a drink from a fire hydrant. Susan was supposed to say she wasn't even thirsty. But she wasn't up to playing along. Maybe last night she had been thirsty.

She said, "It's okay. Today is better than yesterday. Julian's at my house building a fire for me."

"Great. And you're okay?"

"Yes, Natalie! I'm okay. I'm just checking in to tell you I am so okay I don't need company."

She chuckled. "Is that a hint?"

"I guess it is. I know you mean well—"

"Suze! It's all right! You can want to be alone. Try saying that, just for practice. Say 'I want to be alone.'"

She kneaded her forehead and sighed. "I want to be alone. Oh! That sounds so rude!"

"It's just a little honest assertiveness. People don't always know what you want unless you tell them. Okay then, I won't come today. As a matter of fact, I won't come again until you tell me to."

She held her breath. Emmylou probably wouldn't return to the beach, nor the elderly twins, but Gwyn and Tess were likely to check in on her again soon. "And what about the others?"

"Wow. Who is this living inside my sister-in-law?"

"You started it by bringing them in on the situation. You told them I was here."

"This is true. Okay, I will let them know."

"Please thank them for prayers and yesterday's visit and say I'm much better now."

"And you'd prefer no company."

"You don't have to say it so...so forthrightly."

"I'll use my best Susan Starr voice." She laughed. "So what are you doing today?"

"Well, instead of just going through the motions of my normal routine, I think I'll follow the rule book." Susan told Natalie about the conversation with Julian and his made-up rules. "Which means I plan to sit in front of a fire with a book and walk Pugsy in the rain. He thinks he's a duck. And I'll eat some more chicken soup."

"And brownies."

"If you insist."

"I insist. I think it's in Julian's rule book as well. Probably in the top ten."

"Probably. I'd better go. I don't want to abuse Julian's generosity."

"He won't mind. I think he's loaded. What was it he did? Designed and sold some stupendous software the entire world cannot live without?"

"Something like that, but still, I'd better go."

"Okay. Have a good one."

"You too. Bye."

She hung up the phone.

No more monkeys jumping on the bed.

Twelve

Kenzie Starr adored Aidan's mother. First off was her name. *Pepper.* How cool was that? The wildest thing about her name was the way she lived it out. No conversation or situation remained dull for long with her around. She spiced it up in no time. But, as Aidan pointed out, too much Pepper or pepper became an irritant. If his mom got on his nerves, he faked a sneeze. Of course he'd been doing that since the first grade, so Pepper usually called him on it. Then they would rag each other until they ended up nearly rolling on the floor in laughter.

That was another thing Kenzie adored about the woman, how she totally and openly loved Aidan, how she communicated he was the greatest son, brother, musician, whatever, that walked the face of the earth. Why weren't all moms like her? It should come as a package deal with every pregnancy. *If it's genetic, my kid's out of luck getting me for a mom.*

Sitting now in Pepper's eternally untidy kitchen, she watched her rummage through a catchall basket on the breakfast counter.

"What in the world did I do with my keys?"

Comparisons jumped to Kenzie's mind. Her mother never lost a thing. If she did, she'd never admit it. She'd just search and search for it without letting anyone know she made a mistake or needed help. She was so closed up. She should have positively suffocated eons ago.

Now Pepper dug in the canvas bag that served as her purse and a tote for Mickey's toys and snacks. Susan's purses were small, neatly organized, and coordinated with her outfits.

"Kenzie, I really, really appreciate you coming over on your day off to take care of Mickey. If I don't get my time away, I start to pull out my hair."

She laughed. "I know. I've seen you."

"I guess you have."

Good or bad, Pepper's feelings were no secret. Her laughter was contagious, and her hair pulling—she literally grabbed hunks of hair—was…well, it was real. As though negativity was an acceptable part of life, so just blow off some steam and get over it.

Pepper worked three afternoons a week at a musty bookshop that sold new and used copies of every book under the sun. She swore the place had been offering espresso ages before big chain stores with their chic coffee bars existed. It was a favorite of Aidan's and Kenzie's.

How cool was that? Not only did they like the same place she did, it was a *funky* place that regular fortysomething-year-olds like Susan and Drake wouldn't be caught dead in.

Then there was Mick, Aidan's dad, the obvious love of Pepper's life. He was totally certifiable over her as well. At their age! And she even had love handles at her waist! And the two of them even *kissed—really* kissed, none of that air-kissing stuff—in front of whoever happened to be around at the time. And with their open door policy, that meant plenty of people were around day and night.

Pepper gave her a quick smile and jiggled the bag. No keys clanked. "Your mom called earlier. I didn't talk to her, but she left a message. It's still on the machine."

"Oh." After Pepper's report on how yesterday's meeting went with Susan, Kenzie resolved not to talk about her mom. She probably came across like a doofus, ignoring Pepper's comment now, but it just hurt too much to go there. Despite Susan's lame effort to communicate with Kenzie through Pepper, the bottom line was her parents had disowned her and Pepper and Mick Carlucci had taken her in.

Kenzie changed the subject. "You know I love hanging out with Mickey J. Besides, I'm glad I'm available so you don't have to send him to that flu-infested preschool today." She smiled. "Maybe your keys are in the van. I'll go look."

She found them in the ignition, of all places, and Pepper left immediately for work.

Kenzie checked on Mickey J in his bedroom and found him entranced with a construction project. He was so like his dad. Or Aidan, for that matter, except he lost himself in music. Experience told her the little guy wouldn't need her attention until the plastic block city was completely built.

Just the sight of him often sent a wave of intense emotion through Kenzie. It was a vague thing, a mix of melancholy and joy and hope and nausea. Was she really going to have her own kid?

She returned to the kitchen and stared at the answering machine. Pepper hadn't insisted she listen to her mom's message. She hadn't even told her what she said. That was another cool thing about the woman. She respected boundaries.

Actually, her mother did that too. She let Kenzie be. She let her make choices. She let her sing wild rock music and quit college and go to Europe without harassing her about her off-the-wall decisions.

But with Susan, it just looked as though she didn't care.

Kenzie punched the answering machine button.

"Uh, Pepper. This is Susan. Kenzie's mom. I mentioned I'm leaving the beach house on Friday? I, uh, plan to head out around four o'clock." That fake singsong beat of hers fizzled. "I wanted to remind you just in case Kenzie was…thinking of coming down." Another pause. "Thank you."

"Oh, Mom," Kenzie whispered.

Thirteen

On the freeway, through a drizzly rain, Pepper drove her full-size van like a semi driver strung out on one of those supercharged caffeine/gotu kola drinks and making up for lost time.

Mickey Junior was healthy as a rock. He had been since the day he was born. Why did Pepper act as if not sending him to preschool was her own fantastic idea? The thought not to expose him to possible flu had never even entered her mind. Nope. It was Kenzie's remonstration that did it. She said her pregnant body was vulnerable, and if Mickey brought home germs, she would be exposed and endangered. The grandbaby's welfare was at stake. That was the reason Pepper decided he should stay home.

Eww. She was blaming her unnecessary choice on Aidan's girlfriend's opinion?

Resentment crept in, stiffening her neck.

She jerked the steering wheel and swerved into the exit lane.

And leaving her keys in the van? In the ignition? In their neighborhood? Even an old family vehicle with a dented fender screamed money to someone. What was she thinking?

Probably that she'd lost her son to a young hussy whose model for wife and mother was Susan Starr, the uptight picture-perfect pastor's partner.

Mick's words from last night nibbled at her resentment, the ones about his mother resenting Pepper because she had stolen away her son.

Kenzie was a beautiful person. Not a hussy. She couldn't change the character of her mother or her parents' marriage. She could use a different model. Was erasing her heritage even a possibility, though?

Pepper skimmed along the off-ramp and merged into traffic on a business district street.

"All right, Lord. I admit she is sweet and thoughtful. She always has been. She has not changed. Help me to accept her as a daughter-in-law, even in this technically nonlegal condition. If restructuring my relationship with Aidan is what that takes…Oh, nuts."

If?

If she didn't, their relationship would resemble her own mother-in-law's with her son. Not a pretty sight.

"Okay, okay. I get it!"

She cruised into a parking lot, turned into the first vacant space she came to, slammed on the brakes, and shoved the gearshift into park—all prayed up and outside the shop with two minutes to spare.

Now if only her heart would slow down.

Fourteen

At the beach on Thursday, the sun shone from a cloudless sky. Azure blue.

No monkeys jumped on the bed or weighted down Susan's shoulders. The previous day's cozy fire, Helen MacInnes thriller, and chicken soup had worked wonders. Chocolate brownies had cinched the effect.

Chocolate, Susan? Drake's voice. *A novel? A cozy fire? It's God who works wonders, not secular, material things.*

She shrugged off his opinion and went through the motions of her everyday routine. Shower, two soft-boiled eggs, lightly buttered toast, tea, the one-word prayer and fruitless wait, walk the dog.

She and Pugsy headed north at a fast clip that took them beyond the pier, farther than they had yet explored. The scent of roasted coffee beans saturated the crisp air. She slowed at Kono's kiosk alongside the boardwalk, a place which she vaguely remembered sold a nice variety of herbal teas.

Why don't you drink coffee anymore? Now Natalie's voice spoke in her thoughts.

In the past, Susan enjoyed coffee. She drank it with milk and sugar, just like her grandmother had. About five years ago, after a visit to the doctor, Drake announced that his bouts with trembling fingers and acid stomach were the effects of caffeine. He didn't want to see or smell coffee in the house.

In support, she gave it up as well. After all, if she were forced to abstain, would she want to watch him drink it or smell its rich scent?

She fingered the ten-dollar bill and loose change she always carried in the pocket of her light jacket on Pugsy walks. One never knew…

"May I help you?"

She started, surprised to find herself under the green canopy in front of the counter. "I…I would like…" she exhaled the c-word, *"coffee."*

"What kind?" The young woman reminded her of Kenzie. Too thin, too much black clothing, too much tummy showing, too many ear piercings. And a genuine smile that lit up her face and warmed Susan down to her toes.

She scanned the chalkboard's long list of types and flavors and sizes. "Just regular. Whatever the special is."

"French roast okay?"

"Fine." She eyed the goodies displayed inside a large case.

"What size?"

"Big. The biggest." She smiled. "And one of those apple muffins."

"Coming right up, ma'am."

The motions of everyday routine disintegrated.

Fifteen

Pepper leafed through a cookbook at her kitchen counter in search of a recipe for gnocchi. The recent talk about her mother-in-law produced a craving for one of her old dishes. Not that Bella Carlucci had ever shared an original recipe with her. Nope, she carried those things with her to her grave. Her daughter-in-law, that hussy who stole her son, would never know the correct way to prepare gnocchi.

The door leading to the attached garage opened, and a laundry basket entered, followed by Kenzie.

Speaking of hussies for in-laws.

Kenzie set the basket on the floor beside the kitchen table. She was laundering her and Aidan's things in Pepper's washer and dryer, located in the garage. Although the girl had been at the house less than twenty-four hours ago to babysit Mickey Junior, she hadn't brought laundry with her. Evidently none needed to be done *yesterday.* Pepper thought herself casual, but the young couple carried the adjective to stratosphere level.

"Pepper, are you sure you don't mind me doing our laundry here?"

"Nope." She turned a page in the cookbook.

"Aidan said it was fine."

She looked up again. The girl was folding her second load of the morning, the third was in the dryer, and still she wanted reassurance of her welcome. "Kenzie, you've been around long enough to know how it is in this house. *Mi casa es su casa.*"

"Yeah, but that was before Aidan and I were living together."

Pepper's automatic response died in her throat. She couldn't quite get out, *So why should that change things?* Their living together, their pregnancy, had indeed changed things. Despite Pepper's brave words to accept Kenzie as a semi-daughter-in-law and accept the change in her own relationship with Aidan, and despite the fact that she prayed daily along those lines, discomfort crept in. Mick had nailed it, of course. She resented Kenzie for stealing away her son, for dumping on him the burden of raising a child before he was married.

Kenzie's comment hung in the air between them. The girl turned her attention to folding towels at the table.

Pepper went back to her cookbook, but the print wavered as if she swam undersea. She gazed at Kenzie through her eyelashes. Slight of build like her mother, the girl-woman resembled a fragile urchin who craved love and acceptance and a place to belong.

I think the question is, does Jesus welcome us with open arms? With our faults? Did He die on the cross for us because we did everything right?

Pepper stifled a groan. Words spoken in a huff always boomeranged, flying back to zing her unexpectedly.

If anyone gives so much as a cup of cold water to one of these little ones because he is a disciple, then in truth I tell you, he will most certainly not go without his reward.

There went Matthew again, using her voice to paraphrase himself quoting Jesus.

The point seemed not that a reward was involved. The point was that if any little one needed a cup of cold water, it was Mackenzie Starr. And at the moment, no one else appeared to be available to give it.

"Kenzie." Pepper went to the table, sat down, and met those uniquely shaped, pretty blue-gray eyes that had surely done a number on Aidan. "My son loves you. That means you are family. You are not a guest. You are not just any old band member. You are the mother of my grandchild. Okay?"

Kenzie nodded once and smiled. "Okay."

"How about some coffee? I have those espresso beans you like so much."

"Oh, I can't." She picked up another towel to fold. "Caffeine is a no-no for the baby."

Pepper froze. She had made a special stop the previous day at a special gourmet place and paid a special price—all for Kenzie. "Hmm. Really? I drank coffee with six pregnancies. No problem that I was aware of."

"People didn't know the effects of caffeinated drinks on the fetus back then. Do you have any herbal organic tea?"

Susan Starr drank herbal tea. At Starbucks. "I have black tea. The orange pekoe stuff."

"I don't mean to sound like my mother." She fluttered her eyelashes. "She drinks only tea and only herbal. But I prefer that now. It's best for the baby. Aidan likes it too."

Pepper lolled her head around in a circle. "Well, we'll have to get some. What kind do you and Aidan prefer?"

And to think there were five more children who someday would bring home the love of their lives. Before all was said and done, Pepper Carlucci could have a dozen grown children under her wings and twice that many grandbabies!

She wanted to scream.

Sixteen

On Friday morning, Susan did not notice the weather.

She awoke refreshed with only two thoughts on her mind. The previous day's coffee had not bothered her in the least and no eggs remained in the refrigerator.

She dressed immediately, called to Pugsy, and did not even consider going through the morning routine.

By late morning, however, everyday motions nipped at Susan's heels. Recess was over. It was time to go home.

"Lord, please help me!"

The sound of her own voice praying over a suitcase lying open on the bed startled her.

She had prayed four whole words! Loudly. Distinctly. Emotionally. Without first asking God if it was all right with Him if she requested something.

Where had all that come from?

Pain.

Pain at the mere thought of the word "home."

Of rocks and trees, of skies and seas...

The partial line from an old hymn tiptoed into her consciousness, just loud enough to catch her attention.

Now where had that come from?

She replayed it. Sketchy verses tangoed with jumbled notes. She hummed.

And the ordeal of packing and preparing to go home slowly, steadily dissolved.

∽

At the kitchen counter, Susan hummed and poured hazelnut coffee beans into the grinder. She kept her mouth closed, but the hymn's words now rang out loud and clear in her mind. At last the song she used to know almost as well as her own name flowed, a silent intonation of unbroken praise complete with pipe organ accompaniment reverberating in her head.

Of rocks and trees, of skies and seas—

A soft knock at the front door interrupted the music. Susan paused as well, a tablespoon of ground coffee beans held midair. Drake wouldn't visit, would he? At lunchtime on a Friday? Wasn't he conducting a businessmen's Bible study today? He would not approve of coffee at noon.

This is my Father's world, and to my listening ears all nature sings, and round me rings—

There was another rap, a bit louder than the first. From a back bedroom, Pugsy yipped once, too lazy to bother with more.

The music of the spheres. This is my Father's world.

Lost in the music again, she set down the spoon and went to the door. Opening it, she nearly gasped at the sight of Pepper Carlucci. "Is Kenzie all right?"

"She's fine."

"The baby?"

"Growing." Aidan's mother shrugged. "They're fine. I'm not. Mind if I run away with you?"

"Run away?" Susan stared, uncomprehending.

Run away. Run away. The phrase tumbled about. She hadn't meant to run away. But she had, hadn't she? With the wise, loving help of her sister-in-law she ran away to the beach house where peace reigned and bird-of-paradise grew from concrete. Where the neighbor Julian—in the blink of an eye—provided a space so safe she unburdened her soul. Where the Martha Mavens delivered prayer, food, and hugs. Where Natalie challenged her to let the mental image of Drake go and not allow him to screen every jot and tittle of her behavior.

And now the beach house was where Pepper Carlucci stood on her doorstep. Aidan's mother, the sole link to Kenzie, asked if she could run away with her there.

Yes indeed, this is my Father's world.

She smiled. "It's a great place for running away. Come inside."

Seventeen

Susan and Pepper drank coffee outdoors at the round wrought iron table. With its umbrella folded shut, the full impact of warm sunshine bathed the patio. Along the boardwalk occasional passersby strolled, biked, skated, or jogged. In its rhythmic crush of waves, the Pacific dispensed its namesake. Peace covered everything.

Susan wasn't quite sure what they should talk about. After Pepper's initial question asking if she could run away with her, they had exchanged few words beyond the location of a bathroom, that Mickey Junior was at a friend's, and whether she wanted cream or sugar.

Pepper set down her cup. "So anyway." She flashed her easy grin. "This is a little awkward."

The grin was delightful. Winsome even. It hit its mark and disarmed Susan on the spot. The truth was this woman knew more about her than did the Martha Mavens or anyone at Holy Cross Fellowship. No subject need be off limits with her.

Susan said, "Yes, it is a little awkward, but it actually feels good. I mean, we're in the same boat, aren't we?"

"That's what I think. We could call it the 'Grandmas out of Wedlock Boat.'"

They exchanged a smile.

Pepper said, "It does feel good to share the situation with someone. I seem to be the Christopher Columbus in my circle of close friends. First one in this boat, off exploring uncharted waters."

"There are people in our church who have experienced this, but…"

She didn't want to go into why Drake believed they didn't exactly qualify for personal sharing. "Did Kenzie tell you where I was?"

"Inadvertently. She mentioned the other day that the house resembled a squished red chili on the boardwalk south of the Mission restaurant. I parked and took a walk. It's kind of hard to miss."

"I suppose so."

"Susan, I don't know how to say this, so I'll just say it. I already told you about my lack of tact." She paused. "You don't seem like the same person I met on Tuesday."

She imagined the difference Pepper saw: no chignon, no makeup, no skirt. Her hair flowed to her shoulders.

"I mean," Pepper went on, "Kenzie said you don't drink coffee. And I never would have guessed you wear sweats. Although your pants and shirt can hardly be called sweats in the true sense of the term."

"But they're not a frumpy skirt."

She nodded, clearly curious.

That spread the flowing seas abroad...

A phrase, a snatch of notes. Another hymn. What was it?

"Susan?"

"Sorry. I keep hearing hymn music. I don't know why it's popping up. Ages and ages ago I sang solos. Drake and I even sang together, before he was a senior pastor. Kenzie and I sang when she was little. Always hymns, the grand old classics. I had dozens of them memorized. I guess they're still tucked away in my mind."

"You don't sing anymore?"

She shook her head. "It just sort of went by the wayside."

No...not quite by the wayside. Susan remembered the exact day the public singing ended. She and Kenzie sang a duet on Mother's Day during the collection of tithes and offerings. Her daughter was thirteen. Imagine that. A teenager singing with her mother in church. At Drake's insistence they chose a hymn. Unknown to him, though, Kenzie rearranged its tempo. It became an upbeat, finger-snapping version of the melody.

Drake did not care for it. His disdain revealed itself in his sermon which immediately followed. Subtle, but snide. The private lecture at home cleared up any lingering doubts.

After that, Susan begged off whenever the music director approached her. Once Kenzie gestured an offensive sign toward the woman. That ended her daughter's career as soloist in Drake's church. Years later she somehow found the courage to ask her dad's permission, through the youth pastor, for her band to sing at a youth rally. That disaster hammered another nail in the coffin of father-daughter warm fuzzies.

Eventually Susan stopped singing altogether. Not just up front, but in the pew as well. She wasn't sure when that happened. During congregational singing she sometimes only mouthed the words. At home she rarely played a CD.

Pepper's voice startled her. "Then Kenzie must get her singing ability from you."

She shrugged.

"I told you, she has an angel's voice." She smiled. "I'd love to hear you someday."

Natalie's challenge that she make a decision without Drake had caused her to imagine a number of possibilities. Public singing was not one of them.

I sing the mighty power of God…

"That's it!" Susan clapped her hands. " 'I Sing the Mighty Power of God.' Isaac Watts." She heaved a loud breath that lifted and dropped her shoulders.

Something sounded in her imagination. Not music this time. It was more like a clanking noise. Like a heavy metal chain falling from a great height onto concrete.

Yes. I will sing of God's mighty power.

~

Susan refilled their coffee cups and gazed out at the ocean. Clumps of silver tinsel danced on it, reflections of the afternoon sun. Pepper waited for an answer to her question about the obvious change in her over the past seventy-two hours. What could she say? *Oh, it's just a little something my sister-in-law proposed.*

A little something? It was a heretical concept that attached itself like a parasite onto her imagination. She couldn't shake it.

"Susan," Pepper said. "We are in that same boat, but we don't exactly know each other to the point of revealing innermost thoughts. I don't mean to be nosy."

"That's not what I'm thinking." She managed a wan smile. "It's just that I don't have it quite figured out. You are right. I am different than I was on Tuesday. I blame my sister-in-law, Natalie. She's married to Drake's brother. They always give us a week's stay at the beach here. We've used this house in recent years. It's a favorite. Anyway, she convinced me to come early by myself. And she encouraged me to call you." Gratitude for Natalie shot through her. Susan's throat closed up.

"She sounds like a good friend."

Susan nodded and glanced at the ocean. "She stopped by the other night and...um...well..."

In her mind, Drake's voice suddenly resounded. *Careful, careful. You're treading in very personal waters here. Let's distance ourselves, shall we?*

Organ music filled her head, and then words burst forth. *I sing the mighty power of God!*

That too had been happening since the music first began. Whenever Drake commented in her mind, whenever he screened, then a hymn interrupted, a crescendo blasted and drowned him out.

She was beginning to wonder if unsolicited music was a harbinger of nervous breakdowns.

"Well," she said again. "The thing is, Natalie believes I rely too much on Drake's opinion. She said when I listened to my heart, I took a step toward Kenzie by calling you. I'm quite sure he would not like that. She suggested I, um, try to, um..." *Imagine God's voice. You go, girl.*

Pepper leaned across the table. "She told you to keep listening to your heart rather than to him."

She nodded and relief filled her. The woman understood.

"How's it going?"

"Okay. It was unconscious at first. I rolled out of bed and went for coffee. No shower, wearing these clothes. Later while I was packing, I realized I spent the morning doing what Drake would disapprove of. I don't mean to misrepresent him. He is a good man, a godly man. He's not a tyrant. He doesn't insist I shower and skip coffee and wear skirts. I just know his preferences. I want to be the kind of woman he likes."

"There's a fine line between incorporating a husband's likes and dislikes and being bent toward him."

"What do you mean by 'bent'?"

"It's the idea of being bent toward a creature, the created, rather than being vertical toward the Creator, the Uncreated. I straddled the line for a while." She lifted both palms, raising one, then the other. "Mick hates peas. I love them. I didn't serve them until four years into our marriage. Not that God has an opinion about peas, but I was miserable until I figured out I was more concerned about Mick's opinion than God's."

"Drake's opinion is everything. When I met him, I was just a nobody, so unsure of myself and my faith. And he fell in love with me, little Susie Anderson. He made me feel special." She paused. "I guess somewhere along the way I started listening to him more than to God."

Mighty power. Sing it.

Susan went on. "Well, I guess I've stepped way over that fine line. I'm beginning to see how much I do according to his opinion. I comb my hair, dress, eat, keep house, shop, and study the Bible in the ways he suggests."

Pepper's eyes widened. "Like you need his approval?"

"Probably even to breathe. That's sad, isn't it?"

"Very," Pepper whispered. "I don't think it's healthy, either."

"It's quite sick. I don't think it's what God had in mind when He said the two shall become one when a man and woman marry." She winced. "There it is. And I can't believe I said all that to you out loud." She exhaled a noisy breath. "So, Pepper, why is it *you* want to run away?"

The corners of her mouth lifted. The dark blue eyes glittered. A hint of a chuckle gave way to a snort. "After hearing your story, I have no clue why."

Susan joined her in a loud, unadulterated guffaw.

The power of God was indeed mighty.

Eighteen

Vanilla ice cream melted on Pepper's tongue, followed lazily by a chunk of waffle cone crystallizing into pure sugar.

She sighed. "This is incredibly yummy."

Beside her Susan mumbled in agreement, her mouth full of the same treat.

They stood at the far end of Crystal Pier. Fishermen lined the rail enclosing the large squared area. Far below the surf whooshed at the pilings and the boards beneath their feet swayed.

Pepper savored her final bite. "Mmm. This is extra yummy because today is a Friday, it's the middle of the day, and I don't have a kid with me." She stole a glance at Susan, wondering if such an admission would disturb her.

Apparently it didn't. Her eyes were bright as she swallowed, smiling. "Welcome to my new world. Ice cream in the middle of the day, no kids or husbands to bug us. What shall we do next?"

Pepper nearly choked. The uptight woman's about-face was indeed a sight to behold.

Susan's blond hair blew in the sea breeze. Sun and wind had tinged her pale cheeks pink. She still wore the navy blue knit pants and long-sleeved floral top, an outfit Pepper categorized as dressy enough for church. Not so for the "picture-perfect pastor's partner." Susan admitted that except for that walking outfit, she had packed only skirts for her stay at the beach, clothes she considered the norm for public wear even in the capital of casual.

Pepper glanced at her watch. The too few hours of freedom were slipping away.

Susan said, "Do you have to go?"

"Soon." Pepper smiled to herself. Susan asked the question as if she herself had all the time in the world. But she had told Pepper about her work as a wedding consultant, that a rehearsal was scheduled for the evening.

"You probably have to pick up Mickey Junior."

"Yes." She inspected the rail of peeling white paint and bird droppings, found a somewhat clean spot and rested her elbows on it. "It's the story of my life. Gotta go, babysitter's time is up, school's out, a kid needs me." She shrugged and smiled. "Most days I would not trade a minute of the past twenty-five years of motherhood, but there are times when I will break something if I don't run away at least for a while." Her first experience with needing to run had actually involved a couple of broken plates. Mick stopped her from smashing a third onto the floor. But that might be too much information for present company.

Susan said, "I never felt the desire to run away until now. On second thought, maybe I did and just never admitted it. I didn't even really recognize it this time, not until you called it that." Almost in midsentence she interrupted herself by humming.

To Pepper it sounded like another old hymn. Susan's attention had drifted several times during their conversation. Her eyes lost focus and she hummed softly. How Pepper wished Kenzie could see her mother! Though still somewhat hesitant in manner, Susan was not the woman Kenzie always described.

The humming stopped. Susan turned to her. "Running away seems so disloyal. Weak. Inefficient."

"Nah." Pepper shook her head. "It's admitting we're human and we need a break. A true Sabbath. Sundays don't always get the job done at my house."

"Tell me about it. Neither do Mondays, Drake's official day off."

"He's probably on twenty-four/seven/three hundred sixty-five?"

"Mm-hmm." The murmur slid into a vaguely familiar tune.

"Kind of like us mothers."

The music came to an abrupt halt, and Susan's face crumpled. "I've been such a horrible mother!" Her voice came out a hoarse whisper.

"Susan, we're all imperfect. We can't help but to parent imperfectly. All we can do is ask our kids' forgiveness for however we've failed them."

"You've done that?"

"Of course. I've always told Aidan he was my practice child and the next five were do-overs. Yes, he is the recipient of my biggest parenting blunders, but I tell him to just get over it. I mean, who doesn't have junk to deal with?" She sobered the jocular tone. "Dealing with it means forgiving me and his dad for all sorts of things. And he certainly can't do that without God's help."

"I could never say such things to Kenzie."

"Why not?" Pepper bit her tongue. Did that question come out huffy?

"Because I'm her mother. She'd lose respect for me."

The back of Pepper's neck prickled. She locked her tongue between her teeth to prevent a retort from flying off.

"Wouldn't she?" Susan asked.

"For being truthful?" *Sorry, Lord. Fix it! I really, really want to connect with her.*

Susan faced the railing again, her gaze toward the ocean.

"Look, Susan, the thing is, Kenzie needs you. In about four months she is going to give birth to your grandchild."

Her shoulders sagged.

"And I need you too. Friend to friend."

Susan looked at her.

"Mick is as supportive as I could hope for, but let's face it. He's a man. My closest women friends haven't been through this. I'm feeling all alone with Aidan and Kenzie. I'm having a tough time being mom, semi-mother-in-law, mentor, and out-of-wedlock grandma all rolled into one."

Two knots appeared above Susan's brows.

"Don't get me wrong. I am enamored with Kenzie. I love her. But—"

"You love my daughter?"

"Sure. Because my son does. And she is, after all, the mother of my grandchild."

"She's a handful. She's scatterbrained. She's melodramatic. She's moody." Her eyes filled. "And she's the most delightful girl I've ever known."

Pepper nodded. "Your typical creative personality intensified a hundredfold by mommy hormones."

"Oh, my. And you love her."

"Not as much as you do."

"If I don't hold her soon, I think I'll die. But I know I won't really die, and that makes it even worse. That means I have to live with this pain."

"Can I tell her that? Your exact words?"

She gasped.

"Why not?"

"Because—" She clamped her mouth shut.

As Pepper watched, Susan's face went through a myriad of changes, from furrows and knots to red splotches and eyes clenched shut.

Pepper said, "What's Drake saying in your head right now?"

"That I shouldn't do this. That it will interfere with her suffering the consequences of her choices." Standing immobile, she hummed what sounded a lot like "Joyful, Joyful, We Adore Thee."

After a long moment, Susan opened her eyes and lifted her chin. "Geez Louise."

Pepper nearly burst into laughter.

"As if professing my love to her would reverse her pregnancy." Susan waved a hand. "Okay. Tell her. Tell her all of it. Tell her I love her no matter what. Tell her—no. Ask her to please, please get in touch with me and then I can tell her myself."

Pepper flipped a mental back handspring. *Thank You, Jesus!*

There was hope for reconciliation. Hope for a better start for the young couple. Resisting an urge to leap into the air with a shout, Pepper squeezed her hands together, tensed muscles throughout her body, and steadied her vocal cords. "Susan, it will be my privilege to convey that message."

~

"What do you mean Kenzie's not here?" Pepper spoke to the back of Aidan's head as he shut his apartment door. "I thought this was her night off."

"It is. She went to Dakota's."

"South or North?"

"Ha-ha. It's a girl, Mom." He faced her now. "Dakota's her best friend from high school. You want to sit?"

"Yeah. For a minute." She sat on the loveseat.

Though he told her he was not working, his demeanor said she interrupted something. He pulled around a kitchen chair and straddled it backward. The baseball cap on his head sat backward as well. The entire atmosphere felt backward. It was probably left over from her last visit when she realized there was another woman in her son's life. But still...

She held up her hands. "I got a mom question."

He smiled crookedly and shook his head as if surrendering to the inevitable. "You're allowed one per visit."

"Thank you." She lowered her hands to her lap. "Are you okay?"

"Yep." Too quick. "So what's up? What did you want to tell Kenzie?"

"I visited her mother today at their beach house."

He lowered his chin to his arms crossed on the chair back, his expression blank.

"You're doing a good job there holding in all that disapproval you feel at my meeting with the enemy."

His eyebrows rose briefly, up and down. "The other day you sounded like you didn't care if you ever saw her again."

"That was before I realized she and I should be on the same side. I mean, we're both in the same boat, you know? We even named it the Grandmas out of Wedlock Boat. We are the grandmas. A kid gets only two per life, biologically speaking, anyway. The better we sail together, the better for you and Kenzie and the baby."

"So you went recruiting a shipmate."

"I guess."

"Mom, from everything Kenzie has ever said about her, she's a loser."

"What's that song you wrote about mercy?"

"I forget."

"I'm sure it'll come back to you. Listen, the thing is, Susan was so different today, nothing at all like the tense woman I met Tuesday. Even her hair and clothes—It's too much to try to explain to you. I just have to describe what she was like to Kenzie myself. When will she be back?"

"I don't know. Depends on when her ride heads this way. Probably Sunday or Monday."

"Huh?"

"She's in Phoenix. That's where her friend lives."

"Phoenix? I just saw her yesterday. She didn't mention anything about a trip."

He shrugged. "It came up this morning. Another friend was driving there."

Pepper scratched her head and reminded herself that trying to make sense of the chaotic lifestyle of the young and creative was a hopeless waste of energy. But still…

"You didn't want to go?"

"It's a girl thing. Besides, I have to work. We got a five-night gig at Reilly's."

Pepper crossed her legs, uncrossed them, and crossed them again.

"I know you don't like it, Mom, but it pays the rent."

She knew. "And you sing about Jesus in a bar."

"He's already there. I'm just doing what I can to reveal Him." Aidan lifted his mouth into a tiny smile, the infuriating one he used to forewarn. It conveyed that he was about to express a favorite declaration.

She knew it well and mouthed the words along with him when he said, "I, Aidan James Carlucci, am a product of Mick and Pepper Carlucci's wild and wooly faith."

"Yeah, yeah." She scratched her head again and tried not to envision drunks who didn't like the music and loose young women who liked too much the guys who sang it. Kenzie wasn't even old enough to enter the place.

Pepper stood. "I'd better go."

He walked her to the door. "I'll tell Kenzie what you said about her mom."

"There's a lot more to tell her."

"I'm sure we'll see you before too long."

She heard it again, something off in his voice. "What does that mean?"

"Aw, Mom." Now it was exasperation. He opened the door. "You were just here the other day."

"Yeah? So?"

"The night before that we had dinner with you."

"And a few months ago you told me I'm going to be a grandma and that my semi-daughter-in-law had no place to live or work or means of emotional support beyond your family."

"I need some space."

"Is that why Kenzie left?"

The pained expression on his face said she struck a chord.

He needed space. *I told my mother the same thing.* Mick's words came to mind. *Several times as a matter of fact and it wasn't nonverbal.* Good grief. Now she was sounding like Grandma Carlucci.

"Oh, man," she muttered, stepping past him and through the open doorway. "All I need is an Italian accent." She turned to him. "This is just really, really hard."

"Like I don't know that?"

She wanted to stick a bar of soap in his mouth.

Instead, she gathered him into her arms. Their hug was a silent one.

Nineteen

Pugsy in tow, Susan entered the church's main office, a large interior room with glass walls facing the lobby. It was furnished tastefully with two loveseats, four armchairs, and cherry wood end tables. Soft lamplight lit winter's five o'clock gloom. Pastel blue walls completed the cool, calm, and collected ambience.

The intended effect did not impact Susan. She had no idea what would restore cool, calm, and collected to her spirit. The memory of a rainy day in front of the fire reading a book felt ages old. After Pepper left the beach house a short while ago, she had quickly gotten herself together—complete with chignon and dress clothes appropriate for a rehearsal dinner—crying the entire time. Though her tears dried as she drove on the freeway, her eyes burned now with unshed ones.

The room was vacant, the door to Drake's office closed. She checked the phone on the receptionist's desk and saw that his line was lit. He was busy.

Pugsy yipped excitedly and she let him off his leash. He raced down a hallway to her small room, where he knew food and bed awaited. She followed him, passing empty offices. Everyone must have gone home for the evening.

Her office was scarcely larger than a closet with one slit of a window. She'd moved into it after giving up her duties as Sunday school director. There was no need for her former big office. Occasional meetings with congregants to plan social events like weddings and funerals did not require much space. Tucked away at the end of the hall also made the office an ideal hideaway for Pugsy, who was allowed nowhere else in the building.

She hung up her coat, put out food and water for the dog, powdered her nose, reapplied eye shadow and lipstick. Procrastinating? Enough spare time to greet Drake before the rehearsal began was almost gone.

She went back down the hall to his door, rapped twice, and opened it.

He looked up, phone pressed to his ear. Brows met above his nose, and eyes squinted nearly shut.

She smiled and waved.

He held up a hand and spread his fingers. Five minutes.

Susan backed out and shut the door.

"Susan!"

She turned to see Gwyn in the lobby and went out to meet her. As always whenever she happened to meet Gwyn there, she remembered how they had first met that night many years ago. Gwyn had lain just outside the door, a bloody heap. How the woman managed to even walk over that same spot week after week confounded Susan.

Gwyn grabbed her in a hug. "Am I glad to see you! I know now what your unspoken prayer request was!"

Every muscle in Susan's body constricted.

Gwyn released her and whispered, "It's the Hathaways, isn't it? I mean, dear God! Five hundred invitations! Fourteen attendants! Not counting the flower girl and ring bearer! Catered buffet right here! Two weeks before Easter! No wonder you had to get away."

Gwyn would not have known such details unless she'd somehow become involved. Susan found her voice. "What happened?"

"No worries. Melinda called Drake on Wednesday." She referred to the bride's mother. "He called Tess. She called me. It was a technical issue with the florist. I handled it. Every single petal contracted for will arrive tomorrow morning on schedule."

"Whew. Thank you, Gwyn."

"You are so welcome. I was delighted to find a literal way to be there for you." She smiled. "I thought I could at least give you some moral support at the rehearsal tonight. But I confess, I wouldn't blame you for not showing up. Yikes. Then they'd be looking to me. How do you handle this stress?"

She shrugged. "Weddings don't happen every month."

"Do you feel more rested now?"

She stretched the corners of her mouth upward. "I'm just fine." *No longer hovering on the edge of a nervous breakdown. At least I think not.* "I appreciate you coming. Would you mind making sure all the lights are on in the sanctuary? And maybe see if Melinda is around yet? I'll be right there. I have to talk to Drake for a minute."

"Of course." She flashed her dazzling smile. "Welcome back."

As Gwyn headed the other direction, Susan reentered the main office and sat down to wait.

She noticed a tightness in her chest now accompanied the stomach pain.

The story of Queen Esther approaching the quarters of King Ahasuerus without an invitation took on a brand-new meaning. Not that Drake had the power to sentence the uninvited to death...It was nothing like that. The comparison was silly.

But the pain didn't go away.

⁓

"I've missed you, Susan." Drake hugged her briefly in his doorway. He wasn't into public displays of affection. For him that meant anywhere in the church, even if the entire building was unoccupied. "How was traffic?" He crossed his office and went around the desk.

"Not bad." She wanted a hug, a proper one in strong arms that promised safety. "Rush hour added a little travel time."

"Naturally. It's after three o'clock." He arranged his desktop, shuffling papers, moving pens. Avoiding eye contact. "We almost had a fiasco with the Hathaways."

"Gwyn just told me. She said it's all taken care of."

"Mmm. I thought Tess could handle it."

"Gwyn is a little better at this sort of thing."

"This sort of trivial thing, you mean." The nuance in his voice came through loud and clear. Something about Gwyn bothered him. Not that he'd ever confessed that outright, but he always seemed disinterested in talking with or about her.

Come to think of it, he wasn't all that keen on any of the Martha Mavens. Except for maybe Tess, the one with an official title, director of women's ministries.

Susan said, "I suppose it is a trivial thing. Compared to Tess' teaching of original Greek scriptures, weddings are insignificant."

He slid shut a desk drawer and looked up. "We'd better go."

The tightness in her chest had spread, constraining leg muscles and rooting her to the floor. "Drake, we need to talk."

"You should have thought of that before choosing to stay at the beach until you knew the freeway would inevitably be gridlocked."

"I'm—"

Drake screens every jot and tittle of what you do.

Natalie's admonition shot through her mind. It garbled the "sorry" on the tip of her tongue and shifted her thinking.

Drake was pouting. Drake pouted a lot.

She apologized a lot. She explained her decisions, usually before they were made, looking to him to screen every jot and tittle.

Enough was enough. She unclasped her hands and straightened her shoulders and pushed her voice up a notch to chimp level. "I'm going to check on the bride."

Susan found Melinda Hathaway in the ladies' washroom. Her daughter Bree was in a stall, behind its closed door, being loudly, obviously sick.

"Susan!" Melinda cried.

They exchanged a quick hug.

Susan said, "Gwyn told me the bride is not feeling well." At the sound of gagging, she winced. "Don't worry. This happens often. Nerves and all."

Melinda's smile fell short of spreading joy to her face. She was about

Susan's age and resembled the majority of women at Holy Cross, healthy, wealthy, attractive, chicly casual, tan, blond-streaked hair. Her daughter was a clone. Bree and Kenzie, though in the same class, had never been friends.

"Oh!" Bree groaned the other side of the door. "I hate barfing!"

Susan could see beneath the stall door that the girl was sitting on the floor.

"Mom, I think maybe I'm done— Oh! Nope!"

Melinda scrunched up her face and folded her arms over her stomach.

Susan smiled in sympathy.

A long moment later, all was quiet. Bree unlatched the door. "I don't know why they call it morning sickness." The door swung open. "It's after five o'clock— Susan!"

The surprised gaze passed itself around from one woman to another. It circled another time. Bree's pale face turned pink. Melinda's bronzed tone went yellow.

Morning sickness.

Bree was pregnant.

Just like Kenzie.

Drake did not perform wedding ceremonies to expectant couples. After counseling he might consider marrying them in a small private affair in the chapel.

Melinda and Bree knew that. His stance was no secret to the congregation.

Drake would cancel the Hathaway wedding in a heartbeat. Or would he? Their tithe alone covered his generous salary.

No, Drake was not a hypocrite. He would stick to his guns.

And turn away another young woman who probably needed something besides her pastor's disapproval.

Susan grabbed a handful of paper towels from the pile on the vanity and dampened them under the faucet. With the first genuine smile she'd felt in a very long time, she patted the young girl's distraught face.

"Crackers help. Maybe you could slide one of those cellophane packets under your garter tomorrow?"

Twenty

Late Friday night, Pepper snuggled against Mick's arm. He held the book. They were on page 104.

She said, "There's no other explanation. Someone must be praying for Susan. It's a totally dramatic, overnight change."

"Talk about totally dramatic. You could have knocked me down with a feather when I heard you'd gone to see her again. I'd say your attitude toward her was dramatically changed. Maybe someone's praying for you too?"

No doubt he referred to himself. "Thanks."

He glanced her way with a wink.

Where would she be without her husband? Most days she took his prayers for granted. His love was always there, as obvious and permanent as stars in a desert night sky.

Poor Susan! What a nightmare marriage! To run every thought past a husband's scrutiny!

Mick turned the page. "What's up?"

"Hmm?"

"You're making that mumbo jumbo sound in your throat. It's a dead giveaway you're up to something."

"Not necessarily."

He grunted.

"Well, under other circumstances I'd invite the woman here for dinner."

"Under other circumstances you wouldn't know her to invite her to dinner."

"Yeah, I would. Her daughter's in the band. We've gotten together with other families through Aidan's group."

"Pep. The Starrs have never shown up for a concert except the one in their own church. They weren't even at the airport when the kids left for Europe. I'd say they're not interested."

It was all true. Poor Kenzie! She didn't stand a chance.

Mick laid the book on his lap. "The throat thing again. Invite her to dinner if you want. I don't mind. Aidan might, but he doesn't have to come."

Pepper slid down until she was flat on her back, her head on the pillow. "That's not it."

"What is it?" He leaned over her and put a little finger at her temple, catching the tear rolling toward her hairline. "Hmm?"

"I'm beginning to understand your mother."

"Uh-oh."

"Yeah."

He smiled. "Is that so bad?"

"If it means I feel displaced and not in tune with my son and preoccupied with how to fix relationships so that said son will have an easier time of it, then yes, that is so bad."

"You'll get over it." He kissed her forehead. "All things are possible with God."

Matthew again. Or was it her Lord's words?

Twenty-One

"They were getting married today anyway." Melinda Hathaway dabbed the corners of her eyes with a lacy handkerchief.

Susan reached over and squeezed her hand. They sat on a loveseat in a corner of a large comfortable room used by brides and their attendants as a dressing room. It was Saturday, the wedding day. Bree and her party of seven bridesmaids giggled and talked nonstop, too occupied to notice the teary-eyed, whispering women in the corner.

Melinda said, "She knows it was wrong."

"Jesus forgives."

Melinda nodded. "She knows that too."

Susan smiled.

"Thank you for not telling Drake."

Her smile wobbled. If he ever found out, would he forgive her? *Jesus forgives.*

She probably should have told him. As pastor he had a right to know. A truly submissive wife would have told him.

Or would she?

There were so many things to tell him. Bree Hathaway's pregnancy ranked last in priority, way below other things. Things like the meeting with Pepper Carlucci and Susan's unremitting heartache over separation from Kenzie.

After the rehearsal dinner the previous night, she and Drake arrived home exhausted. Still, she wanted to talk, to begin to describe her days away, but he had dozed off before she brushed her teeth. He mumbled goodnight and turned to hug the opposite edge of the king-size bed. She followed suit.

After a long time, Susan fell asleep basking in the memory of a warm fire on her face, Pugsy snoring in her lap, rain pattering against the window, and a worn book in her hand.

Drake left early that morning for a breakfast meeting, to be followed by other pastoral duties. They would meet up that afternoon for the wedding. Susan had spent her hours alone in a chair in the living room with a cup of tea and wondered yet again if she was losing her mind.

Listen to your heart, Suze. Her sister-in-law's advice struck again. Evidently the more Drake moved from her consciousness, the more the gospel according to Natalie moved in.

The morning passed before Susan budged from that chair. She had listened to her heart and made a very short list of desires. She desired not to lose her mind. She desired not to hover anywhere near nervous breakdown territory. What she did desire, truly and beyond a shadow of a doubt desired, was to reconcile with her daughter.

"What I don't understand is," Melinda whispered, "what did I do wrong?"

Susan squeezed her hand again. Though she had pondered that exact question for three months, she could not allow true empathy to show. She couldn't invite Melinda onto the Grandmas out of Wedlock Boat. No. This was Drake's congregation. The right to inform or not inform them was his.

But she did have an opinion, some of it gleaned from—of all people—Pepper Carlucci. The woman's thoughts had clicked with Susan's heart. Perhaps Melinda could benefit as well.

"Melinda, we all fall short of mothering perfectly. And none of us have been mothered perfectly, either. We're human. Who hasn't suffered from a parent's behavior, whether unintentional, subtle, or direct? In the end, though, when all is said and done, each of us is responsible for our own choices."

"I drilled into her head not to get intimate before marriage."

Me too. "I remember giving Kenzie medicine when she was little. The pink liquid stuff. She'd take it from a spoon and hold it in her mouth for the longest time. When she didn't think I was looking, she'd spit it out into the sink or a cup. I'd put vitamins into her hand and find them later stuffed behind the sofa cushions."

"Bree did that with carrots."

She smiled. "They decide whether or not they're going to swallow what we give them."

Melinda sighed. "I even put sugar on the carrots. And I sweetened the warnings by telling her how extra special wonderful it would be if she waited for marriage."

"Well, none of us can mother without stumbling," Susan reiterated. "I've let Kenzie down in ways too numerous to count and beyond my understanding. But Jesus forgives."

"Right. I just hope my daughter does someday too."

Me too.

Twenty-Two

At the sight of wall-to-wall people eating catered salmon and steak, Natalie thanked God once again for not blessing her with a daughter.

The church hospitality area with its adjacent patio accommodated nearly every member of Holy Cross Fellowship. Of course nearly every member attended the wedding reception because they all knew the Hathaways never spared the horses when it came to entertaining.

Natalie spotted Susan, cocreator of the extravaganza. Her sister-in-law claimed Melinda Hathaway needed very little help, but Susan now appeared downright haggard.

Natalie made her way through the throng and cornered her. "I didn't know this was a costume party."

Susan's eyebrows lifted. It was probably all she had energy to do.

"Suze, you look like the proverbial chicken with its head cut off, racing to and fro."

"I'm fine."

"And I'm a tree. Hey, everything went beautifully. You can relax now! Take your heels off and eat some cake."

Susan attempt to smile failed. "Did you notice the centerpieces?"

The showy red anthurium were hard to miss. They were part and parcel of a typical Hathaway production. The cost of flying flowers in from Hawaii guaranteed they would be noticed.

"Yeah," Natalie said. "I give them a wow factor of ten."

"They remind me of the bird-of-paradise behind the beach house."

"There's one there?"

"Yes. Growing right out of the concrete."

"That wins a big wow factor too." They hadn't talked since Susan called her on Wednesday and asked her not to visit the beach house. "So how did your last few days go down there? Did you read in front of a fire and relax?"

"I did. It was good. But now— I don't know. All I can think about is what you said."

Uh-oh. What'd I say now?

"About the jot and tittle."

"Hmm," she murmured again, treading lightly. "You mean about not listening to him screen them? About listening instead for God's permission? The 'you go, girl' comment?"

Susan gazed around the room and didn't answer. Up close the haggardness worsened. Dark circles rimmed her eyes. She looked too thin in the simple pale blue sheath. Had she even slept last night? Maybe she had come home too soon.

"Suze, do you think you spent enough time away?"

"How would I know? I've never done such a thing."

"Well, how do you feel right now?"

"Like I want to grab the microphone and announce that I'm going to be a grandmother. And please pray for Kenzie because she can't come home and deep down she must feel so lonely and so rejected."

"That would take care of Drake's quandary of whether or not to slip it into some future sermon." Natalie smiled gently. "Why don't you go home?"

"They haven't cut the cake yet."

"Do you know how many former brides are in this room? Not to mention all it takes is a knife and the photographer in place. We'll manage somehow."

Susan shook her head. "There are other things, so many details—"

"Gwyn has been helping. Let her finish this business. Really, Susan, you look like you might keel over any minute. Go. You've reached your limit here. I'll tell Gwyn."

"I shouldn't leave Melinda."

"Look at her flitting between tables. She's having the time of her life. I will make your apologies! Go. That was God's voice granting permission."

At last Susan made eye contact, her expression that of a woman drowning. She whispered, "I feel worse than I did last week."

They stared at one another for a long moment. Natalie replayed Rex's admonition that she not become more involved. But...

She was certain her blood pressure skyrocketed. This was Susan.

Natalie said, "Do you want my opinion?"

Susan closed her eyes.

"I'll give it anyway. Your sabbatical was too short. And, for your information, the beach house is still ours to use."

"Until Monday. Hardly worth—"

"Until the end of the month."

Susan opened her eyes.

Natalie shrugged. "I paid for longer. Who knows? I thought somebody could use it. Maybe even Kenzie. So. If you replaced the key yesterday in the lockbox, then it's still there."

Susan's face went from wild-eyed to wrinkled brow to open mouth with no sound. She clutched her hands to her stomach and walked away.

Natalie didn't move. She'd done it again. Said way too much.

Someone squeezed her elbow. Rex. "Hi."

She wrinkled her nose.

"What'd you say to her?"

"I think I just told her she should leave her husband."

Twenty-Three

Susan left the wedding reception, walked through the building's numerous hallways, and entered the main office. Earlier in the day, after helping the florist and taking care of other last-minute pre-wedding details, she had changed into dress clothes in her office. She would retrieve her things now along with Pugsy and go home.

Natalie was right. Much as Susan wanted to deny it, she had reached her limit. Again. It was becoming too familiar, this inability to handle life's inevitable daily stress. Would she ever recover from the split caused by Kenzie's news?

"Susan."

She looked up to see Drake in his office doorway. He was so handsome in the deep gray suit that matched his eyes and hair. The festive ice blue tie complemented the bride's colors. It had been Susan's suggestion.

"Hi." She went over to him, stopping within arm's reach. "Beautiful ceremony, Pastor Drake."

He smiled. "As always, you did a superb job behind the scenes."

"Thanks."

"You look tired."

"I am. I'm going home."

"I didn't sleep well myself last night. Susan, I don't like this being apart."

"I don't either."

"I'm glad you're home."

It was time to tell him what was going on in her heart, what truly separated them. It wasn't Kenzie's news alone.

Maybe they could spend the remainder of the evening at home in front of the fire. The scene would be perfect for a long, heart-to-heart talk. Surely he ached for Kenzie as much as she did. Surely she could convince him that sending a message through the Carluccis was acceptable. Yes, they just needed time alone to reconnect.

"Are you coming now?" she asked.

"Not just yet. You go ahead, though. There are too many people wanting to bend my ear. They don't get a setting like this too often, you know, to talk up close and personal."

"Neither do I." The words tripped off her tongue, murmuring what she normally would have kept to herself.

"What?" His snappish tone belied that he had indeed heard.

She cleared her throat and repeated it anyway. "I said, neither do I, meaning I don't often get to talk up close and personal with you."

"You're the one who left for five days."

She ignored that. "I need to talk with you, Drake. I need to do that soon."

He placed his hands gently on her shoulders and kissed the top of her head. More often than not he followed up snappish tones with a soft touch. "It has been a rough couple months for both of us. I'll be home by nine."

"Mmm." She pressed her lips together, but they wouldn't stay put. Their Saturday night routine was too ingrained. "That'll give you just enough time to review your sermon notes before bed."

He removed his hands. "By eight then."

Geez Louise. Was she special or what? He'd just scheduled an hour for her.

He walked to the main office doorway. "Get some rest."

She *was* special. Worthy enough for more than an hour on a Saturday night.

She could not, she simply could not wait for eight o'clock. "I met with Aidan Carlucci's mother."

Drake whipped around on his heel. His jaw sagged. Literally.

She'd never seen that before.

"You did what? Why on earth would you…?" He went speechless.

She'd never seen that before either. "Because I had to find out how Kenzie is."

"But we agreed—"

"I know we did. I apologize for breaking that agreement, but I could not handle it any longer. I had to find out what I could. So I met her at Starbucks in Fashion Valley and we talked."

"We cannot communicate to that woman or Kenzie that we condone what our daughter is doing! Susan." He spread his hands, a gestured plea to accept his words.

"I wasn't communicating that I condone her actions. I was taking back my communication of condemnation."

"You're disrupting the process."

"But it's not like she was abusive to us, that we had to send her away because she was on drugs or something and hateful and destructive toward us. The least we can do is offer her comfort."

"I know that would make you both feel better, but our God is the God of all comfort. He will comfort you and as soon as Kenzie turns back to Him, He will take care of her. If we interfere with His work, that can't happen. You and I agreed that the best way to allow her to come to her senses was to let her feel the full impact of consequences."

"Is withholding our love from her a consequence?"

"This is our love, Susan. This is the way God loves us, the way He draws us back to Himself by disciplining us when we need it."

His words of God's truth, spoken in that most compassionate tone, wore her down. She could not lift her eyes to meet his. Yes, God did discipline those He loved. Yes, she wanted Kenzie to—

Drake screens every jot and tittle of what you do…

What had Natalie said? Something about God saying *You go, girl. You don't need anyone else's permission to do what you think is right. You've got Mine.*

Drake hadn't even asked about Kenzie's welfare.

That wasn't right.

It wasn't.

She waited. She felt her chest heave. And she wondered, not for the first time, why she had brought Pugsy along to spend the long afternoon in her office…why she hadn't yet bothered to unload her luggage from the car…why she thought—even before Natalie said anything—about the rental week technically not ending until Monday…

At last she whispered, "Don't you want to know about Kenzie?" She looked up.

Drake's mouth worked as if his tongue pressed chewing gum against the back of his teeth, readying it for bubble blowing. It was that old nervous habit only Kenzie could still provoke into action.

Evidently Susan now possessed the same power.

He avoided eye contact for several silent moments. And then she knew he wasn't going to ask about their daughter.

"Drake, I'm not tired because of last night's lack of sleep or today's wedding or even Kenzie's news. I've been tired for a long time. I'm going back to the beach house tonight. For a little while."

He slid his hands into his pockets and looked at her now, his face caved in on itself like a lost little boy's expression.

"If it's—" *Drake screens every jot and tittle of what you do.* The gospel according to Natalie cut off what she intended to say…*If it's all right with you.* It didn't matter if it was all right with him or not. She knew what she needed to do.

But she didn't like this distance between them either. She began again, "If you'll come too, tomorrow after church, or Monday, we can—"

"I told you I can't come. I have two full weeks until my scheduled vacation time. It's Easter season. If you can't rest at home and come to grips with this, then go." He spun on his heel and strode from the office.

She spun on her own heel and marched down the hall, pulling bobby pins from her hair and letting it fall to her shoulders.

He really was an infuriating man. She wondered why she hadn't noticed before.

Twenty-Four

They were on page 115.

Pepper hunched back against a pillow, rubbed lotion into her hands, and didn't even pretend to read. "Mick."

"Hmm?"

"It's Saturday night and Kenzie's not back yet from Phoenix."

"Tell me you didn't call him."

"Well." Of course she had called Aidan. "I seem to be assuming this role of meddling mother-in-law faster than a speeding bullet."

"I noticed. He didn't hang up on you?"

"No, but I didn't learn anything more from him, either. I should have listened to your mother. I probably could have learned a lot."

He ignored that. "Aidan told you yesterday that there was no schedule for Kenzie's return. It's typical of them. I have no clue how they ever get to a performance on time."

"What if they're fighting?"

"It's none of our business."

"What if she doesn't come back?"

"It's none of our business."

Pepper bolted upright. "Of course it's our business! That's our grandchild she's carrying across the country!"

"Six hours is hardly across the country."

"Young married people don't take separate vacations! They love being together all the time. They can't get enough of each other."

"This is a different generation."

"Not to mention they're not even married. Is there honestly any commitment between them? How could we tell? It doesn't exactly show with her taking off and probably losing her job and him getting all quiet and working extra."

Mick shut the book on a finger and looked at her. "We knew this was going to be a long rough haul for them. Aidan has professed his love and commitment. Kenzie is obviously nuts about him. Do you think we can fix it for them? Pressure them into marriage? Guarantee that they'll live happily ever after if only they look and act just like us? Or her parents?"

She stuck out her lower lip.

"Mm-hmm. Exactly," he said. "Pepper Sprout, this isn't like you to get so unnerved. Why can't you let it go?"

"Because this is about me being a grandma."

"So it's all about *you.*"

"Yeah."

He smiled and opened the book again. "Bingo."

"Shut up."

He chuckled. "Read with me. Give your mind a rest."

The phone rang beside her on the nightstand. Although the clock read ten twenty, she wasn't surprised. Family and friends called all hours. She picked it up. "Hello."

"Pepper? This is Susan Starr."

Now that surprised her. "Hi, Susan."

"I am so sorry to call this late, but I just wanted you to know I'm back at the beach house for a while. By myself."

"Okay." That message of course was for her daughter. "Um, Kenzie's in Phoenix. At Dakota's."

"Geez Louise." She exhaled loudly and then began humming. It sounded like a hymn. "Well, will you just tell her when you see her? Please?"

"Sure."

"You're welcome to stop by again. Better yet, come run away with me." She giggled. "I really enjoyed our visit. Bring Mickey Junior. I'll bake monster cookies for him. They're Kenzie's favorite, so will you tell her that too? Oh, and I have ingredients for fettucine alfredo with chicken. That's her favorite. Actually I'm at the Ralphs in Pacific Beach and my grocery cart is overflowing with her favorites. I'm thinking maybe I can win her over through her taste buds. And will you tell her I want to give her some money? I'm sure they could use it. Oh my goodness, I'm keeping you. I'll let you go. Thanks, Pepper."

"You're welcome. Thank you."

"For what?"

"For joining me in the boat."

She laughed. "Bye."

"Bye." Pepper hung up the phone. "Oh, man!"

Mick said, "Kenzie's mom?"

"I think! Or someone impersonating her. No, on second thought it was her for sure. She started humming a hymn."

"Like the other day?"

"Yes. I think this one was 'Great Is Thy Faithfulness.'" She touched his arm. "Mick! Maybe she's not so bad after all. After the last two conversations, I would swear she wants to shower Kenzie with a hands-on love. She even referred to 'they,' to Kenzie *and* Aidan."

He smiled. "Feel better knowing you've got a shipmate?"

"Yes, I do." She nodded. "Amen."

Twenty-Five

"Kenz." Aidan set down his tea mug. "Do you want to hear the latest?"

Kenzie smiled. "I love you."

He grinned. "Why?"

"That shorthand talk. I know exactly what you're referring to."

"Of course you do." He reached across the table between lunch remains and squeezed her hand.

They sat in the apartment's kitchenette, large enough to hold two chairs and the small table pushed against the wall. The dining set was fifties retro, made of metal. Thin orange vinyl padded the seats and backs. Kenzie loved his Salvation Army decor.

Actually she loved everything about him. Which explained why she was back already from Phoenix. She missed him so much she convinced Jenae, her friend with the car, that if they didn't leave in time to reach San Diego by dawn she'd hitchhike. Jenae and Dakota were angry at her for cutting the visit short. It couldn't be helped.

And it didn't really matter, not with Aidan looking at her in that way of his, with those eyes the color of lapis lazuli nearly hidden behind black, black lashes, curly and thick.

"Kenz," he said again.

No one had ever nicknamed her that. It was part of their private shorthand.

Of course, his voice added its own effect. Her skin tingled at the sound. It didn't matter what he said. She'd fallen in love with his voice long before they met. She was fifteen and heard him sing at a concert. Low and sort of raspy with an unbelievable range, it wrapped itself around musical notes.

Years later he heard her sing. And the rest was history.

He said, "We don't have to talk about it."

"It's okay. What'd my mother do now?"

"Let's start with *my* mother. Achoo."

Kenzie laughed at his pretend sneeze.

"She called after I got home last night."

"After you got home?" The band had played in a club; Aidan didn't get home until after three.

"At least she wasn't on the doorstep waiting for me." He shook his head. "Anyway, she was too excited to sleep. Your mom called her last night from the grocery store in PB and said she had a cartful of your favorite food."

"This is getting weird."

"Yeah. She said she's back at the beach house—alone—and hopes you'll come. She invited my mom and Mickey too. She also said she wants to give you some money. Sounds to me like she's trying to buy your affection with food and cash."

Kenzie didn't reply. She wasn't so sure. Aidan's folks were always giving them food and cash. Not much—she suspected they didn't have all that much to spare—but some. He said those were gifts of love, no strings attached.

"Maybe they're peace offerings."

He squeezed her hand. "Maybe. It gets weirder. On Friday my mom went to see your mom at the beach."

"You're kidding!"

"Nope. Mom saw a huge change in your mom. I laughed and said she'd known her for five whole days. She insisted it's true."

"How has she changed?"

"Mom said she is totally not uptight."

"No way."

"That's what I said and she said they drank coffee together and ate ice cream cones. In the middle of the day. Coffee, Kenz."

"My mom would never— I can't believe it! But I have to because your mom wouldn't make it up. This is totally bizarre."

"Let's face it. We've thrown them for a loop. Mom says they're on a boat together. She calls it the Grandmas out of Wedlock Boat."

"They've got a little club going? Off the charts bizarre."

"I know. So anyway, that's the message from your mom to my mom to me to you. If it's like the telephone game, we'd better disregard the whole thing."

"Aidan, I want to go see her."

He stared at her.

"I don't know where that came from, but I think I really do."

"Kenz, don't let them guilt you into this."

She shrugged. "She's my mom."

"You're always a basket case after being with her. Four months away in Europe was the best thing for you." He paused. "For us."

"She's my mom."

"You'll come home a basket case."

"Probably."

"Not probably. For sure."

"Okay, for sure. Will you still love me?"

He picked up her hand and kissed the palm. "Yes, I will still love you."

But what if he didn't? What if he got tired of putting up with her? She was usually a basket case over something. Just ask her parents. And look what they did to her.

What she truly wanted was her mommy.

But…had that person ever even existed?

Twenty-Six

Susan bent over in front of Faith Fontaine's ancient oven and pulled out a baking sheet of fresh hot cookies, humming as she worked.

Hymns flowed in her mind, one after another like the waves rolling toward shore. "All Creatures of Our God and King." "O Worship the King." "How Great Thou Art." One...after...another. Verse upon verse. Crescendo upon crescendo.

Chasing away the guilt.

There were so many reasons for the guilt, not the least of which was how she'd spent that morning. She'd *dawdled* it away—the *entire* morning, the entire *Sunday* morning when she should have been in a church—with a long stroll with Pugsy, coffee at Kono's, and more than an hour's observation of an artist at work on the boardwalk. The woman painted the pier as the early sun stroked it, capturing all the fresh pink and yellow brilliance in water colors. Susan felt swept away in beauty and wanted to buy it.

Instead she returned to the beach house and mixed up a batch of cookies. They baked now, a slow process with only one cookie sheet and the old unreliable oven. The rhythm of kitchen work and the luscious scents of baking cinnamon and sugar and chocolate whittled at her doubts. Eventually the apologies to God and the defensive conversations with Drake faded from her mind. The music gained ground and she hummed more loudly.

She blamed her broken heart for such uncharacteristic behavior.

Leaving home? Leaving home angry at Drake and he at her? Staying away from home? Unbelievable conduct from the pastor's wife.

But the pain of the broken heart burned like a hot fire under her, forcing her to see things differently, to react to a new set of priorities. She was in a battle for reconciliation with Kenzie. It could not be fought hiding at home, carrying on as if nothing had happened, hoping their daughter would forget she was an outcast and come back with marriage plans. Or better yet, with a marriage license.

Yes, setting up camp at the beach house was outlandish, foolish behavior. In the heat of that fire, though, she intuited that the house was neutral territory, the only way to make herself available to her daughter.

Other than staying there, she didn't know what else to do except bake cookies and pray. She was up to an eight-word prayer: *Lord, please fix my relationship with Kenzie. Please.*

Maybe it was only seven words since "please" entered in twice.

There was a knock at the door.

Pugsy barked and jumped up from the braided rug in front of the fireplace. Before Susan removed the hot pad mitten from her hand, he skittered across the room. Yapping for all he was worth, he spun in circles in front of the door.

He knew.

And then Susan knew.

Kenzie stood on the other side of the screen door, a tentative smile on her face. "I heard there were monster cookies here."

And then she was in Susan's arms.

Susan clung to her daughter, feeling eternity begin and end in that moment.

"Shh, Pugs!" Kenzie said, her voice muffled against Susan's shoulder. "You'll get your turn."

The dog obeyed and resorted to whining and pushing his little body against their ankles.

Susan became aware of a round bump between her and Kenzie and blinked back tears. "Oh, my. Let me look at you." Unable to completely let go of her, she grasped Kenzie's arms and saw the big red plaid flannel shirt she wore. It was a maternity top! She smiled. "Oh, my."

Grinning, Kenzie patted her abdomen. "Yeah, there he is. Or she. We don't know which."

"Oh, my."

"Mom, your vocabulary is shot all to pieces."

She laughed. "Have you felt him move yet?"

"I don't think so."

"You will soon. I remember a little fluttery sensation."

"Like there's a butterfly coming and going, a faint, tickly feeling?"

"That's it."

"Really? I thought it was my imagination. Or something I ate." She sank to the floor to Pugsy, releasing Susan's hold on her. "Okay! Okay! You silly dog."

He went wild again as Kenzie nuzzled him.

An immediate sense of emptiness engulfed Susan, the same emotion she'd lived and moved in for three months. She looked down at Kenzie's stiff spiky hair that moved with her head like a cap. Dangly silver earrings bounced, at least one pair per ear. The upturned nose was buried in Pugsy's furry neck.

No. She refused to let her daughter go again. She would not give in to the emptiness.

Susan pulled her skirt out of the way and knelt on the floor beside Kenzie.

"Mom." She sniffed. "The cookies are burning!"

"It's okay. I have plenty."

"Mom!" Kenzie popped up and scurried to the oven, Pugsy at her heels. "Do you know how long it's been since I've had monster cookies? I could eat dozens." She busied herself in the kitchen. "I think they're okay. Where's the spatula? Oh, here it is."

Susan sighed quietly but didn't budge.

"Do you want me to put more in to bake?"

"I want you to come back here for a minute."

"Just a sec." She spooned batter onto the cookie sheet.

Susan realized a subtle shift in roles. Kenzie, the in-your-face imp, was avoiding her mother. Susan, the avoid-conflict-at-all-costs shrinking violet, felt like a bird-of-paradise breaking through solid concrete. She rearranged her skirt, sat cross-legged on the carpet, and waited.

At last, a new sheet of cookies in the oven and a handful of warm ones in her hand, Kenzie turned. "Is there some milk?"

Susan nodded.

She opened the fridge. "All right! Two percent. You're spoiling me."

"No, I'm not."

Kenzie turned, surprise in her raised brows.

"I'm just trying to love you. Please, sweetheart, come sit down."

Kenzie replaced the milk, set the cookies on the counter, and walked over. "What?" She sat on the floor.

"I am so sorry for sending you away."

"I know. I'm sorry for being such a pain—"

Susan held up a hand. "I'm sorry. I'm sorry for not being a better mom these nineteen years. Please forgive me. I hope you can forgive me, for your own sake."

Kenzie stared at her.

Of course she was speechless. She had never heard such words from her mother.

"Hon, you don't have to say anything. I just wanted you to know. And…here." She dug into her skirt pocket, pulled out a folded pack of bills, and handed it to Kenzie. "Five hundred dollars. It's not much, but maybe you can use it. We were always short on money when we were first—" *Married.* Back up. "When you were a baby."

"Mom! Are you on something?"

Faith. Freedom. Courage. Drake not screening…She shook her head. "Music."

"Huh?"

"I'm just," she pointed to her head, "singing."

"This place needs a CD player. At least a radio. I can't believe there's still no television here."

"It is electronically challenged, I'll give you that."

Kenzie stared again. "Um, thank you for this." She held up the money.

"You're welcome."

"We might have an extra CD player around."

"Does it play cassette tapes? I really want to listen to your music."

"That reminds me, we're making a CD! Professionally!"

"Really?"

"Yeah. It's pretty awesome." She still held the bills in her hand, as if unsure what to do with them. "It won't happen for a while, but there's this producer who's totally interested. He loves Aidan's work. What are you smiling at?"

"Just you." She grinned. She could not take her eyes off her child. No one else would notice the subtle roundness in her face, a soft but mature touch. "By the way, you can keep the money. No strings attached."

"Well." Kenzie looked down at it. "Okay. If you're sure."

"Honey." She put a finger under Kenzie's chin and lifted it. "I've never been so sure of anything in my life. Now, how about some milk and cookies?"

They stuffed themselves with cookies and talked about Kenzie's pregnancy, due date, and work as a barista at a funky coffee shop. They steered clear of the Carluccis, Aidan, Drake, medical insurance, and marriage.

The afternoon shadows lengthened in the beach house and Susan grew anxious that Kenzie would leave soon. Her daughter remained tentative, as if unsure of the situation. Susan could hardly blame her. There her mother sat beside her on the couch, on vacation without her dad, speaking more openly than she ever had in Kenzie's entire life.

But Susan knew there would be no healing until they addressed issues that still separated them. She jumped in.

"I like Pepper Carlucci a lot."

Kenzie bobbed her head. "She's fresh, isn't she? All of them are like that. They all say exactly what they're thinking. Mick is a great guy. It's so obvious he and Pepper are totally crazy about each other."

Envy crept in, a worm chewing at the newfound peace. Why weren't she and Drake like that? Had they never been like that? She didn't think so.

"There's always lots of commotion at their house. Lots of laughter."

That summarized the exact opposite of what Kenzie experienced growing up. No wonder she was enamored with the family.

Susan said, "What's Aidan like?"

"Passionate about music, about creating it."

"Like you."

She shook her head. "He's way beyond me. He writes it and it absolutely consumes him at times. He needs his space. And that's okay."

Susan wondered.

"I just do my own thing when he's in the zone. He's thoughtful like his dad. Romantic with little gifts." She shrugged. "It's kind of weird telling you this stuff."

She smiled. "It's kind of weird hearing it. Do you talk about getting married?"

Kenzie glanced away, her chin rising slightly in the movement.

Drake's did the same when he got defensive. "Hon, I'm not pressing. I'm just curious about what you're thinking."

"We consider ourselves already married. Why should a piece of paper make a difference? Or a ceremony in a church? Of course, that's not going to happen anyway, not in your church."

The charge sliced through Susan, cutting off her breath. "If your dad changed his mind…"

"Yeah, right. Like that's going to happen in this millennium. Ninety-nine percent of his sermons sooner or later get around to moralizing about how wicked and nasty sex is."

"That's not exactly—"

"It is, Mom. It is exactly what he preaches and how often. Why can't you see that? How he really is?"

"He just wants the best for you."

"Well, I found the best. I love Aidan. He loves me. We're committed to each other. And sex is not wicked. It's the most beautiful, holy, amazing thing."

"In marriage."

"Is it in yours? Has it ever been?"

"Kenzie—"

"Forget I asked that. I don't really want to know. But it makes a marriage, Mom. The two become one and then they're married."

Susan tried to focus. Why had she brought up marriage? That was what set Kenzie off. That was the main issue with Drake, and she was so hurt by her dad, she exaggerated everything about him and saw only the negative.

Kenzie said, "Never mind. You can't understand."

"What does Aidan have against marriage?"

She hesitated. "Nothing."

"His parents have a healthy one, right?"

"Yeah. It's not that. It's just we don't see any reason to have someone pronounce us husband and wife when we already are."

Was it Kenzie and Aidan who thought that, or just Kenzie? Was Kenzie so afraid of marriage because of what she saw in her parents' relationship?

"Honey, what have you seen in me and your father that turns you so against marriage?"

Kenzie nearly flew from the couch. She whirled around and raised her hands. "This! This, what you're doing right now. You're aping Dad like you don't have an original thought in your head! You kowtow to him like he walks on water. You're like that old TV wife June Cleaver, all cardboardy, saying her lines sweetly, never ruffled, never *real*."

"That's not fair or accurate."

"You're always defending him. You're never on my side."

Susan's entire body ached. "I'm here now."

"I don't want to wait nineteen years to be here now for my kid." She pressed fists to her eyes and walked toward the door. "I knew it would get to this. We'll never agree and you won't accept me as I am."

Every fiber of Susan's being cried out in agony. She caught up with her at the door. "I just want the best for you, sweetheart. I love you."

"I have to go." Kenzie pulled the money from her pocket.

"Keep that. I said no strings. You don't have to get married to use it."

"Okay. Thanks. Bye."

"Let me hug you."

She stood still long enough for Susan to wrap her arms around her and give a quick squeeze.

And then she was gone.

Susan wanted to curl up in a fetal position.

Twenty-Seven

"I know exactly how you're feeling." Natalie watched Susan slumped in the opposite chair, Pugsy snoring on her lap.

Her sister-in-law's forehead knotted, one lump above each eyebrow. She wasn't buying it.

"Okay, Suze, I'll rephrase that. I've never had a pregnant unwed daughter who called me June Cleaver, so I can't possibly know how you're feeling."

Susan gave a slight nod.

"Maybe a string of pearls would help."

Susan gazed out the window. The knots on her forehead were nearly golf ball size.

At least she had called. Natalie couldn't believe her sister-in-law had actually swallowed her pride and uttered that one life-changing word, "Help." Hearing it made Natalie weep. God had moved a mountain. He didn't need her to keep pushing at it.

Rex, bless him, said his macho wife driving to the beach alone at night in a weepy state was not a good idea. Besides that, he loved his sister-in-law. He invited himself along and gave their teenage sons a choice: They could either eat at a favorite restaurant with Mom and Dad and Aunt Susan or fix their own dinner. The three of them waited now at the place not far down the boardwalk, probably inhaling large amounts of tortilla chips and salsa.

"Suze, listen." Natalie leaned forward, elbows on her knees. "This dialogue with Kenzie was a good thing. It means advancement. It's like you've moved the forwards deep into the opponents' territory. Not that the Carluccis are opponents, but you get the picture."

"You're talking about soccer."

"Yeah."

"Kenzie's right, then. She thinks we're on opposite teams. She said I never take her side. I don't want to take sides at all, not hers or Drake's."

"Okay, forget that analogy."

"We should be on the same team."

"I know."

"They both could be here right now. Drake isn't doing the service tonight; he doesn't have to be anywhere in the morning. Kenzie's not working now or in the morning. We all like being at the beach house. Why am I here by myself?"

"Think of it as if they were traded to other teams for the season. They were offered what looked like a better deal elsewhere. They'll find their way back. You are a team."

Susan looked at her.

"I'm just the rookie called up for a while."

"No, you're my team, Natalie. There's no one else."

"Of course there is. There's a whole slew of rookies waiting."

"The Martha Mavens."

She nodded. "It's time, hon."

"I don't know." Susan sighed loudly. "Kenzie's right. I'm just not a team player."

Natalie swung toward the window and tried not to roll her eyes in vexation. *Lord!* She turned back. "You've just never played in the big league. And you've definitely never played goalie."

"Goalie?"

"You're protecting the goal, your family. You think you're all alone back there at the end of the field, but you've got all of us out in front, protecting you. And we are good. We are not going to let the opponent get anywhere near you."

"Who's the opponent?"

"Don't be so literal. I don't know. Whatever keeps your family from being a team. Anyway, you are the Martha Mavens' main concern right now. Our defensive line is in place. Or it will be as soon as I call Gwyn and Mildred."

The forehead knots flattened out, and Susan smiled. "I just had a picture of Gwyn in shin guards."

Natalie laughed. "Gwyn, cover girl material at thirty-seven, in shin guards? Maybe I'd better leave out the soccer talk."

"Maybe." She paused. "You think I can really be part of a team?"

"Yes, Susan, I know you can. Now let's go eat!"

Twenty-Eight

The white-haired twins, Mildred and Leona, insisted on cooking breakfast for everyone. They bobbed around the beach house kitchen like windup toys.

"Everyone" included Gwyn, busy now with tea preparations, and Emmylou, who set the table, waddling between it and the cupboards. She carried plates on the shelf of her rather large, rounded eight-and-a-half months abdomen.

Susan tightened the belt of her bathrobe and watched them. Talk about forgetting the morning routine. When the women had knocked on her door moments ago, she was still half asleep. The sun had barely risen, and yet there they stood, bright eyed and bushy tailed, jabbering about how great the commuter lane was in rush hour traffic.

"Good morning, sunshine!" they'd said and bustled inside, a group of magpies.

"Natalie called."

"Need we say more?"

"She'll come later."

"Tess has appointments and simply can't get away, even for breakfast."

"Are there eggs? We brought bacon and ingredients to make blueberry scones and forgot the eggs!"

"How about juice?"

"Emmylou is having labor pains."

"No. Ooo. Ow." Emmylou puffed out words between breaths. "It's just those Braxton Hicks things."

"Same difference. One of these times they'll be for real."

"Pugsy wants out. I'll take him."

"Shoo, Susan. Go do what you need to do. Shower, whatever. We know our way around a kitchen."

What had her sister-in-law told them about her this time? True, Susan asked Natalie for help. Kenzie's visit had drained her. And then there was that sweet dinner with Rex and the boys. They made her laugh and they didn't avoid the subject of Kenzie's situation. Their company convinced her she needed others; she needed friends and prayers. She told Natalie it was all right with her if she let the Martha Mavens know she was hurting.

Evidently Natalie had not wasted any time.

Would the women have come if she were in her own house? They'd never done anything remotely similar to what they were doing at the moment. After her hysterectomy, they used Natalie like a UPS man, giving her gifts and food to deliver. Susan had felt that was proper. Others could have their open door policies when they were out of commission, but she wouldn't want them laundering her underwear and seeing her kitchen up close.

Was it the beach house that gave them permission to invade her life?

Or was it the beach house that gave her permission to let them?

"Susan."

She refocused.

Leona addressed her. "I said, shoo. Can we get you anything?"

"Um, well, I'd like a cup of coffee."

Four pairs of eyes zoomed in on her.

No doubt about it. The pastor's wife lived under a microscope. They all knew she didn't touch coffee, hadn't for years. Every coffee hour between services, every wedding reception and funeral lunch and what-not celebration included a large pot of herbal tea made especially for Pastor Drake and the Mrs.

It couldn't be helped. If they viewed her through a microscope, sooner or later they would notice the damage. Surely pain would etch itself into wrinkles, lackluster expressions, sagging shoulders. They might imagine all sorts of horrid scenarios. She might as well tell them the correct one.

She straightened shoulders already in an unmistakably droopy condition. "Yes, I really would like a cup of coffee with milk and sugar. And by the way, Kenzie is pregnant and she doesn't want to get married. I'm going to take a shower now."

~

The shower was a long one.

Susan remembered Natalie's suggestion that she imagine God with her, right there and then, cheering her on. *You go, girl. You have My permission to…*

To what?

Tears mingled with the hot water.

Permission to cry?

Permission to hurt over Kenzie and Drake?

Permission to receive the love of friends, the love of God through them?

You go, girl.

And she knew then—in that deep heart of hearts where things were known without benefit of the mind's explanation—her world would never ever be the same again.

~

They lingered at the table, no one moving to clear the breakfast dishes.

Mary tendencies had definitely shoved Martha's to a back burner.

Mildred, Leona, Gwyn, and Emmylou listened to Susan talk about Kenzie. She stopped short of the New Year's Day story, how she and Drake had sent her from the house.

The women sympathized and they empathized.

Leona said, "My granddaughter is living with her boyfriend."

Mildred said, "My grandson isn't married to the mother of his two children."

Emmylou said, "Robbie and I, were, uh, you know, *together* before we got married. Before we got saved. Is it all right if I tell you that?"

Gwyn patted her arm. "What's-his-name and I more or less lived together for six months before we got married and that was *after* I got saved. You know what?" She sighed. "It feels good to finally say that to you all. I never could admit it for fear you'd condemn me. I remember hiding his toothbrush and shoes once when Tess came over for something. It wasn't until after our divorce that I admitted I never felt quite right about our premarital ways." She smiled sadly. "It took me ages to even tell you we were divorcing."

Mildred said, "Leona and I also have divorced children. We have grandchildren involved in alcohol, drugs, school failure, jail time, abortion, and the occult. Did I forget anything, dearie?"

Leona said, "One of my sons is having an affair."

Emmylou said, "My father is an alcoholic."

Gwyn said, "My sister is gay."

Susan could only stare at them.

Leona grinned. "The skeletons are fairly jumping out of the closets, aren't they? I think I hear bones clattering across the floor!"

Mildred chuckled. "See, Susan? You're not alone. We understand. And just because you are the pastor's wife does not mean your world is untouched by pain and difficulty and sin. God's forgiveness and mercy cover it all—if we let them."

Leona added, "We are your sisters and we don't condemn you or Kenzie or Drake. We never did expect you to be completely healed of all your life's wounds. That won't happen for any of us until we leave this world."

Everyone sat in silence for a long moment. They exchanged dazed looks. Slowly and quietly those mellowed into ones of affirmation.

At last Mildred smiled. "There is healing in dialogue. Leona and I have our own prayer group, you know, all of us old fogies. We don't like to bother you young'uns with our troubles. Leona, dear." She turned to her twin. "Could that be a form of pride?"

"I do believe that's a possibility, sis. Though we have always sent our requests along the prayer chain without reservation."

Gwyn shivered in an exaggerated way. "Natalie and I refer to the prayer chain as the gossip chain. I know it's a wonderful way to share emergency situations, like when Rex was in his accident. But my goodness! There are something like fifty names on that list. I don't open up all that well with you ladies. No way could I tell this deeply personal kind of stuff to people who are virtual strangers to me."

"Me neither," said Emmylou.

Leona shook her head. "Of course not. But something is happening here. I think you three—and probably Natalie too—have each other to confide in. You have your own prayer chain."

"So, Susan." Mildred homed in on her with those doe eyes enlarged behind thick lenses. "Where are we? What shall we pray for, exactly? The baby, of course, that precious new life growing in His sight. Kenzie and Aidan, that they will seek God in all this. You and Drake, that guilt and embarrassment won't disable you."

Susan nodded. "Mmm." She cleared her throat. "That about does it. Um…Drake…um." Did all this openness include telling on her husband?

But without Drake beside her, she felt like a one-armed lumberjack. Was it telling on him so much as asking for help for herself? One thing she knew for sure: She needed all the help she could get.

She said, "I don't mean to disrespect him, but, well, he banned Kenzie from our home."

All four pairs of eyes widened.

"Out of love for her. We— He believes if left to suffer the consequences, she will return to God."

Mildred leaned forward, interrupting. "Has she turned away?"

The question stopped Susan's thoughts cold.

"What I mean is, has she denounced her heavenly Father? Is that what the premarital relations and the decision not to marry are based on? Disbelief?"

Susan covered her mouth with her hand.

"She and I used to chat now and then." Mildred winked. "I'd compliment her on a new hairdo or pair of earrings. We discussed her music a lot. One time she said, 'Millie—'"

They all laughed.

"She called me that. Anyway, she said, 'Millie, it's like coloring books. I never could stay inside those idiotic lines with my crayons. My brain kept seeing other pictures and I'd color those instead. Music is like that. We sing a chorus in church, and the whole time I'm rewording it.' Then she kind of swung her arms and snapped her fingers." Mildred demonstrated. "She said, 'And my body is moving to some other beat.'"

Susan's breath caught. Kenzie had told her such things. Until that very moment, though, she never understood what she was saying. "Her music doesn't always make sense to me. The songs seem full of such longing and sadness or outright condemnation of society. But...they always point to God, to Him as the ultimate hope, even if His name isn't specifically stated."

Mildred nodded. "I know."

"You do?"

"Yes. I told her I was hard of hearing and couldn't quite catch everything in the songs that were popular with her generation. She'd write down words for me so I could read them."

Smiles went round the table.

"Susan." Mildred patted her hand. "Kenzie believes in Jesus. She's just trying to color in pictures of Him that are different from what we can see. Sooner or later, she'll get to the one of Him in which He floods her soul with His reality, and then her heart will burst with love for Him." She paused. "Why don't we pray?"

And then the Prayer Warrior squeezed Susan's hand and began to pray for her single, unwed daughter who never had liked coloring books.

Twenty-Nine

Twenty minutes after reaching the beach community, Pepper found a curbside parking space large enough to accommodate her van. It was on a side street three blocks from the sand itself and at least two beyond that from Susan's squished red chili pepper of a house. There was no meter to feed, just a sign indicating a two-hour limit and a meter maid cruising along in her nifty little vehicle, eagerly enforcing the rule.

How on earth did people live full-time in an overpopulated neighborhood inundated year round—on a Monday afternoon in March, no less!—with ocean-worshipping commuters?

Pepper hopped down from the van and pushed up her shirt sleeves. Spring was well underway with bright sunshine and warmish temps that promised more than they could deliver. Shade or a brisk breeze would instantly cool her down. Young people in scant summer gear headed toward the beach in pursuit of goose bump sunbathing. Did they think early season tan lines proved their courage or something? That they were better than others?

Oh, man! Was she in a funk or was she in a funk? Hopefully the hike would help. No sense in greeting Susan with a growl.

Some minutes and a few blocks later, with what felt like a sheen of perspiration covering her entire body, Pepper arrived at the white picket fence out of breath. No oxygen in the lungs might eliminate fussy speech, if not speech altogether.

As she unlatched the gate, Susan appeared at the side of the house, coming from the direction of the backyard. Her hair hung loose to her shoulders.

"Yoo-hoo!" She waved and grinned. "Hi!"

Pepper nodded, attempting to smile and suck in air at the same time.

A woman accompanied Susan. She was taller with an athletic build obvious in her outfit of shiny soccer-style top and shorts. Her reddish-brown hair was pulled back into a bouncy ponytail.

"Is Kenzie all right?" Susan asked.

They crossed the patio toward each other.

"She's just fine."

"Oh, thank God. After yesterday— I'm sorry. This is my sister-in-law, Natalie Starr. And this is Pepper Carlucci, Aidan's mother."

Natalie's friendly expression broke into a wide smile and she thrust out a hand. "Hi! It's a pleasure to meet you. I'm the aunt."

Susan added, "She's married to Drake's brother."

"Kenzie's my favorite niece." They shook hands. "My only one as well, but who's counting that?"

A pleasant relative who adored Kenzie! An immediate sense of comfort washed over Pepper. "I'm so glad to meet you too."

Susan said, "Do you think we can expand our boat to include aunts?"

Pepper nodded. "Yes, by all means. Welcome aboard, Natalie."

She raised her brows at them.

Pepper explained. "The Grandmas out of Wedlock Boat. I hereby rename it the Grandmas and Aunts out of Wedlock Boat." She turned to Susan. "I told Aidan about it. He called us shipmates."

She laughed. "Well, come inside, maties. We'll make some coffee, and…" She reached into her handbag and pulled something out. "Ta-da! And play with my brand-new cell phone!"

Pepper burst into laughter. For all the world Susan resembled a little girl giddy over a new toy. She wondered what the woman was on. Maybe she could get some of it for herself.

They left the outside door open. Soothing sounds of ocean and seagulls floated through the screen door and reminded Pepper why people flocked to the area year round. Given the chance, she could get accustomed to the crowds.

After the usual generic chitchat about weather, beach, and freeway traffic, they settled on the living room couch and chairs with mugs of freshly brewed hazelnut coffee.

"Pepper, I'm so glad you came again. Hey, now with my phone…" She touched the new silver toy she clasped on her lap. "You can call ahead to make sure I'm here. Are you running away again?"

She hesitated, taking her internal temperature. "I think I must be. Maybe it's only PMS, but life seems totally out of whack. Nowhere near under control."

"Kenzie and Aidan?"

"Yeah. I don't mean to blame you in the least or my husband, Mick. It's just that schedules and situations leave me in the forefront. And now Mick's going out of town. He's in road construction and has to do this every so often for work. He'll be gone for months to Los Angeles. Sometimes he'll get home on weekends." She turned to Natalie. "I still have three little ones at home, a four-year-old boy and two girls in elementary school."

"Mmm, lucky you." Natalie's tone indicated she thought otherwise.

"Exactly. I usually thrive when I'm at my wit's end. It's where I do my best work. The busier, the better, and I can handle Mick's absence. But I tell you." She shook her head. "I'm coming unglued. So I guess I came to share the fun with you, Susan."

"We are in the same boat."

"Thanks. The thing is, Kenzie and Aidan live in a tiny one-bedroom apartment. There is no space for a cradle, let alone a crib. They're not thinking through practical things like that or how they're going to afford diapers, even. Kenzie hardly has any clothes that fit her. Not that she ever complains."

Natalie said, "It's time Aunt Nattie stepped in."

Susan said, "What do you mean?"

"Well, my first thought is that I want to run out and buy them every-thing they need. But Drake would have a cow and Rex would probably draw the line at that. He'd tell me I'd better work full-time at something that pays real money. Coaching high school girls isn't exactly big league bucks. So maybe I'd better start small. Duh!" She slapped her forehead. "I know! A baby shower! If they'd gotten married I would have hosted a wedding shower, right? Why can't I host a baby shower now? I don't care if it's out of politically correct order."

"She's only five months along. Isn't that kind of early?"

"That doesn't matter either. She needs to know now that we love her. And we could have it here at the beach house, neutral territory."

Susan turned to Pepper. "Do you think she'd come?"

"I don't know. Do you think she would?"

"I don't know."

Natalie said, "Why don't *I* call her and ask her?"

Pepper hesitated barely a fraction of a second. "I'll give you her number." After all, Kenzie never said don't tell Aunt Nattie.

She sipped her coffee.

⌢

Natalie found paper in a kitchen drawer and began writing a to-do list for a baby shower. They worked together on a guest list—a few friends from Susan's church, Aidan's sisters—and exchanged phone numbers.

Susan laughed when she recited her new cell number from memory. "I'll program both of yours in this. I can do that, right?" She looked at Pepper. "Natalie convinced me I need this. I never thought I did, but already it gives me such a sense of freedom! I don't have to go next door to use the neighbor's phone. And Kenzie can call me directly. If she ever wanted to."

"I'm sure she'll want to."

"I don't know. Did she tell you about yesterday?"

Pepper shook her head. "No. I haven't talked with her since last week."

"She came here. By the way, thank you for giving her my message, that I was back and baking cookies."

"I told Aidan. He must have told her. How did things go?"

A myriad of expressions crossed her face. First the womanly uptight appearance overtook the delighted little girl, and then they flip-flopped positions. "Um. They went okay. Kind of hopeful. Disastrous."

"Suze." Natalie laid down her pencil. "She came. She gobbled your cookies. You asked for forgiveness but didn't demand it on the spot. You hugged her more than once. You touched her tummy. You gave her money. All the way around it was major movement in the right direction."

Aunt Nattie was one straight talker. Pepper liked her more and more.

Susan said, "But then I blew it. I asked what they were thinking about marriage."

Pepper nodded. "They always go defensive on that one."

"You've asked?"

"Sure. Although I'm accepting them where they are in their own journey, I do believe they're out of God's order, so I ask. I hint. I get shrugs, frowns, and 'give me some space' looks."

"Kenzie said they consider themselves married already."

"Mm-hmm. I mentioned legalities like last names. They said the baby can be given either or both, but it'll be different from at least one of theirs. That's always a confusing thing for a kid, I think."

Susan nodded in agreement. It felt so good to unload feelings to an empathetic ear.

Pepper continued. "I've noticed now and then it seems Aidan and Kenzie are out of sync."

"How's that?"

"One time, early on, Kenzie was upset, very emotional, and she said she didn't want Aidan to marry her just because she's pregnant. He's never mentioned that concern, but he told his sister Lisel that he bet if she were in Kenzie's shoes, she wouldn't want to wear a maternity wedding dress. Now he could have just been teasing her about being concerned with her looks—which Lisel is, but Kenzie isn't so much. Or maybe he was serious and it's a reason not to marry now."

Natalie said, "Pregnancy can reduce any woman to tears because let's face it, our appearance is not what it once was and there's not a whole lot we can do about it." She waved a hand. "Been there, done that."

"I think there's a chance they do want to marry, but not just yet."

Susan said, "I used to think this was my worst nightmare, Kenzie pregnant and not married." She sighed. "Now I know it's not. That was all for show. That was what the pastor's wife should feel. Now I know my very worst nightmare is they would marry because they feel like they have to and then she spends her whole life wondering if she did the right thing."

"Huh?" Pepper said. What happened to the pastor's wife who more or less agreed her daughter should suffer the consequences of her choices?

Natalie leaned forward. "Susan, what are you talking about?"

"Me. I'm talking about me." She fiddled with the phone on her lap. "I was pregnant once, three years before Kenzie was born. I had a miscarriage before anyone knew what was going on, but in the meantime Drake and I got married. We thought the pregnancy meant we had to. And now…well, I've just been wondering, that's all." She opened the phone. "How do I use the speed dial?"

Thirty

Wednesday afternoon Natalie was back at the beach house. She stood in the kitchen at a total loss for words. Absolutely speechless. An absurd condition of which heretofore she'd had little personal acquaintance.

And to think that of all people, her sister-in-law put her in such a position.

Forty-eight hours before, Susan divulged that she had been pregnant when she married Drake. That was news to Natalie. Not that she expected all family members should be informed of such a thing—especially an in-law like herself who met Rex years after Drake and Susan were married—but still! Rex didn't even know! The brother and best man!

And now Kenzie was pregnant before marriage, and her dad—who'd been in the exact same situation—wouldn't even speak to her because of it!

"Natalie." Susan leaned back against the kitchen counter and straightened the plastic silver cape draped around her shoulders.

Their friend Emmylou, the pregnant hairdresser, was in the bathroom arranging things. She was going to cut Susan's shoulder-length hair. She was going to cut it short. She was going to cut it shorter than Kenzie's.

That was another reason for Natalie's speechlessness. She'd never seen her sister-in-law with short hair. She didn't even know she had been wanting to get it cut for years.

Susan said, "Are you furious?" She was not referring to the planned change in her hairdo.

"Furious?" Natalie shook her head. "Incensed is the word. Not because I didn't know, but because as far as I can tell, Drake has not revealed a hint of compassion toward his daughter, who's in the exact same situation he was in at one time."

Susan hummed under her breath. It was a bar from some hymn. The same thing happened the other day when they'd gone out to get the cell phone. A couple times Natalie had to wait through one or two verses before speaking.

They hadn't talked privately since Susan's revelation on Monday. Natalie had had to leave before Pepper did in order to get to soccer practice. Then their brief phone conversation on Tuesday did not present the opportunity for a heart-to-heart.

Susan finished the song. "The compassion is there, inside of him. Drake loves Kenzie. If he accepts her situation, though, then he would have to confess his own past. We buried it so deep, I don't know that he can face it now, even within himself. Twenty-four years ago seminary students in our school did not engage in premarital intimacy. There was no way they could become pregnant."

Natalie crossed her arms and shifted her weight onto the other foot. "It was a major taboo?"

"Yes. We truly believed it would have ruined his future to serve as a pastor."

"Forgiveness never entered the picture?" She bit her lip.

"Pastors don't need to be forgiven. They're already perfect." Susan's smile was gentle. "We were probably always under that false impression, even as children. The man in the pulpit and his wife were Christlike. That meant they were perfect. Of course, neither of us were, so we pretended. I guess we've been pretending for a long, long time."

Natalie almost disbelieved her own eyes. The change in Susan astounded her. Not only was she forthright in her talk, her entire demeanor exhibited a new softness. Her old fragility, which had made her appear brittle, was gone. Even the blueness of her eyes and her light complexion fairly sparkled.

Natalie said, "I think you've stopped pretending. You glow like you've just had some heavy-duty facial peel. Make that body peel."

"Well, praise God." She chuckled. "You didn't know how right you were when you said this whole thing isn't about Kenzie. It's about me and Drake."

"But you don't really believe your marriage was a mistake, do you?"

"No, not really. We loved each other as best we knew how when we got married. We still do. Kenzie is the result of that love. We've done good work in the churches we've served. But," she paused, "twenty-four years of faking perfection is wrong."

"This is huge. Now what?"

"Oh, Natalie! Now there's freedom. I cannot begin to describe how incredibly free I feel. Telling the others about Kenzie just got me started. Then admitting to you and Pepper and to myself that I am not perfect was like taking off a straitjacket." She flapped her arms. "Whew! I can fly now. And to think—Jesus loves me no matter what I've done or ever will do! I think He even likes me. This is all that matters. This is what I want Kenzie to know. I don't want her to marry Aidan because she thinks that's how she will earn His forgiveness. Or her dad's."

Natalie doubted her hearing as well as her sight and remained speechless.

"Your mouth is hanging open."

Natalie closed it.

"I do want her to marry—but only out of her love for God, a love that moves her to serve Him." She smiled. "I talked to Drake. Aren't cell phones great? Thanks again for talking me into getting one. Anyway, he's coming here for dinner tomorrow night. There goes your jaw again. It's dropping."

Natalie let it drop until her mouth formed a large oval.

Susan laughed. "I feel like Cinderella. I'm wearing the glass slippers and the ball gown. The difference is, I'm not climbing back into the pumpkin coach or the straitjacket."

The bathroom door squeaked, and a moment later Emmylou

appeared at the end of the hall, all eight months plus of her abdomen well in advance of the rest of her. "Okay. The Beach House Salon is now open for business. Are you ready?"

Like a six-year-old, Susan clapped her hands. "Yes. Let's do it!"

Natalie trailed behind them, hoping she'd be able to speak again, preferably before that afternoon's soccer practice.

Thirty-One

Susan drove through the deepening dusk. Five lanes of red brake lights led the way. She felt on edge, half expecting a timer to ding and then poof! Her car would shake and rattle and roll itself into a pumpkin with a bunch of white mice jumping around it.

An unscheduled meeting had delayed Drake. He couldn't make it to the beach house for dinner and recommended they meet at a Thai restaurant. Located just off the freeway in a strip mall, it lay equidistant between the coast and home.

At least he had called. At least he had called before she cooked the pasta. The spaghetti sauce could keep; the table could be unset later.

With every passing mile the hymns grew fainter in her mind, the warmth of the scene of a candlelit dinner in front of a cozy fire grew dim. She felt cold.

Lord, please stop the silly imaginings. You are my song. You are my warmth. You don't live exclusively at the beach house.

Her teeth chattered, and she turned the heater fan to high.

At last she reached the exit, parked in the mall lot, and entered the restaurant. Drake wasn't there yet. Would he want her to wait at the door until he arrived or should she—

Drake screens every jot and tittle of what you do…

Susan asked for a table, followed the maître d' across the dining room, and then redirected him to a booth. She sat, drank tea, and read the menu.

You go, girl. You don't need anyone else's permission. You've got Mine.

She checked her cell phone. No missed calls were indicated. The power was on, the ringer volume set to high. The time glared. He was twenty-five minutes late.

Traffic? Endless meeting? Accident? Or simply no consideration for his wife…

As the waiter approached with a fresh pot of tea, she decided to order.

You go, girl. Fly. Fly for all you're worth!

Drake arrived along with the Tom Kha soup.

"You already ordered?" He slid into the booth across from her and, without benefit of menu, told the waiter he wanted Phad Thai.

The young man left.

"Sorry I'm late. You know how those guys can talk on and on— Your hair." He stared now.

Susan smiled and touched it, dipping her head every direction to give him a full view. "What do you think?"

"What did you do?"

"I had it cut."

"It's, uh, different."

"Mm-hmm." She loved it. Obviously he didn't. It was extremely short and layered and, she thought, flattering. And unbelievably carefree. "It'll grow." She frowned and rephrased that. "You'll get used to it."

He tried to smile, but the corners of his mouth wouldn't stay up. "I suppose the ladies will like it. It's a, uh, a more contemporary style than what you normally have."

"The chignon is a timeless classic, but I've worn one for twenty years. I was just ready for a change."

He only stared. He looked tired, but elegant as ever in a lime green tie and deep brown suit.

"Nice tie."

His smile turned genuine. "My wife gave it to me."

She smiled again. "How are you?"

"Busy. Usual Easter season preparations. Palm Sunday is this week."

She nodded. She knew that. She didn't want to talk about that. "I hoped we could finish our last conversation."

The waiter interrupted to serve Drake's soup.

While he took his first sip, she explained. "The one about our being apart."

"I don't know what else there is to say, Susan." He shrugged. "We're not together on Kenzie. You went behind my back and met with the kid's mother. Do you know what that makes me look like?"

"I said I'm sorry for going behind your back." She pressed a hand to her stomach. "But I think there's something else to discuss." Her appetite was gone, and she sensed her memorized talking points disintegrate on the spot.

"Like what?"

"Like…"

He set down his spoon. "Things are beginning to appear odd. You were at the wedding Saturday night but not in church Sunday morning. I've been making excuses for you for a week and a half now. When are you coming home? I really need you beside me this Sunday."

That wasn't the issue, was it?

"I do need you, Susan. What exactly are you waiting for?"

To tell people the truth. To stop pretending. *You have My permission.*

She cleared her throat. "I didn't want to talk about this in public. I really wanted you to come to the beach house for dinner."

"That couldn't be helped. If you want private, there is always our own house just up the freeway."

She would not be thrown off track. "Drake, what I'm waiting for is for us to stop pretending. To be open about Kenzie with the congregation. To admit to each other that we were in the same situation she's in right now when we got married."

"Susan!" His tone in those two syllables spat chagrin, a spray of darts pierced her being. "That's far behind us. God has forgiven us and forgotten it."

She ignored the pain. "But sometimes I don't know if I've forgiven myself. I know I haven't forgotten." Her eyes filled with tears, and a new thought drenched her soul. "I never mourned our baby. I have never even acknowledged his or her existence."

He inhaled sharply.

"We've forced Kenzie to believe she has to be perfect to win our approval or God's. She needs to know we have feet of clay."

"Like mother, like daughter."

His words whipped more harshly than a slap on the face.

Something welled up within her, something she'd never felt before. Her body went hot, and then, in a flash, it went cold. A stillness settled into the very core of her being. The room faded from view. Her thoughts zeroed in on one thing.

"Yes, I got pregnant out of wedlock. But you know what, Drake? You were there when it happened." Somehow her purse was in her hand. "I'm going to leave now. You know where to find me. I even have a cell number." Somehow she was standing beside the table. "It is so pathetic I didn't even have my own phone because you didn't think I needed one."

A few moments later she sat in her car, shaky hands stabbing the key everywhere but into the ignition, unable to remember how she'd gotten from the table to there.

⁓

Susan tromped barefoot at the ocean's edge under a starry sky, and little by little the rage burned itself out.

Pugsy chased darting sandpipers and pawed at tiny crabs wriggling into the sand in the backwash of receding waves. With only occasional glances in her direction, he raced and halted and raced again, choosing his own route, wild with delight at not being attached to his leash.

Susan understood. Not that she'd quite grasped the wild with delight behavior yet, but her self-imposed leash was gone. She alone was responsible for herself. What freedom existed in that!

The whole thing frightened her to pieces.

"Lord, are You in it?"

Something was broken between her and Drake. If they did not face that fact, it couldn't get fixed, could it? If she continued to kowtow and to tell him he was right no matter what, didn't she simply prolong the dilemma? Surely God did not mean for a wife to totally suppress her own heart and mind, did He? Perhaps, after all, there was truth in Natalie's opinion that Susan's version of submission had gone haywire.

"Lord, if You are not in it, stop me."

Put me back in the straitjacket?

She shuddered at the thought. It would be worse than a straitjacket. It would be more like death. Like climbing again into a tomb and being trussed up for a second time in a burial shroud.

She plunked down in her dry-clean-only lined powder blue business suit skirt, pressed the heels of her bare feet into the cold damp sand, and crossed her arms over her bent knees. Boundless sky and ocean filled her vision.

"Lord, You didn't raise Lazarus just to die again, did You? He must have been living proof of Your love and power. A constant reminder to his family of Your reality, of Your hand in their lives. Please." She sighed. "Oh, please make it so with me."

As the next wave rolled toward the shore, an organ prelude came with it. Susan hummed along, and then she lifted her chin and her voice.

"'Christ the Lord is risen today. Alleluia!'"

Thirty-Two

Several doors north of the squished red chili of a beach house, Kenzie sat on the seawall, legs dangling beneath her long black skirt, booted heels tapping rhythmically back against the concrete. Through a continual stream of joggers, amblers, bicyclers, and in-line skaters along the boardwalk in front of her, she watched her mother in the distance.

At first she didn't recognize Susan. Her hair was *short* and she wore a multicolored skirt unlike anything that had ever hung in her closet. It flowed to her ankles and the setting sun glittered off its sequins or rhinestones or something sparkly. Instead of the usual blouse and blazer, she wore a plain short-sleeved, green top. If Kenzie didn't know better, she'd guess the outfit was bought at a shop down the street, the one that sold hippie-style clothing.

Susan greeted women as they arrived on the patio. Pugsy bopped around, overly excited with the commotion of having company. The Marthas lingered outdoors before going into the house, jabbering and laughing in the warmish spring air. Everyone came for the baby shower.

Kenzie's baby shower.

She wasn't sure she wanted to join them.

Aunt Nattie was there, of course, the party giver. She'd been the one to call and invite her, the only reason Kenzie sat almost within shouting distance of the beach house now. She promised it wasn't a big deal. Only the Martha Mavens and Pepper Carlucci were available to attend.

Kenzie was at least acquainted with all the women and—the true test—Aunt Nattie liked them. She also promised no dorky games.

Although Pepper ran a close second, Aunt Nattie won first place as the coolest woman Kenzie knew. If she sang in a band, her style would be bluesy jazz. Her voice was smoky, hoarsened from a lifetime of shouting at high volume on athletic fields.

Her aunt had introduced Kenzie to soccer, Jack Kerouac books, and U2 music. She seldom got bent out of shape, even with her two sons who behaved like total brats at times. As far as her husband went, absolutely no Starr family resemblance existed between Uncle Rex and Kenzie's dad. Grandma and Grandpa Starr must have adopted one of the brothers and kept it a deep secret.

Emmylou Bainbridge arrived now. Kenzie grimaced when she saw her. She was humongous and walked as though she'd been riding on the back of a horse for days on end. Was that what pregnancy did to a body? Maybe Emmylou was expecting twins. Or triplets. Quadruplets? Kenzie really hoped so, hoped it wasn't the norm.

Emmylou was funny and sweet. Definitely a country western style. No one could understand half of what she said in that thick drawl of hers. If her husband showed up, lingering doubts about going inside would vanish in a heartbeat. Robbie was a Marine, just as friendly as his wife, and—more importantly—the hunkiest hunk at Holy Cross Fellowship.

Mildred and Leona, the elderly twins, hobbled into view now. They were—

"Hey, sister!" The friendly voice came from behind her. "Is that you?"

Kenzie recognized the voice before she turned. It belonged to Zeke, a guy who knew everyone at the beach but seldom remembered a name. He addressed them all as "sister" or "brother." Considering how he talked a lot about Jesus and often carried a Bible, it sounded natural coming from him.

"Hey, Zeke!" She shook his outstretched hand and grinned.

Zeke's exuberance was enough to fill her with laughter, but his looks carried it to another level. If he were a musician, he would definitely sing reggae, Bob Marley style. She once asked him if he was born in Jamaica, but he said no, San Diego was his birthplace. His long deep brown hair sprouted every which way in countless twisted dreadlocks, and his dark brown eyes were like magnets drawing her in. She had no idea how old he was.

She said, "How you doing?"

"I am fantastic, sister. Fantastic. Living and breathing in God's grace day by day. Watching Him work wonders in the souls of my homeless brothers. How about yourself?"

"Fine." She groaned. That was so her mother's voice. "Actually." She wore a denim jacket of Aidan's that covered what now resembled a serious beer paunch. Holding it aside she patted her stomach. "I'm pregnant."

"Praise God from whom all blessings flow!"

She laughed. "Yeah. I'm down here for a baby shower. My mom's staying at Faith's house." Zeke had known Faith Fontaine and was friends with Julian.

"Who's the daddy of this little one?"

"Aidan Carlucci."

"Oh, oh! Look at you blush, just saying his name. You are in love, aren't you? I hope he's a good one."

"He's a good one. We sing together. He writes most of our band's music."

"No kidding? He's gifted then."

"He is. We're going to make a CD. You know, a real professional kind of thing that stores will sell. We didn't plan on a baby already but…" She shrugged.

"Our Father knows this baby, knows when it's time for him to be born. He sees him right now and loves him more than even his mama or daddy can."

Kenzie sure hoped so.

Comfort flowed from Zeke, and she wished she could bottle it up and take it home.

He glanced toward the beach house. "Looks like quite a group. How come you're over here and not over there?"

She sighed. "I don't know. I guess because I don't feel welcome over there."

"Say what? I thought you said this shower was for you."

"It's a bunch of churchwomen. And Aidan's mom. She's cool. But see, Aidan and I aren't married and my dad—" Her throat closed up.

"Hmm. He's a preacher, right?"

She nodded.

"Mm-hmm. Probably got a reputation to uphold in front of his congregation. He thinks this puts him in a bad light."

She nodded again.

"That happens, sister. That happens. And not just with preachers. All kinds of people let their false self rule their hearts. They just don't know how to let out the true self, the forgiven one who's freed up to love and be loved. Then they gotta blame someone else for reminding them how miserable they are."

Kenzie swallowed. "What do you mean?"

"Your daddy just took his eyes off the cross. He'll come round. He's going to be a grandpa!" Zeke grinned, a white slash against his dark chocolate skin. "I got one question for you, little sister."

She waited.

"You think all those women would come if they didn't want to see you?"

The Martha Mavens would help out her mom in any way they could. But Emmylou looked ready to pop; she couldn't be comfortable. The twins had traveled far and through rush hour traffic; old people avoided those things. Aunt Nattie probably should have been at a soccer practice; she always hated letting an assistant take charge. Beautiful Gwyn should have been out on a date. Pepper had come straight from work and literally had a hundred other things to do at home. And now there was Tess Harmon greeting Susan. Surely the director of women's ministries had more important business.

Kenzie smiled at Zeke and shook her head. No, they wouldn't come unless they wanted to see her.

Thirty-Three

On the patio outside the beach house, Susan accepted Tess Harmon's hug. As usual, intimidation wormed its ugly self into her consciousness. She liked Tess very much, but she always had to fight down discomfort in her presence. Once more she wondered why.

Was it the title, director of women's ministries? The master's in theology? The knowledge of Greek? The impressive gift of teaching? The tall dancer's stature? The unwavering confidence, whatever the situation?

Or Drake's almost daily glowing reports of her incomparable attributes?

"Susan," Tess murmured, "I love your hair."

"Thanks."

"Oh, hon." She straightened and grasped her hands, a gift bag hanging from her own, and looked directly into Susan's eyes. Concern permeated the hushed voice and tone. "Natalie told me, of course. This is a baby shower, after all. You're going to be a grandmother! Do I say congratulations?"

Praise God from whom all blessings flow.

Tess spoke in her quick, confident way. "I'm not quite sure. You and Drake must be so stressed, bearing this burden all alone. It's understandable why you haven't shared the news with the congregation. The secular media would have a heyday."

Susan couldn't follow the leap and felt her forehead knot. "The media?"

Tess squeezed Susan's hands and let them go. "Drake is quite an important public figure. Newshounds are always on the lookout for opportunities to cast aspersion on someone in his position."

"We're talking about a baby. It's not like our daughter committed some felony."

"Of course not. But just the hint of a skeleton in the family closet is fodder. We want to be careful."

"I can't be concerned with the media!"

"And you shouldn't be. That's not your job. I'll worry about it, and Drake can worry about how and when to inform the congregation. I'm sure he already has a plan."

"I'm informing. I told the Martha Mavens."

"Well, we Marthas are different. We don't need to be told how to handle things, how not to gossip."

The frustrated sigh building in Susan's chest flung itself outward, probably loud enough for passersby to hear.

Tess' thin brows formed two inverted *v*'s on her forehead.

Susan turned aside to shut out the intimidating sight. Words swirled in her mind and threatened to spew forth incoherently. She struggled for control. "This isn't news to be spun."

"I know, hon. It's about you and Drake carrying on in the face of adversity. You'll get through it, and then everyone will see God's faithfulness in your lives."

No, it wasn't about them carrying on as if nothing had happened and pointing to God afterward! She pressed her lips together. Tess didn't get it. They were in the middle of a nightmare and needed help. The thought of admitting that to this woman made her feel as though she were standing on her head. Rushing blood squeezed her brain until the world tilted crazily and flipped upside down.

But…she had shed the straitjacket and known what it was to fly, to even sing again. Such sensations always came on the heels of saying out loud to another person that she, Susan Starr, was imperfect and needed help. That was the antidote. Even with cool, calm, collected, intimidating Tess.

She willed herself to meet those steady determined eyes. "First and foremost it's about a baby. It's about Kenzie needing my support.

It's about me needing your support. It's about Drake needing your support."

"Susan, I support you. That's why I'm here. But I can't function in the middle, in between you and Drake. You've told us that Kenzie's pregnant. *He* hasn't, and he's my boss. How can I show support if he doesn't realize I'm aware of the situation?"

"I left him a voice mail first thing this morning." She thought it only fair to inform him; obviously she never got the chance at their dinner. "I told him about the shower and the Marthas coming. He realizes that you know."

Some of the steely gaze faded from her eyes. "He didn't say a word."

"I think maybe…" Susan blew out a breath, "maybe he needs to hear directly from you that you know and that you haven't disowned him."

"Why isn't it enough coming from you?"

Because she was only the wife. No master's degree, no comprehension of Greek, no giftedness beyond helping a bride order cake. "It will mean more if he hears it from someone he respects on the church staff."

Now Tess sighed. "All right."

"Thank you."

"You're welcome." She tried to smile and straightened her shoulders. "Okay. Are the others inside?"

"Yes. Go on in. I'll wait outside for Kenzie a few more minutes."

Tess walked to the doorway and then turned. "Susan." The smile succeeded this time. "Congratulations, Grandma."

She grinned. "Thank you."

~

Susan watched Tess enter the house and put a hand to her mouth, holding back a giggle. Had she really just spoken her mind to Tess Harmon? Yes indeed, praise God from whom all blessings flowed! *Praise Him, all creatures here below. Praise Him above, ye heavenly host. Praise Father, Son, and Holy Ghost.*

Now if only He'd bring Kenzie to her own baby shower. Natalie reported Kenzie had sounded agreeable to the idea on the phone. Pepper said she wanted to pick Kenzie up, but Kenzie insisted Pepper not go out of her way, and besides, Aidan offered his van. She'd drop him off for his performance and drive herself.

"Mom."

Susan smiled and turned. There she was, unlatching the gate. "Kenzie! Hi." *Thank You, God. Thank You.*

"Hi."

As usual, she wore lots of black: short clunky combat-type boots, a long skirt, a denim jacket masculine in style and at least three sizes too large. A familiar worn knapsack hung across her shoulders. Through the unbuttoned jacket, Susan glimpsed a white T-shirt too short to reach the skirt's waistband. It only partially covered her little round tummy.

She went to her daughter, arms open. Kenzie stepped into them, and they hugged for a long moment.

"Mom, your hair looks great!"

"You really like it? Emmylou cut it."

"It's got *attitude.* Way to go, Mom. I like the skirt too. Wow! And sandals? *Toenail* polish?"

"Your aunt's influence. We shopped down the street."

"No way."

"Yeah." She smiled. "And look at you. You're blossoming."

"I'm getting fat."

"Can I touch him?"

"Him?" Kenzie pulled aside the large jacket. "How about her?"

Susan laid a hand on the small bulge partially covered in cotton. "I guess a 'her' would be all right too. If she was like her mommy."

Kenzie blinked.

"Wild and crazy and creative and delightful." She removed her hand. "And if Aidan is anything like *his* mother, I think a 'he' would be a masculine version of all that?"

Kenzie nodded.

"I'm so glad you came, honey."

"Well." She cleared her throat. "Aunt Nattie promised no dorky games."

Susan smiled. "Shall we go inside?"

Kenzie glanced around the patio. "Where's Pugsy?"

"Gwyn has probably locked him in a back bedroom by now."

"She's not a dog person, is she?"

"If Pugsy sits on your lap and not hers, she'll be okay."

Kenzie hesitated. "I can't stay late. I have to pick up Aidan when the band's done."

"That's fine."

Now she bit her lip, clearly unsure about going inside.

Please, Lord.

"So how did your Marthas react to…to the baby news?"

Susan smiled gently. "No one was shocked and appalled. Not a hint of condemnation surfaced. There was sympathy because unplanned, out-of-wedlock pregnancies bring their own set of difficulties."

Kenzie narrowed her eyes and defensiveness flashed in them. Her impish nose tilted further skyward.

A wave of panic washed over Susan. The feeling felt odd and yet familiar. Too familiar. It was like when Drake screened the jots and tittles. Did Kenzie screen as well? Did Susan choose her words according to what their impact on Kenzie might be?

She thought of her songfest last night under the stars. All shred of straitjacket and burial wrappings had vanished. Easter arrived early for her. Instead of Resurrection Sunday, she experienced a Resurrection Thursday. She wasn't about to climb back into the tomb.

Even if Kenzie ran away from her.

"Honey, I'm just trying to be honest here. This situation has caused problems for everyone involved. For starters, your dad's embarrassed, I'm angry with him and you, and you and Aidan have all kinds of adjustments to make. But," she said, smiling, "there is an upside. I can now admit I'm not perfect and I don't have to pretend that I am. Of course that brings its own set of adjustments. Your dad won't speak to me. Well, we did try last night. It didn't go well. I don't think he knows what to do with me. I refuse to go home if you can't go there. So I don't know.

Does that mean we're separated? Pepper and I are getting hooked on ice cream in the afternoon. Not exactly a healthy practice. The gospel according Natalie is making more and more sense, which confounds me to no end. I'm singing, and that makes Pugsy howl—"

"Mom!"

She refocused her eyes and saw Kenzie grinning. "What?"

"You're running off at the mouth."

"Oh."

She laughed. "It's okay."

"Yes, of course." She ran her fingers through her hair, feigning nonchalance. "I know it is."

Kenzie laughed harder.

"So, are you coming inside or not? We don't have all night."

Wiping at the corner of her eye, she nodded.

Thank You, God. Thank You.

Susan smiled to herself and led the way.

Praise God from whom all blessings flow. Praise Him, all creatures here below. Praise Him above, ye heavenly host. Praise Father, Son, and Holy Ghost.

Thirty-Four

Pepper's love for her semi-daughter-in-law pounced on her time and again, sneak attacks that caught her unaware.

Like now at the baby shower. There Kenzie sat by a front window, the last flash of the setting sun encircling her comical sprouts of stiffly gelled hair with a glow, looking for all the world like a little kid in a candy store as she tore wrapping paper from gifts. Who would have thought? She was not a material girl, but something in her responded to the love represented in the stroller, the car seat, the tiny pj's, the silky blankets, and the bags of disposable diapers.

Pepper didn't know if she was more surprised at Kenzie's delight or at the love-gift givers. With the exception of maybe Natalie, the chatty churchwomen filling the room were the last ones Pepper would have guessed able to touch Kenzie in such a way.

Whoa! The tone of her judgmental voice spun Pepper off into a private little confessional time with the Lord right then and there in the middle of the party, sitting on the couch next to Mildred, one of the delightful white-haired twins.

The thing was that for Pepper, condemning Drake and Susan Starr and their entire hoity-toity evangelical, thousand-plus member congregation from a distance had felt...Well, it had felt downright fun in a twisted sort of way. It probably soothed her own ego. Only a bunch of hypocrites could turn their backs on Kenzie. Not so Pepper Carlucci.

Jesus in a short, pudgy body with an Irish temperament.

And no wonder the girl had gotten herself into such a situation. She craved love and attention. Why wouldn't Aidan fall head over heels for such a needy, talented, attractive, funny woman? True, he had behaved foolishly, but at least he turned to his parents. He knew they were available to help him figure things out.

Oh, Lord! I am sorry for thinking myself better than others.

The Martha Mavens from Holy Cross Fellowship were the most gracious women she'd ever met. Reverend Starr might be a snoot, but nothing short of God's power had transformed his wife. His sister-in-law, Natalie, was earthy and undoubtedly the most positive influence in Kenzie's short life. The others—Emmylou, Gwyn, Mildred, Leona, and Tess—all treated Kenzie like a princess.

Lord! I am sorry for drawing a denominational line in the sand, for believing only my side knows Your ways.

Beside her, Mildred patted her knee. "Tell me about Aidan."

Pepper smiled. The woman was the epitome of cordiality from some bygone era. She truly wanted to hear about her son.

"Well, he is handsome. He looks like me. Black hair and sapphire blue eyes."

Mildred laughed.

While the others carried on different conversations and Kenzie unwrapped, Pepper described Aidan to Mildred. "He's twenty-five, our oldest. He's like Kenzie, creative, moody, talented. Have you heard their music?"

Brown eyes twinkled behind thick lenses. "Yes. It's wonderful. Intriguing words. Kenzie told me he writes the music and lyrics."

"Most of them. I don't understand all the words myself, but I think they're a record of his faith journey. You know, full of questions, often without clear answers."

Mildred bobbed her head. "Like the psalms. Asking, wondering, yet turning to God for hope. Like Peter saying to Jesus, where else would we go? Who else has the words of life?"

Amazed that the elderly woman connected with Aidan's struggle and offbeat music, Pepper could only nod.

"There is power in your Aidan's work. Power not of this world. However did you raise him to be like this?"

Pepper chuckled. "If it's good, I wasn't responsible."

"You prayed." She stated it as fact.

Pepper grew somber. Mildred wanted to dig deep. "Yes, I prayed. Nonstop. My husband and I thank God for the faith He has given us. It's never looked traditional, though. Aidan calls it wild and wooly."

Mildred grinned.

"And I blame my parents. They were downright weird, original Jesus freaks." She laughed. "In a good way. They raised me and my eight siblings in northern California in what might be called a commune. I think it was more like a monastery, even though we all had our own simple houses. As a group we were fairly self-contained with farm animals, crops, a school, and church. It wasn't like we were closed off from society, though. Most of the men worked elsewhere, even some of the women. Some of the kids went off to high school or college. The common thread that tied us together was a radical dependence on Jesus."

"Really?"

"Yeah. Prayer and worship and music defined the group. The main thing I took with me from my childhood was an acceptance of the mystery. That God is real and yet unexplainable." She smiled. "I'm sorry. I'm preaching."

"To the choir." Mildred giggled and slapped her hands together, a smack of cymbals for emphasis. "What happened? Why did you leave?"

"Like with most experiments, things didn't seem to take by the second generation."

"Mm-hmm. We all have to find our own way."

"Yes. And I met Mick around the time my older siblings were leaving. He was working on road construction nearby. Love at first sight. I was barely seventeen and he was twenty-one, but we both just knew. We married as soon as I turned eighteen and then we moved down here. Aidan was born eleven months later."

"You and Mick found your own way, then."

Pepper nodded. "He loved my unconventional parents and my far-out faith. Eventually we settled into a mainline church whose pastor didn't mind if we acted a little odd now and then."

Mildred leaned toward her and whispered, "Because you still trafficked in the mystery, right?"

Pepper grinned. "Yeah."

"That's why Kenzie is in your family now." She winked. "She's always colored outside the lines too."

Another sneak attack.

Despite the upheaval Kenzie and Aidan had brought to the Carlucci family, Pepper wouldn't have wished it any other way. A girl who colored outside the lines was made to order as a daughter-in-law. Semi or not.

Thirty-Five

Natalie grew more incensed by the minute.

Faith Fontaine would be so disappointed in her. The deceased woman's beach house exuded an indescribable, tangible sense of peace and love. It always had. On the two occasions Natalie had visited Faith with Rex, she assumed the woman's personality responsible. But she knew better now. Renting her house as a vacation place, she believed Faith's character actually lived on. In the air. In the walls. Wherever, however. That could produce the heebie-jeebies in some people. The exact opposite occurred every single time she visited, though. Peace permeated. Peace and love, goodness and mercy—

Until now.

As far as Natalie could tell, Kenzie and Pepper and the Martha Mavens were thoroughly enjoying themselves. Her niece had thanked her already no less than three times for organizing the shower. Susan absolutely beamed, more attractive than ever in her new clothes and haircut. Even Tess had loosened up and left her role as director of women's ministries behind at the office.

Natalie poured water into the coffeemaker and punched the "on" button and tried not to think about what she'd rather be punching. Or rather, *whom.*

"Natalie."

She jumped at Mildred's voice right behind her and turned.

"Are you all right, dearie? You seem a bit nettled."

No use pretending with the Prayer Warrior. "Try mad as a wet hen."

"Ah. Anything I can do for you?" She smiled. "Besides pray, I mean."

"Thank you, Mildred. I don't know what it would be. Besides pray." Natalie clenched her teeth. They could leave it at that, like an unspoken prayer request. Mildred wasn't asking for details. She never needed to know them. But that seemed like a coward's way out.

She touched the old woman's arm. "Can we talk?"

"Certainly."

"Let's go back here." Natalie led her off the kitchen, past the side door and a bathroom, into a closet-size bedroom at the rear of the house. It was a favorite hideaway of hers. She would read in it, undisturbed while Rex and the boys did other things.

The room contained a daybed against the far wall, one window, an armoire, and a hardback chair. Those few things totally filled the space.

Natalie pulled the trundle out and smoothed the coverlet. Mildred's short legs would never get her up atop the daybed. "Have a seat."

They sat beside each other.

"Mildred, I have to tell someone."

"Before you pop a gut?"

Natalie burst into laughter. How did such words drip from that honey-sweet smile? "Yes, before I do that." She paused. "I want to murder my brother-in-law."

"That would be Pastor Drake."

"Uh, yeah. Here we are, loving on Kenzie, trying to take care of her needs, show her support. But it's like putting salve on an open, gaping, bleeding wound. It won't solve anything. She'll leave here tonight with that great big hole still there. Her dad won't speak with her or acknowledge to his congregation that she's alive, let alone expecting his grandchild. Totally asinine."

"Well, dearie, you're sticking your neck out pretty far."

Natalie sat back and blinked. No. Not Mildred. The Prayer Warrior would not say there was no place for a father's unconditional forgiveness in this situation.

Mildred took Natalie's hand between her own and zeroed in on her face. "But I feel exactly the same way."

"Huh?"

"The question is, what are we going to do?"

"Uh, you mean besides pray."

"Yes, besides pray. We must have the right response in our anger. I don't think we should simply pretend it's not there."

"Mildred, I was thinking a gun."

"Well, now, that is a little drastic. I have something else in mind."

"Please don't say let's kill him with kindness."

"Unfortunately, I don't know if he would notice that."

"Mmm."

"I'm thinking a boycott."

"Boycott?"

Mildred nodded. "Boycott. Now, let's pray. We really need Tess on our side, and you know how devoted she is to her human boss." She shut her eyes, squeezed Natalie's hand, and raised her other hand toward heaven. "Father."

As if a plug had been pulled from a tub filled with water, Natalie's anger drained from her.

Maybe Faith Fontaine hadn't abandoned her after all.

Thirty-Six

Kenzie cuddled Pugsy in her arms, nuzzling his neck. She wished she could take him home with her, but pets were not allowed in the apartment.

"He'd love to go with you." Susan petted his back. "Wouldn't you, Pugs?"

Kenzie peered with one eye over the dog's head, hiding astonishment again at her mom's extreme chattiness. It wasn't that she'd never been chatty. Most of the time Kenzie thought her too much so. This was something different.

They stood behind the beach house in the dim carport light. Natalie had driven her to the parking lot where she picked up Aidan's van and returned to the house so they could load the shower gifts into it. Her aunt was gone now, as well as Pepper and all the Marthas. Much to Kenzie's surprise, she remained the last one to leave. Earlier she had fudged about being unable to stay late. Aidan and the band sang until two. Although she could sit in the club and wait, she wasn't exactly behind schedule.

"I'd love to take Pugs, but pets are not allowed in the building." She gave Pugsy one final kiss and set him on the sidewalk. "Be good. Okay. I'd better go."

"Thanks for coming, honey."

"It was fun. And I can't believe all the stuff they gave me. I had no clue a baby would need so much."

Susan put her arms around her. "Drive safely."

"Okay. Thanks, Mom." She walked around the vintage VW van, its size perfect for hauling band equipment and now baby things.

She climbed into the vehicle, started it, slid the floor gearshift into first, and put her hand on the parking brake release.

June Cleaver hadn't shown up. Not once in four hours.

Nor had there been a single question or remark or even thinly disguised hint about a wedding, where the apartment was, the address of the coffee shop she worked in, when her mom could meet Aidan, or what her dad needed from her. And although Susan had given Kenzie her cell phone number, she hadn't asked for Kenzie's. She hadn't even pressed for a time when she would see her again. To top all that, none of the Marthas breathed a snide remark about there not being a wedding shower first. They all seemed genuinely concerned that she get what she needed to welcome a baby into the world. Period.

Kenzie shifted into neutral, leaned across the front passenger seat, and rolled down the window. "Mom."

She stepped to the car. "What?"

"I programmed my phone number into your cell."

Susan smiled.

"It's number two."

"Like speed dial?"

"Asked the technologically challenged mother."

She chuckled.

"That's what it is. Just press 'two' and 'send' and it'll call me."

"Thanks," she whispered.

She gazed at her mother's face half hidden in shadows. An ache tightened her chest and spread to her throat. She wanted more...more of something she couldn't put into words. Something between her and her mom. She wanted to express her love. She wanted to tell her she would bring Aidan, that she truly wanted Susan to meet him. What kept holding her back?

"Kenzie, it's almost eleven. Aidan will wonder what happened to you. He probably can't imagine you'd hang out with a bunch of old women this long." She smiled again.

Kenzie hesitated. She didn't want to leave. This new Susan Starr might disappear the minute she turned her back. This *real* woman who spoke freely and didn't resemble any fake TV mom in history might vanish like a puff of smoke.

She had to ask. "So how come June didn't come tonight?"

"June? Oh, June Cleaver." Susan chuckled. "No, she didn't come. I didn't invite her. Actually, I told her she wasn't welcome."

Kenzie swallowed and whispered, "I didn't miss her."

"Me neither. I love you, honey."

If she could have found her voice, she would have returned the sentiment.

~

"But, Kenz." Aidan let go of one of her hands and stroked her face. "Can you trust her?"

Kenzie rested the side of her face against the back of the couch and yawned. She had just finished telling Aidan all about her evening, from the conversation with Zeke to the Marthas to the gifts and food, ending with her mom's extraordinary behavior. "I know. It was only for one evening."

"And her friends were around, and your aunt and my mom." He kissed her forehead.

"Even after they left though, she was great."

"You are desperate for a mommy."

She smiled. Why did she want anything beyond what she already had? She told Aidan everything and he remembered it all and talked with her and helped her think things through. She didn't remember her dad ever talking in such a personal way to either her or her mom.

"Well," she said, "I do want her to meet you."

He shuddered, shaking arms, legs, and head in exaggerated movements.

"Stop that." She pushed his arm playfully.

He jerked again. "Stop what?"

"That. She is not a monster."

"She's had the same effect as a monster on you."

"But not tonight."

"Granted. Not tonight. You're not exactly a basket case after this visit." He touched her face.

"Not exactly? Not even a little bit!"

"There is something."

She lowered her eyes. His ability to connect unnerved her at times. "It's what you said. Can I trust her? Was she just pretending tonight?" She looked up. "I don't think she was."

He nodded. "God does change people when they're willing to let Him. It sounds like your mom is willing."

"She must be because if she doesn't change, she'd just follow my dad's rules and end up never seeing the baby."

"Right. It's all because of the baby. That's what got her attention."

Kenzie laid a hand on her tummy. Was it the baby that got Aidan's attention too? Would he have committed himself to her otherwise? Could she really trust him?

Once again a familiar darkness eddied around her like a whirlpool, threatening to swamp any trace of well-being.

Thirty-Seven

Saturday morning Susan rinsed the carafe under the running faucet. It clanked against the porcelain sink.

"Doggone it!"

She inspected it carefully, grateful not to see a crack, and set it on the countertop. After turning off the water, she clasped her hands together, squeezing so they wouldn't flutter about and knock something over.

"What I mean is, Lord! Help! I'm losing it. Calm me down. Please, please calm me down." A song sprang to mind and she sang aloud. " 'Leaning, leaning, safe and secure from all alarms. Leaning, leaning, leaning on the everlasting arms.' "

Drake was on his way to the beach house. Cause for alarm? Or for hope?

"Hope. I choose hope. I do. Hope is from You. Fear is not. The straitjacket is not."

"Susan."

She turned and saw Drake on the other side of the screen door.

He grinned and stepped inside. "Are you talking to yourself?"

"Me, myself, and I." She shrugged. "And God."

Drake walked across the room, his arms held wide. "Sounds like good company."

The memory flashed through her mind of Thursday night's dinner. Her sharp words to him replayed. *Yes, I got pregnant out of wedlock. But you know what, Drake? You were there when it happened.* She thought of the voice mail she'd left for him, informing him of the baby shower.

His only response to both communications had been to call her that morning. He'd asked, somewhat tersely, if she was available that afternoon. He would come to the beach, after an early lunch meeting. They could talk.

At least it was a start.

She stepped into the circle of his arms.

"I miss you, Susan."

She slid her arms around him and laid her face against his chest, cutting off her response. The truth was, she didn't miss him. In some bizarre twist, life had been simpler at the beach house. Alone. In particular, alone without him.

What on earth were they going to talk about?

They turned the armchairs to face the large front picture window and watched people pass along the boardwalk just the other side of the patio and picket fence. Surfers disappeared in the glare of the afternoon sun bouncing off the ocean.

Weather talk and freeway conditions used up the time it took to shove the chairs around and settle into them.

"Your hair does look nice in that style."

What was going on? He actually arrived and on time and now he complimented her.

"You don't believe me."

"Today's April first. I thought you might say April fool!"

He chuckled. "No. I mean it."

"Thanks." She combed her fingers through it, up the back, making sure it didn't droop. Making sure the *attitude* didn't droop. "It's easy to take care of."

"Tess said she liked it."

"You talked to Tess?" The director usually didn't work on Saturdays.

"She stopped by the office this morning." He leaned forward, propped his elbows on his knees, and laced his fingers together.

Susan sank against the back cushion and crossed her legs. He and Tess discussed her hair?

"We can probably thank Tess for getting me here. She told me she came to the shower. That she knows. That she understands. And loves us both to pieces. She even cried a little."

Susan folded her arms. "What did she say about Kenzie?"

"That she…seemed…okay." He searched for words.

What else had Tess said? *Okay* did not scratch the surface. Did she describe Kenzie's glow? The fear in her eyes? The obvious camaraderie she enjoyed with Pepper? The laughter that filled the little beach house while she was there?

Drake continued. "She believes that our daughter's missteps are not a reflection on our character. It helped me see that you were right. We should share this burden with friends, those closest to us. Then, as word gets around, perhaps I can say something from the pulpit. Something along the lines of a difficult time, but our faith will see us through. She thinks, though, that I should head things off at the pass. Address the issue before it becomes gossip. Susan, you look distraught. What's wrong?"

"I don't know." That wasn't true. She knew. When would she ever quit this pretending with him?

She kneaded her forehead and thought of Kenzie, pregnant, scared, lonely, and in need, despite the love the Carluccis poured on her. They weren't her family. Susan and Drake were wrong to turn their back on her.

Something stirred inside of her. A long-asleep Mama Bear growled awake. She lumbered about Susan's mind, knocking aside all fears that prevented her from protecting her child.

She lowered her hand. "I have to take that back. Yes, I do know what's wrong. The thing is, I'm angry. Really angry. With you."

A surprised moment passed between them. In all the years they'd known each other, she had never even hinted at such a thing. Submissive women did not feel mad. Ticked off maybe, irritated. Annoyed. Peeved. But not this. Not this white-hot rage.

"Anger is an emotion, Susan, neither right nor wrong. It just is. Can you explain the reason why you feel it?"

How to start?

"It's all right." He smiled crookedly. "I promise I won't blow a gasket. Tell me what you're thinking."

Okay, she had his permission. "I'm thinking it's wrong for a submissive wife to feel this way. I've always thought my duty is to keep your world a peaceful harbor, to keep storms away."

"Do I teach that?" He shook his head. "I would never intentionally suggest such a thing."

"I am the keeper of the home environment."

"Well, I have said that, yes. But…Oh, Susan. Storms come. We can't avoid them."

She swallowed. He could be incredibly thoughtful and understanding. It was no wonder people flocked to him for counsel. She was being silly. Overreacting. Life wasn't that bad. He was only doing the best he could.

She realized her arms were crossed over her middle, so tightly the elbows nearly touched. It was like being wrapped in a straitjacket.

Was Drake forcing her back into it?

Or did she step into it herself?

He couldn't force her to do something she didn't want to do. Even if her choices were made unconsciously, she alone was responsible for them.

She untwined her arms and inhaled so deeply her throat made a gasping noise. "Well." She exhaled loudly.

Time to fly.

"Well," she said again. "We're in a storm right now. I bet you knew that."

He smiled in a self-deprecating way.

"And I think I'm angry because you and Tess had a heartfelt conversation about our daughter." Her voice wavered.

"What?" Total surprise. "That's just Tess. You know we have that sort of relationship. She's more a righthand man than Vince is." He referred to his very capable associate pastor. "It's a spiritual but business connection. She's happily married."

"I've asked you to tell people about Kenzie. Why is it Tess' opinion counts more than mine? You even like my hair now that she okayed it."

"That's not true, Susan."

"I've cried for three months. You've never referred to my tears as sweetly as you just did to Tess'. How could you? No one knows there's a reason for me to cry. And another thing. It's Kenzie we should cry for, not ourselves because this makes us look imperfect." Her shoulders sagged, but she did not cross her arms.

"Is there anything else?" He spoke in a hushed tone.

Before she could say a word, tears gushed from her eyes and she sobbed. "You blame me for sleeping with you before we got married."

"No, Susan."

"You blame me for getting pregnant. For tarnishing your image."

"No."

"Yes!"

"No."

"It's subtle, Drake." She wiped at her damp cheeks. The accusations tumbled off her tongue. Frighteningly, as if they had a life of their own, they kept coming. "When was the last time you took my opinion seriously? Or thought one of my ideas worthy of your consideration? How could you? They come from someone you consider unworthy."

She didn't see him move, but now he was beside her, gently pulling her from the chair. His arm at her waist, he helped her to the couch. They sat side by side and he drew her into his arms.

Rage and pain tore through her, a physical sensation beyond release through crying. She felt as though she were falling into a gaping black hole, rushing headlong into oblivion.

Thirty-Eight

Without any effort on her own part, Natalie glided into speechlessness again. What was it about Susan and Drake?

"So." Susan set down the coffee mug on Natalie's kitchen table and lifted her hands, palms up. "What do you think?"

Natalie could only stare at her sister-in-law. Her new hairstyle still looked great, but then how could one mess up hair scarcely two inches in length? She wore the other long skirt and matching blouse they'd purchased in the hippie store. It was a rose color; silver threads were woven throughout it. Her toenails, peeking from dainty pastel green sandals, were painted in the same shade.

But her nose matched the pink color. Red rimmed her eyes, and the lids were puffy. Thirty minutes ago she had called from the freeway, crying as much as laughing, and said she wanted to stop on her way home. They had talked earlier in the morning—Natalie had been eager to hear what Kenzie thought of the previous night's shower—and Susan informed her Drake was going to visit. Now she wanted to tell her in person what happened.

The fact that she and Pugsy were on their way home in time for Palm Sunday service tomorrow indicated one thing had occurred: Drake got his way.

"Natalie, we are making progress. Today was a giant step forward."

She nodded. After hearing that Susan and Drake had discussed Kenzie's situation and the miscarried baby of twenty-three years ago and that Susan had spoken her mind and cried her eyes out, Natalie agreed. Progress, yes. Incomparable progress. But…

"Oh, Natalie, I'm flying. I told him exactly how I feel and he accepted it. He *apologized* for treating me all these years like I didn't count. He asked my *forgiveness.*"

"And now you're going home."

"Yes." She beamed. "We'll go back to the beach house after Easter. Together. We'll rest and talk more."

"A compromise."

"I suppose. Marriage needs an awful lot of that. So this means the house is available. Maybe you and the kids can use it. Don't they have a few days off this week?"

"Kenzie's still out there."

"I think she and Aidan are fine in their apartment."

"I mean, Kenzie's still out there. Not welcome at home."

Susan paused. "That's true, for now. But I left her a voice mail about my plans. And I told Drake I will not quit communicating with her."

Thank God for small favors.

"Kenzie is first and foremost on my mind, but like you said, this is about me and Drake. Natalie, we have to figure out *us* before we can be any good to her."

"You'll stay strong?"

Her brow furrowed. "What do you mean?"

Natalie recalled last night's talk with Mildred. The old Prayer Warrior felt the same as she did and carried the opinion so far as to throw in the crazy notion of a boycott. Which meant Natalie wasn't completely out of touch with reality. Actually, the fact that Mildred agreed with her probably meant she was nearer true reality than ever before.

"Suze, I don't mean to rain on your parade. It's wonderful progress. But promise me you will stay strong. I mean no more straitjacket."

She grinned again and stuck a thumb in the air. "Absolutely no more straitjacket. I've been singing at the top of my lungs all the way here. I can't wait to sing with the choir tomorrow."

"The choir?" Natalie couldn't remember the last time Susan had participated. She didn't even think she sang from her seat in the pew.

"The director may throw a hissy fit. I don't blame her, considering I haven't practiced with them for years and she is such a stickler for attendance. This may be one time when I'll just have to pull rank. The pastor's wife is entitled to breaking a rule now and then." She laughed.

Natalie joined in. "Wow. I never would have imagined the Holy Spirit created monsters."

"I'm not a monster." She stuck her thumbs under her arms and flapped her elbows. "Just one joyful bird."

Thirty-Nine

Susan stood at the dining room table, flicked on the long-necked lighter, and held its flame to the first of four yellow tapers in tall crystal holders.

Next to her, already seated, Drake said, "I can't remember the last time we ate in here without guests."

"Neither can I. The kitchen is so practical, but I thought we could use a change." She finished lighting the candles and surveyed the setting. Glossy oak wood reflected candlelight. Bone china with its silver and pale yellow primrose design. Polished silver. A simple quiche, green salad, French bread, and sparkling white grape juice in crystal goblets. "There. An intimate dinner for two at a table that seats twelve. What do you think?"

"It works. Very romantic."

She walked around the table and sat across from him, surprised to see yet another smile on his face. Since her outburst at the beach house that afternoon, he had been extraordinarily attentive. If it weren't a Saturday night, he said he would have stayed there. She agreed, though, that their Sunday morning routine would needlessly be complicated and agreed to go home as well.

Drake stretched his long arm over the wide table, and she placed hers in it while he said the blessing. After a quick squeeze, they let go.

"This looks scrumptious, Susan. Thank you."

"You're welcome. Thank you for rearranging Saturday night's routine." Usually they ate at seven and then he disappeared in his study for the remainder of the evening to finish preparations on the next day's message.

He nodded. "I guess I thought we needed a change too."

Through her eyelashes, Susan watched him eat. He really was a handsome man. Articulate and charming. No wonder she had fallen for him.

"Drake, I was just wondering why in the world you chose me, shy little Susie Anderson."

He looked up, his fork midair. "You're not serious?"

"Yes, I am."

"Why wouldn't I?"

"You're so…so. Oh, I don't know. You have this bold presence about you. Even in college you had it. You were made to lead a congregation. You come from a solid, upper-class family. By comparison I'm a wallflower who still can't believe she has a hutch full of nice china and crystal."

His smoke gray eyes twinkled. "Susan, God brought us together. We clicked from the beginning, didn't we? When I met you, I knew I'd met the perfect helpmate. The potential was obvious. Besides that, you were the prettiest girl on the campus."

His words echoed down the years from sermons he had given, using them as an example of a happily married couple.

She caught a tear at the corner of an eye with her little finger. She didn't remember ever hearing such things directly. "Have I reached that potential?"

"Of course. Not that either of us are perfectly there yet, but I couldn't ask for more in a wife." He winked. "Except maybe that she doesn't drift on down to the beach too often."

Did he have to add that?

"Just kidding. I understand." He smiled. "This quiche is really good."

They ate in silence for a few moments. She thought about how much information she'd accumulated over the past two decades on the topic of marriage. It did not come from her parents because her father died when she was eight and her mother never remarried. Growing up with her mom, widowed grandmother, and unmarried great-aunt, she seldom witnessed the institution up close. Most of her girlfriend's mothers belittled their husbands, and she understood why. The ones she met scared her to death.

Her knowledge of marriage came from Bible college courses and late-night dorm discussions. It came from women's Bible studies and conferences. It came from sermons—and not just Drake's—and how-to books. She was grateful for the plethora of good, practical advice that encouraged her to do her best, to work hard at fulfilling her end of the bargain.

Somewhere along the way, Susan the Pretender employed Drake's opinion as the ultimate sieve to filter it all.

Somewhere in the past week or so, Susan the Joyful Bird had misplaced that sieve.

"So," he said, "why did you choose me?"

Her elbows nearly thrust themselves out from her sides. With an effort she kept the wings folded and said with a straight face, "I knew eventually you could buy me china and crystal and a table that seats twelve."

He laughed. "Come on. Play fair. I gave you a serious answer."

"Okay." She grinned. "You noticed me. You made me feel special. No one had ever made me feel so incredibly good about myself."

"I..." He set down his fork and pressed a napkin to his lips. "I didn't know that."

"How could I say such a thing to you? It might break the spell."

"And now? Do I still make you feel special?"

No. The exact opposite more often than not.

She shrugged and reworded her response. "Sometimes."

"Because maybe life gets in the way?"

She shrugged again.

"I should work on that."

"Me too. As far as filling my potential, I mean." She wondered about that sieve. "I was just thinking about all the information I've heard and read through the years about marriage. There's one thing I never really understood until now. It's that expression 'Love is a verb.'"

"It's not a feeling, though hopefully that comes as part of it."

"I always *felt* that I loved you. But…I am mad at you about Kenzie and I don't feel it anymore."

He set down his fork again.

She smiled. "You're never going to finish dinner."

"You just said…" He fairly sputtered.

"I said I don't *feel* love anymore. So I thought I'd try the verb thing. I left the beach house and went to the grocery store. By the way, do you consider shopping for food an act of love?"

"Well, they say the way to a man's heart is through his stomach."

"Ha-ha. Like a woman wouldn't feel loved if every meal weren't set before her and all she had to do was pick up a fork."

"You sound a little sensitive."

"Come on. Think about it."

"All right. Point taken. Grocery shopping is an act of love."

"I thought so too. Anyway, then I cooked dinner, I baked your favorite apple pie, I put on this black dress that's too short to wear in public. I prayed God would bless our evening and help you finish early. And I've been kissing you every chance I get."

He rubbed a hand across his eyes. A gesture of discomfort?

"Did you notice?"

He slid his hand down his jaw and nodded.

"It's like magic! Though I'm sure it's the Holy Spirit instead." She grinned and let her elbows bounce a little. "It works."

"You mean the feeling is back?"

"Oh, yes."

"Well." He sat back and cocked his head, studying her. "Well."

She smiled. "Well, well yourself."

"Your potential just grew by leaps and bounds. Maybe you should write a sermon on marriage."

"I have something else in mind. Did I mention you were the most handsome guy on campus?" She laughed. "Now that's what I call a rakish grin on your face, Pastor Drake."

He chuckled. "You didn't say what else it is you have in mind."

"I think you know." She smiled. "First, though, comes the apple pie dessert."

⁓

Sunday morning Drake leaned back against the kitchen counter and sipped orange juice, the epitome of nonchalance. "I wonder how I can use last night as a teaching point in a sermon."

Susan, cooking scrambled eggs at the stovetop, pointed the spatula at him. "That's too much information."

He laughed. "Just seeing if you were paying attention." He leaned over and kissed her cheek. "But speaking of too much information, I think the, uh, miscarriage is in that category."

She turned off the burner and picked up the skillet. "I agree. Are you sure you don't want any eggs?"

"I'm sure, thanks."

She didn't know if she wanted them now either. Her stomach twisted itself into a tight little ball.

At the beach house the previous day, after she'd cried so hard, they'd discussed Kenzie and the situation. He decided he would tell the congregation today. Then they'd declared a moratorium on painful subjects and spent the evening making peace.

It was time to decide on their joint posture. Drake would be leaving soon for church. He always left before she did.

They sat at the kitchen table, in the early sunlight. He sipped juice and she raked a fork through her eggs.

"The way I see it," he said, "the miscarriage is for us to visit again in the future."

"Mm-hmm. I feel it's incomplete. I want to name the baby and tell Kenzie."

"Let's hold off on that one."

She mashed the eggs. *Compromise. Compromise.*

"Now about Kenzie. Here's what I have in mind. I'd like to have you stand up with me, before the offering."

"It'll be an announcement, not part of the sermon?"

"I couldn't work it in on Palm Sunday. And it's not exactly an announcement. More like a special prayer request. I know we do prayer requests earlier in the service, but I don't want to just list this one with everything else. 'Let's pray for Edna's gallbladder and the Starrs because their daughter is pregnant and unwed.'"

"Drake, it's more than that."

"I know."

"It's not just we're hurting because our daughter has got herself in trouble. It's more like 'Help!' What did we do wrong? What do we do now? How do we communicate love and forgiveness and not condone living outside God's order? And it's all about her and the baby and Aidan, about their welfare. Their poverty and their fears. It's about I don't want to lose my daughter and grandchild."

He touched her arm. "I know, Susan. But I can't go into all that. The church is a public place with strangers in attendance every week. I want this to be a general announcement to our friends gathered together, just a straightforward 'we need your prayers.'"

"A lot of them have been here, in this position."

He nodded. "I'm counting on their empathy. Will you stand beside me then? I think this is the most difficult thing I've ever done."

"Of course I'll stand beside you. I love you."

"And I love you."

Forty

Natalie leaned her shoulder against her husband's and slipped her hand into his as they stood side by side in church. It was a large sanctuary, easily accommodating hundreds and hundreds. Its half-octagonal shape, far flung ceiling, and wide, fanlike array of pews gave it a contemporary style. There were traditional stained glass windows though, glorious now, with rays of the morning sun streaming through them.

Palm Sunday always made her ache inside, nearly to the point of an upset stomach. The day was full of such hope. Music and Scripture readings and sermon recalled Jesus' entry into Jerusalem, palm branches lining the road in welcome, the people ecstatic about the possibility of Him bringing peace to their world.

She always tried to forget what happened at the end of the week.

Did He know all along what was coming?

Rex gently pressed Natalie's hand. He knew what she was feeling. Of course, he thought she was nuts, but he let her just be and didn't hassle her.

Lord, will You convince Drake to let Susan be without a hassle?

The large, white-robed choir entered from the back of the church and strolled up the center aisle, singing and strewing palm branches donated by parishioners who had trees in their yards. There was Susan with the sopranos, in a too-large robe. Natalie wondered if she wore one of the hippie skirts underneath.

"'All glory, laud, and honor to Thee, Redeemer, King.'" Natalie raised her voice, which never could have been accepted into the choir no matter who pulled rank. "'To whom the lips of children made sweet hosannas ring. Thou art the King of Israel, Thou David's royal Son, who in the Lord's name comest, the King and Blessed One.'"

As the service progressed, Natalie studied her sister-in-law seated in the choir pews up front, directly behind the pulpit. She could have sworn an ethereal light illumined her face.

Before the offering was taken, Drake himself went through the announcements. Then he asked his wife to join him in the pulpit.

Much as Natalie had been hoping for this moment, watching Rex's brother prepare to expose his pain was excruciating. She might be able to tell a team of soccer players what she thought about regarding every subject under the sun, including her boys' dumb antics, but not in a million years could she stand up and say she'd lost one of them because she refused to forgive them.

Drake put his arm around Susan's shoulders. "As many of you know, our daughter has always marched to the beat of a different drummer. She sees things differently. If I say something is white, she'll insist it's black." He paused. "Vice versa as well."

Polite laughter rippled through the crowd.

"My wife recently gave me an illustration of how she would administer medicine to our little girl on a spoon, but she often refused to swallow it. She'd hold it in her mouth and, when we weren't looking, deposit it elsewhere. Of course a mother always finds out these things." He smiled. "The point is, we can't force our children to follow the example we've set before them."

Natalie's breath caught. *The example we've set?* Which one would that be? Getting his girlfriend pregnant or pretending as though it never happened?

Rex reached for her hand and held it tightly between his.

At the podium, Susan blanched.

Drake said, "Sometimes they choose to leave the fold, and we have to let them go." He paused. "Our prodigal daughter is expecting a baby and she is not married. We cannot honor her choices."

A group inhalation sounded like helium spurting into some giant balloon.

"We wanted to let you, our true family, know before this becomes an ugly rumor with unsubstantiated tales attached to it. We ask that you would pray for Susan and me. As you can imagine, this is a difficult time for us. Thank you for being patient. We may seem a little preoccupied." His smile was the annoyingly self-deprecating one. "Probably because we are."

The air fluttered out of the balloon. The worst was over. People exchanged glances of sympathy and relief.

Natalie argued in her mind with her brother-in-law. *Prodigal? Prodigal! The prodigal son left home because he wanted to and he came back! Kenzie came back and was forced to leave and told not to come back!*

Susan said something to Drake. Her soft voice was inaudible to the audience. His lapel microphone was too far from her mouth to pick it up.

He looked at her.

She spoke again.

Natalie read her lips. Something, something...*pray for Kenzie.* Or was that only her imagination?

Drake gave his head a half shake and lowered his arm from her shoulders. "Well, I apologize for bringing in personal business on this glorious Sunday morning. Let's get back to our regularly scheduled program now." He turned to Susan. "Thank you, honey. Ushers, will you come forward, please?"

Natalie watched Susan move, a stiff-jointed wooden puppet, back to her place in the choir. The luminescence had vanished from her face.

"Lord, not the straitjacket. Not again."

Rex squeezed Natalie's hand and she turned. His eyes were wide and staring at her.

Whoops. She must have spoken aloud.

Susan rose now with the choir to sing the offertory. She looked at Natalie. Across the church their eyes met. Natalie gazed, willing courage into her. Willing her to flap her wings.

And then Susan did exactly that. She closed up her big black music book and stepped in front of the woman beside her, and the next, and the next. Her route took her off the side of the platform, along the far windowless wall, and through a door leading to a hallway near the nursery.

As the choir sang and the ushers began the passing of offering plates back and forth through the pews, Natalie caught sight of two white-haired women rise from the third row, left side. Mildred and Leona, the twins. Slowly they moved down the pew, excusing themselves to those they passed.

Many women headed for the restroom before Drake started his sermon, but…?

Natalie turned sideways and glimpsed the back of Gwyn as she strode through a rear exit. Near the center aisle in the last row Emmylou's husband was helping her stand.

Movement in a middle row, side aisle, drew Natalie's attention. Tess.

Tess?

She marched toward the rear, her habitually composed features distorted in an obvious scowl, visible even at that distance.

Natalie bent close to Rex's ear. "I'm outta here."

He nodded.

Natalie squeezed his knee as she stepped around him and into the center aisle…and onto those palm branches, symbolic of so much hope.

Forty-One

"I totally adore your family." Kenzie turned to Aidan seated next to her at one of two long picnic tables in the Carlucci backyard.

He laughed. "And they totally adore you."

"They adore everyone."

The midafternoon spring sun warmed the grassy area. Palm Sunday dinner was in full swing; rowdy family and friends squeezed together on the benches. Blocking views of neighbors on both sides and behind was a tall peeling gray wood fence in such desperate need of paint even Kenzie noticed. The plants at its base were either overgrown or dying of thirst. Susan would never allow people to see such a yard. Not that hers would ever deteriorate into that condition. Pepper only laughed and said she and Mick had better things to do. Like feed lasagna to thirty people.

Kenzie said, "I can't imagine growing up in this environment."

"Aw, Kenz." Ignoring the hubbub around them, Aidan stopped eating and wrapped his arms around her.

"I'm sorry." She sniffled against his shoulder.

"For what?"

"I don't know. I just feel so sad. Maybe this is what your mom calls mommy hormones."

"What are you sad about?"

"Everything."

He straightened and put a finger under her chin. "Come on. You've got me. You've got my adoring family as your very own."

Well, technically, legally, she did not.

"That's not sad, is it?"

"No."

He kissed her cheek. "If you wanted to, Pepper and Mick would even think it great if you called them Mom and Dad. They'd adopt you in a heartbeat."

She blinked rapidly, but not quick enough to stop tears from spilling.

He said, "But that'd make us brother and sister."

She giggled.

"We don't want that."

"No."

He gazed at her, his deep-set blue eyes penetrating, and waited.

"It...all this...even church this morning...it all makes me homesick."

He nodded.

"I'm sorry, Aidan."

"There's nothing to be sorry about."

She disagreed. She was sorry to drag him into her misery, for his sake and hers. It added more reasons why he would grow tired of her. She was sorry she'd caused her parents so much trouble. At least her mom seemed to be accepting her, but she left a voice mail the previous day. Now she was back home with her dad, who would never give up until he got his way. Did her mom feel stuck in the middle? Could Kenzie help at all?

"Kenz, I'm sorry I don't know how to fix your homesickness. Maybe I can't."

She shook her head. "Your parents are doing everything in their power, but I guess...I guess I want my own mommy and daddy to love me. Unconditionally."

"Hmm."

"I know, I know. My mom has come a long way. And on her voice mail about going home yesterday she said Dad was willing to talk more. Aidan, I have to take my own step. I'm responsible for hurting them."

"But you can't change that. You've apologized. Kenz, I just don't want to see you rejected."

"I have to try, though. One more time. With Mom there with her new attitude and the connection we had Friday night, it's got to be different for him. And, Aidan," her eyes filled again, "they've got to meet you. I just can't stand that they don't know this really cool guy who likes me."

"Who totally adores you." He brushed his thumbs gently under her eyes. "Who is absolutely wild about you. And loves you too. Not to mention is having a baby with you."

"Will you go with me?"

A small hand grabbed her shoulder. She turned to see Mickey J behind them, his other hand on Aidan's shoulder.

"Hey, you two," he said in a stern tone. "No smooching at the dinner table!"

They looked at each other and burst out laughing. Aidan snatched Mickey before he could dash away, and they tickled him without mercy.

Kenzie so totally adored the Carluccis. They almost filled the hole in her heart.

Forty-Two

Palm Sunday night Pepper and Mick settled into bed earlier than usual. The full day ended wearily with them packing his bags. He had to leave at the crack of dawn to drive to a new road construction site. For the next few months his commute would be three hours each way. When not working on Saturdays, he'd spend weekends at home.

It was not an unusual situation for them. Pepper was accustomed to it…and she was not.

Mick turned the page. They were on 182.

She sighed. Although she'd checked out a copy from the library, the sad fact was they would each read the ending on their own.

But that wasn't the most difficult situation lounging about with them.

"Mick, I can't shake it."

"Then maybe it is the Holy Spirit nudging you."

"I just hope it's not that scene at the table this afternoon influencing my emotions."

"The one between Aidan and Kenzie." As often happened, he intuited what she thought. "She is one sad little puppy."

"She's so wounded. I think she and Susan really enjoyed each other at the shower, but it's like finding a corner piece in a jigsaw puzzle that has three thousand pieces. A start, yes, but they have such a ways to go. And then there's the dad. Nincompoop."

"Tsk, tsk. Did you know Kenzie thinks we adore everyone? Make that *totally* adore. Aidan said that she said she never hears a disparaging remark from us about anyone."

"Well, obviously she's missed my conversations about her dad. And your mom."

"Hmm." He turned the page. "So, if it is the Spirit nudging you, what do you think you should do?"

She grimaced. The Spirit nudged all right. "You mean besides pray for Drake?"

"Ah. There's my true Pepper."

"First off, I'll fast for twenty-four hours. And of course I'll pray for all of them. Maybe I should call Mildred. I'd like to get together with Susan. I am drawn to her, and not just because of our Grandmas out of Wedlock Boat. Maybe it's because I'm so astounded at her transformation. She's living, touchable proof of God working in the here and now."

"That's saying quite a lot."

"Yeah, I know."

"Which one was Mildred again?"

"One of the seventysomething twins. They refer to her as the Prayer Warrior. I'm sure she's praying too, asking God to heal this family."

Mick kissed the top of her head. "The walls will come tumbling down. Drake Starr won't know what hit him."

"I hope he does. I hope he feels the full impact of what he's losing."

Mick shut the book and set it on the nightstand. "More importantly, I hope our little semi-daughter-in-law feels the full impact of God's love pouring into her wounds, healing them as only He can."

"Amen." She snuggled under his arm.

"Amen." He turned off the lamp. "Who put Mickey Junior up to his stunt?"

"You didn't?"

He chuckled. "No. If I'd thought of it, I would have."

"Me too. It pulled Kenzie out of her funk, but no one confessed to it."

"Must have been the Spirit then." He held her close. "I love you, Pepper Sprout."

She smiled, and all the world's woes drifted away.

Forty-Three

Late on the evening of Palm Sunday, long after her usual bedtime, Susan's world teetered precariously on the edge of collapse.

It wasn't going down without a fight.

"Okay." She folded her hands in her lap and swallowed the quivery tone. With resolute finality she said, "I quit."

Seated in the other winged-back chair in the family room, Drake rubbed his forehead.

The day had worn on him as well. At least it was not the one Sunday of the month when evening church services were held. Tonight people met in homes instead, in small groups. They fellowshipped. Susan and Drake did not participate.

They hadn't eaten. Somehow she managed to remove the roast from the oven before it burned, but neither of them were interested. Somehow they changed from dress clothes into casual. Somehow Drake built a fire to warm the always chilly family room. Somehow they survived the hours laden with tension.

Somehow Susan had not shriveled once again into a bent posture or slipped her arms into a straitjacket, eager to placate her husband at any cost.

Perhaps the morning hugs in the church lobby from the Martha Mavens kept her going. Perhaps the knowledge that they exited the service in support of her filled her with courage.

"You quit what?" he said.

"I quit talking. I'm exhausted."

Drake lowered his hand. "We both are, but nothing is settled yet. I see two impasses. One, you think we should coddle Kenzie. I absolutely refuse to do that."

"Coddle is your word, not mine."

"Two, you think I should repeat my request to the entire church, asking them to pray for Kenzie."

"It wouldn't be a repeat since it wasn't stated in the first place."

His mouth worked so strenuously she expected a pink bubble to emerge from it at any moment.

"Drake." She leaned forward, arms on her knees, surer of herself than she'd been all day.

The Marthas must have been praying up a storm.

She gave him a gentle smile. "We disagree on this. It's all right for married couples to disagree, isn't it?"

"Certainly."

"I imagine other people do it all the time."

"We're not other people. We have to settle this subject before quitting. I can't lead if you're not on my side."

"It can't be a question of sides, Drake. I can't choose between you and Kenzie."

"We must agree on a workable plan regarding our daughter."

"How about we agree to disagree?"

"Susan." Exasperation pushed his voice up a notch.

They were breaking new territory here. Since midafternoon he hadn't resorted to his just-above-a-whisper volume, the usual indication of agitation. Not that he yelled, but he spoke in a manner different than she'd ever witnessed. His breath came in irregular bursts. It was as if he'd...lost control.

Strange how that comforted her in a way.

His eyes flashed. "What in the world has gotten into you? I've never seen you so non-submissive!"

Ah. Now he'd named the true impasse.

Her muscles froze, holding her in that leaning pose, the one that offered to meet him halfway. "Submission means I have to agree with you?"

"No, not at all. We've exchanged opinions and disagreed. Fine. But now as head of this household it's my duty to decide how we're going to act. As a respectful wife, you'll see the wisdom in following my lead."

Feeling returned to her muscles and she straightened, her spine stiff as a ramrod. "*If* you don't expect me to do something that goes against God's Word."

He blinked rapidly.

"My favorite preacher taught me that."

"I'm not expecting you to go against God's Word!"

"'Parents, do not exasperate your children. Do not drive them to resentment.'"

"'But correct them in the Lord.'"

"She's been— Oh, Drake. I am not going to argue Scripture with you. The point is, I will not turn my back on her."

"I'm not asking you to turn your back on her."

Lord, talk about exasperation! Why can't he let go?

"Susan, please."

His voice carried the pouting tone she could now recognize immediately. His shoulders and face sagged.

And she saw him as a little boy. Like a kid threatened by a normally compliant buddy suddenly transmuted into nasty bully.

She leaned forward again. Halfway. "Drake, I love you. Please believe that."

"Then let's present a united front. Let's—"

The doorbell rang. They exchanged a glance. The time was very late, but Drake was on call twenty-four/seven/three hundred sixty-five. There was no question of what to do.

But he hesitated getting out of his chair. Susan knew they both looked bedraggled, not quite presentable for company. Their minds were a million miles from being able to listen to another's woes. It was the last thing they needed.

On the other hand, it provided the opportunity for Susan to quit talking.

She led the way to the front door and breathed a prayer of thanks.

Forty-Four

Ringing the doorbell at the house where she'd lived much of her childhood epitomized Kenzie's relationship with her parents: locked out.

Lights glowed through curtains, so Kenzie knew someone was awake. She used to have a key, but it had gotten lost and hints had not prompted either her mom or dad to replace it.

As she stood in the dark, comparisons jumped to mind. They always did. The Carluccis were so off the charts when it came to hospitality. The entire family defined the word.

She shook the meandering thought from her head and glanced over her shoulder. Aidan sat in the van parked at the curb, watching her. He gave her a thumb's-up. He had tried to talk her out of this, but in the end simply hugged her and said he'd be there for her no matter what, her own SWAT team in the wings.

Okay. She had to focus on what she had come to do and not whine that she was actually related by blood to the Starrs.

The porch lights flicked on and her mother opened the door, an instantaneous grin cracking her face. Her dad appeared, slower, somber.

"Hi, Mom. Dad." Kenzie's smile wasn't as forthcoming as her mom's. She felt it tuck in and out of her cheeks quick as a rabbit. Dread paralyzed her limbs. *Oh, God.* The prayer worked. Her smile stuck and she spread her arms. "The prodigal kid returns."

Susan grabbed her in a bear hug. "Welcome, sweetheart. Come inside." She shut the door behind her.

Pugsy yipped and raced into view, down the hall from the kitchen as fast as his short legs could pump. Kenzie knelt and caught him up in her arms. No time for dog talk. If she didn't speak the rehearsed words, dread would close up her throat and she'd die on the spot. She propped Pugsy on her soft pudgy tummy and nuzzled him briefly. Then she turned to her father.

Drake stared back at her, no response on his face.

Kenzie's courage drained.

"Well," Susan said, "as soon as you two hug and make peace, I'll order up the fatted calf."

Kenzie blinked first. "Dad, I'm sorry." The words burst from her. "What I did was wrong. I know that. Even if there weren't a baby, Aidan and I should have waited. I'm asking you both to forgive me."

Susan kissed her cheek. "Of course we forgive you."

"Susan, she's not quite finished."

"Dad, what more is there? I really want your forgiveness. We goofed up. I admit that. God had a better way in mind, but we didn't take it."

"What about marriage?"

"We're not there yet."

"If you're there enough to have a baby…" He nodded toward her midsection. "And it's obvious that's going to happen—then you're there enough to take responsibility." His breath came in funny spurts, disrupting his speech. "As married parents." His volume increased and his voice bounced, echoing off the high walls of the open staircase in the entryway.

Kenzie had never seen him in such a state. Now that she noticed, they both looked as though they'd been out in the rain too long. Their clothes were uncharacteristically rumpled. Their faces had accumulated years, making them appear as old as Aidan's great-great-aunt.

Her mother touched Drake's arm. "Let's take this one step at a time. Why don't we go sit in the family room? Kenzie, would you like some tea?"

Much as she wanted to just hug her mom, she focused on her dad.

Way too much baggage lay in his direction, stuff that had to be dealt with before she could move on or even further into the house.

"Dad, getting married isn't going to right things."

"It will right what you're doing now, living in sin with that man."

"His name is Aidan, and I am not going to guilt him into marrying me. He'd resent me for the rest of my life and probably our baby too!"

"That's ridiculous."

"Dad, why don't you ever listen to me? Why don't you ever try to understand my side?"

He didn't reply with words, but his breathing sounded like it came from a runner about ready to keel over.

Her mother leaned toward him, her hand still on his forearm, her knuckles prominent as if she clutched tightly. The chipper expression on her face was gone. "Do you resent me?"

Though her voice was scarcely above a whisper, Kenzie heard.

"What?" Drake said. "Why would I?"

Susan's eyes got big.

Her dad's mouth did its funny pucker thing. It was not a good sign.

"Drake," her mother said, "I forgive you. But it won't continue."

Kenzie felt as though she'd walked into the middle of a conversation. What were they talking about?

Her dad slouched and not just with his shoulders. It was like his whole body and personality wilted. He seemed smaller somehow.

What was going on?

Susan let go of his arm and smiled at Kenzie. "So. The prodigal returns, asking for forgiveness. Let's embrace this moment. It'll have to be with scrambled eggs, though. Last I checked, there was no calf out in the yard."

Her dad said, "I can't go back on my word." His voice was a hoarse monotone. "No marriage, no welcome."

Kenzie couldn't believe her ears. "And no forgiveness?"

"You know what I said. I've taught it for years. What is there to forgive if you don't change your sinful ways?"

"Drake!"

"Susan, the prodigal has not returned."

Kenzie recognized his tone. It was the one he used to wrap up sermons. It meant he had no more to say on the subject. Throughout her teen years it signaled her exit.

She stepped toward the door. "Oh, well. I didn't really expect a fatted calf. Maybe a bone. That would have been nice." She set Pugsy on the floor. He lifted a forlorn muzzle to her. She missed him a lot. She didn't think she missed her dad at all.

"Hold it!" Susan said.

Kenzie spun back around. What *was* going on? Her parents never argued in front of her. She really didn't believe they ever argued, not even in private. And what had her mom meant, *it won't continue?* What wouldn't continue?

Her mom stood straight, hands on her hips. "We are not leaving things like we did in January. Drake, our daughter is welcome in our home."

"I can't agree to that."

"Then I will spend time with her elsewhere. I will see my grandchild."

"I forbid that. Your place is beside me, enforcing consequences."

"She'll be living out the consequences for the rest of her life. What is my not seeing her a consequence of? What did I do to deserve that?"

His face reddened. "The prodigal needs to—"

"You're forcing me to choose between you and Kenzie."

"There's no choice involved. Susan, we've discussed this."

"We have. Ad nauseam. And all that matters is I want to be free to have a relationship with Kenzie. If you feel you have the right to deny that, I think..." She inhaled a shaky breath and trembled.

"I don't have that right. But you know how I feel."

"I think then that...that I have to get away. Again. For a while." Her voice trailed to a whisper. "The beach house is still available."

"Susan, if you go there again, don't bother to come back. That goes for your Martha Maven friends as well, after their blatant show of disrespect this morning. And Kenzie." He paused. "Grow up." With that he went to the staircase and climbed out of sight.

Kenzie stood beside her mom. Neither of them spoke or moved. It was as if time suspended itself. Or that oxygen had been sucked right out of the place. A sense of déjà vu struck her. She had cruised this route before, more than a few times.

Why had she even bothered? It was always going to be her against them.

"Kenzie, honey, I am so sorry you witnessed that." Susan blew out a noisy breath and walked to the coat closet.

Kenzie watched her put on a jacket and lift a tote bag and Pugsy's leash from the hall tree. Then she picked up a small handbag from the table and took keys from it. They slipped from her hands and crashed to the floor.

This was not in the script. Susan was supposed to offer some lame excuse for him and then trot on up the steps after him.

"Mom, what are you doing?"

"Going to my new home away from home." She retrieved the keys and stood. "Maybe the third time will be a charm. Come here, Pugs."

"But he just said—"

"I can't stay here. It will only continue."

"What will continue?"

Susan knelt to hook the leash onto Pugsy's collar. "This preposterous version of submission— Oh!" The leash clanked against the floor.

Kenzie went down on a knee and looked in her face. Tears glistened on her mother's cheeks. "Mom!"

"I'm all right. Can you hook this— No, I am not all right. Natalie would tell me to admit it. Okay, I admit it. I need help. I can't stay here and I am in no condition to drive."

Her own hands shaking now, Kenzie fastened the leash.

"And I can't bother Natalie again. I'll call a cab—"

"We can give you a ride."

Susan stood with her. "'We?'"

"Aidan's waiting."

"Like before."

"My knight."

"Oh, honey, I want to meet him. Later. Thank you for offering to help, but I can't drag you two into the middle of this. It's between your dad and me."

She wanted to plop down onto the tile floor and bawl her eyes out in her mother's arms. *Kenzie, grow up.* Her dad's harsh words replayed, startling her like a splash of cold water. She was responsible for this mess. It was time to stop passing the ball and dribble it herself.

"Mom, you wouldn't be in this situation if it weren't for me. We will give you a ride."

Susan stopped rummaging in her purse and stared.

"Do you need to bring anything else?"

Her mother hiccupped and swiped her fingers under her eyes. "Hair goop and facial creams are still in this tote. What else is there?" Her smile wobbled. "I've learned how to travel light. My daughter taught me that."

"Okay, then. Let's go. I've got Pugs." She opened the front door. "You want to leave Dad a note?"

"I don't think so. He's got my number."

⌒

Kenzie's energizing rush of responsibility fizzled halfway to the street. By the time they reached the van, she felt like a zombie. She pulled open the back door. The overhead light went on and she caught Aidan's questioning stare. She gave him one in return. She had no clue what was going on.

Before Kenzie could climb in, her mother did. There were no backseats in the van; they'd been removed in order to make space for the band's equipment. She watched now, nearly stupefied, as her fragile, prim and proper mother contorted herself around and between large amplifiers. At least she wore slacks and not her usual skirt. She sat on the floor, a silly grin on her face, and thrust her hand between the front seats.

"Hi, Aidan. I'm Susan, your semi-mother-in-law."

He smiled and shook her hand. "You've been talking to my mom."

"Yes, I have."

Instant rapport? Her mother was definitely not following the script tonight.

Kenzie said, "Let me sit here. There's no seatbelt."

"I'm fine."

"Mrs. Starr, I'll sit back there. Kenzie can drive—"

"Call me Susan, please, and neither Kenzie nor I are in any shape to drive. Believe me."

Aidan's glance to Kenzie registered alarm. She slid the door shut; he reached across and opened the front passenger door. Pugsy in hand, she hoisted herself up to the seat. The dog stood stiffly on her lap, eyeing Aidan warily.

"Pugs, this is Aidan. I told you about him years ago."

"Hey, dog." Aidan scratched Pugsy's ears, but looked at Kenzie. "You okay, Kenz?"

Shudders pulsated through her. She was so *not* okay. Her father had more or less just told her she meant less to him than *dirt*. Her mother had just told him off—in a nice way, but she had never before approached such a feat—and left. *Left him.* Her husband of twenty-some years. The solid-rock pastor, expert on marriage and parenthood.

What should she have done? Hadn't she prayed? Hadn't she admitted wrong? Hadn't she asked him for forgiveness? What else was she supposed to do?

"Sweetheart." Susan touched her shoulder and took Pugsy off her lap. "This is not your fault. Do you hear me?"

Kenzie's teeth chattered. Aidan draped his fleece jacket around her and tucked it behind her shoulders.

Her mom was still talking. "It is not your fault. You are responsible for only one thing, and it's a good thing. You're helping me and your dad face some issues we should have addressed long ago. Before you were born. I am sorry you saw us argue, but thank you for coming. Thank you for your courage. God is using you, hon. He most surely is."

And then Kenzie began to cry.

Forty-Five

The next day Susan recounted the Palm Sunday nightmare to her sister-in-law as they sat on the seawall. Chilled to the bone since she stood at the podium yesterday with Drake, Susan had headed to the sunshine. Outdoors was warmer than inside the beach house or on the shadowed patio. Late-morning sunlight warmed their backs, danced on the ocean, and dispelled the horror to some degree.

She said, "Then Aidan walked me to the door here. I told him if he ever hurt Kenzie I'd punch his lights out."

Natalie's slack jaw finally returned to its normal position. "You're kidding."

"I was not myself last night."

"You're not kidding."

"My new motto is: Talk straight. Aidan didn't laugh. He got the message. He will be in big trouble if he doesn't take extremely good care of my daughter."

For a few moments they didn't speak. Susan imagined Natalie was trying to digest it all, a state she hadn't yet reached herself. Not Aidan so much as everything else. Aidan was the bright spot.

"Suze, do you like him?"

"Yes. Very much. He was incredibly tender with her. They're just a couple of young people trying to find their way in this messy world. I don't know what he feels about marriage, but Kenzie finally expressed her fears about it."

"You said she's afraid he'll resent her for forcing him to marry?"

Susan nodded and bit her lip.

"Suze?"

"When she said that, it felt like Moe smacked Curly over the head and I was Curly. She echoed exactly what I was trying to tell Drake here the other day."

"You think he resents you?"

"I know he does."

Natalie sighed loudly. "I thought he asked forgiveness for this sort of thing on Saturday."

"He did, but I see now it was just to smooth things over, either to calm me down or to get me in church on Palm Sunday." She turned to her sister-in-law. "Sorry. That's not completely fair. I don't think he has a conscious clue to this negative power he holds over me. He doesn't do it on purpose. And it's as much my fault that I bend into it. I got pregnant. Ergo, I forced him to marry me. I'm guilty. I owe him. It's my job to keep him happy. To make up for what I did."

"And forget that it takes two to make a baby?"

"Sure. It's the woman's role to consent or not."

"That's one lousy, cockeyed version of wifely submission."

"Yes, it is." She gazed again at the ocean. "When I asked him if he resented me, he seemed puzzled. He asked why would he feel that? I just looked at him. He got defensive, so I think he caught on to what I meant."

"I can't believe he told you not to come back, even in the heat of the moment. And the Marthas too! He is not the brother-in-law I knew. Nor the pastor of ten years ago. Or even five."

"Nor the husband. Nor the daddy of little Kenzie."

"Well, Suze, I'm sure he's threatened by your new independent streak."

She felt an old familiar sinking sensation. "I don't mean to threaten him."

"You should have threatened him a long time ago. This will either make him or break him." Natalie flung an arm around Susan's shoulders and got almost nose-to-nose with her. "How are *you*?"

"Um."

"Suze, come on. What happened to your straight talk?"

"There are these lapses." Especially when it came to Drake. "It looks like I've left him. I don't want to break up our marriage. That's not my intention."

"I know that, but I didn't ask about your plans. Tell me how you are."

"You can be such a bulldog."

"That's good! Keep going." Natalie lowered her arm, but her intense eye contact said she was not letting go. "How do you feel?"

"I feel ugly and worthless and abandoned." Susan blurted the words. "My husband kicked me out! I don't mean a thing to him! I am scum in his eyes. Oh, Natalie, it hurt so bad last night I thought I would die."

"But you didn't."

She shook her head. "I didn't. God brought me through the worst night of my life and this morning…" Tears welled, and she whispered, "This morning I walked Pugsy on the beach, before dawn, for at least an hour. And I sang the entire time! Out loud! It was like I couldn't help it."

Natalie grinned. "The joyful bird."

"Yes, but now what?"

"Now we pray."

"We need Mildred."

"Suze, you're asking for help."

She smiled. "Yes, I am. It's getting easier."

"Great, because I already called in the troops. Those crazy boycotting Martha Mavens will be here by dinnertime."

~

Natalie left to coach soccer practice, promising to return later with Susan's car. She would hitch a ride home with one of the others. Earlier that morning Gwyn had helped her. Using Natalie's key for Susan's front door, they went inside after Drake left for the office and collected her clothes as well as her car, which was parked now at Natalie's.

Susan busied herself unpacking once again. Much to her surprise, Tess caught her at it, arriving long before dinnertime.

"I'm early, Susan." She laughed as she entered and gave her a quick hug. "Like you didn't notice. I hope I'm not interrupting. Can I help you with anything?"

They sat in the living room.

"Thank you, but, um, I'm just doing laundry. Getting, uh, organized." The usual intimidation she felt in the presence of the director of women's ministries seared through her like desert heat. Little Susie Anderson shriveled. What must Tess think? There she was, not even unpacked yet. How could she explain that she'd left her home in such a tizzy she hadn't the wherewithal to grab even a nightgown? Or that Natalie had to gather her things on the sly. It all sounded so juvenile—

"Susan." Tess lifted her elegant hands with their professionally done pearly pink nails and then let them fall to her tasteful, classic, woolen beige slacks. "I don't know where to begin."

"I realize what I did appears wrong."

"Susan, if you appear in the wrong, then we all do. I left the service yesterday too, remember?"

"Of course. I appreciated you comforting me."

"Well, I didn't do it solely for your sake. Nor did the others. We all felt a similar letdown when Drake made his special announcement. He sounded like a heartless automaton, hardly even mentioning poor Kenzie." Her short laugh resembled a harsh bark. "Letdown isn't the word. It doesn't begin to scratch the surface of what I felt. It was more... I don't know. Disillusionment? Indignation? Righteous anger? Perhaps all that and more. No, I'm not here to lecture about right and wrong and Drake's reputation and what you should have done."

Huh? Susie Anderson sat up and took notice. Tess Harmon, the most staid woman she'd ever met, had just performed the equivalent of a break-dance right there in the living room.

"The thing is, Susan— Oh!" She covered her face with both hands.

"Tess?"

After a few deep breaths, she pulled a handkerchief from her blazer pocket. "I'm sorry. Something is tearing me apart, and I haven't been able to speak of it because, well, after all I am this director. I teach and mentor women and suggest, more or less, that if they live life as I do, they'll be fine." Emotion interrupted her speech again.

Susan understood. "You have to keep up an image. You can't be real."

"Precisely. Isn't that a crock?"

She couldn't help but smile at the slang. "It is indeed. These past couple weeks I've found…" Was she actually passing a lesson along to Tess? Imagine that! "I've found that being real is the most freeing experience ever."

"That's what shows."

"Really?"

She nodded. "And I want it."

"Then…" They exchanged a long stare. "Then let out whatever is tearing you apart. It shouldn't control you."

"My son is gay."

Susan moved to the couch and took her hand. "Oh, honey."

"And I didn't have a clue on how to love him until I saw you with Kenzie Friday night." Tears glowed in her eyes. "God doesn't stop loving us when we make foolish choices. Why do we put so many conditions on others? He's my son! I don't understand why he's involved in this lifestyle. I've spent years trying to figure out what we did wrong. It's easy to pretend it's not happening. He lives in San Francisco and has a good job. I just don't talk about his personal life. What I need is wise counsel and direction, but I can't even tell anyone because it would tarnish my image!"

While Tess cried, Susan did what she wished someone would have done for her in January: She put her arm around Tess' shoulders and sat beside her, silent except for wiping at her own tears.

After a time Tess blew her nose. "I was still in denial after Kenzie's shower, though. I still thought you should handle things differently. I offered Drake sympathy and let him know he was still my highly respected pastor. Then on Saturday night our son called. He and his… boyfriend…partner…are planning a civil marriage ceremony. It was devastating news for me and my husband. I don't know how we made it to church the next day, but we did. And then Drake did his announcement thing. All I could see was me standing up there talking about how miserable I was because of my son's choices and not once speaking of him as a human being in need of prayer or of my need for prayer because of how I've hurt him."

Susan nodded.

"That's when I realized Drake had it all wrong. I left the service and decided to get real."

"Tess, you are incredibly real right now. Thank you for letting me in."

"Thank you for showing me how." She gave a tiny smile and patted her chest. "Oh, my. Is this it? Is this how it feels? It's like I just got released from prison."

Susan laughed. "I hear the chains falling to the ground."

"Wow." Tess hooted long and hard, until she had joyful tears to dry. "Now what?"

"Well." She smiled. "I suggest we start with ice cream."

"Ice cream? It's the middle of the afternoon."

"That's the point, Tess. That's exactly the point."

Forty-Six

"Ah-ah…" Aidan covered his mouth with his hands. "Achoo!"

Pepper sneered at her son in the doorway and pushed past him into his apartment. "Don't you dare give me that, bud. You called me, remember?" She faced him as he shut the door. "Otherwise I wouldn't be here invading your space."

He laughed. "Just kidding. Little touchy, are we?"

Maybe she was.

Okay. Yes, she definitely was. She could be woman enough to admit it. But not to him. No way.

Fourteen hours into her fast, she was struggling. Usually when she practiced the discipline, she disengaged as much as possible from the world and tried to do it in secret the way Jesus suggested in Matthew. Her daughters Carys and Davita went off to school, Mickey Junior to a friend's, she cleared her schedule, stayed home, and didn't answer the phone.

The day wasn't usual. Mick had left town early that morning. His absence always left a vacancy inside of her. The twins, Lisel and Sari, were spending their Easter break from college at the house. Good news, bad news: They kept Mickey and the other girls busy, but they kept them busy at home, stirring up all kinds of energy. Then the washer broke. Then Aidan phoned. Kenzie was in a bad way. She needed his mom. Could she stop by?

The whole reason she fasted was to focus on prayer for Aidan and Kenzie and the Starrs. Of course she agreed to go right over.

Her stomach growled. *Lord, I realize these interruptions could be a test. An opportunity to radically depend on You to keep me sane and focused. But I gotta tell You, I'm leaning toward the other explanation. As in this is a total waste of effort!*

Aidan's smile caught her attention, and she noticed her accusatory forefinger was still planted in his sternum.

He winked. "Thanks for coming."

"Sure." She removed her hand and turned to see Kenzie reclining on the loveseat, propped against a pile of pillows and covered with a ratty, colorless afghan Grandma Bella had crocheted ages ago.

"Hi."

"Kenzie." She went over to her and sat alongside her legs. "Got enough room?"

"Yeah." She wriggled toward the back cushions.

"You don't look so good."

The girl shrugged. Her hair was more flat than spiky and her complexion pale.

Aidan squeezed onto the end of the couch and put Kenzie's feet in his lap. "She hasn't eaten since the picnic yesterday."

Well, that makes two of us. "Hon, Baby needs nourishment. He needs— I'm sorry. You know all that. What's wrong?"

Kenzie exchanged a glance with Aidan. He nodded.

"I saw my parents last night. We went to the house. Aidan waited in the car."

The feeling of a fist pressing into her stomach squelched the rumbles. "Your mom was at home?"

"Yeah. They sort of made up on Saturday." She rolled her eyes. "Mom left me a voice mail. Dad actually went to the beach house and they talked and then she went home. I guess I was feeling left out."

"Of course you were."

"Then at your dinner yesterday, I felt so sad. You all treat me like I'm family, even all those relatives I hardly know, but…" When Kenzie wasn't talking, singing, or smiling, her lips remained partially open as if ready to jump into the action. Right now they were shut tightly. Holding in?

"But you're not exactly family." Pepper finished her sentence. "Not the flesh and blood or by marriage kind." She stopped, feeling like she'd lit a firecracker. Holding her breath, she waited for the explosion. None came. "You want to reconcile with your own family."

Kenzie nodded. "Friday night was so good with Mom."

"I know. It was evident to everyone at the shower."

"So." She glanced again at Aidan. "I begged him to take me to their house. I wanted to ask Dad once and for all, calmly, to forgive me."

Pepper touched her cheek. *Thank You, Holy One, for prompting this child of Yours.* "That took a lot of nerve."

"It was more like something I just had to do. Like I didn't have a choice."

"The Spirit can push us like that."

Kenzie's long lashes swept over her blue-gray eyes, as if in dismissal.

Pepper's heart sank. Evidently the dialogue hadn't gone as hoped. "What happened? Did you tell him?"

"Yeah. All he could talk about was us getting married. He said…" She swallowed with difficulty a few times. "He said he won't forgive me until that happens."

Pepper closed her eyes.

"But that's not the worst."

Swell. She looked again at Kenzie. "I'm sorry, hon."

"Then my mom argued with him. She said he forced her to choose between him and me. She said she wouldn't give up on our relationship."

Lord, thank You for my Mick.

"He said if she left…" Kenzie's face crumpled.

Aidan continued. "He said if Susan left, she needn't bother to come back."

"Oh, no."

"We gave her a ride to the beach house."

Pepper leaned over and hugged Kenzie.

"They never argued before."

"It's not your fault."

"But it is!"

"No, it's not. It's not." She held Kenzie's small body wracked with sobs.

Eventually Pepper's silent cursing slowed. The man really needed prayer, but for now her semi-daughter-in-law was the one she carried to the throne.

⤙

They coaxed Kenzie into eating some chicken noodle soup. Still seated on the loveseat under the afghan, she spooned it from a mug.

Aidan sat beside her on the floor, Pepper in the old upholstered chair.

"Mom left a voice mail for me this morning, but I just can't talk with her now."

"That's okay," Pepper said. "Do you two mind if I express my opinion?"

Aidan slapped a hand to his mouth. "Achoo!" He made his eyes abnormally wide.

Pepper laughed.

He grinned. "Opinionate all you want, Mom." He looked at Kenzie, and his voice softened. "It's a special day."

She watched him for a moment. Beneath his impulsive personality beat a solid, tender, loyal heart. "You are a lot like your father, Aidan James Carlucci. You are a good man."

His brows rose. "Thanks."

"I know you'll take care of Kenzie. Whatever that entails." *Like you will figure out marriage is God's best way for a family to function.* Her son needed to hear that from some other voice, though, not hers again. "You know you'll be in deep yogurt if you don't."

He turned to Kenzie who sprayed a mouthful of soup back into the mug.

Pepper said, "What?"

Aidan laughed. "Susan said basically the same thing to me last night. She said she'd punch my lights out if I didn't."

Kenzie giggled. "I still can't believe that came out of her."

Pepper said, "Well, I can. You think mama bears are tough. You ain't seen nothing yet. Grandma bears have triple the hutzpah."

They roared.

"I'm serious." She smiled and waited for them to finish laughing. "Okay, here's what I think. Kenzie, what's happened to your parents is understandably painful for you, but it could be for the best."

"Mom said they're facing issues they should have taken care of a long time ago."

"That's the sort of thing I'm talking about."

"But she *left* him."

"She temporarily removed herself from the situation. It's a healthy thing for her to do. I believe she thought there was no other direction to go right now. If they made up on Saturday, something happened before Sunday night that showed her things weren't finished." Pepper imagined it had to do with their own premarital pregnancy. Kenzie didn't seem to be aware of that story, and she wasn't about to bring it up.

She continued. "With your mom not being at home, your dad is forced to face the problem. He wouldn't have such a large congregation if he wasn't a man who trusts in God. And God is faithful. It'll work out."

Kenzie lowered the mug to her lap. "We got along when I was little. Then I became a teenager."

"And he became a big success." She shrugged. "His church wasn't always this huge, was it? And I imagine his early churches weren't either?"

Kenzie shook her head.

"So who's to say what came first? The terrible teens or the hotshot holy man?"

Kenzie giggled. "He's never been called that."

"I certainly hope not. It's horribly disrespectful." She smiled. "Let God have His way with him. And ask God to help you forgive him. Sing Aidan's song over him, that one about peace."

Aidan scoffed. "I had antiwar efforts in mind when I wrote that."

"I know. So do I." She looked at both of them. "We are in a war, kiddos. As long as our relationships remain unhealed, we cannot live in peace. Forgiving those who wound us is an antiwar effort."

"You're weird, Mom."

She grinned. "I know that too."

Forty-Seven

As far as Natalie could tell, Susan the joyful bird flitted in and out of the present moment. No doubt what chased off her new demeanor was the scene before her: a roomful of gaggling, uninhibited women binging on straight talk that bordered on disrespectful.

Shafts of setting sunlight bathed the beach house living room in a soft glow. All the Martha Mavens were in attendance. They described their grave disappointment in Drake's attitude on Sunday, how they felt even betrayed by it. Tess won the prize, though, for revealing the biggest whopper of a grievous story. The worst wasn't so much that her son lived the gay lifestyle, but that she'd kept the truth bottled up inside of herself for nine years.

At last, Susan squirmed in her chair and spoke. "We can't blame Drake for everything."

"Why not?" Emmylou sprawled in the big chair with her legs outstretched across the ottoman. Her huge belly suggested she should have been checking into the maternity ward, not sitting at the beach.

Susan said, "We can't blame him because he is not responsible for our reactions."

"But he made it sound like Kenzie is some awful punk who made your lives a living hell just because she didn't want to take medicine and her favorite music was different than his."

Natalie nearly burst into laughter at Emmylou's summation.

Mildred smiled sweetly. "He forgot to mention her disdain for coloring inside the lines. That in itself adds several demerits against her."

215

Leona said, "I did overhear her swear one time in the church kitchen. More demerits."

Gwyn tsked. "Well what about those pierced ears of hers? Such garish fashion statements! That's certainly grounds for dismissal from the home. Why, I wouldn't be surprised if she even has a tattoo tucked out of sight."

As if on cue, the four speakers gasped dramatically and covered their mouths with their hands. Susan's panic-stricken face suggested she was ready to fly the coop along with the joyful bird. Unresponsive Tess seemed lost in her own private agony.

Mildred lowered her hand, leaned forward, wide eyes magnified behind her thick lenses, and whispered, "She does! She showed it to me once. Back here." She pointed to her rotund hip. "It's a beautiful, eensy teensy rose. Lavender."

Natalie snickered. Kenzie hadn't kept that tattoo a secret from anyone but her parents. Susan only knew because she'd spotted it by accident and never even mentioned it to her daughter.

"Natalie!" Susan's tone begged for intervention.

"Okay, ladies, we all agree Drake blew it. But we've indulged long enough in bashing and dissing him."

Mildred murmured, "Lord, forgive us."

"Amen. I think we also agree that Kenzie is not a bad apple. She's crying out for her dad's love and forgiveness. The prodigal did return last night. I vote we pressure him to change his attitude. To reconcile with his little girl."

Tess spoke up. "You can't make that man do a thing he doesn't want to."

Mildred grinned. "No, but God can."

"Well, of course." Tess shrugged.

The woman never shrugged. She did not know the meaning of indecisive. Natalie thought Drake wasn't the only person who needed prayer. Tess' needs, though, would have to take a backseat for now.

Natalie exchanged a glance with Mildred. They'd already discussed a plan. "Drake is losing his wife and daughter, but so far he's only digging his heels in deeper. What seems a bit closer to his heart..." She paused, catching sight of the pain etched on Susan's face. Natalie looked away before her anger had a chance to explode. Drake was such a fool! *Sorry, Lord, but we're talking about Susan and Kenzie! His heart should be broken!*

Mildred nodded, prompting her to go on.

"As I was saying, what seems closer to his heart is his reputation with the congregation. So, for his own good, out of our love and respect for him, we attack him where it hurts. We boycott services this Friday night."

Gwyn uncrossed her legs. "My word! Good Friday services? That's a major undertaking. Don't we average over a thousand people on Sunday mornings alone? Easter draws even more."

"Yes, but records show Good Friday is one of those odd times when attendance is usually well below normal."

"Then perhaps we aim for Easter Sunday? Go for the jugular, I say!"

A stab of panic kept Natalie mute. Uh-oh. What were they creating?

Gwyn thrust a fist into the air. "Gosh, I wish I hadn't missed the sixties! I would have made a stupendous protestor."

Phew. She was joking. "Well," Natalie said, "I think Friday will be jugular enough. We're not talking the whole church. I'm sure the vast majority wouldn't even agree with our take on things. Some will learn of our plans, but we're not announcing it to everyone. If we impact a small portion, it will speak to him. Now, Mildred and I have a few suggestions, but please, please give us your thoughts."

Nods all around.

"We think that besides our small group here, we can invite a few others, people we trust to be discreet, those who have an obvious heart for our pastor and his family. Mildred and Leona will recruit from the senior brigade. I'll call parents of middle and high school kids. Emmylou, your influence is with the young marrieds. Gwyn, the singles. Tess—"

"I have a huge women's Bible study class." She pressed her lips together.

Natalie breathed a prayer.

Tess said, "What exactly do we tell our circles of influence, Coach? That our pastor is a misogynistic prig who's twisted truths on submission for years and hoodwinked us all?"

Susan inhaled sharply.

Natalie winced.

Emmylou said, "I'm lost. What does *that* mean?"

Natalie answered, "It doesn't matter what it means. It's too harsh. We just tell our friends the bottom-line facts. Pastor banished Kenzie from home; his intention is right on, but we disagree with his methods. Susan is devastated, torn between her husband and daughter. We want to show our concern for the Starr family. In order to get his attention, we lodge a formal protest by skipping Good Friday service."

Leona said, "That will spark a boatload of ugly, false rumors."

Gwyn nodded. "Of course, that's nothing new, but he may feel pushed against the wall and banish all of us."

Natalie raised her brows in Susan's direction and received a half nod of approval. "He already has."

Shocked expressions lined each face.

"He noticed exactly who left the service Sunday morning and didn't return. He told Susan she needn't come back home and that the Martha Mavens needn't return to church."

There were a few gasps. Tess' complexion had turned a vivid red. She doubled over as if seeking relief from a stomachache.

Natalie held up a hand. "We can't let that get a foothold in our hearts. He was upset. We all say things we don't mean when we're that upset. It just reveals how serious the situation is. All right. My assistant coach has something to say."

Mildred smiled. "We do not do this out of anger, but out of love. Love must be foremost in our hearts. It alone must color our words. If we cannot speak graciously about our pastor, we don't speak about him at all."

Letting her words sink in, the Prayer Warrior gazed at each pair of eyes in turn before going on. "All right. Thank you. I know you understand what I'm saying. Now, because it is Holy Week, I believe we should gather for informal services elsewhere. I miss the old ways of observing the Passion that Leona and I grew up with, Maundy Thursday, Good Friday, and Holy Saturday services. Our Lord's last week on earth should be embraced in all its horror and beauty. I haven't figured out details yet, but the beach here is a perfect place to worship. We don't need anything but two or more people gathered together in His name."

Natalie nodded. "That's it, ladies. What do you think?"

Gwyn turned to Susan. "We need your blessing. After all, you are our pastor's wife."

She puffed her cheeks up and blew out a breath. "I don't want people taking sides."

Natalie shook her head. "Everyone will take the Starr family side. That's what we emphasize. We want you three back together again, whole again."

"Five. There are five of us."

Natalie immediately inferred her meaning. "Right. The baby and Aidan too."

"And I don't want this to be the start of a split in the church."

"None of us do. We keep it low-key."

"What about after Friday?"

Natalie stared. All of a sudden Susan, who never questioned a thing, couldn't stop asking about every detail. "We think Drake will answer that. He'll call you."

"What if he doesn't?"

"Then…then we drop it as a group project, but the Martha Mavens will always take care of you."

"Don't boycotters explain their actions? Who will tell Drake what's going on? How is he to know this is an act of love?"

Natalie waited a beat. She and Mildred had prayed about the right choice. "Rex."

A knowing glance passed between her and Susan. The brotherly relationship was not exactly one of mutual respect.

Natalie said, "He's the only one audacious enough to tell Drake the tough stuff."

"He agreed to do it?"

"Well…he doesn't know about it yet."

"Then we'd better pray." Susan smiled. It seemed at last the joyful bird had roosted.

"Is that a blessing I hear?"

She nodded.

"Amen." Natalie looked at the others. "How about everyone else?"

Leona said, "I'm in."

"So am I." Gwyn nodded.

Emmylou stroked her abdomen and exhaled through rounded lips. A Braxton Hicks moment. "Me…too."

Tess sat up straight. "I apologize for what I said about Drake earlier. I apologize for my own sinful pride. My class should have boycotted me years ago."

Natalie stared.

Tess twisted her head to the right, then to the left, yanked on her blazer lapels, and cleared her throat. The director was getting down to business. "I've harbored concern about our pastor in recent months. He has become too full of himself. Although I am sure he would retract what he said about the Marthas, one does not banish—not even momentarily in anger—the teacher of a two hundred-member women's Bible study class, many of whom have influential husbands. There will be fallout. This plan is absolutely ridiculous and probably nowhere near biblical in principle, but I see no other recourse." She paused. "My core ladies will hear of it tonight."

Natalie nodded somberly. Enlisting the support of the Martha Mavens wasn't exactly a sweet victory.

Forty-Eight

By the time the Martha Mavens had finished praying together, Susan's fears were long gone. Every aspect of the bizarre situation had been presented to the King of kings. She knew in her heart that He would be glorified. Nothing else mattered.

"Amen." Mildred smiled. "So be it."

Pure peace lit the elderly prayer warrior's face. Everyone else appeared slightly dazed.

Emmylou said, "Wow. He really is here, isn't He?"

Soft laughter rippled around the circle of women. Susan was convinced of His presence because for the first time in her life she had prayed out loud unself-consciously.

Natalie stood. "Is anyone else hungry?"

Plans were made for dinner. Natalie, Gwyn, and Tess left to buy takeout Chinese. Emmylou needed a nap and went to a bedroom. Leona busied herself in the kitchen and set the table.

Susan slid to the rug and sat next to Mildred's feet.

"You're humming, Susan." Mildred leaned over and touched her cheek still damp from tears.

"Am I?" *Jesus Christ is risen today, Alleluia!* The words revealed themselves now. *Our triumphant holy day, Alleluia!*

"I saw you in the choir, dearie." She winked. "You haven't participated for years."

"I started singing again."

"God is moving in you. He is faithful. He gave you that voice for His purposes."

Susan reached up to Mildred's lap and held on to her hand. "Am I betraying my husband?"

"On the contrary, you may be saving him." She adjusted her glasses. "I haven't wanted to tell you, but it's time you knew. The rumblings began long before yesterday's incident. We've heard it among the seniors for quite a while. Tess named it when she said Drake is becoming too full of himself. With the phenomenal growth Holy Cross Fellowship has experienced in recent years, it's understandable. But how long will it be acceptable? Last night Leona and I fellowshipped with a group made up of all ages. We overheard disturbing comments. They were just murmured. There was no railing against our pastor. It was obvious, however, that his announcement left a bitter taste in many a mouth and not for the reason he would imagine. No one thinks less of him because of Kenzie's situation."

A chill ran down Susan's spine. "He's lost his way."

"We all do in some way or other. His digression is a little more public than ours. He feels if he admits it, we will abandon him. I want to show him the very opposite is true."

"I should…" *be by his side.* Another chill froze the words in her throat. If she were by his side, he would need her to support him. In the past, that always meant agreeing with him, no questions asked. If she dared voice her own opinion, he could not accept it. His resentment toward her relegated her to the category of…of— "Mildred, I feel like a *concubine!* Like my only purpose in life is to…is to…make him feel good! I can't go back and support him by telling him he's right."

She patted Susan's hand. "Shh, now. God will carry you through this. We prayed for Drake to receive God's healing touch. When that's revealed, you two will be restored in a healthy marriage."

"I can't see that. I see myself asking Rex for the name of a divorce lawyer!"

"That seeing is not from our Lord."

"I wish I had your faith."

"You do, dearie. You do. It simply takes practice to recognize it and to keep leaning on it." Mildred smiled. "Now just quiet yourself."

Susan closed her eyes and Mildred smoothed her hair.

"Give that awful thought to Jesus. He'll throw it away. He doesn't want you to have it."

I don't want it either, Lord. I don't want to even consider divorce a possibility.

"Think on things that are true and honorable and upright and pure."

Only Jesus fit that description. She thought what a beautiful thing it would be if instead of Mildred, He sat in that chair and caressed her head.

After a few moments, Mildred said, "What do you hear?"

She heard what she'd been hearing at the beach house all along. "Music."

Mildred chuckled. "Zephaniah 3:17."

Susan looked up at her.

"'He will rejoice over you with happy song.'"

Susan smiled, listened for the pitch, and then began to sing aloud. "'Hymns of praise, then, let us sing, Alleluia! Unto Christ our heavenly King, Alleluia!'"

Forty-Nine

"You okay?" Pepper braked the van at a stoplight and eyed Kenzie in the passenger's seat.

"Sure." The girl gazed straight ahead, her voice a monotone.

"You don't have to do this. I mean, a slumber party with three middle-aged women at the beach on a Tuesday night?"

"Achoo!" She turned to Pepper, a wide grin spread across her face.

"I guess that means I've already annoyingly voiced this opinion once or twice."

"Uh-huh."

She moaned. "I am supposed to be salt! Why can't I be salt, Lord? Doesn't a rose by any other name smell as sweet? Doesn't salt by any other name—even by the name of *pepper*—doesn't it preserve and make things taste just right?"

"Light's green."

Pepper drove, tortoise speed along the crowded boulevard near the beach. It was the week of spring break for hordes of youth who descended upon Southern California. Parking anywhere near the house was out of the question. Parking within two miles of it was impossible.

"Pepper, are you okay?"

"Sure."

"You're making that mumbo-jumbo sound."

"Oh, man! Is nothing sacred? How do you know about my mumbo-jumbo noise? Aidan doesn't even know about it!"

Kenzie giggled. "Actually, he does. Mick told him years ago how when you start doing it, that means you're up to something."

"Well, I am not up to anything."

"You don't have to do this either. I mean, a slumber party with my mom and aunt—two women you've just met—and me?"

She inched the van forward. "Yeah, I do have to do this. My ship-mate called."

"From the Grandmas out of Wedlock Boat?"

"Grandmas and Aunts. Besides, it sounds like fun. A night away from the three little ones. Pizza, popcorn, sappy videos—if your aunt remembers to bring a television—and girl talk. Sign me up."

"I'm not too sure Mom knows how to make girl talk."

"Maybe she's ready to try. My concern is that I don't want to intrude. I want her to be able to make girl talk with you." A new sensitivity toward her chafing, peppery personality had mushroomed overnight. She blamed it on the fast. Aidan's incessant fake sneezing the previous day could have had a hand in it as well.

"You won't intrude. My mom really likes you."

"Well, there is that boat thing we have in common."

"Do you like my mom?" Kenzie resumed her monotone delivery, a hint again that something bothered her about the night's outing.

"Yes, I like her."

"I'm not sure if I do."

Pepper waited for more. When none came, she said, "Understandable. I don't like Mick when he doesn't do what I need him to do. You've been through a rough few months when you needed your mom in ways she wasn't able to meet."

"The thing is, I'm not sure if I can trust her."

There it was, the thing that bothered Kenzie.

The comment hung in the air. Pepper didn't want to touch it. She refused to get between Susan and her daughter.

At least not any more than she already was.

Did Susan understand that Kenzie could not trust her? Was that why she invited Pepper to the party? Because she needed a buffer?

Yeah. It made sense. Susan needed some salt…to make things taste just right.

Okay. She could live with that.

⌒

Standing in the beach house kitchen, Kenzie gawked at her mother. "A boycott? Are you crazy?"

Pepper contorted her lips to keep from laughing out loud. The girl said exactly what she would have said if she weren't so busy trying to be salt.

Susan turned off the stove top burner under a whistling pot and grinned. "I've definitely gone round the bend. Shall we sit outside? Spring is in the air."

"Dad will never put up with it." Kenzie picked up a plate of freshly baked peanut butter cookies.

"Isn't that the whole point of a boycott, though?" She poured hot water into waiting mugs. "He doesn't have a choice but to put up with it."

"He'll go ballistic in that subtle way of his."

"Probably."

The three of them carried mugs of tea to the patio table and sat less than twenty feet from the boardwalk. Pepper glanced toward it. Talk about crazy. Spring break was undoubtedly at its peak. Throngs of mostly young people jammed the pavement. Bikers and blade skaters crept along on their wheels. Joggers shuffled in place waiting for a chance to get around walkers. Although the sun waned and the air chilled, scantily clad sunbathers lingered on the sand.

Kenzie held her head at an angle, as if in disbelief of her mother's news. "All the Marthas are in on this?"

"Mildred is the ringleader. She suggested it to Aunt Nattie in the first place. Even before Sunday."

Kenzie broke apart a cookie. "You mean they were riled up before his little speech?"

Susan had told them about Drake's announcement during the service, how he hadn't asked directly for prayer for Kenzie. Pepper thought for the zillionth time how the poor girl didn't stand a chance.

Susan said, "Well, I guess you could say that. There are several in the congregation who…" Her voice trailed off.

Pepper cringed. *Come on, Susan, don't clam up on your daughter now.*

"Several who what, Mom? You said nobody else knew about me being pregnant except Aunt Nattie and Uncle Rex. Not until you told the Marthas last week."

"That's true. This part isn't about you. I just learned there are others, not the Marthas, who have been…grumbling for a while…about other stuff." She paused. "They think your dad has changed since he first started pastoring at Holy Cross, especially within the past year or so."

"Surprise, surprise. I could have told them that. And it started before last year." She continued snapping pieces off the cookie, never taking a bite. Crumbs piled up on her plate.

Susan said, "Kenzie, when did it start? In your opinion?"

She shrugged a shoulder.

Susan gave her a moment, but she uttered no reply. She rephrased the question. "What was the last *good* time you remember having with him?"

Silence prevailed. From Kenzie's rapid blinking, Pepper deduced she needn't think long and hard to recall the last good time. The girl had visited the memory before.

Finally she said, "It was here in August the year I was twelve. Aunt Nattie and Uncle Rex and the boys were staying at that other beach house down a ways, and we came to spend a day with them. Dad and I worked on a huge sand castle all afternoon." She glanced up with a tiny smile. "He wouldn't even let my bratty cousins smash it." After a moment, she went on. "The next thing I remember was being thirteen and singing a duet with you in church, Mom."

"On Mother's Day the following May."

Kenzie nodded.

Pepper opened her mouth but quickly shut it.

Evidently Susan intuited her unasked question. "He didn't care for our selection. It was an upbeat version of a hymn. Kenzie arranged it. She's always been incredibly gifted. Do you remember it, honey?"

Kenzie scowled.

Susan cleared her throat and then began to sing. "'For the beauty of the earth, for the glory of the skies, for the love which from our birth over and around us lies, Lord of all, to Thee we raise this our hymn of grateful praise.'"

Goosebumps prickled Pepper's arms. "Your voice is incredible!"

Susan smiled. "Thanks. That was how we sang the first verse. Then we started snapping our fingers." She demonstrated. "And the pianist joined in. Ta-da boom. Ta-da boom. Second verse. 'For the wonder of each hour of the day and of the night—'"

"Hold it! Hold it!" Kenzie raised her hand in a stop gesture. "No, no, no. That's not it. Wait a sec. Let me think." She hummed and snapped and bobbed her head. "Okay. Try this. 'For the wonder of each hour of the day and of the night, hill and vale and tree and flower, sun and moon and stars of light, Lord of all, to Thee we raise this our hymn of grateful praise.'"

The voice of an angel.

"'For the joy,'" the angel's mother joined in, "'of human love, brother, sister, parent, child…'"

Their voices wove in and out of each other's, complementing, enriching. They finished with a cascade of "amens" and some passersby cheered. Pepper felt transported to another time and place. Words were inadequate to express her reaction.

Kenzie stood up and bowed toward the applause.

Susan grinned. "Yes, that was it."

The girl sat back down, her smile fading quickly.

"Sweetheart," her mother said, "I'm sorry I didn't stick up for you that day. I'm sorry for all the times I didn't. Like I said before, I hope you'll forgive me, in time, for your own sake. And I hope you'll forgive your father too."

"It was like he smashed every sand castle I ever made," she whispered.

"I know."

Kenzie sniffed a few times. "Hey, I thought this was supposed to be a slumber party for fun."

"It is!" Susan smiled and handed her a napkin. "That's why I invited Pepper. She's very good at spicing things up, don't you think?"

Mother and daughter turned to her expectantly.

Pepper grabbed a napkin and pressed it to her face. Who needed salt or pepper? The Starr women were more than enough spice for any party.

Fifty

Natalie figured she'd lined up all her ducks in a perfect row. Slumber party accoutrements were loaded in the car: a portable combination television-VCR and a batch of sappy chick flicks. Carpool duties fell to another mom; her boys had a ride home from baseball practice. The high school girls soccer team she coached had finished practice early. A pasta casserole was in the oven, a favorite dinner of all three of her guys. And—most important—Rex had accepted his role in the boycott. He promised to have a heart-to-heart with his brother soon.

In the kitchen she grabbed car keys from a dish and threw her arms around her husband. "You are such a man about this, Rexton Starr."

Smiling, he hooked his arms around her waist. "In a good way this time?"

"Mm-hmm, definitely."

"Why? Because I agree with your wacky idea?"

"Yep. Not every guy is man enough to say his wife is right."

He kissed her soundly on the lips. "Have fun tonight."

"Thanks."

The doorbell rang. She hesitated a split second before following him into the living room. It was time for her to go. But someone was at the door.

Rex pulled it open and there stood Drake. The word *apoplectic* came to mind. His face was beet red and his breathing loud and irregular.

Natalie could have sworn she heard wings flap as every single one of her ducks flew away.

She really didn't want to be there.

Rex pulled his brother inside. "Drake, what's wrong? Come in and sit down. Nat, get some water."

While Rex steered him toward the couch, she went back into the kitchen. Filling a glass with water, she longingly eyed the door that led to the garage and her packed car. Obviously Rex could have his talk right now. She would only be in the way. Drake seldom took her seriously. The wise thing to do was skedaddle. Her keys were still in her hand.

The same hand holding on to the faucet.

"Ick." She and her family never drank tap water, but there she was, ready to offer it up to her brother-in-law.

She flipped off the faucet, dumped the glassful down the sink, and refilled it with water from the bottled gallon in the fridge. How in the world could she totally bypass such an ingrained habit? Was she that strung out over the situation? That ticked off?

That angry at Drake?

The truth was, she didn't take him seriously either. Deep down she considered him a joke. He could teach well, and he did offer unique biblical insights, but ages before news of Kenzie's pregnancy, Natalie blamed him for Susan's inability to express her own opinion about anything under the sun. If she thought long and hard enough about it, she could probably blame him for all manner of ills, from her team's current losing streak to Southern California drought conditions.

She groaned. *Oh, Lord. Are we having a conversation?*

Of course He and she were.

"Okay, okay. I'm sorry. I don't take him seriously. I treat him as disrespectfully as I perceive he treats me. Not exactly the spirit of Your golden rule. I suppose I should do something about this?"

She pressed her lips together and inhaled deeply, her best attempt at listening. Susan was not the problem. Kenzie was not the problem. Drake was the problem—or Natalie herself was.

He's just like my dad. Always insists on being king of the hill. At least my dad had the decency to leave us alone.

The pain cut through her chest, almost as sharp as a real knife slicing through it.

Her father left the family when she was fourteen, never to be heard from again. He fell off the face of the earth and none too soon. She'd wished for years that he would disappear. After he was gone, peace filled their home and they all laughed again, she, her two sisters, and their mom, who made a solid living as a teacher.

But…there was always a hole. Even with God's healing touch on her heart, some hurt remained when she let it surface.

She whispered, "And I resent Drake for hurting Susan and Kenzie."

You need to let it go. Your resentment is not going to fix anything. You need to forgive both of them, Drake and your dad.

"I can't."

But Jesus could. He already had.

"I don't want to. They don't deserve…"

Oh, as though she deserved forgiveness?

Natalie wiped tears from her eyes. What was going on? All she wanted was to leave and have a fun night off with Susan and Kenzie and Pepper. All she wanted was for Rex to explain things to Drake in her absence.

But Drake came while she was at home, and now she held a cup of cold water in her hand. The right thing to do was to give it to the guy.

In Jesus' name.

⌣

"It's all your wife's fault."

At Drake's words, Natalie slowed her entry into the living room.

Rex said in his firmest attorney voice, "It is not her fault, and I refuse to listen to you talk like that, so knock it off."

Go, Rex! She walked over to the couch where the men sat and held the glass out to Drake.

"I don't want your water."

Rex took it from her. "For crying out loud, Drake, stop acting like a whiny brat and drink some." He said to her, "He got wind of the Good Friday plans already."

Not sure yet if she trusted herself to speak in any sort of gracious manner, she gave him a silent questioning stare and sat on the edge of a chair.

He mouthed a board member's name. No surprise. The Martha Mavens expected word would get out to people who didn't agree with their tactics. Natalie only wished it had taken a little longer.

Drake gulped down half the water and glowered at her. "If you hadn't insisted on Susan going to the beach house in the first place, none of this would have happened."

Rex said, "Hold it right there. You've brought this on yourself, Drake. People are grumbling about you and have been for some time."

"That's unavoidable considering the size of my church."

"*Your* church?"

Drake never chewed gum, but his jaw worked as if he'd popped in a piece. Finally words came. "You know what I mean."

"I think you mean *your* church. And that's the problem. You're so caught up in appearances, you're losing sight of the good work God is doing there—through you. He is using you, but you seem to be pointing more to yourself than to Him."

"How do I do that?" His tone scoffed.

"You don't let your heart show anymore." Rex's voice went soft. "I remember when Kenzie was the apple of your eye and you did a series of sermons about how God taught you lessons through her. This past Sunday, when you had the opportunity to reveal your broken heart and ask for prayer for her, you didn't even mention her name. Not once."

Wow. Rex was not following in the least Natalie's suggested tactics.

He went on. "You can make all the excuses you want, Drake, but you're pushing your family and your congregation away. You're keeping them at arm's length when they desperately need a leader who is real, one who's been where they are and isn't afraid to show his pain."

"You don't know what you're talking about."

"Okay, I don't know what I'm talking about." He could be so incredibly diplomatic. "The boycott is simply about a small group of women who are mad at you because— Because why?"

"Because they don't understand how it's necessary to express love by shunning one who continues to engage in a sin."

"Hmm." Rex leaned forward, elbows on knees. "Or—just thinking out loud here—perhaps they do understand all that. Which is why they've decided to shun one of your services, to express their love for you." He paused.

"That's a bunch of baloney. What sin is it I'm supposedly continuing to engage in?"

"Pride."

He barked a laugh and cast a glare at Natalie. "Who told you that?"

"Nobody," Rex said. "Nobody had to. I see it when you don't reveal yourself from the pulpit. I see it when ten families leave the church in two months and not one new one joins. I see it in boycott plans made because a bunch of men and women, not just the Martha Mavens, love you. Drake." Rex reached over and grasped his brother's arm. "Get off your high horse. You look like you did your senior year of basketball when Coach benched you time and again for refusing to pass the ball."

Drake stood abruptly. "You always did see things differently."

"But I came over to your side."

He frowned.

"Or God's side, I should say. Who do you think faithfully showed me the way all those years I was running from Him? Who besides Faith Fontaine and my wife prayed me through my recovery after the accident? That's the brother I want back. And if it takes a boycott to pull him out from behind his mask, well, I guess you won't see me Friday night."

Without a word, Drake strode to the door, yanked it open, and left.

So profuse were her own tears, Natalie almost didn't see the ones streaming down Rex's face.

Fifty-One

Susan stared at Natalie beside her on the seawall. Her sister-in-law had just relayed the conversation that took place a short while ago between their husbands. "It's as if Rex told Drake we're going to give him a dose of his own medicine."

"That's exactly what he told him."

"Oh, my."

"You can say that again."

"Oh, my. I never imagined all this...this fallout about a private family matter."

"Well, in a sense you're not allowed private family matters. You're sort of public people to us. But it's been coming for a while, Suze. You didn't start this. We lost members in January and February."

"We did?"

"Ten families and none replaced them. We've had visitors, but not a single person has officially joined during that time."

"I had no idea..."

Now Natalie's eyes widened in disbelief. "No idea?"

"Drake doesn't talk about those business matters...They must have been people who didn't cross my path?"

"Probably. Since you quit running the Sunday school, your path hasn't made much of a wide swath. But the point is, that happened as well as what Mildred and Leona told us about people noticing things amiss with Drake. And now Tess just called and said her core women and their husbands have felt the same way. They didn't have the nerve to tell her before."

"You've been crying."

Natalie nodded.

Her sister-in-law never cried. "Oh, my."

Natalie's shoulders lifted as she inhaled. "I know I've resented Drake because he reminds me of my dad. I never really saw the goodness in him that you and Rex did. He can teach, I give him that." She paused. "I asked God's forgiveness and Rex's. Maybe I'll ask for Drake's some day. Now I'm asking for yours because I've influenced you negatively toward your husband. I haven't been the best sister-in-law or parishioner."

Susan leaned over and wrapped her arms around Natalie. "You've been a good friend to me. But if you think you've had wrongful attitudes toward him, I forgive you." She straightened.

"Thank you. So." She pressed the heels of her hands to her eyes for a moment and then looked up, the bloodshot whites even redder. "Rex believes—in spite of Drake's nonresponse—that we might have hit a nerve. He's praying that once it all sinks in, Drake will see his pride for what it is."

"And that his heart will melt."

Natalie blinked. "That's exactly what Mildred said when I called her on my way down here."

"Amen." Susan grinned. "Come on, let's go get the pizza. I promised Kenzie fun, and this subject is definitely not on that track. It's time to let it go for a while and party. Party hearty, as they say!"

⌒

The next morning Susan and Kenzie stood on the patio, waiting for Natalie and Pepper to finish packing their things.

Susan embraced her daughter in a long hard hug, mindful not to squish Pugsy tucked under her daughter's arm. "I had such a good time, honey."

"Me too."

They parted and smiled at each other.

"Did you really? With us old women?"

"Really. You and Aunt Nattie and Pepper are the goofiest bunch of old women I've ever known."

"It's that boat thing, you know." She fluttered her eyelashes. "It brings out the goofiness in grandmas and aunts."

Kenzie groaned, but Susan caught the lift at the corner of her mouth. The slumber party had been a success: lots of laughter, lots of silliness, lots of openness.

"Hey, Kenzie, did you see June Cleaver last night?"

Her daughter burst into laughter. "No. I'm beginning to think you killed her off."

"I certainly hope so. That woman should have been, at the very least, muzzled a long time ago." She hugged her again. "I love you, sweetheart. Thank you for coming."

"Thank you for asking me." Kenzie's muffled voice was barely audible against Susan's shoulder. "I love you too."

Susan wondered how her feet stayed put on the ground.

Fifty-Two

Pepper drove her van along the crowded freeway, unable to erase what had to be one major perky smile off her face. From the passenger seat, Kenzie chirped away, apparently voicing every happy thought that entered her mind.

When the girl slowed long enough to take a breath, Pepper said, "If you don't mind my saying—"

"If I don't mind? Now that's a *salty* thing to say!"

She laughed. "Not the usual blast of opinion with both barrels, huh? I guess I've lost my peppery edge, so I guess that means prayer works. Anyway, if you don't mind my saying, you seem more at peace after the slumber party than you did going into it."

Kenzie flashed her impish grin. "I guess that's because I am!"

"What happened?"

"I had a surprisingly good time. Everybody was so totally relaxed. So totally real, even my mom."

"She set the tone for the whole event."

"Yeah? Yeah. I guess she did. Aunt Nattie helped, but she kept saying how this and that was Mom's idea."

"It's very mature of you to be able to give her the credit."

"It's easy to when she's not hung up on looking perfect. Wow. She has come a long way since I told her I was pregnant."

From the corner of her eye, Pepper noticed Kenzie slip a fingertip into her mouth and bite on the nail. "Kenzie, I think God is using your situation to show her she doesn't need to be perfect, but it's not your fault, not the tough stuff."

"What's going to happen to them?"

"Your parents?" Pepper steered down an exit ramp. "They will get through this. Your mom wants reconciliation. Why wouldn't your dad want it too? They'll find their way."

"He's as bullheaded as a mule." She lowered her hand and smiled. "Kind of like me."

"What do you think would get through to him? When you've been bullheaded, what's made you change your mind?"

"Morning sickness." She laughed. "I guarantee a good dose of barfing would give him a new outlook."

Pepper chuckled with her. "So maybe we pray he gets stomach flu?"

Kenzie giggled again.

"Seriously, morning sickness made you view things differently?"

"Sort of. The thing was, I couldn't control it. Yuck. Constant nausea. That made me realize I couldn't really control anything anymore." She shrugged, all traces of smiles gone. "But I dug my heels in deeper, like he's doing now. Like he will do with this boycott thing." She shook her head and touched her abdomen. "Then the fluttering started and Mom told me it was the baby moving. All of a sudden, I got tired of trying to control things. Aidan and this baby need me. They need me to be the best me I can be. If I'm behaving like a brainless mule insisting on my own way, thinking that's control, I'm not really much good to them at all."

Pepper blinked away tears, reached over, and patted Kenzie's arm. "Okay. So we pray your dad experiences a fluttering of new life inside of him."

Kenzie sighed dramatically. "I don't know. I kind of like the upchucking visual better."

Pepper held her breath as long as she could. Then the laugh rumbled and burst forth.

So much for being salt-like.

Still grinning, Pepper braked at the curb, a loading zone outside Aidan's apartment building. "I'll get your backpack." She hopped from the van and hurried around to the other side.

"Pepper, I've got it." Kenzie was already out and sliding open the back door. "I'm not an invalid."

"Stop trying to control things."

She smiled and backed away from the car. "Touché. You get my bag."

"Thank you."

"Sure. Will you carry it upstairs for me too? Maybe even unpack it while you're there?"

"Sorry, no. I don't want to get a parking ticket." She wrapped her arms around the girl. "I only got out so I could give you a proper hug."

Kenzie laughed and returned the embrace. "You are too funny, Pepper."

"Mom!"

Pepper turned and saw Aidan jogging toward them, down the short sidewalk from the building's front door, a gym bag bouncing at his side. He must have spotted them from a window and hurried outside. Reaching them now, he puffed. There was no welcoming smile on his face.

"Aidan? What's wrong?"

"It's Dad. There was an accident."

Life drained from Pepper. Like receiving a giant shot of instant-acting novocaine, her body went numb from head to toe. Aidan, Kenzie, the bright blue sky, and the apartment building faded from view.

Mick!

"He's in the hospital." They were holding her arms, steering her into the van, up onto the front passenger seat.

"What happened?"

"Somebody hit him. A car. A *small* car."

She moaned.

"George called." He named Mick's boss. "Dad told him to call me first. So Dad was okay enough to tell him that. Which is good, right?" Aidan crouched in front of her, brushing his hands up and down her forearms. "The doctor's doing X-rays and stuff now. George didn't know anything else yet."

Pepper started to cry.

"I talked to the girls. We all agree I should drive you up there right now. We'll be with him in three hours. Do you need to go home for anything?"

She shrugged.

Kenzie said, "You've got your toothbrush and pj's. Go."

Still paralyzed with fear, Pepper sensed only one thing. "Pray. Kenzie, you'll pray?"

"Of course." She hugged her. "I'll even get word to the Marthas. One thing I know for sure about them, they know how to pray up a storm."

Fifty-Three

"Susan! Is that you?"

Sitting on the seawall facing the ocean, Susan turned to see Julian saunter across the boardwalk. She gave him a questioning glance. "Hi."

"You look like a new woman! I almost didn't recognize you."

She grinned. A week ago, before the haircut, he waved to her as he drove away. They hadn't seen each other since then.

He tilted his head this way and that, eyeing her from every angle. "New hairstyle. New clothing style. Very nice. Very nice indeed."

"Thank you."

"Not to say your appearance was ever disagreeable."

A flush warmed her cheeks.

"I'm sorry, Susan. Your husband would not be pleased with the forward neighbor. I apologize for causing you discomfort."

"Oh, it's not that! On the contrary, you have a gift for making me feel safe." She pressed her hands against her cheeks. "I'm just turning pink because I'm delighted someone would notice."

Smiling, he crossed his arms and slid sideways onto the wall. "Actually, I think it's something beyond the physical changes that has captured my attention. There seems to be an inner glow emanating from you. Hmm. Might I deduce the sabbatical is working?"

She laughed and nodded. "Yes, I think you might deduce such a thing. I believe that's exactly what's happening."

"Marvelous. What do you credit? The time away from your ordinary world?"

"Yes, and other things. There's Faith's house dripping with peace and joy. Friends and their prayers and laughter. We had a baby shower here, and last night I hosted a slumber party. You'll never guess who came. Well, besides my sister-in-law, Natalie."

"Who?"

"Kenzie and the boy's mother!"

He widened his eyes behind the glasses in an exaggerated way. "No!"

"Yes!"

He laughed with her. "That's wonderful."

"It is." She basked in the shared moment. "So much has happened. Have you been gone? I haven't seen you for a while."

"Yes. I've been in Florida visiting my son and his wife." He pulled at his jaw a few times, and then a broad grin broke out. "And my very first grandchild. A boy. I was right there when he was born. Well, right there in the next room."

"Julian! You're a grandfather! Congratulations!"

"Thank you." His face almost could not contain the smile. "I must say, there is nothing to compare it to. It's quite indescribable. You will love it, Susan, in spite of the difficult circumstances your family is in at the moment." He grew somber. "I may have told you or Natalie about my divorce many years ago. Naturally, that was the main reason I fiddled with the bullet in my pocket."

She nodded. She knew the story of how his business consumed him and his wife left, how she remarried out east and another man raised Julian's children. Only in recent years had his grown children begun to reconnect with him.

"And now," he said, "I was invited for the birth. Imagine that! It's a second chance to love a wee one in the right way."

She blinked back tears.

"Susan, I guarantee Drake will see life differently when he holds that baby. Just never, never give up on him."

Alone again in the beach house, Susan sat in her favorite spot by the window, cell phone in hand, Pugsy snoring on her lap. Julian's words echoed in her mind. *Just never, never give up on him.* They kindled a flame of hope.

"But, Lord, it's so hard to take another first step toward him!"

She reminded herself of last night's laughter and smiled. In the midst of silliness, the women had related on a level deeper than she thought possible. Kenzie, Natalie, and Pepper—all three of them—had mellowed almost beyond recognition. They insisted, however, that if it came to a vote, she won first prize for the most unrecognizable.

She agreed. She pinched her arm now in an effort to convince herself she wasn't dreaming. Positive developments nearly eclipsed all the shadows on her horizon. Communication lines with her daughter and Aidan's mother were wide open. The Martha Mavens hovered about her like guardian angels. She—shy little Susie Anderson—was on the same prayer wavelength as Mildred, the prayer warrior of all prayer warriors. A big soft spot in her heart enveloped the formerly intimidating Tess Harmon. Susan felt like a joyful bird who couldn't stop singing. What more could she want?

Besides reconciliation with Drake.

Even in her atypically weepy state, Natalie had taken issue with Susan's desire to call him. "Let God have His way with him," she said.

Susan replied, "You sound like Drake condemning Kenzie. 'Let her suffer the consequences, then she'll turn back to God.'"

Natalie cricked her neck, twisting her head in that way of hers while she considered how much opinion to verbalize and how much to hold back. "It's close, but not the same thing."

"Kenzie came back after I contacted her. After I expressed as best I could my unconditional love for her. How can I not offer Drake the same thing?"

Natalie had shrugged, but tears glistened in her eyes.

Just never, never give up on him.

Susan opened her phone and pressed Drake's cell number.

"Susan." Drake answered his phone on the first ring by saying her name.

Susan's chest felt the same way it did when she heard Handel's "Hallelujah Chorus." What did one do with such joy except sing?

She restrained herself and only whispered in her heart a prayer of thanks. Drake recognized her number on his caller ID! He evidently had the phone at his fingertips! Was he eager to hear from her?

"Drake. Hi." A nervous giggle escaped.

"Hi."

"I…I was just wondering how you are."

No reply.

"Drake?"

"I'm here. I'm…well, I guess you could say I'm not myself. Which, according to some people, might be a good thing." He heaved a sigh. "I didn't mean for you not to come home."

"I know."

"Or for your friends not to come to church." There was no hint of condescension in his tone.

"I know. And that has nothing to do with why they're planning— But how are you?" She didn't want to talk about the other thing yet. "Are you eating and sleeping?"

"More or less. How are you?"

"I'm doing really well." She recalled Julian's description; it said it best. "The sabbatical is working."

She heard his sharp intake of breath.

Withholding a quick reply to downplay how great she felt—she didn't want to sound calloused to his depressed state—Susan placed a hand at her chest and prompted herself. *No more straitjacket. No more binding myself.*

He had to hear the truth about her as well as things about his daughter. The tension drained away.

She said, "Kenzie spent last night with me. We got along fine. Probably the best we have in years."

"Hmm."

"She's working at a coffee shop. She's been to a doctor. The baby's heartbeat is strong and regular. She's healthy. The band is scheduled to record a CD. Aidan keeps busy writing music. And they have quite a number of engagements scheduled, weddings and parties. Sometimes the guys play in clubs. Not Kenzie, of course, since she's not old enough." Whew. She'd told him everything, even the part about bars. "So I guess that's all her news."

"Hmm."

She didn't let his lack of enthusiasm dismay her. At least he gave a response. At least he was listening. She went on.

"I called to see how you are. I miss you."

"Will you come home?"

"I will when…um, I just…I just need to feel comfortable about you and Kenzie. I need to know that when I call her or go see her or when she comes to the house, you'll be all right. You won't condemn our relationship or…or send us away."

"What about Friday night?"

His subject change eluded her. "What do you mean?"

"Your friends' antics."

"My friends—? Oh." The boycott. "Drake, I'm sorry it looks like antics, like they're choosing sides. They simply want to show their concern for all of us. They believe it was the only way to get your attention."

"Well, they were right about that. It got my attention all right. No doubt whatsoever."

"It's understandable if you're furious, but I hope you'll see their love in what—"

"I was furious at first." He paused. "Now I'm confused and hurt."

She ignored the hint of a sulky tone. "Of course. The thing is, they want us back together again. All five of us."

"Five?"

"Five." She waited for him to catch her drift.

It took a moment. "We do not have five people in this family. Kenzie broke us apart. Does your little clique really believe that because they won't be in church Friday night I'll change my mind about our prodigal? Reverse my teaching on letting children suffer consequences?"

"Yes."

"Susan, that is not going to happen."

"Oh!" She didn't hide her instantaneous frustration. "You're as pigheaded as she is! Would what you're doing to Kenzie have worked with you back when we were unwed and pregnant? If you'd been kicked out of seminary, what would you have done?"

"It's a moot point. We got married."

"And didn't have the baby. But if the school found out about us, neither of those would have mattered. It was written in black-and-white right there in the rule book. Intimacy before marriage meant no degree, no support from that institution." Susan felt lightheaded, as if her brain were cut off from oxygen. She couldn't think about what she said; the words shot straight out from her heart. "We lied, Drake. We lied. At least Kenzie's not hypocritical. Not letting her come home is condemning her to a death in the same way you would have been condemned to a death. Getting kicked out of that school would have ruined your life. Your rejection of Kenzie cuts a hole so deep in her heart it will never go away."

She ran out of words.

Drake did not respond for a few seconds. "Susan, I don't know you anymore. You're like a stranger."

"Then let me introduce myself." Evidently she had more things to say. "I'm Susan Starr and I just discovered Jesus *likes* me. As a matter of fact, He's *crazy* about me. Even when I'm not perfect. I believe He wants me to live accordingly."

Drake didn't reply.

"Does that make sense to you?"

"I have to think about it. I met with a few deacons earlier."

She knew he studiously avoided naming names. He didn't want her image of his board members tainted.

His next words came as no surprise. "They back my position a hundred percent."

Her shoulders sagged, and she didn't bother to ask which exact details he'd told them that they would support.

"In the interest of all fairness, I'm meeting with some others later today."

"All right."

"All right."

Silence.

"Drake, are we making any headway?"

"Does it feel like it?"

"I don't know. Is this how it is when you counsel married couples?"

"How do you mean?"

"Do they feel sort of...unfinished after a session?"

"I...I've never been on this end." His voice wavered.

"Should we talk to someone?"

"Between your Marthas and my deacons, I think we're talking to quite enough people, thank you very much." He was backing off, gaining control again.

"I meant to a marriage counselor about us."

"I don't think the church could handle that. Besides, I am a marriage counselor. I'd better go."

I quit, Lord! A flash of anger cut that line of thinking. She would not quit! She was not going to be defeated. By the grace of God, she would not quit.

"All right, Drake. I just called to say I love you and that I'm here for you."

"I'd much rather you were saying that from *here*."

She waited a long moment, hoping for any sort of expression of his love. It didn't come. Which was okay. Her unconditional love for him was independent of any reciprocation. Right? Right.

"Goodbye, then."

"Yes. Goodbye." Crisp. Efficient.

She closed up her phone and told herself he and Kenzie were exactly alike. They could push each other's buttons for the remainder of their lives and neither boycotts nor babies nor a broken marriage would change their minds.

Fifty-Four

"Call it off, Natalie." Susan's voice nearly squeaked.

Natalie moved the phone from her ear. She must look like an idiot walking through a parking lot pushing a cartful of groceries, frowning at a cell she held at arm's length. No doubt she had looked silly inside the store as well. During the entire checkout process she listened to Susan's woeful tale of a conversation with Drake. What felt like permanent grooves carved themselves into her forehead.

At last the urge to shout at her sister-in-law passed and she replaced the phone to her ear. "Susan, you're going monkey on me. Come on, girl, get a grip. The straitjacket is gone. Drake is not in your head screening every jot and tittle. Jesus, the Lord Himself, is right there with you and He's crazy about you."

"Call it off! A few people skipping church is not going to faze him. He will not budge from his convictions."

"Do you doubt God's ability to melt his heart?"

Susan went quiet.

"Of course you don't. Things seem a little scary at the moment, that's all."

"He's digging his heels in deeper."

"So God will just have to yank a little harder."

"I don't want the church to split over this."

"It won't, Suze."

"This is how splinter groups form."

"Listen." She reached her SUV, opened the back end, and unloaded groceries while she talked. "Those of us involved simply want Drake to know we're concerned. We're the ones who care deeply about him. We'll be there for Easter. We'll be there to work from the inside, praying you all through this time. We don't want to go anywhere else. We're not condemning Drake. On the contrary, we're rooting for him."

"You're *rooting* for him?"

"I hadn't thought of it like that before, but yeah. That's it! We are. I am. Suze, I told you. I've been in the wrong, always mad at Drake. I don't want to be like that anymore. Oh, hon, are you crying?"

"I don't know how to root for him."

Natalie listened to her sniffle and pushed the cart to a return slot. How could Susan root for him? He hadn't responded to her need. He hadn't promised he would stop disapproving of her relationship with Kenzie. She was so torn, still forced to choose between her husband and her daughter. Should she go home? What about their vacation schedule for next week?

"Suze, his vacation time starts Monday. Is he coming to the beach?"

"We…we didn't talk about it. I have no idea what to expect."

Natalie sighed and climbed into her car. "You know what Mildred would say to expect. Expect God to show up."

"I'm losing hope."

"Glory."

"What?"

"Glory. I'm not sure. The word just popped into my head. 'Glory!' Go sing, Suze. Go walk with Pugsy on the beach. Walk and walk and sing and sing. That's how you root for Drake. God inhabits the praises of His people. Praise Him and He will show up and He will melt Drake's heart."

Natalie propped her arm on the steering wheel and rubbed her forehead, listening to silence from Susan's end for what felt like minutes.

At last there was a final sniffle and she cleared her throat. "All right. 'Glory be to the Father.'" She sang the words. "'And to the Son, and to the Holy Ghost.'"

"What is that?"

"The 'Gloria Patri.' Second Century traditional. 'As it was in the beginning, is now, and ever shall be, world without end. Amen, amen.'"

"And amen."

Fifty-Five

As Kenzie imagined Aidan and Pepper speeding toward Los Angeles, she carefully inched his van into the carport beside her mother's sensible white four-door car. There really wasn't enough space for it. The rear bumper stuck way out into the alley, but that was the least of her worries. She crunched the parking brake and shut off the engine. It shook and shuddered and rattled.

And then she did the same.

"Oh, God."

Mick couldn't die. He couldn't. Pepper might be the heart of the Carlucci family, but Mick was the soul. He was the essence. He kept them together. All the kids adored him. Kenzie totally adored him. And how she loved Aidan!

She totally adored the entire family. They had taken her in when her life fell apart.

Still…she wasn't a Carlucci. She might be carrying one, but she wasn't one. Aidan didn't need her by his side. He didn't need her to work on his latest composition because, unlike ones of the recent past, he hadn't shared it with her. Pepper didn't need her to take care of Mickey Junior or the other young ones. Mick didn't need her at the hospital.

"Oh, God!"

She shuddered again. Unhooking the seat belt took a while. Only the sight of her mother's car cut through the anxious thoughts that clung like black cobwebs jamming her mind. Her mom was near. Traces of last night's slumber party beckoned. Peace and laughter.

Kenzie made her way around to the front of the beach house and approached the door. She didn't want to knock. She wanted to be a little girl bursting into the house with news. She wanted to be *home*.

As she touched the doorknob, the door opened and her mother greeted her with a fading smile. "Kenzie, what is it?"

She stumbled into Susan's open arms and sobbed. "Mommy!"

⌣

Hours later, after tears, the Carlucci family news, Susan's prayer, a nap, milk, cookies and an apple, Kenzie smiled. "At least it was my day off. I didn't miss work."

Her mother sat on the edge of the couch where Kenzie lay and smoothed her hand. "I'm so glad you came, honey. Do you want to call Aidan? They should know something by now."

She shook her head. "He said he would phone when he got a chance. They've got so many other people—*relatives*—to contact. Do you know how many brothers and sisters Pepper has?"

"A lot."

"Yeah. Mick does too."

"Do you want to spend the night here?"

A wave of euphoria swept through her. She didn't think it was a cookie sugar rush. "You mean it?"

"Oh, sweetheart, of course I mean it. What a treat! To have you with me two nights in a row? Wow. This is a slice of heaven. I wish—" She closed her mouth.

"What? You wish what? Come on, Mom, you're into speaking your mind."

She smiled. "Okay. I wish we could spend more time together."

"We have been lately. Maybe it'll catch on."

"You'd be all right with that?"

"Sure. You're different than you used to be. You're not so uptight and perfect anymore and driving me nuts. I don't even feel compelled to call you June!"

She laughed. "Praise God from whom all blessings flow. Do you feel like going outside? There's a couple hours of daylight left. We could just sit or walk with Pugsy."

"Can we play in the sand?"

"The rest of the day is for you to be spoiled. We can do whatever you want."

~

Hunched over in the middle of a small shed in the backyard, Kenzie moved aside wetsuits, a heavy surfboard, fins, boogie boards, beach chairs, and bicycles. "Aha! I knew these were in here."

"What?" her mother asked.

"These." She backed out of the shed, carrying a large mesh bag full of plastic sand toys. "Shovels, buckets, and look! Molds for castles and parapets. Faith Fontaine sure knew how to stock a beach house."

"I was impressed with the tea."

"Tea? It's the beach, Mom! Think sand and ocean."

Susan fluttered her eyes and grunted in disgust. "Whatever!"

Kenzie laughed. Where had this Susan Starr been the past nineteen years? She even wore blue jeans. Baggie ones, but still. They were the first pair Kenzie had ever seen on her. She said Aunt Nattie had bought them.

They plunked down on the sand a little way from the water's edge. The tide was making its slow return. Before getting her hands gritty, Kenzie slid her cell phone from her back pocket and checked for messages again. Of course she would have heard it ring if Aidan had called, but she couldn't help checking anyway.

"Anything, hon?"

"No." She closed up the phone and put it away.

"Why don't you call?"

"I don't want to be in their way." She upended the bag and emptied it. Mickey Junior would enjoy this. Someday maybe she could bring him to the beach.

The lengthy silence between her and Susan grew comfortable. Compatible. Kneeling in the sand, they dug moats, filled molds with wet sand, and constructed towers. Pugsy raced around like a crazy dog and eventually settled into nosing every shell in sight. After a time, Kenzie became lost in the simple activity of playing, oblivious as a kid to the yuckiness of life.

"Kenzie, may I ask something?"

"Just say what you mean, Mom."

"I thought I was doing that."

"No. Why would you ask if you can ask a question instead of just asking it? You're really concerned about something besides the question. Like whether or not I'll go berserk. I bet that's what you mean to say. For good reason. Berserk has always been my modus operandi."

Susan smiled. "All right, here goes. First of all, I hope what I'm about to ask does not set you off. It's just a question, not a backhanded way of giving you advice. Please don't take it as such."

"You got it." Kenzie continued work on the castle, glancing now and then at her jeans-clad mother digging with all the earnestness of an artist creating a permanent masterpiece. "Promise, no berserk-ness."

"Thanks. I'm wondering, do you feel left out of things with the Carluccis? With this emergency?"

"Why should I? Aidan took Pepper to the hospital. It was what he needed to do for his mom and dad. He didn't need me along. I'd just be in the way." She heard the whine in her voice and bit her lip.

They dug in silence for a few moments.

"Kenzie, why do you think you'd be in the way if you went with them or phoned him now?"

Say what you mean, Mom. Well, Susan was doing exactly that, more and more even without Kenzie's not-so-subtle hints. And Pepper always talked real. Seldom shuffling around a subject, she'd give her blast of opinion with both barrels. Why couldn't Kenzie do likewise? She laid down her little plastic shovel, uncurled her legs, and sat in the sand.

"Hon, sometimes we feel things we'd rather not feel. Even your dad says emotions just are. They're not right or wrong."

"If he believes that, he sure has a funny way of showing it."

Susan settled back on her shins, the purple shovel on her lap, and met her eyes.

"Mom, I'm telling you to talk real, but I can't because Dad always tells me what's wrong with how I feel."

"I know," she whispered.

"How do I get over this?"

"Forgiveness is the only way to healing. Forgive me for not intervening. Forgive him for communicating your feelings are wrong. Once you decide you want to, for your own sake, then God will give you the grace and power to forgive."

"You already told me this stuff."

She nodded.

"I'm...not there yet."

"Okay. Let's go back to the other subject about how you feel toward the Carluccis. If you want. I'm learning that it helps me to express my feelings out loud. It seems to soften the rough edges of the pain."

That euphoria gushed through her again. Her mom wasn't forcing her to talk about her dad or about forgiveness. She gave Kenzie the freedom to go a different direction, to be...real. How she wanted to trust her!

Susan said, "But I understand if you're not ready to open up with me."

"I think I need to." The confession flew off her tongue. She followed it. "Aidan didn't invite me to go along. He hardly even acknowledged I was there. I mean, I know he was horribly upset. He loves his dad so much. I just felt totally invisible to him and Pepper. If I were his sister we would have talked. He talked to his sisters and figured everything out about what they should do. They haven't called me, either. I could help with Mickey Junior and the younger girls. I'm just—" She wiped her short sleeve across her face. "I'm not part of the family! That's why I can't call. I don't count! I'm not a Carlucci!"

Susan crawled around the castle and grabbed her in a bear hug.

It was a long, wordless, rocking bear hug. Kenzie's tears flowed, cleansing, healing, freeing. Her mom was her family.

Fifty-Six

As slanting sunbeams glinted directly on Susan and Kenzie's faces, the incoming tide engulfed the castle's moat and lapped at its wall. The late afternoon breeze turned cool. No one else lingered on the beach; few people jogged past. Still they worked, adding wings and buttresses and towers. Susan smiled to herself. A new burst of energy had seized both of them.

She moaned. "Kenzie, we're going to lose it."

"Mom, you didn't think it'd last through the night, did you?"

"Well…"

Her daughter laughed. Dried tear tracks wove unevenly on her sand-dotted cheeks. "It's the nature of sand castles. Here today, gone next high tide. Which usually comes twice a day."

"I never realized how much these castles resemble life. We dream and work and build, as if something so incredibly fragile as life is going to last. Then, before we know it, poof. It's all gone and we're dead."

"Thank you for that depressing observation."

"You're welcome." Susan patted a wall into place. "Maybe they're like the works talked about in the Bible, where it says some will burn up, but others will stand forever because they're made up of eternal elements. We shouldn't worry so much about the transitory stuff." She glimpsed Kenzie's arched brows. "Whoops. There I go preaching again."

"You really ought to get yourself a pulpit." Her tone clearly teased. "But seriously, that can't mean we quit dreaming and working on this life."

"And giving birth and making a home and creating music." Smiling, she shook her head. "I'll get you a pulpit too."

Kenzie laughed, and they returned to their silent construction.

A short while ago, as Kenzie wept in her arms, mother and daughter bridged a great yawning gap that had lain split open so many years between them. Since then, Susan couldn't stop humming and murmuring songs.

Earlier in the day, Susan followed Natalie's advice. She trudged along the beach, forcing herself to sing the entire time. It had been a struggle. The music escaped her. The image of God singing over her faded. But she kept at it, repeating the "Gloria Patri" again and again, the only words she managed to recall.

What felt like hours later, her voice hoarse, her calves aching, she returned to the house. Not exactly carefree, but she was—at the least— no longer hopeless.

And then from the kitchen sink she spotted Kenzie through the window, head down, walking around to the front door.

And then her little girl called her "Mommy."

And then nothing else mattered except closing up that gap.

Now there remained only one thing between them, one fissure unsealed. If she died within the next five minutes, Susan would regret for eternity not attempting to reach over it with her hand toward Kenzie.

"Honey, there is something I've been wanting to tell you about."

"Are you really saying 'don't go berserk' again?"

She shrugged with an air of nonchalance. "You gotta do what you gotta do."

"Way to go, Mom!" Kenzie thrust a shovel skyward and sputtered as sand flew at her mouth. "Bleagh!"

Susan smiled sadly. The movement was so Kenzie, flinging hands and feet and remarks willy-nilly, heedless of consequences. What a handful she had always been! Delightful, yes, but a handful.

"Okay." Kenzie laughed, still brushing sand from her lips. "I'm listening."

"Okay." Susan steadied herself with a deep breath and set aside her shovel. "It's about your dad and me. I had hoped we could talk to you together— What's wrong?"

All color had drained from Kenzie's face and tears welled in her eyes. "You're getting divorced! Because of me!"

"Oh, no, honey! That's not it at all." She leaned over and grasped her forearm. "It's what I mentioned before, that we're dealing with issues from our past. All right?"

Kenzie nodded. Avoiding eye contact, she scooted away, out from Susan's hand and to where Pugsy lay. She lifted the dog onto her lap.

Dear Lord, help! "Okay. You know how your dad and I met at school. I was an undergrad and he was in seminary. This might be hard to believe, but we were absolutely crazy about each other from the first day. I mean, we couldn't get enough of being together. I was your age, nineteen."

She ruffled Pugsy's fur, a tiny smile on her face. "Yeah, that is kind of hard to picture."

"Well, it happened. And ten months later, when I was a little over twenty, I got pregnant."

Kenzie whipped her attention to Susan. Although her mouth hung wide open, she didn't say a word.

"Your dad would have been kicked out of school if anyone knew, the future as he saw it completely ruined. We eloped. We figured if we married right away, the timing would be concealed." She listed the events in a monotone. "A few weeks later, I miscarried. We never told anyone about it." Her voice wavered and tears stung. "You should have known long before now that we are not perfect. I am so sorry we always avoided revealing our true selves to you."

"You were in the same situation I'm in? Pregnant and not married?" Her face reddened. "And Dad has the nerve to *condemn* me?"

Susan had no reply. She could not defend herself or Drake, nor did she want to attack him. Kenzie and Drake's relationship belonged to the two of them. The point of telling her daughter belonged elsewhere.

"The thing is, Kenzie, I don't want you to get married if you're not ready. Your dad and Natalie and Pepper and most of the church would disagree with me. But I know from experience. *I wasn't ready.* The circumstances were wrong. I got married out of shame. Ever since I've been trying to hide it by hiding myself. I guess that's what this stay at the beach house has been all about. It's about me no longer hiding or pretending."

Kenzie still appeared angry and shocked, but she didn't speak.

Susan went on. "I am not saying 'Get married' and I am not saying 'Don't get married.' You and Aidan must decide whether or not and when. Whatever you decide, I'm your mother and this baby's grandmother. You have my full support anyway you need it." She paused. "There is just one other thing. About your living together? You'll have to answer to God about that one. And that's all I have to say."

Kenzie scooted back through the sand. Pugsy yelped at being disturbed, but she ignored him and put her arms around Susan's neck. "Oh, Mom! I love you."

She held her daughter close. "But do you like me?"

Kenzie chuckled. "Yeah, I like you. I think…" Her shoulders heaved. "I think I even trust you."

Thank You, Lord. Thank You. Thank You.

Arm in arm, they slogged through the sand. Twilight had fallen, and they headed to the beach house. Kenzie carried Pugsy under one arm and Susan pulled the bag full of toys. Enough serious discussion and tears had passed to last them the rest of their lives, Susan thought. They were into silly mode.

Kenzie said, "We could do another slumber party. Chick flicks and junk food." She groaned. "I don't think I really mean that. Baby wasn't too happy with last night's pizza and popcorn and chocolate."

"Why don't we go out? To a real restaurant with cute solicitous waiters and lemon in the water and real greens in the salads and seafood with gourmet sauces and yummy desserts?"

"Wow, yeah! But is it in the budget?"

Susan smiled to herself. They had always counted pennies, first out of necessity, and then later in an effort not to appear materialistic. "Your dad hasn't cut me off, at least not yet. Yes, it's in the budget."

"Mom, he wouldn't, would he? Cut you off?"

"I don't think so, but that's sober talk. We called a moratorium, remember?"

"Yep."

They reached the seawall, sat atop it, and swung their legs over. In the distance Susan caught sight of a tall slender man walking away from them. Salt-and-pepper hair styled like Drake's. Why did she keep looking for him? Why was it the hope of reconciliation pestered her like some relentless salesperson?

"Kenzie, there is one more thing."

"Mom!" She chastised as they crossed the boardwalk.

"It's just a little thing. Well, no, it's a pretty big thing. I want to name my baby. Will you help? All those years ago we didn't go to the trouble and expense of finding out why I lost it or if it was a boy or girl. So I want a name like 'Pat' or 'Chris' that would suit either."

"Jordan, Shay, Kai, Shannon, Bailey."

"You've thought about this."

She grinned. "Yeah. My all-time favorite, though, is Jade."

"Jade. That's nice."

"It's beautiful, isn't it? Perfect for either a boy or a girl. Who wouldn't want to be named after a gemstone? I don't know if it's precious or semiprecious, but it conveys color and nature and strength and beauty, all rolled into one."

"Jade. Hmm." They walked through the picket fence gate. She let the name dance around in her mind. By the time they reached the door, it had settled into a niche. "Jade. Yes, I like it. But you like it! Maybe you'll want to use it?"

Kenzie shook her head. "Aidan hates it. He has a cousin by that name. This kid sounds like a worse nightmare than my cousins. I could never name my son Eric or Adam. And besides, if it is a girl, we've decided on a name."

"Can you tell me?"

"Sure. Pepperocini June. After her grandmas. Pepper-June for short."

She laughed. "Good grief!"

"Seriously, we like 'Rose-Marie' for a middle name, with a hyphen between both of your middle names."

"Aww. That's so sweet."

"That's us. Anyway, I am sure about Jade. It's yours."

"All right, thanks. It's perfect." At the front door she swung her arm around Kenzie. "Someday, honey, I hope we will meet your sibling named Jade."

"Me too, Mom."

Somewhere deep in her heart Susan knew her time of mourning her unborn child was finished.

Fifty-Seven

Painkillers kept her husband in a comatose state, but still Pepper sat beside Mick's hospital bed, tightly grasping the hand not hooked up to an IV. Near midnight, the room was lit by one soft light.

He was alive. Bones were broken, every inch of his body bruised. All would heal. He was alive.

Thank You, God. Thank You, God.

Before succumbing to the drug-induced sleep, Mick had teased with her and Aidan. "Flying through the air, my life flashing before me, I had only one thought." His grin didn't quite hold. "'Hey, when this over, I bet I'll get to go home early and finish that novel with Pepper!'"

She and Aidan had cried.

"Okay, okay." Mick protested. "Seriously? I thought 'Man, this hurts like heck. I'm not sure I want to be there when I wake up. But then I sure would miss my Pepper Sprout, so maybe I'd like to hang around, wait for a different grand finale.'"

Always, always about her. She laid her face against the stiff sheet alongside his arm.

"Mom, why don't you sit in this chair?" Aidan referred to the lounger he sat in on the other side of the bed. "Or lay down on the cot. They brought it in for you."

She turned her head to look at him. "I'm okay for now."

"Are you sure you don't want to go to a motel?"

"I'm sure."

"He's fine. He's going to be fine."

263

"Yeah," she murmured.

No two ways about it, Aidan had carried her through this one. At his father's insistence, their son had even spoken with the kid who smashed his car into Mick's body. The eighteen-year-old was at the hospital with his family, unhurt but scared, waiting for news of his handiwork.

Pepper never could have done what Aidan did. She would have sprayed the entire group with caustic, unforgiving remarks. Mick, of course, had already forgiven the boy for ignoring road construction signs, driving too fast, and fiddling with his stereo instead of seeing the orange-vested worker. The police couldn't even find a skid mark.

Now Aidan walked behind her and squeezed her shoulders. "I'm going outside to call Kenzie, let her know what's happening."

Pepper sat up and turned to face him. "You haven't talked to her yet?"

"No."

"She'll be so worried! You talked with all your sisters and Mickey and even the *driver*—"

"I know!"

"Kenzie's family, Aidan!"

"No, she's not."

That shut her up.

He shrugged. "I don't know what she is. We're in this gray twilight, in-between place. Committed but…it doesn't feel like committed. Not totally. Not in a solid way, like you guys." He gestured to Mick and shook his head. "Dad lying here. All of a sudden it all looks different. I'm going to be a father like he is, and I don't know the first thing about it. Kenzie's going to be a mother, and she's still such a kid herself."

Pepper dared not speak.

"I don't know where she fits in. Where *we* fit in. There's a definite disconnect going on between us. Whenever anything comes up that even hints at permanence, she turns flibbertigibbet on me and does things like takes off for Phoenix. Right now I just don't know what to say to her."

He was thinking about permanence? "Maybe," Pepper chose her

words carefully and spoke in a hushed tone, "maybe it's mommy hormones. They can really do a number on you. But no matter what, Aidan, she really needs to hear that your dad's going to be okay."

After a moment he nodded, stood, and shuffled from the room.

A definite disconnect between them? Oh, Lord.

Aidan returned, his face unreadable in the shadowy hospital room. He'd been gone for at least an hour.

Pepper sat in the lounger, her feet up, covered with a blanket, a pillow behind her head. Exhausted as she was, she could not fall asleep while her son was on the phone with Kenzie. His earlier unsettling talk hinted that their future was up for grabs.

"Out, Mom." He pointed his thumb toward the cot at the foot of Mick's bed. "You get that."

"No, it's got your name on it. Trust me, I'll be up in the night checking on him."

"It's almost morning." He sank onto the cot and pulled off his shoes.

Maybe he wasn't going to tell her anything about the conversation. Should she ask? Nah. The new salty Pepper understood he needed his space. Her prayers for him and Kenzie over the past hour fulfilled her role. She knew when to put a lid on it.

"Get this, Mom."

She blinked.

He lay on his side, elbow crooked, head in hand. "She's staying at the beach house with her mom."

"Hmm." Two nights in a row? "Well last night's slumber party was a good bonding time for them."

"But get *this*. Susan told her we shouldn't get married."

Uh-oh. Where had that come from? Oh! Susan's out-of-wedlock pregnancy. She must have finally told Kenzie the story about why she and Drake married, about her lack of self-worth through the years. That would have opened up a can of wiggly worms.

She asked, "Did she say why Susan said that?"

"Yeah. A bunch of stuff about getting married just to cover up their shocking deed." He shivered and hissed. "Such nasty stuff."

She ignored his smart-aleck routine. "Susan told me and Natalie the whole story."

"Really?"

"Mm-hmm. It's their issue, Aidan. Susan's and Drake's. She does have a point, though. She hopes you two don't marry for the reasons they did: to pretend you're perfect and escape other people's condemnation. You're not perfect and people are going to condemn you anyway. But she didn't exactly say 'Do *not* get married.'"

"Yeah, she did."

"Honestly, I really think that had to be what Kenzie heard. It's a partial interpretation. There's more to it than that."

"Whatever." He fell back against the pillow with a sigh. The light caught his grimace. "Kenzie's scared to death of repeating her parents' life. We do manage to agree on one thing: The tradition of marriage is not all it's cracked up to be."

Her temperature shot up and the new salty Pepper disintegrated on the spot. His wavering had gone on long enough. "Aidan, your dad almost got killed today. As you said, things look different. Suddenly, I don't give a rip if I come across unsupportive. You, young man, are stuck."

"You think I don't know that?"

"Well, then get off the dime! You don't play at marriage. You either are or you're not. The tradition, instituted by God Almighty Himself, is imperfect in this imperfect world and our imperfect lives. But it's still the best choice available. If you or Kenzie are not ready, okay. I can live with that. We'll make the best of it." A sob out of nowhere clutched at her throat and cut off the flow of words. Her grandbaby might end up living with that fool Drake Starr! Or in Phoenix with someone named Dakota!

"Mmph!" The muffled sound came from Mick.

Pepper and Aidan leapt to their feet and dashed to either side of his bed.

His eyes were shut, but he spoke, his voice low and thick. "Feel better, Pepper Sprout, getting that off your chest?" He smiled. "Aidan, what your mom's trying to say is: Be a man. But you should hear that from me, not her. So." He rumbled a deep chuckle. "Be a man. You know how, son. I've seen you. It's in your music. Follow your heart. That's where God writes His word. Now, you two, keep it down. People are trying to sleep around here."

With that his head sank deeper into the pillow and a loud snore flapped his lips.

Across the bed, Pepper met Aidan's stare. His surprised expression reflected her own. Their stunned silence lasted a long moment. Then the giggles started. They grew into uncontrollable howls, suppressed only after one very stern nurse paid them a visit.

Fifty-Eight

"You are such a man about this, Rexton Starr." Natalie linked her arm through her husband's and smiled as they walked across the church parking lot Thursday evening.

He laughed. "Because I told Drake's assistant I was coming in at five fifteen?"

"Well, yeah." She stretched the last word into two syllables. "You didn't *ask* for an appointment. You just announced what you were doing."

"But I scheduled my visit around his meetings."

"Still, there was that slightly macho attitude involved. Not to mention you left your office early. Canceled appointments even."

"Mm-hmm."

"Mostly…" She went up on tiptoe and planted a kiss on his cheek. "It's because you're not giving up on your brother."

He looked at her and winked. "Some would say—like said brother—that I'm doing all this because I'm so whipped over you, woman."

She grinned. "That's the real reason you are such a man."

They reached the building and went inside. Natalie forced herself to swallow one last snicker. Under the circumstances, Drake might not appreciate mirthful expressions. She wondered if he would appreciate the point of their visit. Two points, actually. Her point was to ask his forgiveness for her disrespect of him. Rex's was to invite him to join them for a communion service at the beach house later that evening.

Knowing Drake, her hopes were not what one would label high.

She had asked Mildred to keep them in prayer. Now wouldn't she chastise her for entertaining such negative thoughts? Expect God to show up, the old prayer warrior would say. Hopes should be sky high.

They crossed the lobby. Lights were turned low throughout the building. The staff was probably already gone for the day. Tomorrow, Good Friday, would be full of activity.

She walked through the open door of the main office ahead of Rex. The door to Drake's private room was shut, and the front desk was empty. A young man sat on a chair, drumming his fingertips on the end table and looking at a magazine on his lap.

He glanced up and nodded at them politely.

Natalie smiled and sat on the couch. Lowering himself beside her, Rex said, "Hi."

The guy looked familiar to Natalie, but in a church as large as theirs, names often did not accompany the sight of a face.

The twentysomething wore khakis and a colorful Hawaiian-style shirt, loose fitting and hanging out. His youthful face said he wasn't old enough to shave, but his shadowy jaw disagreed. His hair was a deep brown, almost bushy with curls, and hung below his collar. A brilliant blue made a brief appearance before he lowered his gaze back to the magazine. His drumming fingertips tapped now, a definite rhythm rather than a release of nervous energy.

There was something beautiful about him. A peace. Even as he was aware enough to greet them and to—apparently—read the magazine, he appeared focused on whatever music he heard—

"Oh my gosh!" She felt Rex's stare and turned.

His brows were raised.

Not quite sure what to do with her revelation, she mouthed a name. *Aidan.*

The brows nearly collided with the blond crew cut.

Although Natalie had seen Kenzie's boyfriend a few times when the band played at area youth rallies, it had always been from a distance. They had never met.

Drake's door opened and he ushered out a smiling young couple whom Natalie might or might not have met. She couldn't think straight.

While they gushed thanks, exchanged hugs, and headed out to the lobby, she racked her brains trying to figure out a gracious way to exit. If the boy was indeed Aidan, something was in the works that shouldn't involve her and Rex.

"Rex." Drake nodded to him. "Natalie." He half turned to the young man now standing. "And this is...?"

The guy offered his hand. "Aidan Carlucci."

Drake whipped his attention back to his brother. "How dare you bring him here!"

Rex shrugged. "I didn't. I've never met him." He thrust his hand toward Aidan. "Hi. I'm Rex Starr."

A smile spread across the boy's face and the blue eyes, set deep under thick brows, sparkled. "Kenzie's uncle." They shook hands. "It's a pleasure to meet you, sir."

"This is my wife—"

"Aunt Nattie." He finished the sentence, and with another smile he shook her hand. "I'm very happy to meet you, ma'am." His voice was low and whispery, his handshake firm. Taller than Rex, he wasn't as tall as Drake.

"Thanks." She couldn't help but return the smile. The kid was perfect for her niece. Gracious, charming, cute. Nervy as all get out to show up unannounced at Drake's office.

Rex said to Drake, "Okay, now I've met him. I assume he wants to talk with you, so Nat and I will leave. We'll chat later."

"I don't have anything to say to him, and I'm quite sure he has nothing to say to me that I'm interested in hearing."

"Drake." Rex's one syllable expressed untold compassion as well as chastisement.

Her husband never ceased to amaze her.

Aidan said, "Sir, I just want to ask one quick question. May I have your blessing to ask your daughter to marry me?"

The silence wasn't quite total. Natalie heard her heartbeat. She heard the hum of electricity.

As if waiting for the dust to settle from his little bombshell, Aidan stood perfectly still for a long moment before speaking again. "I love

Kenzie. I love our unborn child. I want to take care of them for the rest of our lives. I am sorrier than I can say for getting the cart before the horse, for not treating her honorably. I've confessed to God that I chose my own way and not His. I take full responsibility. Now I'd like to take full responsibility as a husband in the eyes of God and man. Sir, your blessing will mean a lot to both of us."

Drake's complexion turned ashen. "I don't…I can't…" His voice quivered. He cleared his throat a few times.

Natalie wanted to yell at him to kick the ball. What more could he want? The goal was wide open, nobody guarding it. Wham! Take the shot! Win your family back!

He tilted his head.

Half a nod?

He raised his chin. "Yes," he croaked. "But it's Kenzie's decision."

Now Aidan stared in obvious disbelief. "Yes?"

Drake blinked rapidly.

Natalie wondered if he had gone into true shock, as in oxygen was not reaching his brain.

Aidan grinned. "Thank you, sir." Again he stuck his hand toward Drake. "Thank you."

Stiff as a board, Drake raised his hand and let Aidan shake it.

"Thank you, sir." Aidan pumped his hand, let go, and turned to shake first Rex's hand and then hers. "Thank you. Thank you. All right. I guess I'll see you. Sometime." He gave a little wave and glided through the office doorway.

Natalie heard a distinct whoop as the lobby door banged open.

Drake sank onto the couch. Elbows on knees, he propped his forehead in his hands.

"Drake." Rex sat beside him and placed an arm around his shoulders. "You did the right thing."

And then Natalie heard the most heartbreaking sound imaginable. Pastor Drake Starr, her brother-in-law, sobbed.

Rex swung his other arm around him and held him fast.

Fifty-Nine

Kenzie melted into Aidan's embrace.

And silently chewed herself out for finding comfort in his strong arms, in the intensity of his sapphire blue gaze, in his kiss that prickled from unshaven chin, in that low raspy voice that had mesmerized her for years.

Was that how it had been between her mom and dad? They were supposedly crazy about each other when they were young. Did Susan give herself to Drake and get pregnant because she loved him...or because she was starved for affection? Was she blind to Drake's obvious faults? Did she melt into his hugs and think that was where she belonged no matter what?

"Hey, Kenz." Aidan whispered into her hair.

"Hey," she whispered back, thinking her decision to get off work early that afternoon was a good one. She wouldn't have missed this reunion for the world.

It was Thursday night, almost time for the Marthas' communion service inside the beach house. She and Aidan stood in the dusk beside the seawall, oblivious to passersby. He had phoned her after he parked his mom's van in a lot a mile south of the house. Idiot that she was, she'd raced out the door barefoot and down the concrete boardwalk in that direction and, when they met, leapt into his arms with a squeal. He'd been gone thirty-three hours. The separation felt like months.

"I'm so glad your dad's okay."

He nodded, his head still nestled against hers. "Mmm. I missed you."

He missed her? That was why he didn't call until the middle of last night? Kind of a funny way of showing it.

She felt herself go still. The words she had said about her dad echoed, that if he truly believed emotions were neither right nor wrong, he had a funny way of showing it by always belittling her thoughts and feelings.

"Kenz?" Aidan straightened and looked at her. "What's wrong?"

Mush filled her veins again. There he went, seeing deep inside her heart like no one else could.

He touched her nose. "Hey, you can tell me."

She gave him half a smile. He wasn't her dad. She really could tell him her thoughts without fear of getting trashed. "If you missed me, it seems like you could have called sooner. At least to tell me he wasn't dying."

He nodded. "I know, I know. I'm sorry. I can't...exactly...explain. Things were a huge mess. There was Mom and the doctors and nurses and Dad's boss. Aunts and uncles on the phone. It took a while to reassure my sisters and then there was Mickey. Poor kid. He was in bad shape."

Well, *she* could have reassured Mickey Junior. They had a special connection. Everybody said so. Some even said they clicked better than he did with any of his four sisters.

She watched Aidan closely as he went on and on with his half-baked apology. The corners of his mouth kept curving up, as if a puppeteer pulled strings attached to his lips. She interrupted him, "You're really psyched about your dad, huh?"

"What?" His puzzled look gave way to another smile. "Oh, yeah! For sure. I mean, he's going to be all right. Well, after he lays in bed for who knows how many weeks and his pelvis heals. And at least he can come home and Mom can be his nurse. Yeah, it's pretty exciting. Like I was saying..."

She tuned him out again. All of their talk about being "one" didn't amount to a hill of beans. If she truly were his wife—marriage license or not—he would have called her first, not dead last.

Well, she knew one thing for sure. She wasn't signing up for her mother's life. Living like a second-class citizen was not for her. If Aidan couldn't treat her with any more respect than he'd just shown her, it was time to set some new ground rules. She could melt in his arms and love him all she wanted, but there would always remain a tiny corner of herself she would never, ever allow him to invade.

~

Aidan hustled Kenzie along the boardwalk. He'd told her how eager he was to meet the Martha Mavens now gathered at the beach house. Pepper had ordered him to thank them personally for their prayers for Mick.

The corner of herself that Kenzie had declared off limits to Aidan already protested. The ache in her chest was almost unbearable. Should she give it one last shot?

"Aidan, you said you have to go back up to the hospital tomorrow?"

"First thing in the morning. I'd better spend the night at my folks' house so I can pack some things Mom and Dad need. Then tomorrow I'll take Mickey with me. We'll see how it goes. The doctor wasn't too optimistic about Dad leaving before Sunday. But Mickey and I might spend the night there, in a motel. Since I've got Mom's van, I don't need mine. You can keep using it, no problem."

"I wasn't asking for a vehicle. I'm suggesting I could go with you and help out, especially with Mickey J."

"Thanks, but that's all right. You've got work tomorrow and Saturday. Dad wants me to take seats out of the van so he can lay in the back. Ha! Mr. Tough Guy. He really shouldn't move at all. An ambulance has to bring him home. But who knows? God could glue him all back together by then."

He squeezed her shoulders and kissed the top of her head.

She figured that happened only because she was the nearest object. At that moment he probably would have kissed a fence post.

Like the day he and Pepper rushed off, she felt totally invisible to the Carlucci family. She wasn't sure which hurt worse: cutting herself off or letting them do it.

The invisible routine continued at the beach house. It expanded to her own mother and the Martha Mavens.

Kenzie stood just inside the front door. No one even bothered to wait for her to introduce Aidan. The Marthas knew who he was, of course, and they went a little nuts meeting him. A bunch of full-on delirious magpies. Her mother kissed his cheek. Millie blushed and giggled, looking seven instead of seventysomething. Frosty Tess hugged him like some long-lost relative. Emmylou shook his hand and then laid it on her abdomen. "It's his foot!" Leona gave him two cookies. Gwyn offered him tea.

Kenzie watched his reactions with surprise. Aidan could be moody and standoffish, especially when he was composing and arranging music. Onstage, singing and playing keyboard, he was totally at peace, oblivious to the world around him, lost in worship. But rarely, very rarely, was he extroverted like now, and never with strangers.

What was up?

He thanked the women nonstop for their prayers for his dad. They wanted to hear details, and so he expanded on the story.

Kenzie left them and searched the house in vain for her aunt. Besides the Marthas, at least two dozen other people filled the living room and kitchen area. More were outside on the patio. Many she recognized from the church; quite a few were seniors like Millie and Leona. They greeted her with hugs and best wishes.

She also saw Emmylou's hunky Marine husband, the neighbor Julian, and the wild-looking street pastor Zeke. She found Pugsy cowering under a bed and nuzzled him for a while. But Aunt Nattie and Uncle Rex were nowhere to be found.

The group had assembled for a communion service right there in the beach house. Millie and Leona had organized it and asked Zeke—who said he held preacher credentials, although her dad disbelieved him—to lead it. Millie told her they were commemorating the Lord's Last Supper.

Since nothing was going on at her dad's church that night, the real boycott wouldn't happen until tomorrow, Good Friday. The twins planned to hold a solemn memorial-type service then in remembrance of Christ's death.

As she reentered the living room from the bedrooms, she noticed the lights had been dimmed. Aidan caught her eye and pointed to the loveseat where Emmylou sat, her husband on the floor beside her. Other people were sitting down in whatever space they could find, the older folks on the couch, armchairs, and kitchen chairs, younger ones on the floor. Conversations quieted.

Aidan smiled. "Loveseat's reserved for soon-to-be mommies."

Soon-to-be mommy? He had never referred to her like that.

She sat next to smiley Emmylou, who reached over and patted Kenzie's stomach. Aidan slid onto the floor, leaning against her leg.

The rectangular kitchen table had been moved so it ran lengthwise, making it look sort of like an altar facing the living room. A white linen cloth covered it; white tapered candles glowed from four tall crystal holders; an open Bible lay in the middle. Beside it were the communion elements: bread and wine. A chunk of whole-grain bread, torn from a loaf, sat on a small plate. The wine sparkled in a crystal goblet.

Behind the table, the countertop was covered with baskets and trays. Earlier, before Aidan arrived, Kenzie had watched the Marthas complete their preparations. Leona's homemade unleavened bread was torn into bite-size pieces and piled into napkin-lined baskets. Mildred uncorked bottles of red wine—real red wine with alcoholic content and a California label. Tess nodded in her somber "right on" expression. Susan's eyes got big, but she didn't say a word as she helped pour wine into the cough syrup-size tumblers on the trays. Gwyn's lips scrunched as though they were holding in a smile. She murmured something about how a thimbleful wouldn't hurt anyone, except for maybe her two recovering alcoholic friends, but they would know better and besides, they weren't coming.

Now Zeke stepped behind the makeshift altar and a broad smile split his face. He looked imposing. His deep chocolate skin and dark hair contrasted with the whites of tablecloth, candles, and shirt. "Brothers and sisters! Welcome to our Lord's Table! We gather here to remember Jesus when He instituted the sacrament of the Eucharist. It was the night He was arrested, the night His Passion began, the night His blood started to pour out for our sake."

He lifted the open Bible. "In Luke 22 we read, 'And he took bread, gave thanks and broke it, and gave it to them, saying, This is my body given for you; do this in remembrance of me. In the same way, after the supper he took the cup, saying, This cup is the new covenant in my blood, which is poured out for you.'"

Zeke looked up. "In essence He told them He was going to be sacrificed and that they should not forget it. Tonight, we do not forget it. We remember it. We know Sunday's a-coming, but for now we turn our hearts toward His Last Supper and we linger there a spell. We remember that God's own Son prepared to take the world's sins into Himself. He shared supper with His friends with the shadow of tomorrow's cross looming within His sight. And we ponder His offer. He says to take and eat and drink this new life He makes available through the breaking of His body and the shedding of His blood."

Zeke set down the Bible, placed one hand over the goblet, the other over the bread, and shut his eyes. "Lord, we ask Your blessing on these gifts of bread and wine. We ask that we might receive them in remembrance of Your Son's death and that through His sacrifice we might receive remission of all our sins."

He opened his eyes. "Sister Millie has made copies of an ancient prayer for us to read together to prepare our hearts before we come to the Table. Does everyone have one?"

Papers rustled. Aidan held a sheet of paper high enough so Kenzie could read along with him the typed words. In unison, the group spoke.

"We do not presume to come to this thy Table, O merciful Lord, trusting in our own righteousness, but in thy manifold and great mercies. We are not worthy so much as to gather up the crumbs under thy Table. But thou are…"

The print jiggled. A whooshing noise filled her head. Kenzie could read no further and heard only the last phrase. It reverberated in her head: *not worthy so much as to gather up the crumbs under thy Table, not worthy so much as to gather up the crumbs under thy Table, not worthy, not worthy...*

No way could she eat His body and drink His blood.

Blindly, she made her way through the crowd, people seated on the floor and in chairs shoved together. Some now stood; some moved toward the table. The Table.

She walked to the back corner of the kitchen, through a doorway, past a bathroom and the side door that opened onto the sidewalk between the house and Julian's. She went into a small bedroom where she kept her things.

Aidan spoke from behind her. "Kenz, what are you doing?"

She found her backpack on the floor. "I'm not worthy. I'm out of here."

"What did you say?"

"I'm not worthy," she mumbled again, ignoring the concern in his voice. Her vision cleared long enough for her to see his face, but she couldn't read it. She could only read her heart, and it was black. Christ didn't want her. Her own family didn't want her. The Carluccis didn't want her. And even if Aidan thought he did, that wouldn't last. It was already on its way to becoming history.

"Kenzie, are you sick?"

"No. I just need to be alone."

"Now? Before the service—"

"I'll go to the apartment. Please, Aidan, this is just too much right now, okay? All this church stuff. All these people from my dad's church. I can't handle it."

"I'll come with you."

"Please don't. I want to be alone. And I need you to tell my mom for me. Please?"

Before she could slip around him to the side door, his arms were there, pulling her to himself. "It's going to be okay, Kenz. It's going to be okay. Everything is going to be okay. Your mom and dad. Our baby—"

With force, she untangled herself from his hug. "I know," she lied. "It's just one of those times I need some major space!" More lies.

He would never let her go if he knew it wasn't one of "those times." This was something altogether different and further outside herself than she had ever felt. She tumbled headlong down a black tunnel. She sensed only that she had to leave. That if she stayed with Aidan and her mom and the Marthas and Zeke, she would hit bottom.

"I'm all right, Aidan. Go take care of your family."

"You're my family."

You have a funny way of showing it. She shoved aside the hand he held out and strode from the room.

He followed her outside into the dark night and down the sidewalk. They reached the van in the carport and she unlocked its door.

Pulling it open, he leaned down and kissed her cheek. "Drive safe. I'll call you."

She nodded, climbed in, and started the engine.

He'd always understood when and how to give her space.

Either that or he knew how to let her go. No fuss, no muss.

Not worthy. Not worthy.

Sixty

"You poor baby, you!" Susan cooed the words of comfort in a high-pitched voice. Her face mere centimeters from Pugsy's, she ignored the doggie breath as best she could. "Did Gwyn scold you? Did all those people frighten you?"

Evidently it was a night for breaking rules. First of all Pugsy was *on the bed*, a practice Drake abhorred. At least the dog wasn't on the sheet...although he came pretty close to sharing the pillow with her. A short while ago Mildred had served *wine*, a no-no in the Starr household. At least it happened at the beach house and not, strictly speaking, in the Starr household. Zeke—who, if Drake were correct, purchased his "Reverend" license from some fly-by-night operation—*preached* from God's Word, an event Drake never would have allowed in his church. At least the Holy Cross Fellowship congregants were not sitting within their own church walls when they listened to him and partook of the communion served by him and the twins.

"But you want to know the one that takes the cake, Pugs? The alpha of all rules that I broke tonight? Sorry, it's not you on the bed, big as that is. Nope, it concerns me. I sang." She smiled. "Yes, sirree. I sang a *solo* in public. Well, sort of public. I bet Pepper Carlucci would call singing at an informal gathering in a beach house semi-public. Anyway, it was a rule buster and it was wonderful."

She closed her eyes for a moment. "Thank You, Lord, for tonight. For the breaking of rules that bind us from seeking You. Thank You for music. For the voice You gave me. For the sheer joy of singing for You in semi-public. Amen. Hold on, Pugs."

Susan reached over the dog and turned off the bedside lamp. Scooting back down under the covers, she kept Pugsy in the crook of her arm and stroked his silky coat. The busy evening had unnerved the poor thing.

"You're like Kenzie, I guess, hmm? Things totally unnerved her tonight too. If you'd both just stay by my side where you belong...But that won't work with her. Aidan said she needed space. That the church stuff was getting to her. It's understandable. All those familiar faces, all the gracious welcomes, all the Scripture talk about forgiveness. Reminders of unhealed issues between her and her dad. My poor baby."

Pugsy snored softly.

"That's okay. I wasn't addressing you, anyway." She grinned in the dark. "Lord, am I losing my mind?"

Sleep eluded her. An odd mixture of joy and peace and unease kept her eyes wide open. She prayed for Drake. She prayed for Kenzie, Aidan, and the baby. She prayed for Mick. She prayed for Natalie and Rex, who hadn't shown up for the service or phoned. She prayed for Emmylou, so heavy with child.

What wouldn't go away, though, was the question of her future. How long could she live at the beach house at her brother-in-law's expense? How long could she have phone conversations with her husband that were left unfinished and unsettled her?

She wouldn't pursue a divorce. She could not imagine Drake doing so either. But of course she never could have imagined him telling her not to come home...even if he didn't mean it.

Where did that leave her? It was up to Drake. If he refused to love and accept her and Kenzie as they were, was Susan prepared to sacrifice money, home, prestige? Was she ready to find a job and support herself?

A feeling surged through her like an electric shock. An image of a bird-of-paradise flower sprang to mind. She recognized it as the one from the backyard, the one growing right through concrete. Music filled her ears. It was her voice singing late at night on the beach. She knew it echoed from another special Thursday night. Her personal "Resurrection Thursday" to be exact.

"All right, Lord. I get it." She smiled. "My life is in Your hands and Yours alone. Goodnight."

With that she rolled over, her back to Pugsy. His doggie breath proved to be really just a bit much.

～

Once again the Martha Mavens—except for Natalie—descended upon the beach house midafternoon. Their plans for Good Friday were far less involved than the previous night's communion service. Mildred had said, "What else can we do, dearies, but weep at the foot of His cross?"

Still, there was much to do.

Susan adored the camaraderie and tried not to worry about Kenzie and Natalie. She had left voice mails for both. She knew Kenzie was working. Natalie probably had an afternoon soccer practice to coach.

"All right," Mildred announced from her stance in front of the fireplace. "I think we're finished."

Leona hugged her twin.

With a heavy sigh, Emmylou sank onto the couch.

Gwyn said, "It's perfect."

Tess nodded. "Yes, it is."

If she didn't know better, Susan could have sworn Tess Harmon had never taken charge of a single thing in her life. Her cooperation and deference to the elderly twins was a sight to behold indeed.

Mildred said, "Susan? What do you think?"

She gazed around the room. Much of the floor space of both living room and kitchen areas was covered with folding chairs provided by Julian. Unlike last night, they and the other furniture were arranged facing the fireplace. Votive candles—more than she could count—sat on the mantel and every other flat space, including book shelves, kitchen and coffee tables, and countertop.

Aside from water bottles and plastic cups, no refreshments waited in the kitchen. Several boxes of tissues were placed in various spots, beneath chairs and alongside couches. Almost as many Bibles lay about the room.

The focus was the fireplace. There, propped on the hearth and resting back against the mantel, was a thick rough-hewn wooden cross about five feet tall. Zeke and a friend had delivered it, gently carrying it through the front door. With an almost reverent air, they'd positioned it.

Susan looked at Mildred. "Only one thing is missing. Well, besides Kenzie and Natalie."

The old woman smiled and nodded as if she expected what Susan was going to say.

Naturally she would expect it. Susan's suggestion was what the Prayer Warrior herself would say.

Susan smiled back at her. "Prayer is missing."

"Mm-hmm. It's time, dearies. Shall we sit and invite the Lord to visit?"

Susan thought back to the time the Martha Mavens first showed up at the beach house and Mildred said almost those same exact words. How she had cringed at the thought of prayer! How she had pretended her life was hunky-dory! How awful she could not say aloud the words that Kenzie was pregnant!

"Lord, preserve us from ourselves," Susan murmured.

Gwyn said, "What?"

Mildred chuckled as she waddled to the couch and lowered herself beside Emmylou. "Oh, she's just getting started. She can't even wait for us all to sit down. Susan, will you lead us?"

She stared. "In prayer?"

The white head bobbed, the big eyes behind thick lenses sparkled.

And Susan remembered the bird-of-paradise. Abundant life could indeed blossom in the face of what looked like insurmountable obstacles.

As the sun inched its way toward the horizon, Gwyn and Tess lit the myriad of votive candles about the room. Emmylou dimmed lamps, but turned off most of them. The result was an inviting atmosphere of contemplation. Gwyn even ignored Pugsy. In turn the dog remained calm and chose to boldly nap atop the bed. Susan moved his food and water into the bedroom and shut the door.

People trickled into the beach house a few at a time, their greetings subdued. No hours had been set to begin and end worship. Mildred wanted the entire evening left wide open to the Spirit's leading. The only plan was to read aloud the Gospel accounts of the crucifixion.

To Susan's surprise, Julian and Zeke returned. With them came four men whose grubby appearances suggested they were homeless. She knew Zeke spent most of his time ministering to the homeless; Julian helped him now and then. When the strangers nodded to her politely, her concern vanished. They weren't like some she had noticed on the boardwalk, so obviously mentally ill and almost violent in their voice and behavior.

A steady stream of Holy Cross Fellowship members began to flow through the front door.

Robbie Bainbridge touched her elbow. Married to Emmylou, he was every inch a Marine from the crew cut to the ramrod posture. "Miss Susan." He hadn't lost his Southern manners, either. "You go sit down. I'll stand outside and man the door."

"I don't mind—"

"To tell you the truth, I can't concentrate real good. Those Braxton whatevers have been going strong for a while. And they're pretty regular too. Like the real thing. Emmylou's thinking she'd prefer Easter and not Good Friday night for a birth, but I don't think that's our call. I'd just as soon be standing up and ready for anything."

Susan smiled. "Like whisking her off to the hospital?"

"Yes, ma'am. Thank you again for saving a parking spot in your carport for us. Knowing my truck is close by gives me my only peace of mind at the moment."

"You're welcome, Robbie."

She made her way to the far side of the room, heading toward a vacant folding chair near the hallway. At least forty people already sat, some on the floor like last night. Not many more would fit comfortably inside the room. Maybe some would see it like a come-and-go open house and leave to make way for others.

Oh, Lord, I really did not want this boycott to succeed. Please take more people to Drake's service than to here. Please let him feel only Your prompting that he be more real than he has been.

Then the expressions caught her attention. Many faces registered awe. She saw peace. She saw tears. Every eye not closed gazed at the cross. The sound of a woman's hushed voice broke the silence. "'From the sixth hour there was darkness over all the land until the ninth hour. And about the ninth hour, Jesus cried out in a loud voice, "Eli, eli, lama sabachthani?" that is, My God, My God, why have you forsaken me?'"

And Susan understood that none of it was about a boycott after all.

Susan didn't know how long she sat there, listening to the familiar words read by different people, Scriptures from the disciples' accounts of the crucifixion and from Old Testament prophecies. All enhanced her imagination of Jesus suffering for her, of His taking all of her sins and the sins done against her into Himself.

On the cross.

She caught herself humming and stopped.

Then she heard the silence. No one was reading. No one was moving.

The pitch sounded in her ear, so clear she wondered if it were audible to others. She opened her mouth and the notes took shape and the words seemed to sing themselves.

"'On a hill far away stood an old rugged cross, the emblem of suffering and shame; and I love that old cross, where the dearest and best for a world of lost sinners was slain. So I'll cherish the old rugged cross, till my trophies at last I lay down; I will cling to the old rugged cross, and exchange it someday for a crown.'"

She didn't stop until she sang the next three verses.

As she let the last note fade away, another voice rose in song. Soft, distinct, masculine.

"'Jesus, keep me near the cross, there a precious fountain, free to all, a healing stream, flows from Calvary's mountain...'"

Susan's breath caught.

Drake!

She opened her eyes and twisted around, scanning the room.

Even when he was seated, his head and shoulders towered above everyone. He sat on a folding metal chair near the door, eyes shut tight, the song tumbling sweetly from him.

Susan's muscles tensed, ready to spring and send her flying across the room. To dance for joy before the cross or to throw her arms around her husband? Both. Yes. For certain, both.

Drake should be at the church! Preaching! Praying! Explaining the reason for the cross!

But there he sat, singing in the beach house.

She stared. At last oxygen refilled her lungs.

He reached the end of the third verse. The familiar chorus and tune nearly burst within her, clamoring for release. Lifting her voice in harmony with his, she felt the years vanish. The two of them were young again, singing duets. They were starting at the beginning. Starting over.

"'In the cross, in the cross, be my glory ever; till my raptured soul shall find rest beyond the river.'"

Sixty-One

At the release of Susan's first chantlike note, Natalie sank slowly to the floor, her backside brushing down along the refrigerator. The beauty of her sister-in-law's voice, too long silenced, resonated somewhere deep within her, awaking a sense of holiness.

She went to her knees.

And then Drake's song kept her there.

As the rhythmical weaving of their two voices rose, she almost pressed her face into the linoleum.

A short while ago, she and Rex had entered the beach house. They used the side door located at the rear of the kitchen and didn't go much beyond the kitchen corner. The entire open space was nearly wall-to-wall people.

Good Friday services always undid her. The ache she began to feel on Palm Sunday magnified itself to an unbearable level. The anticipated fears of Sunday exploded into reality. He died, and He died in a most horrific, excruciating way.

Mixed in with her usual reaction to the season was all the emotional drama of the past few weeks. She thought she might have to find a beach house of her own and take a sabbatical from life. Maybe in Hawaii. Six months away sounded like a good idea. Thanks to Susan, *speechless* and *frazzled* were becoming close friends, two states of being Natalie never would have chosen.

In the silent stillness that followed their songs, she recalled the previous night's events in the church office.

Drake had cried in his brother's arms until Natalie thought her heart would break in two for him.

"Rex." At long last Drake used the tissues she had placed beside him and looked out through red swollen eyes, blowing his nose. "I need to confess my sin."

Rex rubbed his shoulder. "Hey, bud, God's listening. I don't have to."

"No, I need to say it out loud. Natalie, sit down. Please. James says to 'confess your sins to one another, and pray for one another to be cured; the heartfelt prayer of someone upright works very powerfully.'"

Natalie sat in a chair angled toward the couch they shared. The depth of Drake's knowledge of God's Word always zinged her, even if it all seemed to emanate from his head and not his heart. It was there inside of him anyway.

Drake's shoulders rose and fell. "I confess my pride as a grave sin against God and man." He paused, eyeing her. "Man as in men, women, and children. I ask for your heartfelt prayers. You two are more upright than anyone I know, and I need to be cured. Preferably before I lose my family." His voice caught. "If I haven't already."

"Oh, Drake," she said. "Susan will never give up on reconciliation."

At that he bawled again.

And then Rex prayed…for his brother to receive forgiveness and healing and restoration.

They had talked late into the night. Natalie's own confession to him of her disrespect led eventually to smiles when he admitted he never really liked her much, either.

"Apologies, Rex," he said, "but listening to your wife feels like the dentist's drill hammering away in my mouth." He grinned. "The truth is, she challenges my thinking. Pulls me right out of my comfort zone."

Natalie nearly fell off the chair.

He went on in a more somber mode. "Pulls me the exact same way Kenzie does. When Susan started affecting me the same way, I didn't know what to do. I felt like my back was pushed against a wall. I came out swinging. And then this kid, this boy, comes in talking about confession, baring his soul…" Referring to Aidan, Drake choked up. "I had an awful image of Susan living happily ever after with him and Kenzie and the baby. I wasn't in the picture."

They had driven him home and left, knowing that although Drake took a giant first step, he would not change overnight. They encouraged him to give himself some time alone, away from the office. He agreed he wasn't ready yet to talk with anyone else, not even Susan.

Evidently he let his associate take charge of the Holy Cross Fellowship Good Friday service because there he sat now, singing in the beach house with a bunch of boycotters.

Natalie looked up. She watched Drake slip through the front door. He would not want to face parishioners.

But what of Susan?

Her sister-in-law stood and, in spite of the crowd, tore across the room and out the door after him in two seconds flat.

Natalie turned to Rex seated on the floor beside her. They exchanged a grin.

Enough of Friday's death watch. It sure felt like the resurrection was already in progress. Maybe Jesus wouldn't mind if she jumped ahead of the schedule.

Sixty-Two

Pepper cupped the half-empty coffee mug between her hands and fiddled with it, twisting it round in circles. She sat with Aidan at a small table in the hospital's cafeteria. It was late Friday night. Few people occupied the room.

She said, "It was good you brought Mickey."

Her youngest slept upstairs in the cot. Earlier he had snuggled against the thick plastic jacket-like contraption Mick wore. The little guy was ecstatic to be reunited with his dad.

"Mom," Aidan said now, "you're wiped out. Why don't you sleep with Mickey at the motel? I'll stay with Dad."

"Why didn't you bring Kenzie?"

He sighed.

Her son shouldn't sigh when she spoke. "Okay. I'll go to the motel. Thanks."

"I told you she had to work today and tomorrow."

"She took off work to go to Phoenix spur of the moment. Mickey adores her. So does your dad."

"So do I. It just wasn't the right time." His voice was low and gentle, but he stood abruptly. Scooping both their cups from the table, he moved toward the coffeemaker.

Just what they needed—more caffeine.

Now she sighed. Surprisingly she, Aidan, Mick, and Mickey Junior had enjoyed the day together, most of it spent in the hospital room. Doctors presented one promising report after another. Mick could recover at home; they almost guaranteed to release him on Sunday. She slipped away to shower at the motel Aidan had checked into, pleased with the thoughtful job her daughters had done in packing her clothes.

Still, she reeled from the events. One minute she was laughing with Kenzie and the next she heard Mick had been hit by a car and seriously injured. Life often resembled a walk on a balance beam. Okay, she could live with that. It served to center her, to keep her eyes focused on the One who walked alongside, holding her hand. But suddenly some unseen force lifted up one end of the beam, gave it a good jerk, and dropped it. She couldn't quite get her bearings.

The coffee cup reappeared at her hand.

"Mom." Aidan slid back onto the chair across the table. "I talked to her dad—"

"Hon, I'm sorry I'm taking it all out on you—You did what? You talked to her dad? Kenzie's dad? Drake?"

"Yeah. I decided to be a man about things. Don't fall off the chair there. I don't want two parents in the hospital."

"What do you mean, a man about things?"

He grinned. "Come on. What did you and Dad teach us about getting married?"

"You mean besides the part about having a baby after the fact?"

"If you're going to strike low blows—"

"Sorry. Um…I don't know. What did we teach you?"

"Something I'd never expect from such wild, wooly, and unconventional people. You told the story about how Dad asked Grandpa for his blessing before he proposed to you. Dad said it was a beautiful thing, sort of a rite of passage. You both hoped I would do it and that the twins' boyfriends would."

"When did we say that?"

"I was five."

She laughed and laughed.

Aidan smiled. "I asked Grandpa about it and he told me how impressed he was with Dad." He shrugged. "Anyway, I always liked the sentiment. It really doesn't matter what Drake had answered. I'd still want us to get married. But with our situation and all the unresolved issues with her family, I felt it was the right thing to do. The Old Testament blessings carried a lot of weight, didn't they? I thought this might help clear the air between him and me."

"And did it?"

He nodded slowly. "For me it did. The guy was speechless, but after a few eternal seconds he said yes, we had his blessing."

"Wow."

"Yeah, big wow."

"What was he like?"

"Tall." He grinned.

"Come on. Seriously."

"*Really* tall." He held up a hand to cut off her protest. "He's just a guy, Mom. I went to the church office. The secretary said he was with someone, but I could wait. She left. Then Natalie and Rex came in. Drake was angry when I told him my name. I said I loved Kenzie and would take care of her the rest of my life and hope he would give us his blessing. He sputtered a bit and finally said yes."

"Wow," she said again as tears welled. "Double big wow Aidan James Carlucci, I am so proud of you."

"Thanks. I guess I'm trying to mimic Dad. I love a woman like he does. I want a family like he has. I want to do the right thing like he always tries to do. It's all about something bigger than us. I guess that would be God. I know Kenzie and I are not in a right place, living in this gray twilight of in between. Marriage isn't a piece of paper, but the piece of paper sort of formalizes or solidifies things. I don't know. It announces that we have taken part in a holy sacrament. That feels good to me now."

Thank You, God. She dabbed a napkin at her eyes. *Thank You.*

"But I don't know if your prayers are answered yet, Mom. Kenzie's backing off, wanting her space."

"Did you tell her about her dad?"

"No. There wasn't a chance with all those people around last night at the service."

"So you didn't actually propose?"

He shook his head. "She was too upset."

"About what?"

"I'm not exactly sure. She said she couldn't handle the people, her dad's church people. But she mumbled something about not being worthy, I think in reference to taking communion."

Now Pepper sighed. The balance beam tilted again.

"I told Millie."

"Millie?"

"Yeah, you know. One of the old twins with white hair. The Martha Maven?"

"Mildred! The Prayer Warrior."

"That's the one. I told her."

The beam steadied itself beneath her feet. She touched Aidan's arm and smiled. "Okay. If Mildred's on top of it, then we can sleep. Let's go."

Sixty-Three

Although Susan rushed from the beach house moments after Drake's exit, his long strides carried him far ahead of her down the empty boardwalk. He moved quickly through the dark between spots of light cast by the lampposts.

Two houses past Julian's she slowed. The ocean whooshed loudly at her right. Her voice would never carry far enough.

Why was she chasing after him anyway? Obviously he didn't care to talk to her.

But he had come! And of course there was that houseful of people. Not exactly ideal for a private conversation.

And he had sung! She could not remember the last time he sang a solo or a duet with her. Now and then his voice carried over that of the congregation's because he was near a microphone, but it never lifted so sweetly as tonight, not since the old days.

The old days…That was why she chased after him.

She broke into a jog, but soon slackened her pace again, defeated at the growing space between them, at her shortness of breath.

Gone again…just like Kenzie.

Then he stopped and sat on the seawall, his back to her.

And she ran.

"Drake! Drake!"

At last he turned and, seeing her, stood, his hand aloft in greeting.

She hurried to him, her heart pounding. Joy and fear somersaulted, playing havoc with her emotions.

"Susan!" He caught her in his arms.

Her face against his shirt, arms around his waist, she gasped for breath. She became aware of his chest rising and falling, but not in a measured way. It heaved as if he…cried.

After a time, when they both had calmed, she looked up at him and smiled. "Hi."

"Hi." His voice was scarcely above a whisper.

"Are you the man who just sang a duet with me?"

The lamplight shone his lips curve upward. "I love you."

"I love you. Where are you going?"

"Home. I didn't want this…" He tilted his head in the direction of the beach house. "I didn't want it to be about me. After I heard your voice, I couldn't help but sing. It just bubbled out. But tonight is all about the cross. If people started talking to me…" He left the sentence dangle.

"Can *we* talk?"

He exhaled a deep sigh. "I'd like nothing more."

Rubbing goose bumps on her arms, she glanced at the concrete seawall and the dark ocean. With a warm houseful of people, she had not dressed for a nighttime stroll. "Are you parked close?"

"Not far." He shrugged out of his suit jacket and draped it around her shoulders. "Shall we sit in the car? Or go somewhere?"

"I'd rather stay put. Let's sit in the car."

"All right."

They walked another couple blocks in silence, side by side, but not touching. After their initial embrace, Susan felt overcome with shyness. Drake seemed almost a stranger. She had seen him cry now and then in earlier years, but he had never clung to her as he had done just now. The kind gesture of him giving her his coat spoke volumes. Likewise his asking what she preferred to do and agreeing without an offer of his own opinion.

He was paying attention to her.

It felt odd. It felt as though she were nineteen again.

If he resembled Drake at all, it was Drake at twenty-four. Five years older than her, he first noticed her in the campus cafeteria where she worked. What charmed her most from the moment he introduced himself was how he paid attention to every detail concerning her. How his manner told her she was real and worthy of attention.

They climbed into the car. Parked at the end of a street, it faced the ocean. A nearby pole lamp dispelled some of the interior shadows. Drake's face was not in total darkness.

Turning on the engine he pointed at the windshield. "Heat and a view."

"What else do we need?"

"Probably quite a few things." He shifted in his seat to face her. "Susan, I don't know where to begin."

Hesitant and vulnerable? Nope. This was not a twenty-four-year-old Drake. This was a Drake she'd never met.

She said, "We could start with why you're here. My goodness, what's going on at church?"

"Vince took over. He jumped at the chance to preach. That is, after he picked himself up off the floor at my offer." A smile flickered. "Eventually he got around to asking what was wrong. I told him I'm tired. That the boycott was an acceptable form of loving protest. It wouldn't hurt the body of Holy Cross, but it did communicate to me that something is off kilter. I also told him I needed to be with you."

"Oh, my. You said all that to Vince?"

"Yes. He asked me what to tell the congregation tonight. And I said…" Drake's voice grew thick and he paused. "I said 'Tell them what I just told you.'"

Susan reached over and he grasped her hand.

Blinking back her own tears, she said, "The boycott brought you here?"

He didn't answer for a moment. "Indirectly. I told you it got my attention. All negative. Rex's rendition of it and his rebuke to get real only angered me more. Some deacons patted me on the back. 'Hang in there. You're in the right. Susan is the epitome of submissive. This is a minor lapse in her judgment. She just needs a little time. She'll come round.'"

She shuddered at the description.

"I know." He squeezed her hand. "I am sorry for surrounding myself with cheerleaders. Not that I've allowed a deacon to disagree with me for some time and maintain his position on the board. They were only protecting themselves from receiving my indignant wrath. So, armed with all that affirmation, I came down here Wednesday to fix things between us. I knew...I'm sorry." He bit his lip.

"Knew what?"

"I knew I could make you change your mind."

She nodded. "I was a cheerleader too."

"Yes."

She gazed through the windshield. Wasn't she supposed to be his cheerleader, to always root for him? Wasn't that the positive spin on submission? To stand by her man no matter what?

"Susan, your unconditional support meant the world to me—until I got too big for my britches. You could have told me and still remained the epitome of submissive. But I wouldn't allow that. I never gave you permission to criticize or even disagree."

"It was a two-way street. I shouldn't have been in a position where you could allow me to or not."

"No, this is my fault. I am sorry for ever intentionally or unintentionally treating you with resentment because of why we married. I hope you can forgive me. In time."

She turned to him. "I forgive you, Drake. Why wouldn't I?"

"Cheerleaders sweep hurts under the carpet. They don't even notice them until some time later when they trip over a lumpy rug."

"Yes, but I've been shaking that rug good and hard now for a few weeks."

He stared at her.

With a wave of her arms she snapped an imaginary rug. "You were not going to change my mind this time."

"Deep down I think that's what I feared. And then when I saw you—"

"On Wednesday? You said you came Wednesday. I spotted you! From a distance, walking away."

"Yes, I—" His voice broke again. "Oh, Susan. I stood on the boardwalk watching you and Kenzie build a sand castle. You were laughing and hugging and jabbering away. I kept trying to climb over the seawall, to come down and reason with both of you that I knew best and if you'd just listen…But I knew you would not. You no longer could. And I knew— Oh, dear Lord. I knew I had lost my wife and my daughter. That I had driven them away. I had nowhere to go with the guilt and the sheer agony."

Susan wiped her face with the lapels of his coat still around her.

"I'm not sure how I made it through the night and the next day. I figured the trick was to keep putting one foot in front of the next. And then Aidan came to the office late Thursday afternoon. He asked for my blessing for him and Kenzie to marry. I gave it, by the way."

"Aidan came! He asked for your blessing! You gave it! Oh, my!"

Drake sniffled a few times, regaining his composure. "Audacious young thing, isn't he?"

Laughing, she leaned over and pulled his face toward hers until their foreheads touched. "You ain't seen nothing yet. Wait until you meet his little brother."

"There are two of them?"

"Six, counting the four girls."

He groaned in an exaggerated way. "Six?"

"But Pepper Carlucci—"

"Pepper?"

"The mom. Now she wins first prize for audacious. Hands down, she even outdoes Natalie. I haven't met Mr. Carlucci yet. He might very well take the grand prize."

He chuckled, but then straightened to look somberly into her eyes. Tear tracks glistened on his cheeks. "Susan, do you think I can meet them?"

"Well, generally speaking, the grandparents of a baby usually meet each other sooner or later."

"Grandparents! I'm going to be a grandpa, aren't I?" His voice faded into an odd hiccup, the place where tears and laughter met.

Susan wrapped her arms around his neck and held him tight.

~

The buzzing of Drake's cell phone disrupted their long silent embrace.

"I thought I turned that thing off."

Susan patted the pockets of his coat. "My thigh is vibrating. Which pocket—"

"We don't have to answer."

"Of course we do. Twenty-four, seven. Three hundred sixty-five. All that. Not to mention tonight Vince— Here it is." She pulled out the phone and peered at the display screen.

"I'm off duty."

"It's Natalie." She glanced at him. "Do you mind? I haven't heard a word from her…" Before he replied she pushed the "send" button.

Drake murmured, "Did we just exchange bodies? We're speaking each other's lines."

She smiled at him, the phone to her ear. "Hi, Natalie. It's me."

"On Drake's phone." Natalie's voice carried a distinct smile. "You're together."

"You sound pleased as punch and not too surprised."

"I had hints. I'll explain later. So what do you want me to do with Pugsy?"

"Where are you?"

"At the beach house, silly. Rex and I slipped in the back door in time for the beautiful songs. We all agree, you and Drake blessed the socks right off us."

She laughed.

"We're on our way out the door. Everybody's headed to the hospital. Emmylou and Robbie are probably there by now. Her water broke. The rug's a little damp in front of that bookcase by the side window. No problem. I didn't want to leave Pugsy here if you're not coming back."

"No, I'll come to the house." She looked at Drake. "We'll come soon. You can leave the front door unlocked. We're just down the board-walk."

"Okay. Well, the Good Friday service has turned into a party, and it's moving to the maternity ward. All the Marthas and at least half the folks who were here. Feel free to join us!"

"I think we'll skip that." She noticed Drake's forehead furrows smooth out. "We're off duty. No pastor visits tonight."

Natalie laughed. "Good for you."

"Give my love to Emmylou and Robbie. My prayers are with them."

"Will do. Bye."

"Bye." Susan pressed the off button.

Drake said, "Emmylou's having the baby?"

"Yes. She didn't want to on a Good Friday."

"Hmm. It's a perfect time, really. The day we remember all is forgiven. We have a fresh start. We're clean."

Susan nodded. "Let's tell her that. Next week. Right now the coast is clear at the house. Want to keep me and Pugs company tonight?"

He exhaled loudly, a sound of relief. "I would like nothing better."

Sixty-Four

Saturday morning Susan and Drake slept late. Shafts of sunlight already danced through the blinds and on the bed coverlet when they awoke, Pugsy snuggled between them.

"Phew." Drake picked up the dog. "How about you and him trade places?"

Susan laughed and wiggled toward the center of the bed so he could place the dog behind her. "The doggie breath tends to overpower after a while."

"Let's get him some gum." He smiled and kissed her cheek. "Good morning."

"Good morning."

"When was the last time we did this? Woke up at the same time?"

"And after the sun was up. It's been ages."

"Maybe I could stop my habit of tea at the crack of dawn and you could stop puttering around the house until midnight."

Her chest pinched. Ignoring the discomfort, she focused on Drake peering at her as though she was a long-lost treasure. His gray eyes twinkled and a Mona Lisa smile persisted even when he spoke.

"How about some French toast?" he said. "I'll make the tea."

The pang returned, stronger than before, twisting her neck and chest into what felt like a thick rope.

He touched her eyelid. "What's wrong? The light blue just went navy."

"Really?"

"Really." The smile remained, but his crow's feet scrunched and the narrowed eyes registered concern. "They do that. It means you're disturbed about something."

He noticed? The rope tension slackened. "You're being very perceptive."

"Is that bad?"

She stroked his short hair, matted down from its usual moussed perfection. "It's what you did when we first met. Remember what I told you at dinner last week?"

"Quiche in the dining room and you in a short black dress." He nodded. "You told me I made you feel special."

"Yes. You did that by noticing *me*. You noticed details. It always made me believe that I was worthy."

"Worthy of what?"

She shrugged a shoulder. "Of taking up space on this earth. You haven't treated me in such a way for…a long time. That's probably what's disturbing me. Not that you're charming me again, but our history, that you stopped it and…" She paused.

"And what?" He took her hand between his. "I might stop it again?"

She nodded.

"I don't want to stop it ever."

"Did you want to before?"

"No, of course not. It was unconscious. A by-product of my mishandling success. Some success, huh? The church grows and I grow away from you and Kenzie." He thought a moment. "Susan, we're at a new place. But we're coming from an old one. We probably still have one foot in both worlds. It's natural that you don't trust me. I have to prove myself to you. Don't worry about when the mistrust rears its ugly head."

"But what do I do when it does?"

He gazed at her. "I guess you ask God to help you forgive me and heal your hurt. If you want."

The rope totally unraveled itself, and she grinned. "And I can tell you what I'm truly thinking?"

"I suppose you want me to truly listen?"

"And not whine."

He winced. "Curses on my sister-in-law for dragging you to this beach house."

She laughed. "Okay, here we go. I don't like French toast and I don't drink tea with breakfast anymore. I drink coffee."

His brows inched upward.

"Now this is my morning plan for today. By the way, it varies from day to day. Spontaneity is the key word here."

The brows kept moving.

"Anyway, you are welcome to tag along or not. Kono's serves a great egg burrito. They might have French toast. They might not. I will walk there, in public, in sweats, before I shower. I suggest you wear a cap."

Drake rolled onto his back, convulsed in a belly laugh.

Susan stared in wonder. Drake Starr did not do belly laughs. What was the world coming to?

◡

Paper coffee cup atop the pier railing, Susan checked her phone for voice mails. At her feet, Pugsy sat. At her elbow, Drake gazed out at the ocean, evidently unconcerned about his own messages. His phone was back at the house. Indifference for his appearance was obvious as well. He wore yesterday's tan dress slacks and sky blue long-sleeved shirt and someone else's brown Padres cap found at the beach house.

The sun shone brightly from a clear blue sky. They had enjoyed eating breakfast outdoors on a patio, people-watching. Crowds had flocked to the beach, no doubt drawn by the spring warmth. They swam, surfed, strolled the pier and the boardwalk.

She closed up her phone and smiled. "Emmylou had a boy last night."

"Nice. Robbie must be ecstatic."

"Natalie said he whooped and hollered when he told them all in the lobby."

"All that military stoic self-discipline out the window."

"For good reason."

Drake smiled down at her. "For good reason."

"I've heard grandpas sometimes react that way."

"Oh, I hope so, Susan." He placed an arm around her shoulders. "Any word from Kenzie?"

"No. I left that voice mail yesterday afternoon—I know she was at work then. She'll see my number under missed calls for last night and this morning. I won't bug her anymore. She'll call when she's ready."

"I don't know exactly what to do with her."

She rested her head against him. "You'll know when it's time."

"The only thing I do know is I can't preach tomorrow."

Susan straightened and stared up at him. "It's Easter."

"Don't you Marthas have anything planned?" The Mona Lisa smile showed up again.

"No."

"What were you going to do?"

"Um." She tried to remember her thought processes from the previous afternoon. The short time since then felt like weeks. "I don't know. The others were going to Holy Cross. The little boycott was just for Friday night. I wasn't sure what I would do. Of course now I want to go."

"Well, I don't. I'll call Vince and let him know."

"Drake, are you sure? What are you thinking?"

"I'm thinking, like I said last night, that I'm very, very tired. I'm thinking of asking the board for a sabbatical starting today. If they say no, I'll resign."

"Drake!"

"There are more important things to do. I need to win you and Kenzie back. I need to restructure my entire life. Let me reword that. I need to let God work in me. Change me. Forgive me. Show me what a husband, father, and pastor looks like when false pride and hypocrisy begin to fade." He shrugged. "I need a few friends—maybe just Rex—to walk through this with me."

"For how long?"

"I'd say six months. Our savings should carry us that long." He met her stare. "Maybe you and I could see a counselor."

Comprehending what he said took her a number of seconds. He asked for help! She didn't know this Drake Starr in the least.

She smiled at him. "That husband, father, and pastor you mentioned? I think he looks a lot like you."

Sixty-Five

Kenzie's feet hurt. Her head hurt. Her stomach hurt.

Alone in Aidan's apartment late Saturday night, she lay on the deformed loveseat. Legs propped up on pillows and television remote in hand, she surfed channels.

It wasn't pregnancy yuck or flu aches. She couldn't even blame working overtime. She'd gone to the coffee shop early and worked half the morning plus her own afternoon shift. Business was steady, but not hopping like mad. She took her fair share of breaks and then some.

No, it was more. She hurt somewhere deep inside. A place she couldn't touch.

Or wanted to think about.

She flipped the television to another station and engaged her attention on a brainless comedy about football. Not one of her relatives or friends had anything whatsoever to do with football. They never even knew who was playing in what bowls. Bowl. Now there was a stupid synonym for a flat field of grass.

A key turned in the door, startling her. As she began to rise, Aidan walked in.

She laid back down. "What are you doing here?"

He dropped a backpack on the floor and walked toward her. "I missed you."

"Yeah, right."

"Kenz." He sat on the edge of the loveseat beside her.

She ignored the exasperation in his tone, the "give me a break" expression on his face. "How's your dad?"

"Good."

"Good."

She peered over his shoulder at the television.

"He's coming home tomorrow, by ambulance. All my sisters came up today. Lisel's staying with Mom until tomorrow. The rest of us just drove back. They dropped me off."

"Guess there wouldn't have been a seat for me. No space in the hospital room with all eight of you in there. How many cousins and aunts and uncles squeezed in with you?"

"Kenz, don't do this. Don't shut me out."

"Excuse me?" She coughed a noise of disdain. "Me shut you out? Who left whom?"

"I'm sorry. I had to figure out some things."

"You're changing your tune here. Last night it was because things were so hectic. Phone calls to make. Doctors doing this and that. You holding your family together."

"I didn't know how to say it last night. The truth is I had to figure out where we stand with each other."

She gazed at the colorful television images...turned her hearing to the upbeat rock music athletes supposedly moved to in the midst of games—

"Can we turn this down? Off?" He took the remote from her lap, pointed it over his shoulder, and shut off the power.

"Hey! I'm watching that."

"Did you hear what I said?" He tossed the remote onto the floor. "I had to figure out *us*."

She rubbed her eyes. "That *was* figured out until you took off with hardly a goodbye and didn't phone. I'm invisible and an afterthought to you."

"You're not." Aidan grasped her hands and slid to the floor to his knees. "I didn't know what you were, but now I see it clearly. Mackenzie Anne Starr, I love you. I love everything about you. I even love how you exasperate me like you're trying your best to do right now. I want to spend my life with you. I want the piece of paper that says the government knows I do. I want a pastor to join us together and say the Spirit of God knows I do. I want to marry you, Kenz."

There it was. The Proposal. And there she was. Lying on an old colorless loveseat, feet up, fat belly protruding from under her T-shirt. Preferring to watch TV and not make eye contact with him. The air crackled with argument.

This was not part of the fairy tale.

She squirmed. "You didn't want to before. We didn't want to. We decided we already are."

"Does this look like we already are? You know, if I were dying in a hospital, they might not let you in my room because you're not family. Our kid could come in, but you couldn't."

"Aidan, that sounds like something my mother would say!"

"So what? It puts things in perspective even if the odds are against it happening. I want you and our baby to be my family in every which way." He squeezed her hands. "Will you marry me, Kenz? Wait a sec." He let go, reached into his pants pocket, and pulled out something. "Here. I think this is part of the dorky tradition." With a lopsided smile, he put a tiny box in her hands.

It was soft, covered in gray fabric. Obviously there was a ring inside.

He said, "Thought I'd go the whole nine yards."

Her headache pounded now, a steady kettledrum beat, six-eight time.

"My Grandma Bella gave it to me. Out of all sixty-two or whatever of her grandkids, I don't know why. I guess she liked me best."

"I can't—"

"I didn't spend a dime, not that we have one. And it's not a diamond. I know you don't particularly like diamonds. She never had one, so that worked out." He touched her cheek. "Please open it."

An eerie sense of floating enveloped her. Perspiration drenched every inch of her body.

"It reminds me of your eyes, Kenz."

She had to shut him up. With shaking hands, she lifted the lid of the ring box. A bluish square stone caught the lamplight and winked.

He said, "She told me it's aquamarine. Not the exact color of your eyes. It's the clarity that reminds me of them." He took out the ring and held it up to the light. "Look at that. You can see right through."

That described how he always saw her, right through into her deepest being.

How could he be so far off the mark now?

He went on, eyeing the stone. "Clean and pure and beautiful inside and out."

"No."

Aidan looked at her.

"No, I'm not like that. And you'll know it soon enough. You don't want to marry me. What got into you? It's probably your dad. His getting hurt. You're bonkers. It has nothing to do with us." She sat up and climbed around him. The box fell to the floor. "I can't marry you. I don't want to."

"Kenzie!"

She heard him follow her into the bedroom, but the banging in her ears muffled his voice. Forcing herself to reason, she moved like a robot. Knapsack. Wallet. A handful of underwear, shirts. Sweater. Skirt. Jeans. She slid her feet into sandals.

"Kenz! What are you doing?"

"I gotta get out of here."

"You're running again. You're always running."

"I just need some space."

"That's getting a little old, you know? We all need our space, but sooner or later you have to face life and share some of your space with those who love you."

She walked across the living room. "I'll go to Dakota's. I'll get the van back to you—"

"Phoenix? You're going to *Phoenix*?"

"She's living in San Diego."

He waved his arms. "That is so typical. She's here, she's there. You're here, you're there. I can't keep up with you. Why are you so afraid of staying put for once in your life?"

She pulled open the door.

"Kenzie, if you leave tonight…"

She whirled around. "If I leave tonight, what? I shouldn't come back?"

"I didn't mean that."

"Uh-huh. Neither did my dad when he said it to my mom. Somehow I don't believe either one of you."

Before he could reply, she'd rushed through the door and slammed it shut behind her.

Sixty-Six

"He took a nap after church. A few minutes ago he left for the grocery store." Susan giggled into the cell phone. "Do you believe it, Natalie? Drake never naps or shops for groceries. Not to mention he doesn't even have a change of clothing here yet."

"I'd believe anything right about now. Good grief. Rex and I walk into church this morning and the senior pastor is nowhere to be found. On Easter! Then Mildred tells me you called her and said you planned to attend a service down there this morning. Pastor of a thousand-plus and he goes to church *on Easter* at the beach—*on the sand*—where he knows only two people, Julian and Zeke, men he obviously disdains."

"Disdained. Past tense. Oh, it has been a whole week of unbelievable, hasn't it? I'm still trying to imagine Aidan asking Drake to bless their marriage."

"Truly mind-boggling. I want the guy to give lessons to my sons. But what I'm still trying to imagine is you and Drake singing a duet at the beach house during a boycott. And I was there when it happened!"

Susan smiled and stretched her legs across the ottoman where Pugsy snoozed. Through the window she noticed the boardwalk jam-packed with people, bicycles, and skates. It was another warm sunny day at the beach. Resurrection joy permeated the air.

"Natalie, the most unbelievable thing is what's happening right here and now. Drake and I haven't stopped talking for almost two days. We keep learning new things about each other. We even named our lost baby. Jade Anderson Starr. And whenever Drake starts to sound like the old

311

Drake, he catches himself and rephrases his words. I know we have a long haul ahead of us. We've barely touched on Kenzie's dilemma except to agree it's up to him to pursue reconciliation with her. One step at a time. Right now, though, this honeymoon phase is pretty wonderful."

"I'm so happy for you, Suze. You'll stay there all week then?"

"Yes. I don't know how to thank you, Natalie, for everything. Not just for this annual stay at the beach house, but for insisting I come here ahead of schedule. And for bringing in the Martha Mavens. And for telling me the hard stuff, like the jot and tittle thing."

Muffled sounds came through the earpiece.

"Natalie?"

"Mm-hmm. I'm here." Her alto voice rose to a falsetto. "I can't stop crying. I am so amazed at what God can do. At what He does. At what He did."

"Amen."

"Amen. I gotta go. I'm out of tissues. Bye."

"Bye, Natalie. I love you."

"Love you too!" Definite soprano.

For Susan the uncontrollable came not in the form of tears but in smiles, cheek-stretching and jaw-aching grins. Her mourning had indeed been turned into dancing.

⁓

The front doorknob rattled, and Susan looked up from her book, eager to greet her prince. The door swung wide and as it banged against the wall, Kenzie stumbled inside. The screen door slammed shut behind her.

"Mom!" Tears streamed. Her dark hair sprang every which way, disheveled, not styled. Clothing overflowed from the knapsack she clutched to her stomach. She wore dark green baggy flannel pants and a black T-shirt. For all the world she resembled a pregnant urchin. "Mommy!"

"Sweetheart." Susan went to her, pried the bag from her hands, and hugged her tightly.

"I'm losing my mind!"

"Shh. It's okay. It's okay."

Susan prayed silently, waiting for the flood to slow, fighting down fears that the baby was hurt…Aidan hurt…Mick worse…

At last Kenzie pulled back and rubbed her palms across her face. "Oh, Mom! I don't know what to do."

"Let's sit." She led her to the couch and they sat beside each other. "Come on up, Pugs. He is your dog still."

Crossing her legs, Kenzie pulled Pugsy onto her lap and nuzzled him.

"What's wrong, hon?"

"Ha!" She sat up straighter. "What's wrong? More like what's not wrong! Aidan wants to get married! He's nuts. He doesn't love me. How could he? I'm a basket case."

"He proposed?"

"Yeah. Last night. On his knees! With a ring that belonged to his grandma!"

Susan couldn't help but smile.

"But it wasn't right, Mom. It wasn't. He's just upset about his dad and thinks if he acts the way Mick wants him to, Mick will get better."

"What does his dad want him to do?"

"Get married. He told him that from the beginning."

Susan kept her smile inside. Totally opposite of her first impression, the Carluccis were traditional, probably more so than she ever was.

"Not that he was ever pushy about it." Kenzie lifted her chin, eyelids fluttering. "Not like my dad."

"What did you say to Aidan?"

"No. And I left." Her lips trembled.

"Where did you go?"

"Dakota's. But she's no help. If anybody could be in a worse mess than me, it's her."

"So." She rubbed Kenzie's arm. "How did you leave things with Aidan?"

"I told him I'd get his van back to him. Dakota and I took it back just now. I left the keys in it and she brought me here."

"But what did you say to him last night? Besides no."

"I told him I needed space."

Susan bit back her first response. Why did she run away all the time?

Then she recalled Kenzie as a little girl. She had always craved her own "space." A second response took shape in Susan's mind and she followed it.

"You know, Kenzie, even as a toddler, you'd scurry off when people were around. I'd discover you later, perfectly content in a quiet corner, spinning your own fairy tales and humming original music. That's just you. It's the way God made you and it's okay. You need to find your quiet corner and let this song write itself out."

She stared at her. Tears pooled again. "I can't find the corner anymore."

Susan heard movement through the screen door and looked up. Drake approached, his arms laden with paper grocery sacks, a bouquet of flowers in one hand.

Kenzie inhaled sharply. "What's *he* doing here?"

Unease tore through Susan like a charging bull. Every muscle tensed. Her throat went dry.

Drake reached the door and paused, looking at them through it. His eyes met hers.

And she saw fear and hope and compassion. Maybe it was her imagination, but those were the emotions he voiced when he spoke of Kenzie. They were there inside of him. All brand new.

Susan recognized her own response as all old. Something to discard. *I am not their referee anymore.* Her muscles relaxed.

"Kenzie, your dad is here because he loves us. And you know what?" She touched her daughter's chin and turned her face toward her. "He just might know where your quiet corner is."

The reunion between father and daughter soared somewhere beyond awkward.

Drake stumbled over words. Kenzie actually kept her mouth tightly closed up. Susan's emotions bounced back and forth. Referee or walk off the field?

"Kenzie," he said, "I don't know where to begin." It was his third or fourth repetition of that phrase. "I want to fix things between us. No, I don't mean that. I do, but I don't mean that I can force a fix. Or that I even want to try. I want us to dialogue. Both of us talking and listening. Without preemptive judging."

He went on like that, describing what he wanted to talk about but never doing it. Finally Susan stood. "Excuse me. May I make a suggestion?"

They both looked up at her, their expressions blank.

"I'm going to the bathroom. Then I'm going to put my flowers in a vase and the groceries away. Why don't you two take Pugsy for a walk and get to know each other again?" She smiled brightly, spun on her heel, and walked down the hall.

They're all Yours, Lord. Please, please do something!

Sixty-Seven

Spotting her dad through the door made Kenzie feel as though she'd walked into a blast of desert heat. Tears dried on the spot. Emotions puffed away, good and bad alike. Not that she'd felt a good one in recent history except for ten minutes ago when her mom said God made her the way she was and that was okay.

Which probably explained why she didn't have a thing to say. He could blabber on and on, but the usual hate and anger toward him just didn't show up.

She wasn't so sure, though, about taking a walk with him.

He smiled. "Your mom's been—how do you say it?—pretty 'right on' through this whole, uh, situation. Maybe we ought to follow her suggestion."

"Huh?"

Now his teeth showed and his eyes crinkled. "Yes. I am agreeing outright with your mom. Will wonders never cease, eh? Let's walk. I suppose we should put Pugsy on his leash?"

That one did it. Drake Starr was going to walk the dog? She unfolded her legs and set Pugsy on the floor.

Her dad turned around in a circle, his face a question mark.

"It's on the hall tree by the door," she said.

"Ah." He went to it and lifted off the leash. "Okay. Pugsy?"

The dog tilted his head, his dark muzzle as scrunched and questioning as her dad's face.

Kenzie rolled her eyes, walked across the room and took the leash from him. Within a few moments, she'd hooked Pugsy's collar and walked him out the door.

At the patio fence's gate, her dad reached around her and unlatched it. "You know what I'd really like to do?"

Leaning down to hold the gate, he was nearly at eye level with her, only inches separating them. Struck with the dark grayness of his eyes, she froze. Were they always that color?

He stared back at her. "May I tell you what I'd really like to do?"

"Sure."

"Build a sand castle with you."

"Why?"

"We used to do it."

"Yeah, when I was like five." That was a partial truth. They always built one when they were at the beach until she was twelve.

He shrugged. "It might be…fun?"

"Dogs aren't allowed on the sand in the afternoon." She didn't mention that she and her mom had ignored the rule. Her dad and rules were a different story. And there were more people on the beach today than last week.

"Pugsy won't bother anyone. All he does is sit at your feet." He pulled a plastic bag from the pocket of his pleated dress slacks and smiled. "For clean up."

Way too bizarre. She nodded. "The shovels and pails—"

"Are in the shed behind the house. I remember. I'll get them." He strode off. "Be right back!"

Kenzie heard unspoken words: *Don't go anywhere.* He'd always said that to her when she was little and he'd have to leave her for a minute.

Dodging an inline skater, she crossed the boardwalk to the seawall, Pugsy at her heels.

And she didn't go anywhere, her feet rooted to the concrete by a pair of dark gray eyes.

⌒

They worked in silence for a long while. Digging, carrying water in the pails, packing damp sand into walls. Pugsy slept in the shelter of the highest one.

Kenzie stole sidelong glances at her dad. A breeze fluffed his hair all directions. He'd rolled his pale blue dress shirt sleeves above his elbows. He sat flat on the sand, his tan pants a mess, full of sand and wet spots. He seemed oblivious.

"Well." He rested an elbow on his raised knee and surveyed the castle. "It's looking good. Plenty of towers."

"Mm-hmm."

"So anyway. I don't know where to begin. But I guess I already said that."

She nodded and kept on patting and smoothing a wall. "Once or twice."

"I guess I should just jump in anywhere. Kenzie, I'm sorry. I am so very sorry for hurting you."

She stilled her hand.

"I ask for your forgiveness. I've been a proud fool, too concerned about my own comfort and reputation to love you unconditionally. I've been wrong all up and down the line."

Kenzie looked at him.

The dark gray eyes were on her face. "I love you and your mom more than life itself. And I pushed you both away. By God's grace, I will spend every waking moment undoing that, repairing what damage I can. Will you give me a chance? Please?"

She blinked rapidly. What was it with this eternal fountain of tears?

"I feel like I left you hanging about the time you turned twelve or thirteen. Honestly, I didn't know what to do with you. We were kind of like buddies up until then. Weren't we?"

She nodded. The old memories were there from so long ago. Their aftertaste was always one of regret because the good times were short-lived.

"You grew into a young woman, and to tell you the truth, Kenz, that scared me. You were so pretty and boys are such jerks. I treated your mom disrespectfully. I hated the thought of a guy...And so I turned tyrant. You will not do this or that. I used the pulpit like a weapon, thinking the sharp sword of my words could protect you and all the young people in our church. I wanted to control everything."

He paused, raking his fingers through the sand. "And somewhere along the way God brought all these people. The pews filled up. They came to listen to me. Or so I thought. My head swelled up like a mushroom cloud." He smiled at her. "Hallelujah, holy winds are blowing through that cloud now, dispersing it to the ends of the earth."

Holy winds? She wrinkled her brow at his goofy grin and odd choice of words.

"It's a Zeke quote."

"Zeke?"

"He and I had a talk today."

She went speechless again.

"Aidan and I had a talk on Thursday."

"Aidan!"

"Strange." He shook his head as if in disbelief. "I get blown away by a young kid I wanted to strangle and a flakey street preacher. God is getting more mysterious by the hour."

"Aidan? Thursday?"

"You don't know about that? He didn't say anything to you?"

"No. We're sort of…separated. For now. I don't know."

"It's okay. Things will work themselves out in time. Don't worry. Your mom and I are together, we're with you, and we love you."

It was okay? Don't worry? He loved her? And thought she was pretty? Her head spun.

"The bottom line is, I realized I would lose you and your mom and my grandchild if I didn't do something. Only there wasn't anything I could do in the sense of force or control. I had to lean solely on God. You'd think I would have known how to do that by now. But here we are." His shoulders rose and fell. "Kenzie, you are welcome to visit or live with us anytime. Pregnant, married or not. No conditions whatsoever. Our home will always be your home. And it'd be all right if you bring Aidan along too."

As tears spilled from her dad's eyes, she really didn't think hers would ever stop again.

Sixty-Eight

Susan pinched her arm and didn't wake up. Evidently the scene before her happened in real time.

Husband and daughter shivered in front of the fire. Kenzie sat on the brick hearth and Drake stood next to it. They huddled under beach towels, their clothes damp and covered with sand. Traces of tears streaked both faces.

The aura they'd carried in with them through the door surprised Susan most of all. Peace, tenderness, and a trace of joy radiated from them.

They hadn't even mentioned the delicious garlicky scent from her chicken cacciatore cooking in the oven. Nor had they seemed impressed with her fire-making abilities. Those things mattered not at all in comparison. She sank onto the couch and simply stared as they told her about the enormous castle they'd built.

She had seen it from a distance. Wild horses couldn't have kept her in the kitchen. Every so often she stepped out onto the patio and gazed their direction. After a while, she could tell they conversed. Then clouds rolled in and the wind increased. The temperature dropped considerably, but none of that seemed to affect them. They still talked, worked on the castle, and even ventured out into the ocean, rinsing hands and splashing each other.

"I think I'll go soak in the tub," Kenzie announced. "Mmm, I smell dinner. Is there time?"

"Plenty." Susan smiled.

Drake said, "And I'd better shower. Did you see the sweats I bought?"

"Mm-hmm."

"Found them at the grocery store. Do you believe they sell that stuff there?"

"Welcome to the new world, Dad. You know, your head's been in the sand way too long." Kenzie grinned. "Actually, it looks like it's been literally buried."

He laughed with her. "Yeah, well yours looks like you stuck your finger in an electrical socket."

Kenzie scrunched her nose at him. "I'll let you use some of my styling goop. You obviously didn't do a thing with your hair today."

Susan stared some more.

Kenzie stood and walked past Susan. "Hot tub, here I come." At the end of the couch she turned on her heel. "But first, I'll tell you two what I'm thinking so you can discuss it when I'm out of earshot." She grinned again.

Drake said, "Only if you're ready, hon. No rush."

Kenzie's smile faded. "It's no rush. It's one of those things you just know when you know. Deep down." She propped a hip on the couch arm. "I want to move back home. If it's okay with you, Mom. Dad already said it's okay with him. You're not going to faint, are you?"

Susan realized she had slumped backward, her legs and arms sprawled.

Drake touched her hand.

She turned to see him seated on the other couch arm beside her. His gentle expression told her everything. He had asked Kenzie for forgiveness. He had welcomed her back home.

"Oh, my." Susan looked at her daughter. "Oh, my."

"Is that a yes?"

She nodded. "I would love to have you and my grandchild live with us."

"Thanks, Mom." Kenzie took a deep breath. "Here goes with the rest of it. I don't want to marry Aidan. Not now. Maybe never."

Drake said, "That's okay."

Susan was getting whiplash looking back and forth between them. He said it was okay and that was all he was going to say? She squeezed his hand and he squeezed back.

"I just…"

Susan swung around again to Kenzie.

"I just want to feel safe. I want to be quiet. I want to take time to figure things out. I'll get a job closer to home. I want to—" Kenzie cut off her words with a mischievous smile. "I want to know where June Cleaver is. Here Dad and I sit, our sandy wet bums on Faith's flowery couch. I'm sure this is a no-no."

Susan blinked. "I didn't even notice."

"Yahoo, Mom! Way to go!" Kenzie leaned over, her palm raised.

They exchanged a high five, and Susan said, "Get out of here. Take your bath. Dinner's almost ready."

"Uh-oh. Shades of June." She hopped off the couch and strode through the kitchen toward the small bedroom beyond it, the one she liked best.

Susan met Drake's smile with her own. "Oh, my."

"My sentiments exactly."

"You two talked."

"Yeah. Basically I told her how much I love her."

"And you invited her home."

"Unconditionally." He nodded. "Good news, bad news."

"What?"

"You know that second honeymoon we thought we'd celebrate here at the beach house this week?" He winked. "Moving back home means with us. Wherever we are. Starting tonight."

"Oh."

And then they burst into laughter.

Sixty-Nine

Pepper wanted to crawl into bed and snuggle next to Mick with a book.

But the bed was a narrow hospital one and it sat in their front room and five of their six kids hung around him and he wore that awful plastic thing that made him four times larger than he was and a nurse was arriving soon.

So instead on that Monday afternoon, the day after Easter, she remained seated at the picnic table in her backyard, forcing herself to listen to Kenzie, who sat across from her. After the girl had warmly greeted Mick and spent a few minutes with him and the others, she dumped the news on Pepper: She'd turned Aidan down.

"Pepper, does any of this make sense to you?"

No! "Yes. No. Yes. No." She sighed. "I'm in more of a dithery state than usual. Does it show?"

"I understand. I'm sorry for the timing with Mick and all—"

"That can't be helped. I'm sorry for being unavailable. Just give me a minute, okay?"

She nodded, her countless hair shoots neatly bobbing as one.

She shut her eyes. *Lord, I love this child like she's one of my own. We're all hurting so bad here...*

"Pepper." A minute for Kenzie meant something like the blink of an eye.

She looked at the girl, at that familiar smile playing about her lips, at the upturned nose. "What?"

"You could always try blasting out your opinion with both barrels."

"There really is an imp inside of you, isn't there?"

She grinned.

"Okay, Kenzie. I love you like you're one of my own. I love my grandchild, the one you're carrying. My son loves you. But if you're not ready for marriage, you're not ready." She pressed her lips together.

"But you think I should be."

"I wish you would be. That's a different thing."

"Getting married at a young age worked for you, but I'd make a horrible wife. I have to get my own act together first. Hopefully in time to be a mother so I can get *that* act figured out. Aidan says he understands." Kenzie had talked with him at his apartment before coming to the house. "You know, he's the one to blame for all this *reconciliation* nonsense."

Pepper smiled. The news about Kenzie's dad welcoming his daughter home floored her…until she remembered that a lot of women had been praying for exactly that to happen.

"If he hadn't gone to my dad and said those absolutely amazing things, I don't know what would have happened. Maybe if Mom stuck it out long enough and the Marthas kept boycotting, maybe he would have gotten the message eventually. But it was Aidan who cinched the deal. Dad even said so."

"Do you love Aidan?"

"He still turns me to mush when he looks at me with those eyes of his or hugs me." She smiled softly. "And he did that just a while ago. He is such a beautiful person, but I'm so mixed up inside. I can't drag him into my mess. I don't know what I feel except afraid he'll regret us getting married. Or, worse, resent me." She paused. "And I know I feel safe with my mom and dad. I don't remember ever feeling that way with them. Of course, we haven't even been together twenty-four hours yet. Dad and I already went at it again, arguing about some stupid thing this morning. All of a sudden Mom shouted, 'Hold it!' Then she pulled us close together and put my finger on Dad's nose and his on mine." She tapped her own. "She said when we wanted to fuss at each other, we had to literally push at each other's buttons. We cracked up. I don't know what's going on with those two, but it feels good to me."

Lord, You are a wonder.

"We've talked about maybe I'll see a counselor. One who professes faith in Christ, naturally, else Dad wouldn't pay for it. Would that disturb you and Mick?"

"Good heavens, no. The more help and prayer, the better." She held in another sigh.

"Pepper." Kenzie lowered her eyes momentarily and then looked at her. "I love you too. Your grandbaby is going to adore you…please don't cry."

She wiped at her eyes. "I'm going to miss you and your mom so much. And the baby—"

"Miss us! We'll still see each other! As soon as Mick's ready for company, Mom's coming to meet him. Dad might even tag along. She said to tell you she's available for coffee and ice cream anytime. But Dad's not allowed to tag along for that."

Pepper smiled.

"And the baby, well, shoot. Who's the baby expert around this place? I'm counting on you to show me the ropes."

Oh, Lord, let it be so. "I'm going to hold you to that, Kenzie. And I expect you and the little one here for family dinners."

Kenzie faked a sneeze.

"Hey, get used to it. If I can't be a pushy mother-in-law, I can still be one pungent Grandma out of Wedlock."

Seventy

A few months later, August 1
A hospital waiting room, maternity ward

Susan shared the navy blue vinyl couch with Pepper. The past six hours carried a timeless quality. They both dragged and flew by, filled with coffee, tea, soda, breakfast and lunch, conversation, and prayer. Sighted through the single window, predawn clouds gave way to morning sun, morning sun to high noon blaze. Now and then a nurse popped in to give them an update on Kenzie.

"Baby's making progress, Mommy's a trooper, Daddy's a sweetheart."

Drake and Mick paced the cozy room, sometimes venturing out into the hallway. Twice they had gone to the cafeteria, Mick reluctantly sitting in his wheelchair while Drake pushed. Pepper insisted her husband had used up his allotted on-feet time by 9:00.

Pepper squeezed Susan's hand. "This is worse than giving birth myself."

Overcome for the umpteenth time with a wave of emotion, Susan patted her friend's shoulder without comment.

"I guess we didn't have to come so early," Pepper said.

They exchanged a chuckle. When Kenzie awoke at four o'clock with serious contractions, Drake called Aidan and Susan called Pepper. They met up at the hospital. A nurse said there was still plenty of time. Her suggestion the grandparents leave and return later was met by four glares.

Mick settled into his chair now. "Ladies, we're going to the cafeteria again. Want anything?"

Pepper ordered an ice cream bar.

"Make that two, please," Susan said.

"With a coffee chaser?" Smiling, Drake grasped the wheelchair's handles.

"Sure," they replied in unison.

After the men were out of earshot, Pepper said, "Still amazing."

"I know. Drake getting us coffee and ice cream."

"I was thinking along the amazing lines that Mick and I are friends with your husband."

Susan smiled. "And with me."

"Ah, you were easy."

"Not at first."

Pepper laughed. "And now Drake's on sabbatical and you two come to our church."

And that, Susan thought, was only the tip of the amazing iceberg. Holy Cross Fellowship graciously gave Drake a year off at half pay and didn't expect him to attend services where people might treat him as available. They understood his need for a deep rest. He spent much of his time writing. She wondered if he would have a decade worth of sermons by the time the year was over.

Some days were a struggle, but, like the baby, they were making progress. Redefining their relationship with each other and with Kenzie proved to be a faith-stretching adventure. Nobody's personality changed overnight. Friends, family, and counselors helped.

"Susan," Pepper said. "Are you okay with this?"

"With what?"

"Sitting out here. Some parents get invited into the labor room."

"Yeah, I'm okay with it. Are you?"

"No."

She laughed. "Well, I find it best to be okay with things I can't change. I sleep better at night."

"Yeah, yeah. I deserved that remark. But seriously…"

"Seriously, Kenzie and I are good friends. She's crazy about you. But this is her and Aidan's time."

"I am glad she wanted him with her, at the birthing classes and now. What do you think will happen with them?"

"No clue."

"Me neither."

"He's been a perfect suitor. I swear Drake is taking lessons from him. He asks me out for dates. He brings me little gifts. It's working on me."

"Amazing. Simply amazing."

"Amen."

A nurse entered the room, a wide grin on her face. "It's showtime, Grandmas. Back soon!" She hurried away.

Like two little girls, Susan and Pepper grabbed each other with a squeal probably loud enough to be heard all the way down to the cafeteria.

Epilogue

Late March, the following year
The Beach House

Susan wiggled her toes and, like a little girl, peered down to admire their polish. Flecks of sunlight danced off her sequined flip-flops, throwing tiny rainbows willy-nilly through the air.

If she were outlined in a coloring book, only one crayon would be needed to fill in the blank spaces. Pastel pink virtually covered her, from nails to shoes to jewelry to rosebud corsage to linen embroidered dress and jacket. She felt so pretty that if the person wielding the crayon were to stray outside the lines, Susan would not mind in the least.

How could she mind? The past year had been one major, incomprehensible scribble that eventually looped itself into a beautiful picture of grace for the Starr family. Though she, Drake, and Kenzie were God's works in progress, all was well with their souls.

Kenzie squeezed Susan's elbow now, and they exchanged a smile. Her daughter glowed, as only a bride could on her wedding day. Now twenty years old and mommy of an eight-month-old baby, she wore a simple cream-colored tea-length dress with capped sleeves. Sprigs of baby's breath adorned her dark spiky hair, and she held a bouquet of early spring flowers. Her eyes sparkled more brilliantly than the sequins on Susan's flip-flops.

From the other side of Kenzie, Drake moved his mouth. It landed somewhere between a smile and the expression of a man going down for the third count. Susan couldn't help but grin at him.

Drake wore his charcoal gray suit and a pale pink silk tie. His nod to unbreakable rules ended there. He was barefoot and he was going to conduct, on the beach, the ceremony to unite his daughter in holy matrimony with the father of her child. Going shoeless like the young couple was his idea. Slipping into minister's role was Kenzie's.

In his own words, the year had pummeled his heart. Forget the image of God as the potter molding and shaping with strong but gentle hands, he said. When clay was as brick hard as he was, it took a smashing to smithereens before a new lump could even be picked up for kneading.

He winked at her. Or was it a twitch? The poor guy was nearly a basket case.

She smiled and nodded. "You can do this." She mouthed the phrase oft repeated earlier that morning.

A gentle breeze fluttered the dress about her ankles. Only Kenzie would choose a March afternoon for an outdoor ceremony on the beach. *March. At the ocean.* Susan had emoted with much anxiety over such a plan until Mildred gently suggested they pray for beautiful weather. The day dawned so brightly that most attendees wore sunglasses. As if that weren't enough, an unpredicted Santa Ana desert wind softened crisp spring temperatures. Shoe-clad guests might very well feel sand between their toes, but they wouldn't shiver.

From her perch with Drake and Kenzie atop a concrete staircase that led from the boardwalk up and over the seawall, Susan surveyed the scene before her, well aware of curious bystanders lining up along the boardwalk looking at it as well.

They'd chosen a spot in the sand not far from Faith Fontaine's house and collected enough beach and lawn chairs to accommodate the small crowd of family and close friends. Everyone was there now, seated and facing the ocean, the large extended family of Carluccis and Pepper's side, the Martha Mavens, and a handful of others. Band members stood off to one side. They'd left the electronics at home and played classical selections on guitar, violin, and flute.

Julian had come. Kenzie jokingly referred to him as one of Drake's best friends. Her dad's other best friend was Zeke, the street preacher who stood down front with Aidan.

Dear Aidan. He hadn't given up on Kenzie. He courted her, went to counseling with her, and changed diapers. It was an amazing balancing act, an amazing display of his love. He stood tall and handsome now, in black pants and an oversized white linen shirt. Beside him was his father, Mick, serving as best man.

Susan's books on wedding etiquette didn't cover half of what she and Kenzie had arranged, and so they colored outside the lines. As Susan watched it unfold now, she liked the effect. Pepper stood next to Mick. They'd insisted she be part of the wedding party. What better role than as grandmother in charge of the youngest, most important guest?

Little Shay Rose-Marie Carlucci sat in Pepper's embrace, one chubby arm wrapped around her grandma's neck, her sweet yellow dress bunched up like a puffy pillow around her. She bobbed her head about, her deep-set sapphire blue eyes taking in the entire scene. She could easily steal the whole show with a flicker of a playful smile that already resembled her mother's.

Zeke signaled to Drake. Susan heard him and Kenzie draw in deep breaths, and she smiled. *Thank You, Lord, for this moment.*

As the musicians played "Jesu, Joy of Man's Desiring," she and her husband walked their daughter down the four gritty concrete steps, onto the squishy sand, and along the makeshift center aisle between the chairs. When they reached the end, Zeke formally greeted everyone and asked the question "Who gives this woman in marriage?" Both Drake and Susan replied. After kissing their daughter's cheeks and watching her step over to Aidan's side, they took their places. Susan moved to Kenzie's left to serve as matron of honor. Drake stood beside Zeke. He'd asked his best friend to stay close, in case he couldn't quite make it through the ceremony with voice intact.

Drake's tongue stumbled now and then through the familiar words, and his eyes glistened. Susan silently encouraged him, all the while marveling at the journey they'd taken.

Although Aunt Nattie suspected that her niece and Aidan would eventually marry because they were absolutely perfect for each other, Susan wasn't so sure. Kenzie outright did not believe it. Doubts plagued her for months as she struggled, but she sought wise counsel and blossomed from a hurting child into a young woman secure in the love of her parents and God.

Not until late November did something click in her heart. It was around the time when Aidan met a radio station manager who agreed to play one of his new songs on the air. Phone calls poured in; other stations picked it up, secular and religious. One thing led to another. His band's earlier recording hadn't led to a contract for more, but this single hit opened all kinds of the right doors.

Sung as a solo with only his keyboard for backup, Aidan titled the soft ballad simply "Kenzie."

Now, as part of their wedding vows, he began to sing it to her. Susan pulled a handkerchief from her sleeve, placed there in anticipation of the inevitable. A few stray tears were not going to be the end of it. During rehearsal the previous day, she'd blubbered like Shay in dire need of a nap.

Susan knew it wasn't the song or the taste of fame that allowed Kenzie to finally accept Grandma Bella's beautiful aquamarine ring and set the date. It was God's healing of hearts that did it.

She remembered the exact hour Kenzie's doubts fled. Natalie and Rex were visiting. It was a Saturday afternoon, and they all chatted in the family room by a cozy fire, making plans for Thanksgiving. Great-Aunt Nattie rocked the baby. In the midst of the pleasant setting, without warning, Kenzie burst into tears. Susan and Drake rushed to her side.

The display was not all that uncommon. The months since Kenzie had moved back in with them had been, to put it mildly, emotionally charged.

"I want to marry him!" she cried. "I want to marry Aidan. I'm ready!"

"All right," Drake said matter-of-factly.

Susan thought they needed more information. "That's wonderful, honey. Do you know why you're ready?"

"Because of Dad." Kenzie turned to Drake. "Because of you, Dad."

He stared, a blank expression on his face.

"Because I want my little girl to have a daddy like you. Aidan loves me and Shay the same way you love me and Mom, but he can't do it long distance. We can't receive it long distance."

Drake smiled softly.

His minimal usage of words still boggled Susan's mind.

"Do you think he'll ever ask me again?"

Drake coughed discreetly, hiding the sob Susan figured was close at hand. "I could say something to him. I could mention that the blessing I gave is still in effect. Something along those lines. Shall I?"

"Oh, would you? I love him so much it hurts!"

That afternoon dissolved into more tears and laughter.

Aidan did ask again, on Thanksgiving. Kenzie accepted.

And now the knot was tied. Simple wedding bands were exchanged. The bride and groom kissed.

Susan swallowed her tears and cleared her throat. Drake stepped next to her, taking her hand. They were going to sing at their daughter's wedding. Who could have thought such a thing possible a year ago? Even six months ago?

He squeezed her hand. She gave him a slight nod and began to sing a cappella. On cue, Drake joined in, and their voices wove in and out of each other, carried aloft by the gentle breeze. They sang the words of an ancient marriage blessing over the newlyweds.

Susan imagined that God Himself sang His own blessing over them all.

Questions for Discussion

1. With news of her unwed daughter's pregnancy, Susan begins a journey to wholeness, a painful process of becoming broken and letting God put her back together in a new way. What are some of the first difficult steps she takes in giving up control of her world?

2. In what ways do others help her along the path? Natalie? Julian? The Martha Mavens? Pepper?

3. What are some turning points that reveal she is living more from listening to her heart and less from listening to what she thinks Drake would say?

4. Why is Drake threatened by her newfound strength? Describe his and Susan's relationship at the beginning and at the end of the story.

5. Have you, like Susan and Drake, been thrown for a loop that led to God performing some healing work in you?

6. Susan feels God blesses her through the gift of song. This especially speaks to her because of her interest and talent in music. How has God touched you in a way that you feel is unique to your personality or abilities?

7. While the journeys of Pepper and Natalie are not as dramatic as Susan's, these women deal with faith-stunting issues as well. Talk about their personal changes.

8. What do you think are some of Kenzie's wounds? How are they revealed? How are they resolved?

9. Susan and Pepper dealt with their children's situation in ways that stemmed from their own personal experiences. How did you agree or disagree with the choices Susan and Pepper made? How might others respond?

10. Natalie urges Susan to listen to her heart, to live from its center. Do you relate to this advice? How do you/don't you live from your true center?

*Other Books by
Sally John*

THE OTHER WAY HOME SERIES
A Journey by Chance
After All These Years
Just to See You Smile
The Winding Road Home

IN A HEARTBEAT SERIES
In a Heartbeat
Flash Point
Moment of Truth

THE BEACH HOUSE SERIES
The Beach House
Castles in the Sand

About the Author

Sally John is a former teacher and the author of twelve books, including the popular Other Way Home series and In a Heartbeat series. Illinois natives, Sally and her husband, Tim, live in Southern California not far from the beach. The Johns have two grown children, a daughter–in–law, and two granddaughters.

Sally always appreciates hearing personally from you, her readers. Please feel free to contact her via mail at:

Sally John
c/o Harvest House Publishers
990 Owen Loop North
Eugene, OR 97402

or
via her website at:
www.sally-john.com

or
via e-mail at:
sallyjohnbook@aol.com